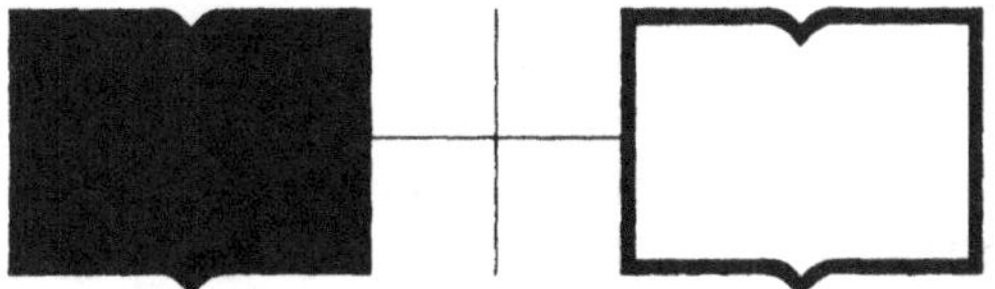

Toronto Reprint Library of Canadian Prose and Poetry

Douglas Lochhead, General Editor

This series is intended to provide for libraries a varied selection of titles of Canadian prose and poetry which have been long out-of-print. Each work is a reprint of a reliable edition, is in a contemporary library binding, and is appropriate for public circulation. The Toronto Reprint Library makes available lesser known works of popular writers and, in some cases, the only works of little known poets and prose writers. All form part of Canada's literary history; all help to provide a better knowledge of our cultural and social past.

The Toronto Reprint Library is produced in short-run editions made possible by special techniques, some of which have been developed for the series by the University of Toronto Press.

This series should not be confused with Literature of Canada: Poetry and Prose in Reprint, also under the general editorship of Douglas Lochhead.

UNIVERSITY OF TORONTO PRESS

Toronto Reprint Library of Canadian Prose and Poetry
© University of Toronto Press 1973
Toronto and Buffalo
Reprinted in paperback 2014
ISBN 978-0-8020-7502-4 (cloth)
ISBN 978-1-4426-5179-1 (paper)

No other editions.

"DOT IT DOWN;"

A STORY OF

Life in the North-West.

By Alexander Begg.

Toronto:
HUNTER, ROSE & COMPANY.
1871.

HUNTER, ROSE & CO.,
PRINTERS, BOOKBINDERS, ELECTROTYPERS &c.

Dedication.

My Dear Friends,

In dedicating to you this, my first literary effort of any importance, I do so from a just appreciation of the many kindnesses you have shown me ever since I came to Red River. Arriving as I did in the country a perfect stranger, I was deeply moved by the very considerate manner with which you took me by the hand; and I must say, that ever since you have done everything in your power to make my residence pleasant and happy. It has caused me much trouble and indignation to see the kind-hearted people of Red River vilified by scribblers in the public press, and if I have done anything towards correcting the unjust impression received abroad concerning the settlers, I will have my reward. Trusting that you may enjoy long happiness and prosperity, the just due of all who, like you, prove themselves sincere friends,

I remain,

Yours very sincerely,

ALEXANDER BEGG.

To Mr. and Mrs. Bannatyne.
Winnipeg, Manitoba.

CONTENTS.

CONTENTS.

CHAPTER VII.

CHAPTER VIII.

CHAPTER IX.

CHAPTER X.

CHAPTER XI.

CHAPTER XII.

CHAPTER XIII.

CHAPTER XIV.

CHAPTER XV.

CHAPTER XVI.

CHAPTER XVII.

CHAPTER XVIII.

CHAPTER XIX.

CHAPTER XX.

CHAPTER XXI.

CHAPTER XXII.

CHAPTER XXIII.

CHAPTER XXIV.

CHAPTER XXV.

CHAPTER XXVI.

CHAPTER XXVII.

CHAPTER XXVIII.

CHAPTER XXIX.

"DOT IT DOWN:"

A STORY OF

LIFE IN THE NORTH-WEST.

CHAPTER I.

HE fine steamer *Phil Sheridan* had just touched the levee at St. Paul, when an active youth sprang from her side on to the landing, and hardly deigning to look at the craft which had borne him so far on his journey, he jauntily turned his steps in the direction of the city. By his manner one would judge him to be a mixture of the sailor and the landsman; his easy careless steps betokened the former, while his dress indicated the latter. Humming a favorite air, he strode on in the direction of the nearest hotel, the "Merchants'," and while he is engaged in entering his name on the register and securing his room, we will return and take a look at some of his fellow passengers in the *Sheridan* who are destined to play conspicuous parts in our tale.

On the levee, surrounded by a heap of boxes and trunks, sat a family of five persons,—father and mother, two boys, and a girl. The latter is especially deserving of notice; rather over the medium height, exquisitely formed, with regular and

B

beautiful features, the most remarkable of which were her eyes; these were dark and flashing, full of expression, and when you looked into them, you saw a strange mixture of boldness and gentleness, a something withal that drew you towards the girl, feeling in your mind that while she might be quick in her attachments, she would be very likely in the end to prove a staunch and true friend. Such, indeed, was Grace Meredith; full of impulse, yet warm-hearted and generous to those she loved. Her two brothers, Jack and Tom, were rough, uncouth specimens, brimful of mirth and pleasantry, and not afraid to put their hands to hard work when it was required of them; unlike their sister, they were as plain-looking as she was beautiful; a couple of good, stout, hearty, honest lads they were however. It seemed a mystery to all who knew the Merediths, where Grace derived her good looks from, for neither father nor mother could boast of the least signs of beauty.

The father was a man standing about five feet six inches in height, very stout, in fact with a decided tendency towards corpulency. His face was large, round, ruddy, and good-natured, eyes twinkling with humour, and a nose that, as Jack used to jocosely remark to his sister, "looked as if a mosquito had just dined there." Mrs. Meredith was directly the opposite of her husband, tall and thin, sharp-featured, and possessed of a tongue which, when once let loose, fairly silenced all other competitors. Grace was the only one who seemed to have any success in weathering the fury of her mother's unruly member; not so much in the way of "tit for tat," as by not appearing to notice the storm.

And now that we have described this rather remarkable family, as far as necessary, we will proceed with our story.

Mrs. Meredith sat on a trunk, and, for a wonder, kept a

profound silence, while her husband and sons stood by wiping the perspiration from their foreheads, after the exertion of hauling the baggage ashore.

Grace, who acted as a sort of mentor for the family, now suggested the propriety of looking for lodgings for the night; when Jack interrupted her by slying remarking: "I guess, father, Gracie wants to be after her beau; eh, sis?"

"I wish you would mind your own business, Jack. What's George Wade to me, I'd like to know?"

"You need'nt take on so," said Jack; "I'm only joking; but were you not a little spooney together on the trip up? Now, come sis? What say you, Tom?"

"Looked like it; but I guess he was in a big hurry to leave the steamer; suppose he thought we'd ask him to help with the trunks; its the way with those fine gallants."

"For shame, Tom!" said Grace. "George Wade is not the man to sneak off to avoid helping a friend. That speech is not like you, brother."

"Well," returned Tom, "I don't think Wade a bad sort of a fellow, but what was his hurry in leaving so, without giving even the shake of a hand to a chap?"

"He told me," remarked Jack, "that he is going on with us to Red River, so what was the use of his saying good-bye just for a while?"

"Maybe," said Tom.

Mrs. Meredith here interrupted the conversation, by asking in a loud shrill voice, "How long they were going to stand there talking while she was left broiling in the sun; but," she continued, "I'm getting used to it. It's my opinion you're all gone daft, and I am in the company of lunatics; there's your father leaving a good farm and comfortable house in Canada to go up to a country where they say there's nothing but bears, wolves, and rats, Indians and ice.   I suppose we'll be keeping hotel at the North Pole before we stop."

"I wish," said Tom, throwing back his coat from his shoulder, "that we were somewhere near that spot at present, for its darned warm here."

"You're just like your father, Tom," said Mrs. Meredith, "always puffing and blowing about the heat. Why don't you take an example from me; do you ever hear me grumbling ?"

" Never," answered Tom.

"How long are we going to sit here, Mr. Meredith ?" the good lady then asked, turning to her spouse.   That gentleman was on the point of answering, when the young man, mentioned in the beginning of this chapter, and who we will know hereafter by the name of George Wade, came up, and addressing himself to Mr. Meredith, said ;—"Landed all right, I see, sir.   Well I thought I'd just go ahead of you a little and secure berths for the party.   There's a good many passengers by the boat, you know, and I feared lest we would be left in the lurch ; but I've got comfortable rooms for us all at the Merchants' Hotel.   Hope I did right, sir ?"

" We are very much obliged to you," answered Mr. Meredith ; " we were just discussing the point about getting shelter for the night when you came up."

" Then if you will accompany Mrs. Meredith and Grace to the hotel, Jack, Tom, and I will see to carrying the trunks over to the railway station, and join you afterwards.   You see, sir, you go that way (pointing up the street) ; take the first turn to the left, and then the " Merchants' " is only a few doors from you.   Mrs. Meredith, you look very warm !"

" Kind o' ; thank you."

During this conversation, significant glances passed between

Grace and her brothers, and as soon as she had departed with her father and mother, Tom went up to George Wade and said,—"Wade, I'm not much given to backbiting a fellow, but I've done it to-day, and I'm sorry for it. You see I thought you left us in such a hurry that I said you did it to get out of helping us with the trunks; it was mean of me, I know, for we were able enough for the work ourselves, and I did'nt exactly think what I said. I hope you won't feel hard about it ?"

"Not a bit, Tom. I left because I thought I'd be more help ashore than afloat. When I saw so many passengers on the boat, I was afraid we'd be shut out at the hotel; and its just as well I went as I did, for I had hardly secured our rooms when the crowd poured in, and such a clamouring you never heard; some could'nt get fixed anyway."

Tom's conscience having now been made easy, the three young men went to work with a will, and soon had all the baggage conveyed over to the railway station, a short distance from where they had landed.

They then betook themselves to the hotel; and after dinner, George Wade, having letters of introduction to the agent of the Hudson Bay Company, asked Mr. Meredith to accompany him to that gentleman's office.

In the meantime, we will take the opportunity of saying a few words regarding our friend Wade. While yet young, he had conceived a fancy for a seafaring life, and to satisfy this desire, his father had procured for him an appointment in the East India Service, in which George remained for some years. Becoming dissatisfied with the life however, he, unlike many who take early to the sea, resolved upon carving out his fortune on land. Several fields for energy and activity presented themselves, but at last he chose the North-West as the one most likely to afford him opportunities for adventure, of which he was passionately fond. His father was wealthy, and as he was the only son, he had very reasonable grounds to expect a windfall at some future day; although, in justice to him, we must say he never built his hopes upon it. George was of an independent nature, and had made up his mind to fight his own way irrespective of any aid from his father. How far he kept this resolution will be seen in the course of our story. Through the instrumentality of his friends he had procured letters of introduction to parties of influence in the North-West, and this he had determined would be the last assistance he would avail himself of from that quarter, until he had given his own exertions a fair trial.

George Wade was not what might be called a handsome lad, although there was something very fascinating in his countenance; he was rather tall and well built, with frank, honest features, surmounted by a mass of rich, curly brown hair. His careless manner, peculiar to him, which we have before noticed, was in fact more a matter of appearance than reality; for, as it will be seen, he was thoughful in regard to those around him, especially if he liked them. Slow to anger, he was, when fairly aroused, almost a merciless opponent, but he was not given to taking offence easily.

At the time we first introduced him to our readers, he had no regular line of action laid down for himself. He was on his way to the North-West, to take advantage of anything that might turn up, and was resolved upon putting his hands cheerfully to the first piece of honest work that offered. The Merediths had "taken to him greatly," as they themselves expressed it, for he had, from the first day he joined them in Chicago, about a week previous to their arrival in St. Paul, shown so much kindness and consideration in his manner, that he completely won the good opinion of his newly found friends. Even Mrs. Meredith was forced to acknowledge that he was a nice young man. One of the family in particular found her heart telling tales whenever he approached her; but of this anon.

When George and Mr. Meredith entered the office of the agent, Mr. K——, they found him in consultation with one of the free traders from Red River, over a lot of furs that lay scattered in heaps on the floor. Mink, marten, and several other kinds of skins, were in different parts of the room, and it was evident a sorting process had just been completed.

Mr. K——, however, rose immediately on their entrance, and graciously desired them to be seated; when George presented his letters, and Mr. Meredith.

On Mr. K—— offering to aid them in their arrangements, Mr. Meredith stated that he was desirous of purchasing some good horses and a couple of stout waggons, and as he was a stranger in the city, he wished to be instructed as to where he would be most likely to obtain what he wanted. An appointment was then made with Mr. K—— to meet him later in the day, when he promised to go with them, and assist them in procuring their outfit. They then were introduced to the trader, as a gentleman living in the country to which they were going, and, after some further conversation they left the office, just as a Jewish looking gentleman entered it, apparently with an eye to the furs for sale. At the time of our friends' arrival at St. Paul, it was the usual season for the annual visit of the Red River traders to that city, for the purpose of selling their furs and laying in a stock of new goods, and Mr. K——'s office was their principal resort, he being their agent as well as that of the Hudson Bay Company. The most of these fur dealers stayed at the "Merchants'," because it was the nearest house to the places of business, and also for the reason that it had been their headquarters for years past when they were on their visit to St. Paul.

When George and Mr. Meredith returned to the hotel, they found that the two ladies had retired to obtain some rest from their fatigue ; but in the bar-room they discovered the worthies, Jack and Tom, in the midst of a number of stout hearty looking men (evidently Nor'-West traders), laughing and talking, and apparently in the best of spirits. George proposed standing to one side to see what was going on, when Jack was overheard to say,—

" As for bears and such like, I don't care a snap; and I'd rather like a crack at a wild Indian."

" But," said a tall, thin man in the crowd, " they're apt to take a slice out of a fellow for breakfast, especially when they don't like you."

" They've sliced you down considerably then," said Tom, eyeing the thin man with a patronizing air.

" Come Doc," said two or three, laughing, " you had better treat on that."

The discomfited trader accepted the terms with a bad grace, muttering that he couldn't see the joke ; and all turned towards the bar and called for their " drinks."

" I declare," whispered Mr. Meredith, " there's my two youngsters calling for cock-tails, a bright beginning to a new life."

" Oh," said George, " I'll warrant neither Jack nor Tom will give you trouble in that line."

" Well, you see, Mr. Wade," returned the old man, " I'm not over particular about taking a drop myself, but I'm seasoned. I don't like to see my boys going that road. I must talk to them kindly about it. We'll go up and join them, but we'll not take a glass just now, please Mr. Wade."

" Not I," said George.

The trader whom they had met in Mr. K——'s office now came up, and all three proceeded to where the unruly crowd were standing, when Mr. Meredith and George were made acquainted with several men, with whom in after years they became closely connected, and whom, when the proper time arrives, we will introduce severally to our readers. One of them, however, comes so early on the scenes of our story, that we must attempt a description of him, while the Merediths are becoming more intimate with their future neighbours.

We have reference to the thin man, whom his companions addressed as Doc! Although slim in appearance, he had not the slightest idea but that he was as stout as the stoutest of the party; in fact he felt himself as big as the biggest of his acquaintances, and of quite as much importance.

His frame (what there was of it) gave token of wear and tear. The expression of his face was a mixture of simplicity and cunning, of frankness and deceit, with a very decided tinge of venom in its composition, His highly colored nose and thin watery eyes were unmistakable signs of a *penchant* for ardent spirits. Few were aware of how he obtained the title of Doc, for he neither practised medicine nor any other profession. At the time when we first present him to our readers, he was looked upon more with pity than any other feeling by his fellow-traders, and his peculiarities, while they often caused a smile, as often made him an object of commisseration by his friends. Possessed of money when he first visited Red River, he was going through it as quickly as he could manage it, for his trading operations were marked by as much wildness in their speculative character as almost everything else in which he engaged, and he invariably came out behind at the close of each season. His connection with another, whom we will speak of hereafter, did not tend to improve matters with him.   Dr. Flyaway was indisputably a character in the North-West.   As was his custom (whenever he had the chance) with strangers, he button-holed George Wade, thinking him no doubt the most susceptible of impression, and taking him to one side, he began a long tirade of abuse againt several parties then present, and directed a whole volley in the same strain at the Hudson Bay Company.

"Most of the traders," he said, "employ Mr. K——, but I don't.   I know too much for that.   How can a man do justice to those who are in direct opposition to his regular employers? The fact is," he said, " K—— hoodwinks our people, and while he makes them believe that he is doing the best for them, he is at the same time selling them to the Company.   You can depend upon it the H. B. C. is rotten, root and branch, and I don't know how good can come out of evil."

All this was like as much gibberish to poor George, who had as yet no opportunity of knowing the difference between a free trader and the Hudson Bay Company; he however listened good humoredly.

"Now, look here !" continued the Doctor, "up in the North-West the Company people do their best to ruin the trader,— they run him far and near, and often oblige him to pay double prices for his furs.   Of course the Company can afford this, but it goes hard with the trader.   Then here is K——, he gets all the furs, or most of them, to sell for the traders, and he just does as he likes with them.   I warrant you a large portion of them falls into the hands of the Honorable Com-pany.   K—— fills orders too, and makes his customers pay dearly for the whistle."

The Doctor had a very excited manner when he touched upon any of his peculiar hobbies.   " You had better look out," he went on to say to George.   " You are going to a new country ; you'll find lots of fine people there, but a great many rascals too."

"That is generally the way in most communities," interrupted George.

"Of course ! of course ! but you find it exemplified better in our small settlement than in almost any other part of the world. Why, sir, I've travelled a great deal, but nowhere did I ever find such a selfish, grinding, back-breaking corporation as we have up there in Red River ; but thank God we'll live to see it played out yet. They've run me hard I know, and used me hard as well. I shouldn't wonder if they had hired men to shoot me, but here I am and likely to be even with them yet."

George now began to find his patience wearing out, when the Doctor changed the subject, by asking him how he was going up, and what he intended to do when he reached Red River ?

"It is impossible to say at present," answered George. "I suppose I will have to make an arrangement with some one returning home, and when I reach my destination, why I'll tackle any honorable work that turns up."

"All right," said the Doctor, "then you'll come with me. I'm alone and will be going back in a day or two."

"I should prefer if possible," remarked George, " to travel in company with the Merediths, who came up in the boat with me."

"I'll wait for them," volunteered the Doctor. "So it is all arranged."

"I'll let you know this evening," remonstrated George. But the Doctor was off in another fit, and now began on the subject of furs. Without heeding the unwillingness of George to proceed, he almost dragged him up-stairs to his room, and opening the door, he pointed to a lot of furs that lay scattered on the floor, and which, even to Wade's unpracticed eye, looked a "hard lot."

"There," exclaimed the Doctor, "you see I do my own business. I unpack my fine furs up here ; I bring my customers along, and we fight out our own bargains all alone, much better than parading my stock in K——'s office."

"And how do you succeed ?" asked George.

"Well, you see they are not apt to bite immediately ; for instance, they are finding fault with this lot, saying they are poor and so forth ; but I'll fetch them to-morrow. Now let us go down and take a drink."

When they descended to the bar-room once more, their friends had disappeared ; and George, who remembered his appointment with Mr. Meredith, hastily excused himself from joining the Doctor in his " refreshment," and hurried away to the Hudson Bay Company's Office.

Dr. Flyaway consoled himself with two drinks, instead of one.

CHAPTER II.

EORGE WADE, on reaching Mr. K——'s office, found Mr. Meredith there with his two sons, as he had expected, and soon after they all sallied out in search of horses, waggons, and other requisites for their trip over the plains.

They found Mr. K—— a valuable assistant in procuring what they wanted; and through his forethought and experience in such matters, they were induced to lay in a supply of several articles which they found the necessity of ere they reached the end of their journey. In this way the balance of the afternoon was profitably spent.

Before parting with Mr. K——, George Wade mentioned to him the offer of Dr. Flyaway, and that gentleman's willingness to become one of the Meredith party.

Mr. K—— thought it should be accepted, as it was the only chance of the kind that would be likely to occur; "But," he said, "you must make up your mind to be regularly bored with a description of his experiences and complaints, and will most likely have to do his work as well as your own on the way up, for he is not particularly considerate in that line."

"I don't object seriously to the latter," replied George smiling, "but I must confess the former is hard to bear; however, I'll take your advice, and close with the Doctor."

They now shook hands with Mr. K——, thanking him at the same time for his kindness, and returned to the hotel, where they found Mrs. Meredith and Grace in the parlor awaiting their coming.

Mrs. Meredith, when they arrived, was deep in conversation with a lady almost her exact counterpart in appearance ; and strange to say, the subject of their confab was the faults and shortcomings of their respective families. Each from her own story, had a weighty burden of anxiety to bear. Grace, in the meantime, had been doing her best to entertain the husband of the lady above mentioned, a short stumpy in- dividual, with a decided nasal twang in his speech, and wear- ing a pair of large blue spectacles.

Mrs. Meredith was in the height of enjoyment, while Grace hailed the return of her father and the rest of the party with the greatest satisfaction, as an escape from her unpleasant position.

Jack and Tom immediately beseiged her with a jumbled up recital of their afternoon's proceedings ; a description of their horses, waggons, and their other purchases, among which Jack declared there was a night-cap for her to use when the mosquitoes were bad.

"And," said Tom, "George Wade has agreed to drive your waggon all the way to Red River, while I'm to ride with the Doctor. Eh, George ?"

"First I've heard of it."

"I'll leave it to father," said Tom winking.

"I've no objections, if George has'nt," quietly remarked Grace.

Tom who had taken a particular dislike to Dr. Flyaway, and had only uttered the speech to quiz his sister, now began to think he had been a little hasty.

"Then," said Mr. Meredith, "if George is agreeable, it is a bargain."

"Say it's all right," whispered Jack to Wade.

"I'll only be too glad of the change," said George laughing.

"I've no doubt of it," muttered Tom, feeling that he had sealed his own fate.

No one enjoyed Tom's discomfiture more than Grace, who teased him to her heart's content,—making up for it, however, (at least in Tom's estimation) by taking his arm to the tea-table, for both her brothers were not only fond, but proud of their sister, and vied with each other for a place in her favor.

After tea, a visit to the Opera House was proposed, and seconded stoutly by both Jack and Tom ; but Mrs. Meredith could not be persuaded to leave her new friend, nor forego the pleasure of relating once more to a ready listener the trials she deemed herself so subject to. Grace therefore also declined to go, and as George Wade declared himself no admirer of the drama, he too resolved on staying behind. Mr. Meredith and the two boys thereupon set out, and while they are enjoying their treat at the theatre, and Mrs. Meredith, oblivious to every-thing else, is reciting her wrongs, we will pay our attention to Grace and George Wade.

Seated on a sofa, in the anticipated enjoyment of an un-disturbed *tete-à-tete*, George said : "It seems strange to find myself addressing you as Grace on such a short acquaintance, and yet I feel as if I had known your whole family for years."

"I certainly prefer my Christian name to stiff Miss Mere-dith, especially from those I like."

"Then I may infer that you don't dislike me after all."

"I do not know what you mean by 'after all,' for I am not aware that I ever showed any particular dislike towards you."

"Not dislike," said George, "but I have fancied that you

might have deemed me rather forward, and perhaps it was all imagination, but I did think your manner at times evinced a little displeasure."

"It was all fancy," replied Grace, "I can assure you. It was through out-spoken Tom that you first came to call me Grace. Had it been disagreeable to me then in the least, I would have discountenanced it from the beginning."

"I am glad to hear this," said George, "for I now can feel more at my ease when calling you by your Christian name than I did before. And I should be sorry to have given you reason for displeasure towards me. I have learned somehow to look on you all as old friends, and you yourself more in the light of a sister than a friend."

"I have almost enough of brothers in Jack and Tom," interrupted Grace smiling, "but perhaps I could manage another."

"Since I can remember," continued George, "I have had neither mother nor sister to confide in and love, and I can assure you, either is a great want in a young man's life. Many and many a time have I longed for the gentle words of kindness that only a mother or sister knows how to bestow. I have certainly been blessed with a kind and indulgent father, but all his kindness could not fill the blank in my heart. I left home to go to sea when I was very young, and often while I've been on the yard, or keeping watch upon deck, or lying awake in my bunk, I have thought and thought over the pleasure of a mother's tenderness; and many a tear have I dropped over her miniature, which I carry next to my heart. I used to chide myself for being effeminate, but I could not help it. My mother's sweet face is always before me. I believe, Grace, that a sailor, from the very hardships and loneliness he endures, is more of a child in feelings than a landsman. I don't suppose there's any disgrace in it however."

"I should think not," said Grace. " I respect a man all the more for being gentle in feeling as long as his acts are manly ; and now George, we are all going to a strange country, amongst strange people, and I hope you will regard us in the light of true friends to you, for I know that from what father has said, that you'll always find a ready welcome at our door."

"I am sure I feel grateful for your kindness," answered George ; "and if half of what Dr. Flyaway has told me be correct, we'll not find many true friends up there. But I am inclined to believe that we are amongst a frank open-hearted people. The traders I have met with here, with the exception of Dr. Flyaway, seem to be a jolly set of fellows."

"Perhaps too jolly," said Grace laughing.

"Well," replied George, "I've always heard of the Nor'-Westers as partial to their creature comforts, but that's not much of a fault as long as they don't 'splice the main brace' too often."

They continued chatting the time pleasantly away, finding much to speak about in the prospects before them, and the long evening was far spent before they were aware of it. They were at last reminded of the late hour by the two boys bursting in upon them, exclaiming "Hilloh ! there you are."

"And where's your father, you good-for-nothings," cried Mrs. Meredith, suddenly interrupted in her *tete-à-tete.*

"Oh ! such a time," shouted both Jack and Tom.

"I tell you, Gracie," said Tom, " we've had the greatest old fun."

"Did'nt you hear me, boys," again cried Mrs. Meredith, where's your father ?"

"He's all right, mother," replied Jack.

"That's not an answer to what I asked you," angrily returned his mother.

C

"Well now," said Tom, "just let me tell you the whole story and you'll see."

"That's how I'm fixed," whispered Mrs. Meredith to her friend.

"You know we went to the theatre," continued Tom.

"Better have stayed at home," muttered his mother.

"And a man there they called Toodles was staggering about—he was drunk, mother."

"The beast!"

"So he was—for he was always making fun of his wife. Well, Toodles had a white neck-cloth on which stuck up all stiff on one side, and then he tried to knock it down, eyeing it sideways, like you do me sometimes, Grace."

"Go on Tom," said his sister, "what about father?"

"Well, old neck-cloth was making such awful faces at us that the thin chap, Flyaway, who was about as drunk as Toodles, roared out, 'Down with the rag.' Toodles seemed to get sober all of a minute, and Flyaway was chucked out into the street as quick as lightning. Then two or three of the fellows from Red River asked father to go with them to try and keep Flyaway out of a scrape. Jimminy! you ought to have seen him kick when they were taking him out—eh! Jack?"

"You have'nt told us where your father is yet," said Mrs. Meredith.

"Why he went off to look after Flyaway. Jack and I stayed till the theatre was out, and father said he'd be home as soon as us. I guess he'll be here soon."

George Wade now observed a shade of anxiety pass over the features of Grace, and having some idea of the cause, he arose to take his leave, saying at the same time that he thought a walk before bed-time would do him good, and that he might come across Flyaway, whom he wished to see.

" You may see him, but I'll bet he won't be able to see you,"
said Tom.

Grace gave George a look of gratitude at parting, and he set
out fully determined to hunt up Mr. Meredith, and remain with
him until he should return to the hotel.

He had heard from Grace that her father had sold a good
property in Canada to emigrate to Red River, and that the
greater portion of the proceeds of this sale he carried on his
person. George knew that this was dangerous in one of Mr.
Meredith's temperament, for, although not given to excess, he
was fond of good company, and were he by any means to lose
the money he had about him in an unguarded moment, it
would place the whole family in a very awkward and trying
position. This, then, was the secret of Grace's anxiety, and
George knowing it, departed at once upon his mission.

He had not walked far up Third Street when he met his
friend of the morning, the trader to whom he had been introduced in Mr. K——'s office ; stopping him, he asked if he had
seen Mr. Meredith?

" Just left him," was the reply. " You see where that
light is (pointing to a house a short distance off) ; go in there
and you'll find the whole party. I'm tired and am going to
bed ; good night."

George proceeded as instructed, and when he had entered
the restaurant, to which he had been directed, he heard loud
voices in an inner room, the loudest of which he recognized as
belonging to Dr. Flyaway.

" Hic ! Hic ! fill your glasses, no heel-taps ; here's how
confusion to all mo-mo-nopolies."

When George had knocked at the door twice, and finding
his summons still unheeded, he turned the handle, and on
entering found himself in rather riotous company. The in

vincible Doc, who sat at the head of the table, around which were other eight persons, seemed in the very height of excitement, but fast approaching a state of happy obliviousness. The others in the room, although full of merriment, and showing evident signs of having spent a "cheerful" evening, were not, however, so far "gone" as Flyaway.

They had just drained their glasses when George entered, and when they perceived him they gave him a hearty welcome to join them. ·

"Hilloh! who's there ?" cried the Doctor. "Why, its my friend. Come along Mr.—Mr.—what's your name ? Yes, yes! by the way, friend, what the d——l is your name ? (here Doc nearly choked over an enormous sneeze). But what's the difference as long we're odd, eh! B——, hi, waiter! wait—er! (on that functionary's appearance), a tumbler for my friend (hic), and a little (hic)—(hic), more water ; no, I mean more whiskey—the real stuff, eh, B——! Now boys (hic), take care of the new chap."

"Say Doc, tell us how you sold your rats," said one.

"Rats be ——."

"Give us a speech on the Hudson Bay Company, then," cried another.

"Gentle—men, you—you all (hic) know my senti—ments on—on (hic) that question (hic) ; but they'll never—ever—ever kill old Flyaway (hic)."

"Hurrah," shouted two or three ; "go it, Doc."

In this way they joked the poor man, until, at last overcome by the powerful hand of John Barleycorn, he lay back on his seat and fell fast asleep with his eyes shut, but mouth wide open. One of the traders present, more mischievous than the rest, now proceeded with a burnt cork to write H. B. C. on the forehead of the sleeping man, and otherwise adorn his countenance, until his most intimate friend could not have re-cognized him..

But as the finishing touches were being put to the Doctor's features, amidst the laughter of those present, they were startled by the cry of "fire! fire!" ringing clear and sharp on the night air.

Each one in the room (excepting Flyaway), thought of his valuables, papers, etc., left behind him in the hotel, the loss of which would have been a serious matter with some of them. Mr. Meredith thought at once of his family, and George re-collected Grace. A general rush was made for the street; where, to their relief, they found that the glare of the distant conflagration was in the opposite direction from the "Mer-chants'."

Their conviviality was broken up, however, and a separation for the night being agreed upon, the question arose: "What was to be done with Doc.?" That gentleman unex-pectedly settled the point on his own behalf, and in a manner not looked for. It appears, happening to awake from his sleep, he chanced to perceive, in a large mirror opposite to him, the reflection of his own painted features.

The effect on him was as startling as had been the cry of fire on his companions; and bewildered, no doubt, from the effects of his late debauch, he started unsteadily to his feet, and peered almost horror-stricken into the mirror; then with a loud cry he bounded from the room, nearly rolling over his friends as he swept past them into the open air. "The devil! the devil!" he yelled, as he tore from side to side up the street, without hat or cap, and his hair like bristles on end. Those who had spent the evening with him were at first stupified by this sudden appearance of one whom, only a few moments before, they had left sound asleep; but quickly recollecting his painted face, and the probable predicament it might bring him into, they set off in pursuit of the terrified Doctor.

George Wade, however, drew Mr. Meredith's arm within his own, and quietly said : " Let us go back to the 'Merchants"; they'll be anxious about us."

"Of course," said Mr. Meredith; "we've been too long away."

CHAPTER III.

HE next morning, George found on enquiring that Dr. Flyaway had left for St. Cloud by the early train. It appears he had been overtaken the previous evening by his friends in his mad career up Third Street, and after a good deal of persuasion, induced to return to the hotel, where he had been immediately put to bed. George thinking this sudden depart-ure of the Doctor very strange, resolved upon asking at the office whether he had left a letter or any word for him there.

The clerk on being interrogated, replied that Dr. Flyaway seemed when leaving to be in a great flurry, but that he had left a note for the gentleman in room No. —.

"My name is Wade," said George, "and you will see on looking at the register that that is the number of my room—the letter therefore is intended for me."

"All right, sir ; here it is."

George took the epistle, and opening it read as follows :—

"Dear Sir,—I have not had the pleasure of your name, or if I ever heard it, I have forgotten it. I was so confoundedly drunk last night that I felt it high time to 'vamoose,' so I shall leave for St. Cloud this morning. I'll wait a day for you there, but if you don't make your appearance at the end of that time, adieu till I see you in Red River.   Who the d——l blackened my face last night ?   I hope it wasn't you.   I'm not accustomed to such familiarities from strangers.   Don't forget to bring a bottle of grog with you.   I'm *awful dry* this morning.

"Yours truly,

"RUFUS FLYAWAY."

George could not help smiling when he read this characteristic document.   Then, going in search of Mr. Meredith, he acquainted that gentleman with the information he had just received,

"We all leave in the morning for St. Cloud," said Mr. Meredith, "so that you'll be in time ; but if you want to secure your man, why not go up by this afternoon's train ?"

"No!" said George, "I'll remain and help you to get the horses, waggons and other traps down to the depot.   I suppose the doctor will be a man of his word."

"Doubtful," said one of the traders, who was standing by. "He's inclined to be tricky, and I'll wager if *you went* to St. Cloud this afternoon you would find that he had left you ; but you need not worry yourself; some of us will see you through."

"I'm much obliged," said George as they separated.

During the morning Mrs. Meredith and Grace went out shopping, to purchase a few articles which they thought would be of use in the country they were going to, as well as to provide some comforts that had been overlooked when leaving Canada.

Mr. Meredith, the two boys and George, in the meantime, went to work with a will and soon saw their horses, waggons and baggage safely on board the cars, ready for the next morning ; and when finished with their labor, they strolled about the extensive freight sheds on the levee.

Boats were coming in and others leaving—some blowing off steam or whistling, and loud above the din arose the hoarse shouts of men. Altogether a scene of bustle and activity presented itself to their wondering eyes.

Piled up here and there in the sheds were large quantities of buffalo robes, packed and ready for shipment to the east. Several of the free traders were moving about superintending the dispatch of their goods to St. Cloud, or looking after their furs, which were being landed from the cars. A great deal of what they saw was novel to them ; even George Wade acknowledged that some of the sights were quite new to him an experienced traveller. Mr. K—— met them in their perambulations, and laughed heartily when George told him of Flyaway's last move.

"His leaving you behind," he remarked, "depends on how the spirit moves the man ; if he takes it into his head, he will most assuredly consult his own feelings without respecting any promises made beforehand to you. The fact is, the Doctor has made a fool of himself in selling his furs, and the others have been chaffing him about it, so that to escape them, I should'nt wonder if he did leave you in the lurch. But I've no doubt you'll be able to make some other arrangement when you reach St. Cloud, although you may have some difficulty in doing so."

"If it comes to the worst, I can buy a horse and light-waggon," said George.

They now adjourned to the hotel, and after dinner the Merediths and George hired a couple of conveyances and drove to Minneapolis, passing on the way a half-breed camp, being a portion of the last train of Red River carts that visited St. Paul, St. Cloud having been their destination since then.

Mrs. Meredith grumbled a good deal at what she termed the extravagance of driving about in fine carriages, when the money could have been better spent; but on the whole she enjoyed the jaunt very much.

The Falls of St. Anthony were first visited, and the numerous saw and grist mills lining the banks on each side of the river impressed them with the go-aheadism of the American people. Before returning to St. Paul, a pleasant hour was spent at the Minnehaha Falls ; and with the exception of Mrs. Meredith, all were delighted with the beauty of the spot.

"After hearing the roar of St. Anthony," said Grace, "how soothing, if I may use the term, is the sound of Minnehaha—laughing water! How impressive and appropriate is the name. I am sure Minnehaha is worthy of its place in Hiawatha."

"It is, indeed," said George. "It is the most romantic little spot I think I have ever had the pleasure of visiting."

"Let us explore a little further," suggested Grace, " and we may find fresh beauties."

"I'm at your command," replied George.

"I'm not astonished at the water laughing at you," said Mrs. Meredith, "the way you talk ; but if you think I'm going to break my neck down that bank for such foolery, you're mistaken. I'm going to sit under that tree, and when you come back you'll find me there." So saying the good lady left them.

Mr. Meredith had stretched himself at full length on the grass in a shady nook with his handkerchief over his face, and was enjoying a nap.

Jack and Tom could be heard in the distance, shouting and scrambling over broken branches and fallen leaves, up and down the banks of the stream. George and Grace being therefore left to themselves, set out on their tour of exploration.

Descending a narrow path, they reached the edge of the stream and passed quickly over the dilapidated bridge in front of the Fall, getting a partial ducking from the spray as they crossed; then following the winding course of the brook (for it is little more) they enjoyed their ramble to their heart's content; but it must be said their own uninterrupted society was the greatest charm to them.

"George, you're a good fellow," remarked Grace, "for your thoughtfulness last night about my father."

"Why, I did nothing out of the common," replied George. "I know from experience what landing in a strange port is, and I took it into my head that Mr. Meredith might get foul of some craft that would do him damage. There's sharks on land much worse than those in the sea. It was a bit of conceit on my part, too, in fancying that I could detect a rogue better than your father, but you see I've been bit (as they call it) before now."

" The principal fear I felt when the boys told me father had left them at the theatre, was that he might be robbed, and if he had been, I do not know what we should have done. I have asked him so often to leave the money behind him when he goes out, but he says it is safer with him. I'll not be sorry when we're once more fairly on our way to Red River."

"Neither will I," said George, " and by the way, Master Tom is likely to escape his expected torture on the trip,—for I fully look forward, from all I can learn, to find Dr. Flyaway gone when we reach St. Cloud."

" Tom will be sorry," said Grace, laughing.

"You do not suppose, however," remarked George, that I meant to carry out the plan of changing places with Tom. I merely acquiesced at the time to tease him."

"Very flattering to me," returned Grace, feigning displeasure.

" Perhaps," replied George, "you will find fault with me before we reach Red River for tasking you too much with my society."

" We are playing at cross purposes," said Grace, " and had better change the subject—besides, it is time to return ;—we have a long drive before us."

" Just a little while," said George, his voice somewhat tremulous as he spoke—" I may not have another opportunity like the present for some time, and—

Splash came something into the stream at their feet, sprinkling them with a shower of water,—then followed a couple of shouts from the opposite bank.

" Spoons !" cried Tom, thrusting his head out of the thicket.

George bit his lip, and tried hard to laugh, while Grace, blushing deeply, vowed all sorts of vengeance on Tom for his impertinence.

"Perhaps," bawled out Jack over Tom's shoulder, "you were out looking for us."

" It's as well for both of you," replied Grace, " there's no bridge here, so that I could get near you ; you've wet me from head to foot."

" We'll swim over to you, if it will do you any good," cried Tom, " but good-bye, sis !—we're off— and only called out to invite you both to some strawberries and cream up at the house ; don't hurry, we'll wait ; and the two boys scampered off laughing heartily at what to them seemed a good joke, but which, as will be seen, hereafter proved an important turn in the affairs of the two would-be lovers. The opportunity lost was not regained for some time, causing as will be shown, a good deal of misunderstanding between the lovers. George and Grace rejoined their friends at the refreshment saloon attached to the Falls, where they found Jack and Tom looking as demure as two quakers.

" Come along truants," said Mr. Meredith, " here we have a treat (pointing to a large dish of strawberries before him) all at Tom's expense, and which my good wife declares is far better than all the Falls in existence."

"Indeed that's just so," cried Mrs. Meredith. "1 would like to know what good that drop of water tumbling over a rock is to do us looking at it—it's nothing but a humbug to my mind to take people in. I'd make a better show emptying my wash tub, and a heap more froth."

"And a heap more noise, too," whispered Tom to Jack.

Grace and George sat down, and all enjoyed the refreshment exceedingly. Mrs. Meredith especially seemed in her element, and had her saucer refilled so often with the tempting fruit, that Tom at last began to count his loose change to ascertain whether he would have enough to foot the bill.

The afternoon was well nigh spent when they re-entered their carriages and drove back to St. Paul.

On reaching the "Merchant's," and after they had taken tea, it was proposed by Tom, and seconded by Jack, that they should all attend the circus, which had arrived in the city during the day, and was to perform that evening.

Mrs. Meredith seemed horrified at first at the idea, and asked them if they'd not had enough foolery for one day. But on George pressing her to go, the good lady at last consented to accompany them to what she styled as Vanity Fair, adding that she did not know where all this sort of carrying on was to end. Had she foreseen what afterwards happened on this eventful evening, there is little doubt but that she would have insisted upon remaining behind.

As they were leaving the hotel, they observed indications of an approaching storm, which caused them to hesitate about proceeding further; but at last the reasoning of Jack and Tom prevailed, and they decided upon running the risk of a probable drenching than disappoint the two boys.

A peal of thunder in the distance, rumbling in its grandeur, startled Mrs. Meredith so much just as they were entering the circus tent that she expressed a wish to return to the hotel.

"What's the use of going back, mother?" said Tom, "you're sure to get wet if you do."

"And if you stay till we all see the fun," added Jack, "I'll take you to the hotel in a cab."

"I think we have had cabbing enough for one day," answered the old lady; "but I suppose I'll have to wait till its over, for I'm sure none of you will go home with me now."

"If you really wish," George commenced to say.

"Don't trouble yourself, Mr. Wade. You'd only be doing something against your will," interrupted Mrs. Meredith. "But I don't see what we're standing here for talking, when every body else are getting seats."

"That serves you right," whispered Tom to George, "for being so ready to offer."

"You'd better stick to Grace," added Jack, and both the boys laughed at Wade's discomfiture.

They then entered the pavilion just as the rain descended in torrents.

"There, now, mother," said Tom " ain't you glad you took my advice."

"Your advice," quoth Mrs. Meredith, " if I had taken my own way I'd not be here now. Oh! dear where's this all going to end."

Bang, came the crash of the band, introducing as it were the performers, who now filled the inside of the ring, and opened the evening's entertainment by the usual evolutions on horseback.

Mrs. Meredith was fairly silenced at last, for if she made any further complaints they were unheard.

Meantime the storm raged more and more furiously without, and loud above the noise of the band came peal after peal of thunder. The canvas became violently agitated, and the rain began to find its way through upon both performers and audience. As if in defiance of the tempest, the clowns did their utmost to hold the attention of the people ; the gymnasts executed wonderful feats ; the riders, apparently reckless of all danger, performed astonishing exploits, and the band exerted themselves to the very best of their ability ; but all to no purpose ; a general feeling of uneasiness pervaded the assemblage.

Our friends now began to regret that they had ventured out in the face of the storm ; but there seemed to them no chance for escape as they were hemmed in on every side by people equally anxious with themselves to leave the tent.

At this moment a sudden and more powerful gust of wind extinguished the lights. The ropes which served to support the tent began to give way. Women and children screamed in their fear. Men began to battle for a passage through the crowd to escape. Self-preservation overruled better feelings, and the stronger prevailed, and in many cases refused to assist the weaker. A dreadful catastrophe seemed imminent.

At last one side gave way, dragging with it the seats, and precipitating men, women and children on the ground. A desperate struggle for life ensued, in which the blustering bully cowered in an agony of fright, while many a poor weak woman taught him a lesson of heroism. Children were trampled under foot, and altogether there was every appearance that many would be lost.

During this time our friends the Merediths and George were also battling their way from under the canvas, but in the hubbub they became separated, which resulted in a manner that leads to the introduction of a very important actor in our tale.

It appears that Mrs. Meredith, when the seats gave way, was landed a few feet apart from where her husband was, and in the darkness and tumult she was unable to regain his side. In a manner quite characteristic of her, she began to screech, kick and scratch everybody and everything she came in contact with, until finally she felt a stout arm round her waist, and a hand placed over her mouth. In this way she found herself slowly but surely dragged along by some unseen person, and in spite of her struggles she at last was extricated from her dangerous position, and placed in safety in the open air, minus bonnet and shawl, and her dress torn almost to ribbons.

"There you are, Madam," said a gentleman at her elbow " You've had a narrow escape."

" Yes ! here I am," she answered, " but where's my husband and children ?   Oh ! dear, what a fool I have been to listen to those boys.   Was it you that took me out ?"

" It was," replied the gentleman.   " I hope you're not hurt."

" I can't say that I am ; but my bonnet and shawl are gone, and sakes alive ! how my dress is torn."

" Where do you live ?" asked her preserver.

" Live !" she exclaimed.   " I'd just like to know that myself.   If it was'nt a sin, I'd wish I was dead.   What will become of me now.   I suppose my husband and children are smothered by this time."

" If you'll remain here a few minutes," said the gentleman beside her, " I'll go and see what I can do to help some of the others out."

" Of course I'll stay here.   And if you hear any one asking for a stray woman, tell them I'm here."

The gentleman who had thus been of such good service to Mrs. Meredith, now proceeded back to the tent, and exerted himself to assist the people from under its folds.

In the meantime we will endeavour to describe him, as he will play an important part in some of the scenes of our tale.

In the first place, he hailed from Red River, was tall and of a very commanding appearance, and he impressed confidence at first sight, while his manner was so suave and polite that he usually attracted people towards him. His features were good —of a dark complexion, and a plentitude of brown, curly hair. His eyes, however, betrayed two features in his character, which soon showed themselves on an intimate acquaintance with him. Of a shade between blue and gray, they had a most determined habit of turning another way when you looked into them, while the next moment you would be very apt to find them set fixedly upon you. The characteristics this habit betrayed were, insincerity and treachery, both of which were attributes of this remarkable man. Endowed with the faculty of making friends, he used his power for his own personal ends, without the slightest solicitude whether by so doing he injured those who treated him with friendship—a boon that most men love to cultivate and deserve. Almost all those who became intimate or friendly with Mr. Cool, complained of having been taken in, some way or another, and it was this indiscriminate mode of using or abusing his friends that eventually made him an object of dislike and fear in Red River Settlement. On first acquaintance, however, his manner appeared so open, frank, and even kind, that he succeeded in obtaining many victims to his unfortunate habit of "making money out of his friends."

His timely rescue of Mrs. Meredith gave him an opportunity for a further and more intimate acquaintance with the family, a chance which he did not allow to pass, as soon as he learned that they were bound for Red River.

On leaving Mrs. Meredith, Mr. Cool proceeded at once to

D

assist, as far as he was able, in the rescue of the unfortunates who were struggling beneath the canvas of the overturned tent, and in doing so, he came across Mr. Meredith, who appeared to be hunting very anxiously about for some missing one.

Mr. Cool ventured a remark in his hearing, with regard to the rescued lady, upon which the old gentleman addressed him, and asked where she could be found.

The two gentlemen then proceeded to the spot where Mrs. Meredith stood, and soon afterwards they were joined by the two boys, as well as Grace and George, all having escaped without injury. It appears that George, as soon as the tent began to give way, watched closely over Grace, and when the final crash came he bore her away in his arms, cutting his passage through the canvas with his pocket knife. The two boys managed to stick together, and also succeeded in getting out of the tumult without injury.

All more or less had suffered in the way of torn clothes; and Mr. Cool and Mr. Meredith were the only persons belonging to the party who had covering for their heads.

It still continued to pour in torrents, so that as soon as it was ascertained that all the people were rescued from under the fallen tent, the party, accompanied by Mr. Cool, returned to the hotel, worn out, and sadder if not wiser people than when they left it about an hour and a half previous.

The accident to the circus happily resulted only in a few bruises to some of the audience, and fortunately no lives were lost.

When they regained the "Merchants'," Mrs. Meredith, unable longer to control herself, at last burst forth—

"There, you good-for-nothings! didn't I tell you it was nothing but a Vanity Fair: see how its ended—in a slough of despond. I knew pride would have a fall; here we've been driving about like grand folks all day, and look at me now ; look at my dress—cost fifteen dollars when it was new, and now its not worth as many cents—and there's my shawl and bonnet gone. I tell you that country we're going to will have to be a fine place to make money to pay up for all this foolery. If it hadn't been for this gentleman here, I'd have been gone too, although I suppose not one of you would have been sorry, but never mind."

" We'd had better go to our room, mother, and change our clothes," said Grace, " you may catch cold."

" I'm going to bed," answered her mother; " that I am— you'll not get me downstairs again."

George and the two boys had gone to their rooms as soon as they had reached the hotel, and when Mrs. Meredith and Grace had retired, Mr. Cool and Mr. Meredith repaired to the bar room, to obtain something, as they said, to keep the cold out.

" We are very much indebted to you for your timely help to my wife," said Mr. Meredith to Mr. Cool.

" It was by chance," answered the latter, " that I happened to be of service to your good lady ; but I have overheard that you are going to Red River, and this meeting in its peculiar character may be the means of a closer intimacy between us.

" It will give me great pleasure I am sure," said Mr. Meredith ; and on being requested by Mr. Cool, he then gave him his name and voluntarily offered him some information as to his intentions when he reached Red River.

Mr. Cool, on the other hand, stated that he had only just arrived that day in St. Paul from the North-West, but intended to hurry through his business as quickly as possible, and would probably overtake him (Mr. Meredith) on the road ; and at the same time he advised the old gentleman to take no steps towards settling down in Red River until he (Mr. Cool) joined him there, as he knew of a fine opening for a man with means, which he would be happy to secure for Mr. Meredith.

The latter promised to do nothing until Mr. Cool should join him in Red River, and after some further conversation, the two separated for the night —Mr. Meredith fully impressed with the idea that he had met the finest man from Red River, and congratulating himself on his good fortune in having secured the acquaintance of such an open, frank and disinterested person.

Mr. Cool, however, had far different feelings. His were, that he had met a man with some means apparently, whom he would endeavour to fleece in as polite and affable a manner as possible. How far he succeeded in his designs will be seen hereafter. One person, however, fortunately for Mr. Meredith, had that night divined the true character of Mr. Cool.

CHAPTER IV.

HE next morning, our friends started for St. Cloud, by the early train, in company with a few of the Red River traders, who having finished their business in St. Paul, were bound for home, not to return till the following summer.

After seeing the ladies comfortably seated, George and Mr. Meredith repaired to the second-class car to enjoy a smoke, where they found a number of German immigrants on their way to settle in the northern part of Minnesota. Those thrifty people seemed to be all well provided with the necessaries, and many comforts, for starting in their new life. Quiet and orderly, they are by far the best class of settlers whom Uncle Sam receives under his protection. Nothing apparently could disturb their good nature, although they were often treated in a very rough manner by the men in charge of the train and of way stations. It was strange to observe how well, in their simplicity, they managed to deal with the customs of the country, new and foreign as they must have been to them. A funny incident occurred while our two friends were smoking, which, although grotesque in the extreme, nearly resulted in fatal consequences. The news-boy in passing along with a basket of "pop," offered a bottle of the beverage free of charge to one of the German immigrants, on condition that he would agree to pull the cork out with his teeth. The poor man, thirsty from the heat, gladly assented, not being aware of the effervescing power of the liquid offered him. The mischievous boy on quietly removing the wire from the neck of the bottle, pressed his thumb in its stead upon the cork, and presented it to the gaping mouth of the unsuspecting German. A report followed, and then the astonished, and in fact terrified, victim of the trick sprang to his feet, spluttering and gasping as if in an agony of torture. Loud roars of laughter sounded throughout the car, which instantly, however, turned to expressions of dismay, when it was found that the man was actually choking, the cork having lodged in his throat.

George Wade, with great presence of mind, at once struck the unfortunate immigrant a terrific blow on the back, which was the means of making the cork pop out of his mouth as quickly as it had popped in. The uproar caused by this singular affair had hardly subsided, when the train ran into a herd of cattle which had strayed upon the track, killing four animals and wounding three others. They hardly stopped to see the damage done, but the engineer whistling "off breaks," they proceeded on as if nothing had happened.

"It's a wonder," said Mr. Meredith, "that the railway company do not build fences on each side of the track, for if they commit this havoc often, it must turn out an expensive item in the running of the road."

" Our American neighbours," said George, " seem to look on such things as trifles; while in Canada, I am told, they are considered in a much more serious light than sometimes they deserve ; for instance, this accident would no doubt be reported far and near in the Canadian newspapers, while probably we will not hear anything more about it in this case."

They now stopped a few minutes at one of the way stations,

where Master Tom, having alighted to see a little of the country, nearly got left behind.

The whistle had sounded, and the train began to move, and still Tom remained stationary, quietly listening to a discussion between a long, lean and lanky clergyman and an elderly lady. The minister was laying down the law in a most emphatic manner, when Tom, who was near him, suddenly perceived the train in motion, and recollecting that he was a passenger thereby, made a dart forward, upsetting the preacher into a large basket of eggs that stood directly behind him. No pen can portray the scene that ensued, but in the midst of the uproar Tom managed to catch the railing of the car and was dragged on board by Jack.

When the two boys looked back, they saw the station agent, with a most woe-begone countenance, assisting the clergyman from his plight. The contents of the broken eggs could be seen dripping down from the once black but now yellow clothes on the poor man's back. The elderly lady, who had been in conversation with the unfortunate victim, was holding up her hands in unspeakable amazement, while the last seen of the station agent he was shaking his fist energetically in the direction of the train, no doubt calculating in his own mind how much eggs would be worth by the basketful. Nothing else worthy of notice occurred until they reached St. Cloud.

As they were entering the station they observed a number of peculiarly dressed men standing in groups upon the platform, many of whom seemed to view the approaching train with wondering eyes. These, as they found out, were half-breeds from Red River, engaged in freighting goods for the free-traders and Hudson Bay Company. All of them had sashes round their waists, some of which were of the brightest hues. A few, spotted leggings highly ornamented with bead work.   One or two wore long blue coats, with bright buttons, while others were in their shirt sleeves ; and the most of them had moccasins on their feet.   As a general thing, they shewed great strength and activity of body ; their features were chiefly dark, but regular—mild and pleasant in their appearance.   As a rule, they were what would be considered handsome, although many of them gave indisputable signs of Indian origin.   This latter does not apply in all cases to the half-breed (as might be supposed), especially in the case of those claiming Scottish descent, as in these the Celtic characteristics seem to pre-dominate.

The French appear to resemble the Indian more than either the English or Scotch settlers, although in many cases it is difficult to distinguish their nationality until you enter into conversation with them, when you at once detect the difference, the Highland accent being particularly noticeable.

When George and the Merediths descended from the train they observed the free-traders who had accompanied them from St. Paul, in the midst of their freighters lustily shaking hands with each one of them in turn—passing jokes, asking questions and making promises to load up their carts immediately, and so forth.   Near the station, on the common adjoining it, could be seen the camps around which were placed the carts, and here and there were bands of cattle—oxen and horses—grazing in the enjoyment of a rest after their fatiguing trip.

The Merediths and George drove over in the omnibus to St. Cloud, and had to go quite a distance round to reach the ferry which crosses the Mississippi above the town.

After dinner, while Grace and Mrs. Meredith, accompanied by the two boys, sallied out for a stroll, George and Mr.

Meredith returned across the river to the station to look after the horses, waggons and baggage.

When they reached the depot, they saw a scene of bustle and activity; a number of the Red River carts were being loaded up, preparatory to starting for home. These carts are worthy of notice from their peculiar construction. No iron work is to be seen about them, and instead of nails and bolts, strips of Buffalo hide are used for fastening them together. The two wheels are large and clumsily made, with no tires upon them. Although the work upon them is very rough, and one would imagine likely to get out of order, yet they stand the hard usage they are necessarily subject to without breaking down or giving much trouble to those in charge of them on a trip. They will generally last for a couple or three years, and will carry from 800 to 1,200 lbs. weight, the former amount being the general standard. As grease is not considered requisite for the axles, they send forth a very unpleasant creaking noise when the cart is in motion; and, on a calm day, a train of these primitive conveyances can be heard a long distance off as they move lazily along. The number of carts in a train varies from 10 to 100, and there is generally one man in charge of each three carts. The oxen are harnessed in the same manner as horses, one to each cart, minus the bridle, and it would be well for farmers to take a lesson from this, as a collar is found to be far preferable to the yoke.

But to return to the loading process. A number of carts were backed up against the platform and two or three of the free-traders were busy selecting and superintending the placing of their packages upon them. Great care had to be taken in doing this, so as not to overload any one particular cart, or to give to one freighter more unprofitable loads than his neighbours. The half-breeds assisted each other in the loading, and seemed to be altogether above any petty feeling of jealousy, or a desire to be disobliging. All was good humor, and a great deal of merriment was mixed up with their hard work.

When a cart was loaded, it was taken at once to the camp, there to be re-packed, corded, and properly covered, and when one freighter has completed his whole brigade in this way, he generally looks about for another as a partner for the trip, and starts at once on his return home. The number of carts from Red River to St. Cloud in a season varies from 1,500 to 2,000, and allowing one man to each three carts, there are from five to six hundred half-breeds who visit the States every summer. The Red River carts at one time went as far as LaCrosse for supplies ; but as railways extended, the length of their trips decreased in proportion. St. Paul became their destination, then St. Cloud, and so it will go on until the cart will be altogether superseded by the iron horse, and the people of the North-West will receive their goods direct from the seaboard by rail transportation.

While George and Mr. Meredith were engaged in getting their horses, waggons, etc., taken from the cars, one or two of the half-breeds volunteered to help them, which was thankfully accepted, and George remarked how willingly they put their hands forward to assist perfect strangers. With the aid thus unexpectedly obtained, our two friends soon had everything in readiness to proceed once more across the Mississippi ; but before doing so, they resolved upon paying a visit amongst the camps to gain a little insight into the manners of the people they were going to live amongst. One of the most extensive traders in the settlement now offered to accompany them, as he had to hunt up some of his men. This trader is one who is also destined to become familiar to our readers.

Of a medium height, he impressed one at first sight as being very much of the gentleman, both in appearance and manners —quiet, polite, affable, and very considerate towards those he came in contact with. Pleasant features, set off to advantage by a long beard, he had not the same ruddy, hardy appearance that characterized most of the other Red River men,—although he was not by any means behind them in endurance or activity. Full of fun, and even mischief, he was universally beloved by the half-breeds, and his patient, kind manner in dealing with them, led them to place the greatest confidence in his word and judgment. To his good qualities in these respects he, to a great extent, owed his success as a trader, for no one in Red River was more generally liked or trusted in business matters than Mr. Bon.

As the trio were walking out in the direction of the camps, George who had been making diligent inquiries as to the whereabouts of Flyaway (so far without success), turned to Mr. Bon and asked whether he knew what had become of the Doctor ?

" He left for Red River yesterday afternoon, soon after he arrived from St. Paul," was the reply ; "and some of his men are in a fix about their loads. I don't know what to make of the Doctor."

Mr. Meredith burst out laughing at this, and said,—"No one else seems to be able to make him out either. He made an arrangement with my friend Mr. Wade to take him to Red River."

"I am very sorry to hear this," said Mr. Bon, "as I am afraid there will be some difficulty in getting such another chance. I would have been very happy to accommodate you, Mr. Wade, but I have already promised to take up a young gentleman who is about joining the Hudson Bay Company's

service. We will see, however, what can be done when we
return to the station."

"If you could direct me," said George, "where I could be
best able to look up a stout horse and light waggon, I think
I will decide at once upon going up on my own hook, in company with Mr. Meredith and his family."

"That can be easily managed," said Mr. Bon. "It is really
too bad that Flyaway should have treated you in this way."

"I was more than half prepared for it," said George.

"I intend starting to-morrow, and," suggested Mr. Bon,
"if it is agreeable, we can all go together."

"I'd like nothing better," replied Mr. Meredith. "We are
strangers, and the road is strange to us, so that we will be only
too glad of such an arrangement."

"I'll wager," continued Mr. Bon, "we will overtake Dr.
Flyaway, and probably pass him before he reaches Red River."

They had now arrived at the nearest camp, in which the
men were busy re-arranging the freight on their carts, covering them up with dry cow-hides, and securing the loads by
cording the packages well together. A small canvas tent stood
in the centre of the camp, at the door of which lay a stoutly-
built man at full length on the grass, with his face towards the
ground. As they approached he looked up, and Mr. Bon
addressed him,—

"Well, André, making ready for a start?"

"Yes, sir; François and I are off early in the morning."

"Any one else going?" asked Mr. Bon.

"Baptiste may start with us," replied the man; "but if he
goes on drinking as much as he's doing, he won't get off for a
month."

"Try to bring him along with you," said Mr. Bon. "He is
a good man, and it's a pity to see him that way.—*Bon jour*,

Andrè, and a good trip to you. I'll let your old woman know you're coming when I get home."

"All right—*bon jour*," said the man, laughing.

"That is one of our best freighters," continued Mr. Bon, to George and Mr. Meredith, as they walked away—"careful, honest and steady—I never knew him to damage an article on a trip. But in fact there are few instances where we lose much by this mode of transporting our goods. The men are honest, as a rule, and although they have every chance to make away with things on a trip (for we never take a receipt from them), we seldom if ever find a single article missing; and if there is any damage done, it generally turns out to have been unavoidable. They can say what they like about these poor fellows, but I'll wager should almost any other class of men be placed in the same position, they would not prove so trustworthy. Many of them are fond of liquor, yet we never find the casks tampered with, from the time they leave St. Cloud till they reach Red River."

"We did not expect," said Mr. Meredith, "from the descriptions we heard of the half-breeds of Red River, in Canada, to find them the people they are ; for instance, we had no idea that they were so intelligent as they seem to be. The truth is, in a few words, we were led to look upon them as a slight degree better than the uncivilized Indians. This is a strange and unaccountable mistake, and how the impression has got abroad, I cannot imagine."

"I think," said Mr. Bon, "I can account for it in this way ; the few who have visited Red River Settlement have never taken the pains to learn the true character of the people in it, and as it is natural for the half-breeds to be reserved before strangers, this, no doubt, has given rise to the idea that they are wanting in intelligence ; but when you become properly acquainted with them, you find them quite the reverse—quick to learn, and sharp at making bargains, especially the French. They are, however, inclined to be suspicious of strangers, and are wary in dealing with them, but to those whom they know, they are confiding, and will never suspect until they once find themselves cheated. In this latter they resemble the Indian character. The English half-breeds are more steady than the French, but not so much so as the Scotch, who are a plodding, saving, canny class of men, with little, if any, of the Indian character about them. When you see a little of our school system in the settlement, you will acknowledge, I have no doubt, that our Half-breed children are as apt at learning as those born and brought up in Canada."

"I have no doubt of it," replied Mr. Meredith, "from what I have already seen."

By this time they had reached another camp belonging to one of Mr. Bon's freighters, who had only arrived the day previous. Already the wheels had been taken off from two or three of the carts, for the purpose of repairing them ; new axles were being fitted on, and injured parts bound up with soften-ed strips of Buffalo-hide, which, when hardened in the sun, holds the parts together as if in a vice, and at the same time proves very durable. Harnesses, made of untanned leather, were being mended, and a general overhauling was taking place preparatory to their return trip. Mr. Bon addressed himself to one of the men at work—

"When will you be ready to load up, Laboucan ? I want to be off to-morrow."

"This evening, sir, I suppose," was the reply, "but I won't start from here for a couple of days; my animals are tired out."

"I don't care when you start," said Mr. Bon, "so long as I can load you up, and be off myself."

"I'll be ready after supper," said Laboucan.

At the next camp the men were enjoying themselves, to judge from the sound of the fiddle, and loud voices and laughter going on.

A couple of women were busy round the fire, cooking a late dinner for the men, who were playing cards in their tent, and on a small trunk sat a young fellow playing his fiddle and keeping time with his feet.

Mr. Bon now insisted upon having a dance with the youngest of the two women, and laughingly taking her by the hand, led her out and giving the young fiddler a poke in the ribs, said,

"Now, Joe, give us a good one."

The men in the tent as soon as they heard what was going on, scrambled out and welcomed Mr. Bon.

One of them led the other woman from the fire. The dinner was forgotten, and left to cook itself. The fiddler tuned up in earnest, and then away they went at what might be called railroad speed.

Mr. Bon showed himself an adept at the "light fantastic," and his partner was not behind. The step was a spirited jig peculiar to Red River, and easily learned. When at last Mr. Bon became tired, his place was filled by one of the men standing by, who in time gave way for another, and so they went on until at last the two women fairly gave in and cried mercy.

"Mr. Bon, you're always up to tricks," said one of the men, who seemed to be the chief of the party. "Look! you've spoiled our dinner."

"That's your own fault, Pierre; for you should have eaten it earlier in the day," replied the trader.

Our three friends soon after left, while the freighters sat down on the grass to their spoiled dinner, after having extracted a promise from Mr. Bon to give them something stronger than water to drink in the evening, to make up for the injury to their meal.

Mr. Bon as soon as he had made arrangements with the station agent regarding the loading of the balance of his carts, accompanied George and Mr. Meredith in their waggons across to the town; and afterwards went with George to purchase a horse and waggon for the trip. In their perambulations they meet the young man who was to be Mr. Bon's companion to Red River, to whom George was introduced; and after their business was completed, all three walked back to the hotel, where they found the Merediths preparing for the start on the morrow.

Mr. Bon and his companion, whom we will know hereafter as Mr. Barron, were introduced to the ladies and the two boys.

Tom, on hearing of Dr. Flyaway's desertion of the party, vowed he would be revenged on him wherever he met him.

"You may have an opportunity before you reach Red River," said Mr. Bon.

"If I do," replied Tom, "he'll suffer, that's all."

While they were laughing at the boy's vehemence, the tea bell rang, and all gladly obeyed its summons.

After tea, Mr. Bon invited Mr. Meredith, George and Mr. Barron to call with him on an old friend, who then held the office of mayor in the town.

They accordingly set out in search of that functionary, and found him in his own private office, busily engaged over the debits and credits of a large ledger. He welcomed the whole party, and when he learned that Mr. Barron hailed from Glasgow, Scotland, he paid special attention to him as a brother Scotchman. The mayor had lived in the United States for a number of years, but not long enough to forget his native land, old Scotia, so dear to her sons wherever in their wanderings they may chance to live.

In honor of the occasion, a bottle of old Scotch whisky, the real stuff, was produced; and the mayor closing his ponderous book for that night, prepared himself to enjoy a pleasant evening.

"Well! old Bon," he said, "it's a pleasure to see your countenance at any time, but with all deference to you and your good looks, I must say I hope you will bring along a brother Scotchman to see me every time you come. And now gentlemen, tak' a wee drappie o' the barley-bree, just to the honor of old Scotland, and at the same time we'll drink success to Mr. Barron in his new life in the North-West."

All joined in the toast, and then came anecdotes, songs and recitations from Burns, in which Mr. Barron excelled. The mayor was in raptures on hearing in true Scotch style the favorite pieces—"Tam O'Shanter," "Death and Doctor Hornbook," "The Cotter's Saturday Night," and others; and to show his appreciation of the enjoyment afforded him, he drank to the honor of Bruce, Wallace, and all the other Scottish heroes he could remember, invariably winding up, however, with Burns. Thus the evening wore on, until at last John Barleycorn began to assert his authority over the mayor and Mr. Barron, and things with them became rather muddled. Finally, to wind up the evening, Mr. Bon proposed that they should repair to the hotel and have some supper. This being agreed to, they sallied out into the street and meeting a policeman the mayor stopped him.

E

"Oh! that's you Tom, is it? Well, Tom, I suppose you observe I'm drunk; but you must remember as mayor of St. Cloud I'm not drunk. These are my friends, and they are under (hic) my official protection. Good night, Tom; and if you see any more drunken rascals take 'em up."

When they were near the hotel, the mayor remarked,— "Gentlemen, the humor of the hour moves me to propose a short stave of the old song, 'We won't go home till morning,' but in my capacity (hic) as mayor of this town I would have to stop such a proceeding. Now, gentlemen, I believe if I know myself this is your house. All you can get to eat in it to-night I'll pay for. As for me, I'll place myself in charge of the mayor of St. Cloud, and go home with him. My friends, farewell. Mr. Barron don't harrow your feelings, I'll see you in the morning—good night—adieu (hic)," and with this the worthy man suddenly left them, before they could even thank him for the hospitality they had enjoyed at his hands.

Our friends found that the mayor had been perfectly safe in his offer to pay for all they could get to eat in the hotel, for it was with some difficulty that they obtained an entrance at all, everybody in the house having retired to their beds. After repeated knockings, however, at the front door, they heard footsteps on the stairs within, and soon after the bolt was drawn and they were admitted.

The landlord, a stout individual, had not taken time to don his nether garments, but appeared before them candle in hand in the form of a good substantial ghost.

"Gentlemen," he said, "this will not do."

CHAPTER V.

HE next morning our friends were roused out of their beds by Mr. Bon, so as to make an early start. Mr. Barron complained of a severe headache, the result of his late jollification with the mayor; but with this exception, the party were in the best of spirits, assisted a good deal by there being every appearance of a fine day before them.

George Wade had procured his horse and light waggon, and as soon as breakfast was over, all hands assisted in loading up. There were eatables and drinkables, tents and cooking utensils, trunks, and other baggage, besides a few bushels of oats for the use of the horses on the journey. When all these were properly stowed away, they found that it was nearly eight o'clock in the morning. At this stage, who should come along but the mayor, looking as bright as if nothing had been the matter with him the night before. He immediately apologized for his abrupt departure; sympathized with Mr. Barron in looking so dull; and then whispered to Mr. Bon to call at his office on their way out of town, as he had something there for him, which, as it turned out afterwards, was nothing more nor less than a bottle of the "barley-bree," to use on the trip. When everything was arranged, and the ladies comfortably seated in their waggon, they started from the hotel, Mr. Bon leading the way, and George Wade, with Tom as a companion, bringing up the rear.

They paid a short visit at the mayor's office, as requested, and then drove on without any further delay. As they were passing through the outskirts of the town, they could not but observe the indications of rapid progress everywhere visible, in the shape of houses being built, streets laid out, and extended. Where only a few years previously it was open prairie, a good sized town now stood, and from every appearance it gave promise of becoming a large city. Thus it is in the Western States, villages, towns, and cities grow as if by magic, and almost every year, new places of importance spring into existence.

They passed a couple of Red River trains, consisting of twenty-five carts each, leisurely moving along, creaking in such a delightful manner, that hearing them would have made any one not accustomed to it almost shiver on a warm day. They travelled in single file, each ox being tied to the cart in front, a man being at the head of the leading one. It is, therefore, a very unfortunate occurrence when an ox stumbles and falls in the midst of a train, for before the poor animal can recover its feet, or the carts be stopped, its neck will more than probably have been broken. The Red River trains manage to travel from fifteen to twenty miles per day, always stopping about noon for dinner. One would not imagine, however, to look at them in motion, that they could go half that distance in the same time.

When our friends reached Richmond, at which place they stopped for dinner, they were joined by a gentleman who was on his way to Pembina, and who, being acquainted with Mr. Bon, immediately proposed forming one of the party. This gentleman held an important position in the United States service, and was considered a man of influence in the territory of Dakota. Possessed of sharp, shrewd, intelligent features, and a body stout and well-formed; his arms were marvels of strength, but he was almost without legs, having only a couple of stumps in their place, the longest of which being not over a foot and a half in length. He was born with this deformity. In moving about he used a couple of short crutches, and it was astonishing with what rapidity he could limp along on them. But it was still more surprising to see him without the slightest assistance from any one lift himself up at one spring into a waggon of the ordinary height.

As he sat in his conveyance, his bodily defects were not perceptible, but when he alighted on the ground he certainly astonished our friends in discovering to them his dwarfish proportions. Mr. Bon introduced him to the party, as Mr. Shorthorn, and immediately afterwards arrangements for dinner were proceeded with. Tom was despatched to the river for a couple of pails of water. George Wade went to work with a will, cutting wood for the fire, which he soon had burning briskly, while Jack and Mr. Meredith attended to the horses. Mr. Bon had a servant with him, who attended to his wants, as well as those of Mr. Shorthorn. Grace, in the meantime, was not idle, but hurried here and there in the preparation of the meal. Ham and eggs were cooked; tea made; and then the whole party sat down on the grass around the table-cloth spread on the ground, and with hearty appetites, after their long drive, did justice to the good things before them.

It was then proposed that for the future all should mess together, each contributing his share to the general store of provisions; and Grace volunteered to do the whole of the cooking for the trip. Ere they had finished dinner, the weather began to look threatening; and in fact they had not proceeded far on their journey in the afternoon, before it began to rain.

They halted for a short time at a place called New Munich, where they partook of some fine lager beer, and laid in a fresh stock of eggs.

Mr. Barron, not having recovered from his severe headache, procured from the store-keeper a couple of dozen of pills, which in desperation, he swallowed at once, but was afterwards heard to declare, while rubbing his stomach, that the lager did him more good than the medicine. As they travelled along, they could not but observe the tidy thrifty appearance of the farm houses and buildings that lined the road on each side, and which belonged nearly altogether to Germans. The rain now became heavier every moment, until, at last, it was proposed to camp for the night, which was finally agreed to, and immediately acted upon. There were three tents belonging to the party, and so soon as the horses were unharnessed, and let loose to graze, these were pitched, and the ladies got under cover as quickly as possible, the waggons being ranged in a circle round them, so as to keep the animals off. As soon, therefore, as everything likely to be damaged by wet was taken inside the tents, and a large fire lighted by George, in the centre of the camp, all prepared to spend their first night in the open air. The tea was prepared with some difficulty by Grace, who, notwithstanding the rain, insisted upon fulfilling what she now considered as her part of the work. When all had partaken of the meal, they immediately retired to try and sleep; Mr. Bon's servant making his bed of a couple of blankets spread beneath his cart. Mrs. Meredith grumbled a good deal during the night and succeeded by so doing, in keeping others as well as herself awake the greater part of the time.

The next morning turned out fine, although the roads were far from being good. They however managed to travel as far as Sauk Centre in time to have a late breakfast. Here again they found a good sized town, where only a couple or three years previously a few houses stood. Such is the marvelous growth of places on and near the frontier. Beautifully situated on the margin of Sauk Lake, a picturesque sheet of water, Sauk Centre presented an appearance of tidiness and enterprise, creditable to its inhabitants.

Mr. Bon had a good deal of business to attend to in this place, so that after breakfast our friends concluded to make the best of the day before them. Mr. Barron, in company with Tom and Jack, having procured a small boat, started out with their guns and fishing-tackle to try their luck in the sporting line, having heard that the woods in the neighbourhood abounded with deer, and that the lake itself could boast of a plentitude of fish. George joined Grace and Mrs. Meredith in a walk through the town, and our friend, Mr. Shorthorn, visited the hotel to see some old friends. Mr. Meredith accompanied Mr. Bon, while the servant of the latter remained in camp to look after things generally. In this manner they separated. We will, however, leave the others to their fate, and follow only the fortunes of the sportsmen.

The surface of the water was as smooth as glass, and they were congratulating themselves on the prospect of a day's fine sport, when they perceived that their boat leaked badly—such is life; with almost every pleasure there is a thorn, and so indeed our three friends found out. Jack being busy rowing, Mr. Barron and Tom taking off their caps, began to bail, but the more water they threw out, the more there seemed to come in, until at last Mr. Barron proposed being put ashore with his gun, thinking that by lightening the little craft it would not leak so much.

Accordingly they made for land, and Mr. Barron jumped ashore and proceeded into the woods, while the two boys put out and began to troll. The boat, however, demanded as much of their attention as the fishing, so that between the two they had no luck. In the meantime, Mr. Barron could be heard firing away in the forest, and both Jack and Tom ex· pected to see a large quantity of game for the amount of powder expended. They were, however, doomed to total disap. pointment that day; for the truth was, Mr. Barron was a poor shot, and had no knowledge of hunting whatever. With every rustle he would imagine a deer, and to make sure of it, as he thought, he would, without waiting, fire into the thicket, but invariably without any of the results he expected. The boys had no better success, for what with bailing and hauling in their line to find nothing but a string of weeds on the hook, they found they day nigh spent, and still nothing to reward them for their trouble. At last their patience could hold out no longer, and they had determined to land and hunt up Mr. Barron, when that gentleman made his appearance, in hot pursuit after an animal, whose species they could not at first glance distinguish, but which turned out to be a young calf. As the boat grazed the shore, Mr. Barron fired, and, perceiving Jack and Tom, roared out—"I be hanged, if I hav'nt hit the tail." The boys in astonishment shouted to him to know what he was after.

"I don't know, nor I don't care," was the reply from the excited man. "It's the first game I've seen to-day."

"It's a calf," bellowed Tom.

"The d—l!" answered Mr. Barron; "its a lively one then; but I'll be hanged if I don't have a shot at it yet. It'll be something to bring to camp."

The boys had some difficulty in persuading the persevering sportsman to stop in his career.

"Hold," said Jack, "if you have hit the tail, you've done

better than we've done in the fishing line. You must be a good shot to hit a tail when it is wagging." Mr. Barron laughed, and was joined heartily by the two boys, when they perceived the unfortunate calf in the distance, still running and kicking up every now and then.

They then returned to the boat, and rowed down the lake, until they came opposite the town, when they landed—their little craft being nearly half full of water by this time.

When they reached the camp, they found all assembled for tea, and the recital of the day's proceedings produced a good laugh at Mr. Barron's expense. In the evening, Mr. Meredith, Mr. Bon, Mr. Barron, George and Mr. Shorthorn, took a stroll towards the hotel, to meet some friends of the last named gentleman. There they met another Scotchman, who, however, did not prove such an enthusiastic admirer of his native land as did the mayor of St. Cloud. Late in the evening, Mr. Barron (who, by-the-bye, had brought with him the bottle of ". barley-bree" unperceived by the rest) tackled this countryman of his on several points relating to Scottish history, and the two at last came to high words. Mr. Barron finally wound up by declaring himself the better man of the two ; which the other immediately resented, by a challenge to test the point in a practical manner.

Mr. Bon, who never lost a chance of a bit of fun, and feeling that John Barleycorn would prevent them from hurting each other severely, suggested that they should settle the matter at once. Accordingly all repaired to the yard of the hotel, and the two would-be-combatants took off their coats and faced each other. Round them were their friends. Mr. Shorthorn, crutch in hand, acting as umpire. Mr. Barron succeeded in getting his back to the moon, and with the aid of it shining brightly in his opponent's face, he gained the first round.

Little Mr. Shorthorn, who had written B. on the ground with the end of his crutch, now made a stroke beneath the letter, exclaiming, "Go it, Barron, time's up."

It was exceedingly ludicrous to observe the earnestness with which the two pugilists eyed each other; at the same time, there is no doubt both wished themselves well out of it. At last after five rounds, A. failed to come up to time, and Mr. Barron was declared the victor.

"Hurrah for the Barrons," exclaimed that individual. "Pretty good for one day. Shot a calf's tail off, and killed a drunken Scotchman."

The excitement and the "barley-bree," however, was too much for him, and both he and the vanquished A. succumbed, and on Mr. Bon's suggestion, they were both put into the same bed in the hotel. The next morning they were found sitting up looking at each other with woe-begone countenances. Mr. Barron sported a beautiful black eye, while the other had the skin pealed off the whole ridge of his nose.

"The deuce take the whisky," quoth Mr. Barron, when he had risen and looked in the glass. "How will I make my appearance before Mr. and Mrs. Meredith ?"

" You've made a pretty picture of me," said the other, looking over Mr. Barron's shoulder.

" You deserved it," was the reply.

"Come, come," said Mr. Bon, who was present, the teams are waiting for you, Mr. Barron, at the door; never mind the eye; we must try to make up to day for what we lost yesterday."

Mr. Barron, therefore, hastily finished dressing, and bidding his late bed-fellow a cool good by, accompanied Mr. Bon down stairs.

When Mrs. Meredith noticed the appearance of Mr. Barron, she turned to Grace, and remarked, "There now, that's what they were up to last night—drinking again; just look at that young man's eye."

"Hush!" said Grace; "he might hear you, and I'm sure you wouldn't wish to hurt his feelings."

"Feelings!" replied her mother; "do you suppose a man that could stand such a blow on the eye has any feeling?"

"Perhaps he didn't stand it," said Grace.

"I don't suppose he did," muttered the old lady. "I should say he fell down, and served him right."

They now travelled on, passing Osakis Lake, another beautiful sheet of water, and afterwards entered the Alexandria woods, where they camped for dinner. Mr. Barron, who had lost his breakfast, did justice to the meal. As he sat opposite Grace, he said, "My eye looks very disreputable, Miss Meredith."

"Rather a black look out," she replied, smiling.

"I am sorry to say it is," returned Mr. Barron, "but it was in defence of my country; you'll excuse it, I hope, Miss Meredith?"

"Under these circumstances, of course."

Mrs. Meredith was prevented from saying anything, by the whole party rising.

Soon after they proceeded on and found the roads through the woods in a very bad condition, and abounding with ruts and large pools of water, in which the horses sank above their knees, and in some places almost up to their necks. They were obliged to travel slowly; and a short distance from the town of Alexandria, they were delayed a considerable time, on account of the stage coach having upset across the road.

There being only one passenger and the driver, all hands turned out to assist in righting the overturned vehicle. At last, after a good deal of trouble, this being accomplished, the coach passed them on its way to Sauk Centre, the passenger, however, preferring to walk rather than risk his neck in it again, until it got through the woods.

Our friends merely halted for a few moments in Alexandria, which at that time, was little more than a small village, and then passed on. Chippewa Lake is the next spot of interest on the route, and like all the small lakes on this road, it is very picturesque and beautiful. Here our friends watered their horses, and then pressed on to a point where the village of Evansville now stands. There was nothing then in the shape of buildings but a small log cabin to be seen. The point is a very pretty one, on the rising of a hill, with a clump of trees in the back ground.

Mr. Bon decided upon camping for the night at this place, and accordingly the tents were pitched and the horses let loose. The mosquitoes troubled them here for the first time, but towards morning, they disappeared. They made an early start the next day, and soon came in sight of Pelican Lake, which derives its name from a small group of rocks cropping out in its centre, and which, in the distance, resembles a flock of Pelicans floating on the water. The deception is so complete, that it is hard to convince some people that it is really not a flock of birds. The next place passed, was Pomme-de-Terre, an old dilapidated stockade, which at one time, was used to resist the attacks of the Indians ; but at the time of our story, it was merely a way station for the stages en route to and from Fort Abercrombie. Tom visited it to try and get some milk, in which he succeeded, and on his return, described the place as one of the dirtiest, filthiest, holes he ever was in. We may say, however, that since then, it has improved very much, both in comfort and cleanliness. George, when they camped for dinner, remarked that they had not seen any Red River trains since they left St. Cloud.

"There are two roads," replied Mr. Bon, " one called the plain and the other stage road ; the carts usually take the former, while we have taken the latter. The plain road is by far the best, but it is so monotonous that I thought it better to stand a little jolting and hardships, than travel where it is nothing but prairie almost the whole way. Our camping ground, to-night, is the point at which both roads merge into one, and probably we will overtake some carts there."

Early in the evening, our friends arrived at Otter Tail River in time to see a train of carts crossing it in rather a novel manner. The late rains had swollen the stream to such a degree, that fording it was out of the question, and when they came up, the half-breeds were about building some rafts in a manner peculiar to themselves. Two wheels were first taken off a cart, laid flat on the ground, and strapped together, one overlapping the other. A large buffalo parchment skin was then placed under them, and four sides about two or three feet high, built with poles cut for the purpose, and fastened at each corner, one on top of the other with strips of hide. The parchment was then drawn up over these, and tied to the top poles, and in this way, a good four cornered temporary boat was made. These rafts carried a cart load of goods across each trip, and after all the packages were over, the carts were floated to the other side, and the animals driven into the water and made to swim to the opposite bank.

Mr. Bon arranged with these freighters to have all the baggage, traps and waggons belonging to the party, ferried over in this way ; and the gentlemen and ladies were taken across in a small boat, while the horses had to swim for it.

As our friends landed, they were accosted by a tall, thin

seedy-looking man, more legs than body, who addressed himself to Mr. Bon.

"Wal, Squire, back agin ? Kind o' hard travelling this time o' the year. Got some folks with you, I see. I guess I'm going to have a ferry here, next year."

"I hope you will," said Mr. Bon. "Have you got any fish ?"

"Wal ! yes, I reckon I can scare you up one. Me and my son, Uriah, were trying our luck, and we did ketch one. You can have it, for I guess we'll ketch another afore the stage comes along."

This gentlemanly and obliging individual was the caterer for the passengers by the coach to and from Abercrombie, and a profitable thing he made of it, for he used to feed his guests at seventy-five cents per head altogether on the fish he caught in the river before his door, and which cost him only the slightest possible bit of exertion. But, in fact, exertion of any kind was this man's greatest abhorrence. When Mr. Bon had procured the fish, and paid well for it, the whole party proceeded a short distance further on, and camped for the night. The next day, when within about twelve miles from Fort Abercrombie, Mr. Bon pointed out a spot where, he said, there stood in 1862, a fine saw mill and a large hotel, a joint stock company affair. This was Breckenridge, where, during the Indian massacre in Minnesota, several lives were lost, and, at the same time, the mill and hotel were burned down, and they have not been rebuilt since. Breckenridge bids fair to become an important place yet, it being at the present time the proposed terminus of the St. Paul and Pacific Railroad. Early that evening, our travellers reached Fort Abercrombie, having, since they left Alexandria, passed few houses on the road.

CHAPTER VI.

ORT ABERCROMBIE, during the Indian troubles of 1862, withstood a prolonged attack by the savages, and since then a few companies of United States regulars have been stationed there.

The Fort itself is an extensive stockade, in which are some good substantial buildings for the accommodation of the men, and for storing supplies. You have to cross on a ferry to reach it; and on this side of the river are a few houses, comprising a hotel, post and stage office, as well as some primitive looking dwellings.

Our friends camped about a mile from the Fort, and in the morning paid a visit to it. There they were introduced to several of the officers, and spent a pleasant forenoon in their company. Grace, in particular, received a good deal of attention from the military men, much to the chagrin of George Wade, who was just a little jealous. Since the unfortunate interruption to their *tete-a-tete* at Minnehaha, neither George nor Grace had any opportunity of enjoying each other's society alone, on account of the presence of Mrs. Meredith.

George felt miserable, the more so, as Grace seemed to be reserved in her manner towards him of late, and in fact, appeared as if desirous of avoiding him. Stung by this, he resolved at last on endeavouring to feel indifferent, and busied himself more than there was any real necessity for in the affairs connected with the camp.

After dinner, our friends started again on their trip, and travelled nearly twenty miles that afternoon. The mosquitoes now began to be very troublesome, and this night they resolved on hobbling their horses, lest they might be driven off by the flies during the night.

Mr. Bon's servant, assisted by George and Tom, undertook the job, which was, first, to catch each horse, and with a soft strip of untanned leather* fasten its front legs above the fetlock, about one foot apart; in this way the animal can only go at a short jump, and strange to say, will feed better hobbled than when free. It was well they did this, as the next morning they found their horses three or four miles off, and had they not been hobbled, probably they would have strayed to a greater distance. An early start was made in the morning, as Mr. Bon wished, if possible, to reach Georgetown that night.

As they proceeded along, several places were pointed out by the trader, as spots where houses had stood previous to the Indian massacre; and about half way to Georgetown, they passed an old abandoned stage house, which was in use before 1862, as the coaches at that time ran as far as Georgetown. In fact, the Indian outbreak put the northern part of Minnesota back at least ten years. Nothing worthy of mention occurred until they reached within a short distance of where they proposed camping, when signs of an approaching storm became visible. The roads were good, and every exertion was made to reach Georgetown before the threatened tempest should overtake them.

---

* Some parties use straps with buckles, and others irons made like handcuffs, with a short chain attached, these latter are fastened by means of a key, to prevent Indians from unfastening them.

"Sakes, alive!" said Mrs. Meredith, as they drove furiously on, "I believe every bone in my body will be broken at this rate. You have a deal to answer for, Mr. Meredith, for taking me a wild goose chase like this at my time of life."

"You'll forget all about it," said Grace, "once you're comfortably settled in your new home."

"New home!" exclaimed her mother, "I liked the old home we left behind us."

"Well! well! good wife," said Mr. Meredith, "we're old, and needn't mind it much ; it's for the sake of the boys I'm doing it. I'd like to see them fairly started in life before we leave them."

This silenced Mrs. Meredith completely, for she was in reality a fond mother, with all her querulousness.

The sky became more and more lowering as they approached Georgetown, and it was with some difficulty, on account of the darkness, that they succeeded in passing over the rude bridge leading towards the houses.

Georgetown is simply a Hudson Bay Company post, used for the purpose of storing goods in transit to and from Fort Garry, and there are only four houses in it altogether, one of which is occupied by the ferryman. Our friends had hardly pitched their tents, when the storm broke, and a most severe one it proved. Neither Mrs. Meredith nor Grace could be persuaded to leave the party, and go into one of the adjoining houses for shelter. The horses cowered and shook, as they huddled together in a band, a few yards from the camp. Bright flashes of lightning followed each other in quick succession, accompanied by deafening peals of thunder, and the rain came down in torrents. Mrs. Meredith was terror-stricken, and shrank into a corner of the tent, covering her face with

F

her hands, while Grace bent over her and soothed her as well as she could under the circumstances.

No supper was cooked that night, and the men sat silently listening to the violence of the storm, the only one who seemed really careless in his manner was little Mr. Shorthorn, as he sat quietly smoking his pipe.

Mr. Bon, who lay stretched on his robes and blankets, felt some one tugging at his coat-sleeve, and then he heard the voice of Mr. Barron at his elbow. "Take a drop of the 'barley-bree;' there's lots of lightning outside, take a little inside; it'll do you good." The offer was too acceptable to be refused.

George Wade about this time started out unperceived in the darkness and rain, over to one of the houses, where he, after some trouble, succeeded in getting a small tin pailful of hot tea, which he brought to Mrs. Meredith and Grace, and insisted upon their drinking it. No one in the camp enjoyed a good night's rest, even after the storm disappeared, and all arose in the morning unrefreshed and tired out.

This was not a comfortable feeling with which to start upon another day's journey, but when people are travelling over the plains, they must make up their minds to bear with such vicissitudes. The only remark Tom was heard to make during the late storm was, "I wonder how poor Flyaway is getting along."

On leaving Georgetown, they had to cross a ferry, which is worthy of description, as the method used in working it is peculiar to Minnesota and the North-West. It consisted of a flat boat, about thirty feet long and fifteen feet broad, with a railing on each side. At each end of this railing were two large blocks, through which a rope passed, being made fast to a post on each bank of the river. When as many of the waggons as the boat could hold were driven on, the ferryman pulled upon the rope, and in this way propelled the boat to the opposite side of the river.

Some of these ferries are worked in a different manner,—a rough windlass being erected about the middle of one of the railings, around this a rope is wound, and runs to each end of the boat, and then attached by means of two blocks to the main hawser connected with the land. The mode of propulsion is by twisting the windlass, and by that means obliging the flat boat to have a slanting side to the current,—the ferry is thus forced forward, the main hawser preventing it from being driven down the stream. One man only is necessary for working a large ferry on this plan.

Our travellers were now in Dakota territory, and found the roads very heavy, from the effects of the late storm, and had accordingly to proceed slowly along.

They reached Elm River about noon, and camped there for dinner ; and as their horses seemed pretty well used up with the morning's work, they remained about three hours before resuming their journey.

They occupied the greater portion of this time in repairing the temporary bridge over which they had to cross, and which was in a very dilapidated condition.

When using the term river to the stream in question, it is simply a misnomer, it being nothing more nor less than a small brook—and the same may be said of all the other so-called rivers between Georgetown and Pembina.

The bridges over these creeks are built in a rude manner, by the Red River freighters going to and fro. Two large trees are first felled and laid across, and on these are placed smaller logs, over which are thrown branches, and, in some cases, the hides are taken from the carts and laid over all. So long as the bridge serves the purpose for a train to pass over, it is left for others following to repair or rebuild it, as may be necessary.

Our friends, under Mr. Bon's direction, cut down numerous branches from the trees close at hand, and strewing them over the logs, they filled up the gaping holes between them, and made the bridge in a safe condition to pass over.

Jack and Tom made themselves particularly useful in this respect, by climbing the trees and hacking off the smaller branches necessary for the work. As soon as the horses had rested sufficiently, our friends broke camp, and continued their journey; Mrs. Meredith and Grace walking over the bridge, in case of accident. It was late in the evening when they reached Goose River, the next stopping place, and on the way there they were troubled very much by the mosquitoes, as they rose from the long grass on each side of the road, and the whole party began to realize the hardships of the trip.

Goose River is a clear, running stream, with steep banks on each side, and as the bottom is hard and gravelly : no bridge is ever built there, it being easily forded. The mosquitoes, when the sun went down, seemed to increase so much in numbers, that a feeling of suffocation was felt by every one in the party, on account of their buzzing and biting in every direction. Mr. Bon's servant went off some distance from the camp, and collecting a quantity of a peculiar sort of weed that grows on the prairie, he made a fire and covered it over with it; the result was a dense cloud of smoke, which lasted most of the night. Round this the horses assembled, switching their tails and biting their flanks incessantly, while the myriads of venomous insects tormented them; the smoke, however, served partly as a preventative, and on this account the instinct of the animals taught them to hover round it.

Little sleep was enjoyed by any one in camp that night, and

the Merediths began to regret having left their comfortable home in Canada. Grace, however, although suffering as much as the rest, endeavored to cheer them up as well as she could manage it.

Fires, covered with the weed already mentioned, were kept smouldering all round the camp, but to no purpose. Smoke did not seem to remedy the evil in the least. At last daylight broke upon them, and in the cool of the morning the mosquitoes seemed to disappear altogether. The horses began to feed as if forgetful of their late torture, and our friends, taking advantage of a few hours sleep, made a late start.

Grace never relaxed her duties as cook for the party, and proved herself during all the trials of the trip, as indeed she was, a noble and heroic girl. Without her Mrs. Meredith would have sank under the hardships of this eventful journey. As they were fording Goose River, they noticed a dead ox lying partly in the water, where, having probably met with an accident, it had been left by some freighter in the place where it had died. Indeed at several places along the route, they passed the carcases of oxen and horses, which had apparently been abandoned by their owners on the road.

The forenoon of this day was more suitable for travelling than any they had experienced since they left Abercrombie ; and shortly after noon they camped for dinner at a spot called Frog Point. When the water is low during the summer the Hudson Bay Company's steamer *International* can only reach as far as this place, instead of Georgetown. A couple of hours were spent here, when the party again proceeded on, passing Buffalo Coolie, Elm Coolie, and arriving at what is called the Grand Forks, late in the evening.

The had just finished pitching their tents, when a train of

carts, which they had passed only a short time before on the road, came up and camped near them.

Mr. Bon expressed fears that this would be the means of of spoiling another night's rest for them ; and he was not far wrong, as they found out afterwards to their cost. The carts were formed in a sort of circle, and the fire lit in the centre. As soon as the oxen were unharnessed, they were driven down to the river to drink, and in this case one of them got mired, and was with difficulty saved from drowning.

Smokes were made for the animals some distance out on the prairie, but the mosquitoes were so thick in numbers that both oxen and horses plunged about here and there, and those of our friends who were unaccustomed to prairie travelling, could not sleep for fear of being trampled over by the infuriated animals. Both Jack and Tom on several occasions rose, and seizing lighted sticks from the fire, chased the horses far out on the prairie, only to find, when they had lain down again, that the brutes were at their heels and snifting about near the tent.

Mr. Bon had taken great care in smoking the mosquitoes out of the tent which Mrs. Meredith and Grace occupied; and on this account, the two ladies were not much troubled by them, and would have had a good night's rest, had it not been for the enraged animals crowding about the tent.

The half-breeds belonging to the train did not seem to be disturbed at all by the mosquitoes, as every thing appeared quiet in their camp. The next morning, Mr. Bon proposed an early start ; and accordingly our friends packed up, and left just as daylight was breaking in. They passed English Coolie, and drove on as far as Turtle River.

At this place the water is so brackish in its nature, that it is unfit for use, and animals drinking of it are very liable to become sick soon after, so that Mr. Bon, who acted as leader to the party, decided upon driving on as far as Little Lake, about three miles further on.

Before leaving Turtle River, however, some sticks of wood were collected and put on the waggons, to cook their breakfast with, as there was little chance of their finding any at the lake.   This latter is nothing more than a good sized pond, of clear, fresh water, without a tree, or even a bush, in its vicinity.

Our travellers finding it a pleasant spot however, decided upon giving their horses a good rest, they having driven a long distance that morning.   The tents were therefore pitched, and a few hours of refreshing sleep were enjoyed by every one, with the exception of Mr. Bon's servant, who had slept well during the night, and who remained awake now to watch the horses.   In the afternoon they proceeded on, passing Riviere Miré, and camping in the evening at Big Salt River.

For a wonder the night turned out cool and pleasant, with hardly any mosquitoes, but, unfortunately for our friends, Mr. Bon's servant on this account did not hobble the horses as usual, thinking they would feed better, and the consequence was, that when the morning came, not a sign of the animals could be seen anywhere.   Mr. Bon's servant was immediately sent in search of them, but did not return until late in the forenoon, having walked a long distance before finding them.

They then continued their journey, and reached Little Salt River in the afternoon.   A short halt was made there, when they started across what is called the Grand Traverse, which is about nineteen miles in length and abounding with tall grass, which in some places reached above the horses' backs.   While in the centre of this long stretch, they suddenly found themselves in the midst of a cloud of flying ants.   These are about the size of a wasp, and their sting is very painful, leaving a sore, burning sensation for some time afterwards. The horses kicked and reared, and were with difficulty prevented from running away; and when the travellers at last were free from this new scourge, they found their faces and hands in a most tantalizing state of irritation.

These flying ants are very seldom seen, however, on the route, so that our friends were peculiarly unfortunate in meeting with them.

"Goodness gracious !" exclaimed Mrs. Meredith, "I thought mosquitoes bad enough, but these pesty things are ten times worse."

"Mother's right this time," said Jack, rubbing himself well.

The only one apparently callous on the subject was Mr. Shorthorn, who did not appear to have been in the least bitten.

"I think he's a bit of the devil," whispered Tom.

A short distance further on they met the mail man leisurely jogging along in his cart, and allowing his pony to travel at its own gait.

"Did you meet them critters ?" he cried out as they passed. "I'd hard work to keep them from running off with the bags."

Late in the evening they arrived at a point called Two Rivers, and camped. The old story of the mosquitoes was repeated again, and in the morning, to their surprise, they observed a waggon and tent, standing a short distance from them, and two horses grazing by.

"Flyaway! or I'm a Dutchman !" shouted Tom.

"I believe you're right," said Mr. Bon, "if I'm not mistaken in the cut of his waggon."

"Come, Jack," said the boy, "let's go over and see him."

And before Mr. Meredith could say a word of warning to them, they were off at full speed. Arrived at the tent, the two boys could discover no one inside, neither was there any person visible in the neighbourhood. They found a bottle, however, half full of whisky, which Tom quickly emptied on the ground, and replaced with the same quantity of water from a pail standing near. They then began a search for the missing Doctor, and finally reached the river side, where they saw their man up to his waist in the water, enjoying a morning bath.

Quietly, at the suggestion of Tom, the two boys cut each a long pole, armed with which, they made a dash in the direction of the Doctor, frightening him out of his wits by their sudden appearance.

" There you are, are you ?" cried Tom.

" Go away," said Flyaway. " Let me put on my clothes."

" Hold on a bit," replied Jack, giving the water a sweep with his long pole, and scattering a shower over the Doctor's devoted head.

" Wait till I get out !" cried the half drowned, and wholly enraged man.

" Out is it?" said Tom ; " we're not going to let you ; we're going to keep you there, and if you try to move, we'll poke your eyes out ; go a little further in, will you ?"

" Do you want to drown me ?" cried Flyaway, excitedly.

" No !" replied Tom, " we only want to keep you there till you melt."

" Now, I tell you what," commenced the persecuted man, in an insinuating tone, " I like fun as well as any man, but ——

" No buts," said Tom, " I say, Jack, give him a poke in the ribs and send him in further."

In this way they teased the poor man, threatening at the same time to steal his clothes unless he consented to apologize to George Wade, which in self defence he at last promised to do. They then returned to their friends, leaving the Doctor to dress in peace.

It is needless to say that the apology was never exacted, and when Mr. Bon visited the crest fallen man, he decidedly refused to join the party, so they left him behind, and arrived in Pembina early in the forenoon.

Pembina is merely a United States port of entry, and contained at that time five or six houses, amongst which were the Custom House and Post Office. The inhabitants were all government officials, and a fine easy time they had of it.

Mr. Shorthorn here parted from our friends, and betook himself to his house, to which he was welcomed by the balance of the officials, some of whom were glad to see him, while others were not. A train of carts had just passed over the Pembina River bridge, as our travellers drove up, and the process of checking the packages was going on.

The balance of Mr. Barron's bottle of "barley-bree" was here *gobbled* up by a thirsty official, and with this interesting incident, we will at present close our description of the Pembina people, as we have to visit them again in a future part of our story.

About a mile from the Custom House, and just beyond the boundary line, our friends passed the Hudson Bay Company's Post, a stockade with some good substantial buildings in it. No more houses were seen for the next twenty-five miles, until they reached the first house in the settlement belonging to one Klyne. Here they camped for the night, and the next day they found themselves in the Red River Settlement. The houses on each side of the road were all built of logs, some of them being mudded and whitewashed, while others were clapboarded and painted. Most of them betokened neatness and cleanliness, and the farms around them appeared in good condition, well cultivated and fenced in.

About fifteen miles from Fort Garry, they entered the woods, and early in the evening they came suddenly in view of the towers and walls of the Fort on one side, St. Boniface and the adjacent buildings on the other, and in the background, the town of Winnipeg.

"Why! I never expected," said Mr. Meredith, " to see a place of this size away up here. I hope it will bear a closer inspection, as well as it appears at a distance."

" Thank goodness," remarked Mrs. Meredith, "that we are safely over this trip."

" Amen," murmured Mr. Barron.

CHAPTER VII.

ORT GARRY is the headquarters of the Hudson Bay Company in the North-West, the residence of the Governor, and consequently the principal business of that service is carried on there. It is built in the form of a square, the main entrance facing the Assineboine River. The walls enclosing one part of the Fort are built of stone, about two feet thick, with four towers, one at each corner, and evidently it has been at one time extended to twice its original size. The walls of the extension, however, is of hewn logs instead of stone.

The buildings inside consist of the Governor's house, the dwelling occupied by the officer in charge (a chief trader), and five or six large warehouses and stores, one of which is partly used as quarters by officers of the company, with their families. In the centre of the Fort is a large flag pole, the towers are pierced for cannon and small arms, and altogether the place has, at first sight, quite a military appearance. When our friends came to the banks of the Assineboine River, they embarked on a ferry, similar to the one at Georgetown, and were soon conveyed over to the other side of tho stream.

While Mr. Bon is driving his friend, Mr. Barron, into Fort Garry, to introduce him to the officers in charge, we will accompany our friends as they proceed to the town. On their

way there, they passed a number of wigwams on each side of
the road, with Indians lounging about them in a lazy, indolent
manner, while the squaws were performing their work, and
the children, all dirty and ragged, were playing in and out of
the lodges. As they passed one spot they heard quite a hubbub, loud above which they could distinguish the sound of
women's voices high and shrill.

It appears that one of the squaws having done something to
offend her liege lord, that individual had coolly taken a stick
of wood and beaten her over the head, cutting her in a fright-
ful manner. As our party passed the place, the Indian was
standing, unconcernedly, with his arms folded, and leaning
against the door of a neighbouring lodge, while some of the
squaws in the encampment were binding up his wife's head.

The Merediths and George were shocked at this instance of
brutality, but Mr. Bon afterwards told them that when they
had lived some time in the settlement, they would not feel
astonished at scenes like the one just witnessed amongst the
Indians. These poor ignorant creatures take it as a matter of
course, and probably you will see the injured woman in this
case following her husband to-morrow, like as a dog would
follow his master.

They soon after entered the town of Winnipeg, which is
about half a mile from the Fort, containing, at that time, about
fifteen buildings, and having a very scattered appearance. It
being, by this time, rather late in the evening, Mr. Meredith
drove directly to the hotel, and as both his wife and Grace
were tired out, he engaged rooms for them there, and directed
George and the boys to go out a short distance on the plains
and camp for the night.

This arrangement having been carried out, George, Jack and
Tom, paid a visit to Mr. Meredith and the two ladies, and

found them comfortably sitting in a large hall, up-stairs in the
hotel, which was used as a sort of sitting room by the guests
of the house.

Mrs. Meredith seemed especially thankful at having reached
their destination in safety, and, for a wonder, did not utter a
word of grumbling during the whole evening.

Our friends, therefore, enjoyed a pleasant time, Mr. Bon
having called to see how they were getting along. George
and Grace, however, still kept up the feeling of misunderstanding that somehow had crept in upon them, and which
neither of them could properly account for. Their manner to
each other was as kind as ever, but there was a something
that put a restraint upon them, and deterred George from
repeating the question that had been interrupted so suddenly
at Minnehaha.

Grace had, from the first, taken a liking to George, which,
in a short time, became a more tender feeling on her part; but
she felt, at the same time, a maidenly and proper reserve
towards him, when she discovered that he returned her love.
George, who was rather matter-of-fact, and perhaps a little too
ardent in his suit, took her reserve to heart, and in this way
the two lovers made no progress towards a proper understanding.

Tom, who perceived that something was the matter between
his sister and George, did all in his power to bring them together, and, in his own blunt manner, did more harm than
good.

Mr. Meredith looked upon the estrangement between his
daughter and Wade as a lovers' quarrel, which will happen
between young people before they know their own minds exactly, and would have been sorry to see any serious misunderstanding between the two, for he was very favourably inclined

towards the young man, and would have put no obstacle in the way of a union between him and Grace.

Mr. Bon was sitting chatting pleasantly with them, and describing Mr. Barron's reception at the Fort, when the door opened, and the burly landlord of the hotel appeared.

"Nine o'clock, gentlemen! and we're going to shut up the house. Mr. Bon, you ought to know better than to be sitting there at this time of the night. Want to have me fined, eh?"

"Oh! Everling, it is all very well," replied Mr. Bon, "but dont think you're going to frighten us off that way. Hadn't we better have some beer, and bring up some wine for the ladies?"

"Well! now I never," exclaimed the landlord. "Here's a magistrate wants me to break the law. Now, gentlemen, what do you think of that?"

"Get out of this," cried Mr. Bon, "or I'll fine you for not breaking the law."

The landlord, whom we will know hereafter as Everling, now disappeared, and soon after returned with the beverages requested.

George and the two boys soon after returned to their camp, while Mr. Bon proceeded to his own house, a short distance off. The law, at this time, required all bar-rooms to be closed at or before nine o'clock, p.m., and anyone infringing upon it in this respect was liable to a fine of not more than ten pounds sterling for each offence.

The next morning a heavy rain fell, and made walking next thing to impossible, the mud being of such a sticky nature, and the town possessing no side-walks, that it was almost out of the question to move about. In the middle of the day, however, it cleared up, and became warm and sultry; and under the influence of the heat, the roads were dried, so that in a few hours our friends found it possible to walk out. In the forenoon, Mr. Meredith was amused, when sitting with George Wade in the hotel, at witnessing the attempted putting together of a billiard table, the first one ever seen in Red River.

Mr. Everling had imported it from St. Paul, and, taking advantage of the rainy day, he had invited all the young men of the town to take part in setting it on its legs. Quite a number, therefore, assembled, and by their united exertions, the large boxes containing the several parts of the table were carried into the room. The lids were quickly raised, and then came the scene ; one had this opinion, another had that, on the respective merits of the dismembered piece of workmanship before them ; and when the parts were being placed in their relative positions, there were as many suggestions given as would have put together a dozen billiard tables. The fact was, however, that none of them knew anything about the matter, and at last Mr. Everling began to give up in despair, especially when his assistants were actually in a fair way of coming to blows over it. At this juncture, a young man entered the room, to whom Mr. Everling appealed, and, in reply, was told by him that, with the help of another, he would guarantee to put the table together, provided everyone else left the room.

This was, of course, hooted at by all those concerned, except Mr. Everling, who, on the other hand, decided upon accepting the terms, and, in order to appease the wrath and indignation of the others, he invited all hands to order their drinks at the bar.

We will have something more to say about the billiard table affair and its consequences before we finish this chapter. In the meantime, however, we will follow Mr. Meredith and George

in a stroll they took during the afternoon, to visit Mr. Barron—
Jack and Tom being out in the camp, and Mrs. Meredith and
Grace having remained indoors all day.

As our two friends were walking along towards the Fort,
they observed a crowd assembled in one particular spot, and
hearing a good deal of noise in the midst of it, they approached to see what was going on. As soon as they reached the
place, they perceived that it was some sort of Indian ceremony,
and consequently were induced to stop and have a look at it.
A circular sort of hedge had been built of green bushes, and
inside this, seated round, were a number of Indians, males and
females, the chief and medicine men occupying the head, or
seat of honour. As Mr. Meredith and George arrived on the
scene, a couple of the medicine men arose, jumping from their
seat on the ground at the sound of the drum, and began a sort
of double-shuffle dance, accompanied by a monotonous tune,
hummed through their noses. They then began to move round
the circle, and as they did so, they were followed by other Indians of both sexes, who shuffled and droned in consort with
the leaders. A round stone had been placed in the centre of
the enclosure, and as the Indians passed this at a certain spot,
they stooped down, each one in succession, and placed their
hands upon it. Another feature in the dance was, when either
of the medicine men pointed suddenly at an Indian, the individual thus noticed would fall back as if dead, and remain motionless for a few moments, thus acknowledging, as it were, the
power of the medicine. At the close of the " walk round" or
" shuffle round," a large pot, containing the mess prepared for
the feast, was produced, and from it the chief filled the eating
utensil of each Indian. The savory contents of the dish thus
distributed, was composed of boiled dog, berries, flour, and any
other scraps picked up for the occasion. The feast was in hon-

G

our of some one of the tribe being about to receive certain secrets of medicine, for which the novice had paid well beforehand. The dog boiled in the soup used in such a feast as we
are describing, must not have a single bone broken in its body;
it is therefore invariably strangled. After the feast is over,
the medicine is administered to the applicant, and it is said
amongst Indians that the recipient will most assuredly live for
the next three years.

"What a miserable lot of creatures these Indians seem to
be!" remarked Mr. Meredith, as he and George turned away.

"I must say," replied Wade, "that they do not come up to
the standard of the noble savage we have so often seen described in books; but I am told that the uncivilized Indians who
live around the settlement are of a very inferior class to those
found generally in the North-West. There are the Crees and
Blackfeet especially, who are daring, bold, courageous, and
desperate, when attacked, or when they attack."

"I am astonished also to see," continued Mr. Meredith,
"that the Indians about here, by some means or another, succeed in obtaining liquor, although I have heard that it is against
the law to sell any to them. Already I have seen one or two
intoxicated, and this morning I witnessed a most disgraceful
sight."

"What was that?" asked George.

"Why," replied Mr. Meredith, "I saw a villainous-looking
old rascal of an Indian parading down the road, in front of the
hotel, minus everything but his shirt (and that in tatters); on
each side of the old scoundrel was a squaw, both, as I learned,
claiming him as their lord and master. The persons of the two
women were about as much exposed as the man, and the three,
it is needless to say, were hopelessly drunk."

"The law cannot be rigidly enforced," said George, "else

that would not have happened ; although, I suppose, there are
those in the settlement unprincipled enough to evade it for
some reason or another ; but," he continued, "I have never
asked your opinion of Mr. Cool : what do you think of him ?"

"I think," was the answer, "that he is a most gentlemanly
person—frank and honourable, I should say, as far as I could
judge from our short acquaintance. I am certainly indebted
to him for his kindness towards my wife."

"Assuredly you are," replied George. "But, after all, who
would not have done the same as he did under the circumstances. I am sorry to say I cannot agree with you concerning
Mr. Cool ; I'm afraid he's a schemer."

"You certainly are inclined to give him a hard character,"
answered Mr. Meredith.

"I judge a great deal from first impressions," said George,
"and there is a something about the man I can neither understand nor like ; besides, he seemed too anxious—I may say forward—in pressing his services on you ; and I have heard you
remark that you intend consulting him about your own affairs,
before you take any steps towards settling down here."

"Mr. Cool," replied Mr. Meredith, "kindly offered to give
me some information and assistance in obtaining a desirable
location in which to establish my new home, and I therefore
promised to await his arrival in the settlement before doing
anything ; and now, my dear boy, have you not allowed yourself to become prejudiced against this man ? Take your own
acquaintance with me and my family ; it has been short so far,
yet we are on the most intimate terms at present. Might it
not be said that you have been as pressing as Mr. Cool has
been ?'

George flushed to the temples at this speech, but he merely
answered, "You are right, Mr. Meredith ; and still I shall not

ccase watching that man, as far as concerns you and your family."

Mr. Meredith added : "Don't be annoyed with me, George, for you must know by this time that I value both your acquaintance and friendship ; I only said what I did to show you how others might say the same regarding you, as you have done concerning Cool."

By this time they had arrived at Fort Garry, and as they were about entering the gate, they perceived Dr. Flyaway a few yards off, seated on a white horse.

"Hilloa !" cried the Doctor, "I'm not far behind you. I would have been in town by this time had that waggon of mine followed close after me ; and now I've got to wait for it until that confounded ferry brings it over. Well, how do you like the place ?"

"Haven't seen much of it," said Mr. Meredith.

"I didn't ask you," continued the Doctor, "when I saw you last, whether you met Cool in St. Paul."

"Yes, we did," replied George. "Mr. Meredith is expecting him here soon."

"Expecting him !" almost screeched Flyaway,—then, addressing his horse, "Whoa ! Zerubabel."

"Yes," remarked Mr. Meredith, "I am expecting him. Have you any reason to suppose he will not be here soon ?"

Dr. Flyaway burst out laughing, in the midst of which he had again to admonish his horse with, "Whoa ! Zerubabel." He then replied—"They say procrastination is the thief of time ; but I guess you might put Cool in the place of procrastination. Why, sirs ! I have lost more time and money by that gentlemanly individual, than you could count up with your fingers if you took all day to it. Whoa ! Zerubabel. What the d——l is the matter with you ?"

"He told me," said Mr. Meredith, "that he had not a great deal of business to attend to in St. Paul, and that he'd probably reach Fort Garry about as soon as we would."

"Perhaps he will," returned the Doctor; "but if he does, it will be the first time he ever kept his word. Whoa! Zerubabel; confound the horse."

Both Mr. Meredith and George were amused at seeing a couple of half-breed women busy clipping the hairs from the tail of the Doctor's horse. Neither of them could understand it in any other light than a joke, which was being played on Flyaway, knowing him to be an eccentric sort of individual. There being women in the case, they were at a loss whether to reveal the fact to the unsuspecting Doctor, that his horse would be minus a tail in a very few minutes, at the rate the scissors in nimble hands were going. "Zerubabel"—for such appeared to be the name of the animal—each time an extra pull was given, would stamp a hind leg, and this called forth the repeated exclamation of "whoa" from its rider.

Our two friends were certainly astonished at what they considered the audacity of the trick, and could hardly refrain from laughing in the Doctor's face. At last, however, they were relieved from the awkwardness of their position by the arrival of Flyaway's waggon on the spot, and the consequent departure of that gentleman.

As he was leaving them, he turned in his saddle to make some final remarks, when he happened to notice the condition of his horse's tail, which had been actually reduced to a stump.

"Hilloa!" he exclaimed, in astonishment; "Zerubabel, what the d——l has become of your tail. You had one when I last mounted on your back; where is it now?"

Then, perceiving the two women hurrying off in the distance, he immediately galloped after them; and as Mr. Meredith and

George turned to enter the Fort, they saw him gesticulating excitedly, as if he was rating the offenders soundly for what they had done.

"That's a puzzler," said Mr. Meredith. "I didn't know what to do. I felt like telling the Doctor, but upon my word I was so dumbfounded by the impudence of the whole proceeding, that I felt regularly non-plussed."

"I had all I could do to prevent myself from bursting out laughing in the Doctor's face," returned George. "But I wonder what could have been the object of the two women? It was a queer way to persecute Flyaway; the horse is the greater loser of the two."

They now passed under the large gateway leading into the Fort, and found themselves in a spacious court-yard, fronting which was the chief trader's residence. On the right-hand side was the Company's shop, around which were gathered a number of half-breeds, and several carts were loading up from a warehouse on the left, preparatory to starting for the Saskatchewan, as they learned afterwards. Fortunately, our two friends met Mr. Barron about the middle of the yard, and were by him conducted to the offices directly behind the chief trader's house, and where they were introduced to two or three of the Company's clerks.

On mentioning the circumstance that occurred to Flyaway's horse, they were told that it was quite a common thing for the half-breed women and squaws to rob the tails of white or grey horses, for the purpose of using the hairs in embroidering moccasins and other fancy work. The barefaced robbery in question, however, caused a great deal of merriment amongst those who heard of it.

They were told also that when a white horse or a grey one with a white tail is sent out to pasture on the prairie, it invariably returns minus its tail, and that the women generally take care to clip the hair with scissors to ensure its growing again, for if it is pulled out by the roots it will never grow, and the stump will remain a "hairless" stump as long as the horse is a horse. This accounted then, for Flyaway suspecting the two women, and setting out in pursuit of them; but as George remarked to Mr. Meredith, "it was only an example of one of the peculiarities of the country."

Behind the offices, stood the Governor's residence, a more spacious and apparently better finished house than any of the others inside the Fort. As our two friends sat chatting with Mr. Barron and the clerks in the office, they observed a tall thin man walk slowly past, and on being told that it was the Governor himself, they took particular notice of him. They saw a man having a care-worn look about him, his hair; which was of an iron grey color, had not apparently been cut for some years, as it hung long and bushy over his coat collar; his face was rather of a sallow complexion; he possessed a massive brow, under which gleamed a pair of dark piercing eyes, that plainly said, "although my body is sinking, my spirit will never succumb." A stoop in the shoulders, together with the slow pace at which he walked, gave them at first the idea that he was feeble in health and strength. To a certain degree they were right, for he had not at the time our story opens the same bodily activity which he possessed a few years previously; but they there and then had an opportunity of judging that he could not be trifled with, even at that stage of his life. A stout burly man met and accosted him a few yards from the house; and as he did so, one of the clerks, turning to Mr. Meredith remarked, "There will be a row between that man and the Governor." The prediction proved true. The man seemed to be very excited, while the Governor remained cool.

In the difficulty between the two, the man appeared to be getting the worst of it, and at last became abusive in his manner, and finally shook his fist in the Governor's face. Like an arrow from a bow, the Governor's clenched fist was planted in the half-breed's face, sending that individual on his back in the mud. Before he could regain his feet, two men who were standing near, sprang upon him and held him down. The clerks in the office as well as Mr. Meredith and George rushed to the door in time to hear the Governor say,—

"Let him rise." Then addressing the man as he rose, he said, "Oderto, I've treated you more like a son than any thing else since you began to trade. You now are in debt to the Company over four hundred pounds. You will get no more outfit from me; and you must learn after this not to shake your fist in the face of a man twice your own age."

The discomfited half-breed slunk away without uttering a word in reply, and the Governor proceeded on.

As he passed the office door, he remarked to Mr. Barron, "The boats will leave for York Factory in a couple of days, and as you go with them, you had better call upon me to-morrow for instructions." Saying which, the old gentleman continued his walk, no trace of the late trouble being perceptible on his countenance. Our friends and the clerks now re-entered the office, and as it was near tea time, they were invited to join the officers' mess, which was accepted.

Before leaving, however, Mr. Meredith placed his money in the care of the Company's cashier for safe keeping, an act that George knew would please Grace, and which he had strongly urged upon her father to do.

All the clerks in the Fort messed together in the Chief Trader's house, that gentleman presiding at the head of the table. Mr. Meredith and George therefore found themselves sitting down to tea in company with eight or ten individuals, and a hearty lot they were. The viands were plain and substantial, and no effort was made towards show or luxury. Topics concerning the settlement and abroad were discussed in a free and gentlemanly manner, and our friends thereby gained a good deal of insight as to the people and the country they had come to live in.

Flyaway's misfortunes, especially the horse affair, caused a good deal of merriment around the table, and one venerable looking old man present, remarked, "The Doctor makes himself out our inveterate enemy; but, poor man, he is very harmless, while he thinks he is doing us a great deal of injury. If he paid more attention to competing with the Company, instead of ruining it, as he says, his pocket would be the gainer, no doubt. Why, sir," addressing Mr. Meredith, "we every year purchase largely from the free traders, and often pay them better prices right here at their door, than they could obtain for the same furs in St. Paul or England. It is true we are in direct opposition to each other in trade, but we are not such fierce antagonists as it has been represented; although we did endeavour for many years, as far as our power would allow, to monopolize the trade, and had many a hard fight over it, until we found the outside operators too strong for us. But who would not have done the same as we did, with the right we considered ourselves possessed of in the country? The old Nor'-West Company, which afterwards became amalgamated with ourselves, gave us a troublesome time while it existed, and in some cases, blood was spilt over the fur trading business between the employees of the two companies. But those days are past and gone, and the only opposition that now exists between the free traders and ourselves is one of pounds, shillings and pence, and that will continue as long as we are a Company."

After tea, Mr. Barron proposed walking down to the hotel
with Mr. Meredith and George; and in connection with this,
we may say he had an object in view in making the proposition.
The fact was that during the trip he had fallen violently in
love with Grace, which, however, he had not revealed to any
one as yet; but he was smitten without redemption, and the
nursing of the passion within his own heart only made it the
stronger. He had observed the coolness existing between
George and Grace, and had penetration enough to discover
thereby, that they were lovers; but he was man enough at the
same time not to endeavour to take advantage of the quarrel.

When they arrived at the hotel, they found the billiard table
in playing order, and as much hubbub around it as would have
set Dion, Deery or Phalen mad in a very short time. Here
could be seen, one with his eyes and mouth wide open, watching the proceedings, and wondering where the fun was in
knocking four balls backwards and forwards. In another part
of the room were two in hot discussion over the rules to be
observed in billiards. One or two were shouting at the players
to “go it while they were young,” and a few knowing ones
were standing with their fingers on their chins, observing to
each other that no one else knew any thing about the game but
themselves. What with discussions, shouting, sarcastic remarks, and the broad grins of those who did not seem to appreciate the game, the players had a sorry time of it, and at last
gave up before they had finished their string.

Mr. Everling flew here and there as well as his corpulence
would allow, but he was heard to remark “that if he had known
that the ‘hanged’ billiard table would have kicked up such a
row in his house, he would have left it in St. Paul.”

At last, to cap the climax, the two who were holding the
discussion became so hot and violent over the matter, that

personalities were exchanged, and Mr. Everling threatened to turn out the light and shut up the house. The two disputants thereupon agreed to adjourn to a neighbouring house, and play a game of "poker" to decide the question—and that game cost one of them £25 sterling before it was finished. Thus ended the first match in Red River.

Our three friends in the meantime had joined the two ladies, and found Jack and Tom keeping them company. All had a hearty laugh over the scene in the billiard room.

The two boys told their father that they were camped next to a family of half-breeds, who lived on the prairie, and that they had left the waggons and tent in their charge, all the small things being locked up in the boxes.

After having spent a pleasant evening with the Merediths, Mr. Barron left on his return to the Fort, more in love with Grace than ever; but when he considered the short time he had to remain in the settlement, he felt that his case was hopeless, and at the same time he felt it wrong to take any steps towards declaring his passion, not only from a feeling of uncertainty as to how he would be received, but also on account of the peculiar position George Wade held in the matter.

While he walked along musing over his miserable condition, he heard the noise of a drum and shouting in one of the wigwams alongside of the road. Curiosity induced him to investigate the cause of this, and accordingly he directed his steps to the spot. It was now dark, and as he approached, he came suddenly upon an Indian, who however merely offered him his hand and motioned him to enter. This Mr. Barron immediately did, and found about fifteen of the savages, male and female, seated round the edge of the lodge, in the centre of which a large fire was burning. One Indian was dancing and whooping inside the circle, and keeping time with his feet to the sound of the drum, beaten by one of those seated on the ground. In the glare from the fire, with their painted faces made still more hideous by the grimaces they put on, they looked more like demons let loose upon earth than human beings. As Mr. Barron entered he was pulled down to the ground by one of the squaws, and motioned to be seated next her; she then snatched the pipe he was smoking from his lips, and taking a few whiffs from it herself, she handed it to her neighbour, and so on it went, one giving it to the other until it finally came round to Mr. Barron again. That gentleman felt himself in a predicament, as he could not make up his mind to smoke the pipe again; so he refilled it with tobacco, and handed it back to the squaw, who had first taken it from him, and while it was going the round once more, he, finding the smell and the smoke of the fire too much for him, quietly slipped from the wigwam, and made his way to the Fort, glad to escape. When he reached the side postern, he found it locked, but on knocking, the watchman, having first been assured who it was, opened it and let him in.

CHAPTER VIII.

HE next day was the Sabbath, and the weather being fine, the Merediths and George walked to the English Cathedral, about a mile and a half from the town, down the Red River, and listened to an eloquent sermon preached by Archdeacon McLean, whom Mr. Meredith remembered to have heard once before in Canada. But as we will have something to say about the clergy of the settlement before we close our story, we will without dwelling on the subject at present leave our friends in the quiet enjoyment of this Sabbath day, while we take a look back on a character whom we have already met; we mean Mr. Cool. That gentleman, contrary to Flyaway's prediction, had hurried through with his business in St. Paul, and started for Red River only a few days after the departure of our friends from St. Cloud. About half way to the settlement he had overtaken a friend of his travelling in the same direction, and with whom he was on most intimate terms, for in fact they were bosom friends. It is soon after this meeting that we again introduce Mr. Cool to our readers.

He and his friend, whom we will know hereafter as Mr. Whirl, had camped in the middle of the day, and after dinner, while lying at full length on the grass, they whiled away the time by plotting mischief that ultimately nearly ruined them, and well nigh did the same for many others.

Whirl was a man of large stature, dark complexion, with eyes that showed him to be unscrupulous and mean in his dealings, notwithstanding he was possessed, like his friend Cool, of an affable and courteous manner. He however did not succeed as well as the other in making friends at first, for anyone being in the least a judge of character could not help suspecting him when looking into his eyes—the windows of a man's soul.

"I say Whirl" said Cool—"That confounded Flyaway is going to the devil as fast as he can, and I don't know what to do with him."

"Let him go," replied Whirl, "don't hold him back—and you'll soon be rid of him."

"That is all very well," said the other, "but while I have so much in my business belonging to him, I can't very well give him the cold shoulder altogether."

"Why don't you lose the money," suggested Whirl, "there's nothing easier."

"You beat the old gentleman," said Cool.

"Perhaps I am in reality His Santanic majesty" returned Whirl.

"I shouldn't wonder," Cool replied, laughingly ; "but what would you suggest about Flyaway, for he is a regular drag upon me at present ; and if you and I are going to play our cards together, we must first get rid of him."

"Then I tell you what it is," said Whirl. "As he is interested in your business to a certain amount, I'd suggest to him, if I were you, when you reach home, to take an outfit*

---

* An outfit means merchandise taken out amongst the Indians for the purpose of trading with them for furs.

from you for the amount you owe him, which you can sell him at good prices; and on the plea of wishing to be free from the fur business, you can say that you'd prefer he would take the goods on his own account and derive any benefit there might be from their sale. Get him then to go to the plains, and I'll wager if he continues to be so fond of whisky as he is now, the winterers will clean him out, stock, lock and barrel before he comes back. You will be free from him, and probably when he finds himself completely out of pocket, he will leave the country."

"Do you think he will agree to take an outfit for his debt," said Cool.

"Butter him well, and you'll manage it. It is your only course, unless you wish to show a sheet with the balance on the wrong side."

"I could do that, if I tried," replied Cool; "but I prefer your first plan, if it will work."

"Try it," said Whirl, "your character will suffer less by it than it would by the balance sheet plan, for everyone knows you're making money."

"Character!" sneered Cool, "how I despise that word — character forsooth as it is known in the nineteenth century is a myth. What is the difference between a pickpocket and a man who will swindle you in a trade. I can't see any. They both steal in an underhand way, yet the one will talk about his character—will attend church—will give donations to the poor—and will be received into society—and why? Because he has a character! and the pickpocket, because he's honest enough not to hide his 'profession,' is scouted at and hunted down by the very society that receives the other thief. I tell you what it is, character in reality is where a man tries in his own heart to deserve a good name. As we know it, however, it is bestowed upon the man who is smart enough to hide his shortcomings ; and knowing this, I am careless about the estimation others may form of my character.   I will make all the money I can, and in any way I can ; and the only regard I mean to have for my character is, that I'll steal or swindle in trade in as respectable a manner as possible ; and I have no doubt by sticking as close as I can to that rule, I will be accepted into society, having a character as good as the usual run of men now-a-days."

When Cool had finished, Whirl lay on his back, and laughed loud and heartily. " By Jove," he said, " I'll be hanged if you are not a first-class philosopher."   Then, sitting up, he continued, "what is this I heard you say about some family you expected to meet in the settlement.   Any money amongst them ?"

" There is considerable, from all I could hear about them in St. Paul," replied Cool.

" And how do you propose working them ?" asked Whirl.

" Well you see," answered Cool, " in the first place the Merediths (for that is the name of the family) want a farm in the settlement ; and I've been informed they are going into stock raising as well. Now there is Harrican's farm. Robert has lived on it for upwards of twenty-five years ; he owes me some money, and I think by a little manœuvering I can get him to sign over to me his claim on the land, whatever it may be. I believe that when a man lives a certain number of years on a place it gives him the right of possession—at all events, if I once get the thing signed, sealed and delivered over to me, I'll try it on a point of law, and I'll give them some trouble to oust me."

" But," interrupted Whirl, " Jack Harrican has the first right to the land ; it was willed to him."

" That makes no difference," answered Cool.   ' Robert, from having occupied the place for so many years will have the precedence in law; at least, its worth trying for."

"And what has all this to do with the Merediths?" asked Whirl.

"Everything," replied Cool. "I sell or let one place to them, and by doing so I will gain an intimate footing in the family,—that once obtained, the balance is quite easy. I'll at the least secure a good account on my books, and perhaps will be able to get the use of some of the money the old man has laid by. I'm in want of money badly just now."

"I never knew you to be anything else," replied his companion.

Without appearing to notice the remark, Cool went on to say "that there was a young fellow named Wade attached to the family whom he did not like, and who, if he was not greatly mistaken, returned the feeling with interest. This Wade," he continued, "I must beware of, and if possible destroy in the opinion of the Merediths."

"I wonder," said Whirl, laughing, "what this Mr. Wade would say if he heard your kindly disposed remarks regarding him?"

"When I reach home," Cool remarked, "I'll set Mrs. Cool to work, and I rather think she'll settle his hash in a very short space of time."

"Bravo!" cried Whirl, "your resources are unbounded."

"Of course I'll have to be guided a good deal by circumstances," continued Cool, "but this I do know, that the old man, Meredith, is a simple sort of confiding man that I can easily control, once I get him under my thumb."

"You remind me of a spider, and Mr. Meredith of a fly," remarked Whirl, "and if I may express my opinion, a deuced clever sort of spider you are at that; and now that we have

H

discussed Flyaway and the Merediths to our benefit and their disadvantage, let us talk over our plans for the future. We are supposed to be working for a change in the settlement, but what the d——l is it to be, and how are we going to be the gainers by it?"

"Well," said Cool, "I'm a little at a loss to know how to act in the matter. We have taken one step forward in inducing the *Buster* to run down and abuse the H. B. C. Government, and as the newspaper is supposed to represent the people, it has given the public abroad an idea that we are intolerably ill-used in Red River; but whether the United States or Canada is going to bite, I cannot tell; one or the other must take the matter up, I am sure."

"In an undertaking such as we are going into," said Whirl, "it is always well to look at the real state of affairs to enable us the better to shape our course. Now how do they stand? In the first place, although the law is not powerful in its execution, and can be evaded by those who are inclined to do so (nothing personal, Cool), yet take it on the whole, it would be hard to find a happier or more contented people than the settlers. It is only men like ourselves who stir up things with a long pole, to bring fish to their own net, who preach dissatisfaction and sow the seeds of discontent. Already we have succeeded in making several believe that they are a persecuted people and so forth. But I am puzzled to determine how these same people will feel after they find themselves on the eve of a change. Will it be acceptable to them, and will they not look back on the past and even present time, and at the last moment kick against the pricks? I tell you what it is, if they do, we will not make the money you are counting on."

"I have thought of all that," said Cool; "but as for the people of the country, their opinion or feelings will not be consulted regarding any change that may take place in the North-West. The half-breeds are bound to give place to new people coming into the country ; like the Indians, they will have to fall back on the approach of a more civilized state of society. There is no doubt of this in my mind, Whirl ; their habits and customs are so peculiar, and have become so much a part of their nature, that it will be impossible for them to keep pace with the times. It is not what the people of the country may think or do in the matter that troubles me, it is the uncertainty we are in, whether we are to be Americans or Canadians, and this perplexity makes it the more necessary that two having a common object in view should be engaged in urging a political reformation in the country."

" May I ask," said Whirl, " what the common object is to which you refer ?"

" Our two worthy selves, my dear Whirl."

" Oh !" exclaimed the other, smiling, " I see—well ?"

" Then," Cool went on to say, " as we are in doubt as to how things will run, I would suggest that you take one side while I take the other : publicly we will be in opposition ; privately we will compare notes and see how things are working."

" This is all very well," said Whirl, " but where is the money in all this ?"

" That is easily explained," replied Cool. " By being on friendly terms with the *Buster*, and inducing it to run the Hudson Bay Company, we are attracting attention abroad to this country. Canada has had an eye to the North-West for some years past, and is only too ready to swallow anything that is said against the Honourable Company, whether true or not, and is willing to accept any statement that tends to show us in the light of a down-trodden people, because it will assist them in their demands on the Imperial Government for the country. At the same time, Uncle Sam has an eye towards the North-West as well, and it is at present a question who is going to get the country. Now suppose you go in and work for the United States, while I uphold Canada; do you not see very clearly that the winning power is sure to reward the man who has assisted it. Fat contracts will be on hand, good offices, and a hundred other things, besides what they call pap."

"Ahem!" interrupted Whirl, "and suppose Canada wins, where will I be?"

"We'll go in snooks, of course," answered Cool, "the winner to share with the loser."

"In other words," returned Whirl, "we're going in for a big strike on a very small capital."

"Pshaw!" interrupted Cool, "it's as clear as day to me that there is to be a change very soon in the country, and I mean to say that the man who works to bring about that change will make his mark with the government coming in."

"And I mean to say," replied Whirl, "that it is very doubtful; but I'll think over it, and let you know when we get into the settlement."

By this time the two conspirators found they had remained in camp long enough, so they soon afterwards started on their way, and in four or five days reached Fort Garry.

CHAPTER IX.

S they drove up to Mr. Cool's house, they were met by Mrs. Cool and three or four little Cools; thereupon Mr. Whirl, who was a confirmed bachelor, and consequently disliked any family scenes, hurried on to the hotel where he boarded.

Mrs. Cool met her husband in a very affectionate manner, at the same time she expressed some surprise at his returning home so much earlier than she expected. The little Cools, who stood in awe of their father, kept a respectful distance from him, and if the truth was told, they were not very well pleased at seeing him home again so soon. They could manage their mother, but their father they knew to their cost was not to be trifled with.

Mr. Whirl became acquainted with our friends the Merediths at the tea table that evening, and soon afterwards he paid a visit to his friend Cool.

In a small room, neatly furnished, sat the two worthies facing each other.

"I've met the Merediths," said Whirl.

"You have, eh! Well, did they ask about me ?"

" Yes, the old gentleman enquired whether you had returned, and I told him you had. He felt rather inclined to come over with me to see you, but I put him off, thinking, perhaps, that you'd prefer not seeing him just yet."

"You were right," said Cool; "and now I must go and see Harrican this very night; there's no time to be lost, and I want you to come with me."

"All right," answered Whirl, "but, at the same time, I would like to know how you are going to manage things?"

"That is reasonable," returned Cool, "and very soon answered. In the first place, Harrican is not such a fool as to sign away his property in his sober senses, even if he owes me quite a sum of money; and although I can scare him into doing almost anything I want, therefore, if he don't do it in his sober senses, we must get him to do it when he's drunk."

Mr. Whirl whistled. "I see," he said, "but suppose it comes out afterwards, where will you be then?"

"I don't care a mite as long as I can get his signature to the document I have prepared."

"Let me see it," asked Whirl.

Cool then rose from his seat, and going to a desk, he produced a paper which he handed to his companion.

Whirl read it, and re-read it, and then turning to Cool said, "You'd make a d——'d good lawyer. If you get Harrican to sign that, I'd not be afraid to bet my last dollar on your chance."

"I should rather think not," returned Cool; "but I think we had better start." Then going to a cupboard, he took from it a bottle of brandy, and placing it on the table, he remarked, "There, that will do the deed."

Whirl now asked for a tumbler, and proposed that they should take a drink before setting out. The two worthies then drank to the success of their scheme, and afterwards left the house on their villainous errand.

It may be well to explain here that the property which Cool wished to get possession of, was willed to Jack Harrican by his father ; but his brother Robert had built a house on it in which he had resided for upwards of twenty-five years, at the time our story opens.   Robert Harrican was a thriftless sort of man, very fond of the bottle, and consequently he became deeply involved.

Jack, his brother, on the other hand, was plodding and careful, and from a good feeling towards his brother, he had never disturbed him in the occupancy of the farm.   Robert was indebted to Cool for a considerable amount advanced him chiefly for whisky, and this gave the latter a good deal of influence over the miserable man.

For some three months previous to the night we are describing, Robert had eschewed liquor altogether, and his wife and family were beginning to feel the happy effects from the change in the husband and father.   Mrs. Harrican was a quiet and very worthy woman, and through her goodness of disposition, her children were being brought up in a creditable manner. But a deep thorn rested in the mind of this noble woman ; she could not trust her husband ; it was therefore like a new life dawning on her, the three months experience preceding the night on which Cool and Whirl visited her house.   Alas! what a blow was in store for the poor woman.

Robert Harrican was sitting in the midst of his children, when the knock came to his door, announcing the arrival of his two visitors ; and as they entered, poor Mrs. Harrican, who knew the characters of both Cool and Whirl, felt her heart oppressed with a dread of some evil threatening them.

After some conversation Cool asked Robert to give them a private interview, as they had something of importance to communicate to him.   The unsuspecting man led the way to an unoccupied room, and then Cool, placing the bottle of brandy on the table, said as they had come on business that was likely to take up some time, he had brought something to keep their spirits up ; and at the same time he asked for glasses.

When Robert went out to the room where his wife was sitting, she went to him softly, and putting her arms round his neck, she whispered, so that the children would not hear her, "Robert, these men are going to tempt you; but you won't drink, will you, my husband ? Oh ! think how happy we have been the last three months. Think of your children and me. You have three tumblers in your hand, let me keep one, Robert; take in the two, and that will show them, if they are men at all, that you don't wish to drink. Oh ! Robert, you won't be angry with me, for you know your weakness, and you've been so strong of late."

"Don't be afraid, wife," said Harrican, " I'll take the three tumblers in, but one of them is for show ; if I bring in only two they'll think me a coward, but I'll not drink if they offer me any. I don't know what their business is, but they say it will be late before we're done with it. You and the children had better go to bed soon." Saying which, he turned to rejoin his guests.

The heart of the poor woman sank within her ; she knew the unscrupulousness of the men her husband had to deal with, and she was aware that he owed one of them a large sum of money ; she however put her children to bed, and then sinking on her knees, she sobbed forth an earnest prayer for her erring husband. Then extinguishing her lamp, the anxious woman crept stealthily towards the door of the room where sat Robert and his guests. Was it wrong that she should thus doubt her husband, and play the eavesdropper on his conduct ? Alas, no ! she knew the temptation he had to resist, and the power of the two tempters over him, and she was determined on making an effort to save him ; and as she stooped to listen at the door, she prayed the Almighty to forgive and help her.

She was too late ; as the sound of her husband's voice reached her ear, she knew that the tempter had succeeded, and that Robert Harrican was already very much intoxicated.

"My God !" she exclaimed, " this is hard to bear."

Unwittingly she had allowed her voice to go above a whisper, and this called forth a remark from Cool that somebody was at the door.

" It's all fancy," replied Whirl.

" I'll go and see," said Cool.

Mrs. Harrican instantly flew to her room, and when Cool opened the door, no one was to be seen.   When he had disappeared, however, the watcher regained her post, and overheard the following conversation—Cool was speaking.

"Now, Robert," he said, " you are in debt to me for a long time.   I've never pressed you, and I don't mean to do so now, but here's a chance for you to free yourself at once, and you'll not feel it.   You have lived on this place for a long time ; the house and all the buildings on it belong to you, and by right the land itself is yours, by having lived on it for so many years."

" It's not mine, I tell you," said Robert, " it is Jack's property, and I've no right to sell it "

" Jack has a good farm of his own," interrupted Whirl, " enough for him.   He's not going to grudge this bit of land to free you from debt ; besides he's not able to buy your house and improvements."

" You sign this paper, Harrican," said Cool, "giving over to me your house, and any right you have to the land, and I'll fix it all right with Jack.   I'll then give you a receipt for what you owe me, and you can move up to your place on the Assineboine.   It's a better farm, any way, than this one."

"Jack has been a good brother to me," said Robert, "and I'm not going to do anything to hurt him.   This place belongs to him, and I'll see you d——'d first before I'll sign that paper. You can lock me up on pemmican and water, if you like, for what I owe you ; but you know well enough I'll pay you some day."

"Well, take a drink, anyway, on it.   Whirl pass that bottle; you needn't keep it all to yourself," said Cool.

Mrs. Harrican had heard enough.   Without a moment's hesitation she hastened away, and, throwing a shawl over her head, left the house, and hurried over to Jack Harrican's, a few rods distant.   Finding everyone retired for the night, she knocked loudly at the front door, and, on its being opened by her husband's brother, she related to him, as well as she could, the trap Cool and Whirl were laying for Robert to fall into.

"But," said Jack, "the land does not belong to him, and how can he sell it ?"

"Cool is trying to convince him that his having lived on it so long, gives him the right of possession, and they are giving him brandy so freely, that I'm afraid they will get him to sign the paper, when he does not know what he is doing.   I wish you'd put on your coat and come over with me, for I don't know what to do."

Jack Harrican was taken aback completely by this unexpected turn in affairs.   As we have already mentioned, the farm on which Robert lived had been willed to Jack by his father, but he had allowed his brother to remain in undisturbed possession of the property, never dreaming that by so doing he was jeopardizing his claim on the land.   From the hurried statement of Mrs. Harrican, he was at a loss to know what to do, but he immediately put on his coat and accompanied her over to the house. As they hurried along they perceived two figures walking quickly away by the edge of the river bank.

"There," said Mrs. Harrican, "I'm sure that is Cool and Whirl, and I am afraid we're too late."

When they reached the house they found that Mrs. Harrican's words were only too true. In the room they found Robert in a drunken slumber, seated at and leaning over the table, with his head resting on his arms ; near him were two sovereigns, evidently dropped on purpose by one of the two men who had just left.

Mrs. Harrican, when she perceived the state in which her husband was, raised her pale face and said, " My God, I prayed for the sake of my poor Robert, but it has been Your will not to hear me." Then drawing herself up with a look of intense bitterness in her face, she continued. " I now pray that the curse of an injured woman may follow those two men to their graves ; they have nigh broken my heart."

Can it be wondered at that the otherwise gentle woman should curse the villians who had robbed her home of its happiness ? Jack succeeded in dragging his brother to bed, and leaving his stricken wife seated by his side, he wended his way home, sad and sorrowful, more at the condition of his brother, whom he loved so well, than any threatened loss of his property.

Cool and Whirl, in the meantime, had returned to the house of the former, and were exulting over the success of their scheme.

" That is one good thing done, at any rate," remarked Cool.

" If the results turn out as well," returned Whirl, " which I must say I am doubtful of."

"Leave all that to me," said the other. "I think I can manage now, with this paper in my possession. By Jove, Harrican caved in suddenly. I think that last glass of brandy you gave him did the deed."

"I was tired," replied Whirl, "of his obstinacy, and therefore gave him a good stiff one."

"And now," continued Cool, drawing his chair closer to Whirl, "what do you think of our political scheme ? Will you go in ?"

"I may as well, if it's to be all fair in war."

"Honor bright," said Cool. "And, by the way, the arrival of the Merediths can be made use of, for I mean to stir up a public meeting. I have to see the old man to-morrow about the Harrican farm, and I will also open the subject of politics to him at the same time, by declaring how ill used we are, and the necessity for a change. Then I will point out our duty, as Canadians, and wind up by asking him to help me about this meeting."

"Go ahead," remarked Whirl. "What next !"

"After we have passed a series of resolutions, censuring the Company, and calling for a change of government, I will get the *Buster* to come out heavy in its favour, of course making special mention of the patriotic speech I intend to deliver on the occasion."

"Cool, you are invincible ; but what am I to do all this time ?"

"You are to throw cold water on it," was the reply. "There are enough Americans in the town and settlement for you to form a party. If you do, then go in heavy for the United States ; this will tend to get up some excitement at least, which is necessary in this milk and water place. I have a good deal of faith in the *Buster*.

"I have no doubt of that," said Whirl ; "but its more than any one else in Red River has. I'll do my best and talk them up."

In this way they planned and schemed till near midnight, concocting several measures to bring about their purposes, the chief of which was the downfall of the Hudson Bay Company. As Cool was showing Whirl to his room for the night, it being too late to obtain an entrance to the hotel, the latter worthy remarked, "I be hanged, Cool, after all said and done, it was a shame to leave Harrican as we did, without notifying his wife."

"Pshaw !" replied the other, "she is accustomed to that sort of thing."

"Cool, by Jove," muttered Whirl, and so they parted.

CHAPTER X.

HE next morning Cool called on Mr. Meredith, and offered him the option of leasing or buying the Harrican farm, stating at the same time, that he preferred to rent it, as there was some difficulty about the title to it. "You can drive down with me," he continued, "and when you see the place, you can judge for yourself."

"When can I occupy the premises?" asked Mr. Meredith, "as I am under a heavy expense at present, and will be glad to get settled once more in a home of my own. My boys are still camping out with Mr. Wade; not that it will do them much harm, but I am anxious to see them regularly employed."

"As far as I can judge," said Cool, "you could get into the house in a day or two; in fact, I will arrange that you do so, if you conclude to take the farm."

Cool, who had his horse and buggy at the door, then drove Mr. Meredith down to Robert's house; and as they approached the door, they were met by that gentleman himself, still suffering from the effects of his late debauch.

"Cool," he cried, going to the side of the buggy, "you are a scoundrel! you thought to make me a robber last night, but you never will do that. Here is your two sovereigns you left behind you—and that paper you showed me.   If I signed it, I did it when I was drunk, d———n you."

"Come! come! Robert," said Cool, apparently unaffected by the words thus addressed to him, "I have brought this gentleman down to see the place.   He is a stranger in the country, so if you have any differences with me, let us settle them by ourselves."

"Neither you nor that gentleman will set foot in my house, as long as I can prevent it,—but I am going away from here, and I will leave the keys with Jack, you can fix things with him.   As for that paper, I'll swear I never signed it when I was myself; for both my wife and Jack will take their oath that they found me dead drunk, after you and Whirl left me, last night."

Mr. Meredith felt very awkwardly placed during this conversation, and turned to Mr. Cool for some explanation of the difficulty; but that collected individual merely asked how he (Mr. Meredith), liked the appearance of the place outside, and regretted not being able to show him the inside of the house, on account of the stubbornness of the person before them.

"Stubbornness is it?" said Robert.   "You may call it by any name you choose, but it is nothing more nor less than what I have said.   You will never enter the door of my house as long as there is life in my body to keep you out.   And you, sir," turning to Mr. Meredith, "I don't know you, but all I can tell you is, that you are in bad company; and if you are looking after the place, I warn you that the man beside you has as much right to it as the horse before you.   I'm leaving it, and it's time I did; but, Cool, you'll never own it, if I have to stand in the court and tell my own disgrace, to show you up."

With this, the conscience-stricken and indignant man entered the house, and shut the door in their faces.

"I regret this scene very much," said Cool, "on your account; but it is easily explained. The man who has just left us, has been indebted to me for some time for a large amount, and I saw no other way of securing it than by obtaining possession of his property. He is a good-for-nothing fellow, who is drunk more than half the time, and is seldom steady enough to transact any business. On my releasing him from his indebtedness to me, he signed over this property in my behalf; but his brother, who professes to have a claim on the land, has induced him to try and withdraw from the arrangement with me—and this is the difficulty about the title I referred to at the hotel. I will, however, see the brother, and probably arrange matters with him in a satisfactory manner, if not, there will be a necessity for a law-suit; but in any case, you can rest assured, that you will occupy the farm in a day or two."

"I would dislike," said Mr. Meredith, "having been in the settlement such a short time, to become involved in any trouble with people living in it."

'You may rest perfectly easy on that score," replied Cool, "as I would be the last one to lead you into anything of the sort. I will see Jack Harrican, however, this afternoon, and let you know in the evening."

When they separated at the hotel, Cool mentally cursed Robert for the scene that had occurred before Mr. Meredith, but he resolved upon putting the best face on the matter, and fighting it out to the last.

Mr. Meredith felt disappointed and troubled, notwithstanding the assurance of Cool, that everything would turn out well; and meeting George Wade, he explained to him what had happened.

"It is nothing more than might be expected from the man."

"Which one?" asked Mr. Meredith.

"Cool, of course," said George.

"Well, there are always two sides to a story, and Mr. Cool, apparently, is not very far wrong in the matter. This Harrican has owed him a large sum of money for some time, without showing any disposition to pay it. You can hardly blame him for endeavouring to get his debt secured."

"A man, of course, has a right to what properly belongs to him," answered George ; "but there is a foul as well as a fair way of collecting an account. Something must be wrong about it, else Harrican would not have acted and spoken as he did."

"It is a strange affair altogether, I must confess," said Mr. Meredith, "and I heartily wish I was out of it. But I cannot hear of another place that will suit me ; so what am I to do?"

"Wait till this evening, and if Cool, does not call upon you, according to promise, go to the Harricans, and arrange matters, if possible, with them. I'll go bail Cool will not interfere with any bargain you make ; only I'd stipulate, that in case he has a claim on the land, you will hold the rent-money in your own hands until the legal possessor is decided upon."

"You're right," said Mr. Meredith, "and we'll give Cool the first chance."

During the afternoon, however, George Wade walked down to the farm, and in the course of his perambulations he came across a man, who was lying at full length on the bank of the river opposite his house, and looking very disconsolate. George, in a free and easy way, sat down beside him, and opened the conversation by asking several questions regarding the settlement and the people, during which he ascertained the fact that he was talking to Robert Harrican.

On making this discovery, George described parts of their

I

journey to the settlement, and in the course of his remarks, he mentioned the circus-scene in St. Paul, and how Cool rescued Mrs. Meredith.

"1 suppose," said Robert, "that is the wife of the gentleman he drove here this morning ?"

"It is," said George, "and I heard from Mr. Meredith there was some unpleasantness during the visit. We are all, comparatively speaking, strangers to Mr. Cool."

"You'll know him before long, to your cost," interrupted Robert, who there and then gave George an unvarnished statement of the previous night's proceedings. He hid nothing about himself, but gave a frank, honest account of what occurred ; how he had given up the use of liquor, some time previously ; how they tempted him, and when he gave way, how they endeavoured to get him to rob a kind brother of his birth-right.

"He told Mr. Meredith," said George, "that you owed him a considerable sum of money, and that he had got possession of this property to secure his debt."

"Well, the fact is," said Robert, "I've been a fool all my life, and squandered my means, and I confess I do owe Cool a good deal of money ; but for what ? Whisky and such like ; and he has taken advantage of my drinking, to heap debt upon my head ; but if he thinks I'm going to do Jack out of his just right, to pay my debt, he is counting on something that won't happen."

"How do you know but that the paper you signed may give Cool the right to the property ?"

"It won't, I tell you," said Robert excitedly. "I'll stand in the open court and denounce him for the way he got me to sign it."

"Why are you leaving the place ?" asked George.

"Because I have a farm of my own on the Assiniboine, and I cannot remain here after what I have done. I'll go there and try to be a better man. I've a good woman for a wife, and I've nigh broken her heart. I'm going to help to heal the sore a bit."

"I believe Mr. Cool is coming to see your brother this afternoon," said Wade.

"So he told me. They can fight it out; but I told Jack that paper amounts to nothing, and if it does come to the worst, I'll go to jail for a while; but it will be better for Cool to give me a chance."

Robert now excused himself for having taken up so much time reciting his wrongs; and then George having given him kindly encouragement for the future, departed, fully convinced that Harrican had been imposed upon, and therefore he was more strengthened in his distrust of Cool.

In the evening, that individual called on the Merediths, and stated that he had been able to come to no agreement with Jack Harrican about the possession of the farm, but that he had made an arrangement with him to let Mr. Meredith have it on lease.

"I expect the thing will be decided at the next court, and until then you will not be required to pay the rent over to either Jack or myself."

"And how about the man who lives in the house at present ?"

"He is leaving to-morrow, to go to another farm on the Assiniboine belonging to him," said Cool, "and I think my having brought him up sharp will be a lesson to him."

George Wade, who was present, smiled while he thought how the lesson had been administered. It was finally arranged that the Merediths should move into their new house in a couple of days, a fact that pleased Mrs. Meredith and Grace very much, they having become tired of the monotonous hotel life. No one had called to see them, and they felt that they were indeed in a strange land amongst strange people.

"Sakes alive!" Mrs. Meredith would say, "its nothing but eat and drink all day, and those two boys they're running to seed as fast as ever they can."

After all the arrangements had been completed satisfactorily about the farm, Cool drew Mr. Meredith to one side, and told him his intention of getting up a public meeting in favor of Annexation to Canada.

"The truth is," said Cool, "we must agitate this matter. It is bound to come some day soon, and a few willing hands will do much to further it."

"But is this quite fair or right to the Company that governs at present. Will not this action on your part be premature, and serve to weaken the hands of the Hudson Bay Company. These public demonstrations are apt, at this stage especially, if the settlement is on the eve of a change, to create party feeling and strife. Now the fact is, I'm not very sure from all I can learn that there are many settlers in Red River favorably inclined towards Canada or Canadians. And from my short experience here, I should say the people are quite contented as they are, and certainly I cannot see much to grumble at."

"You have not lived here long enough to judge," said Cool.

"I acknowledge that," said Mr. Meredith, "but the more reason why I should not at present mix myself up in any political question until I am able to judge."

"You say there is nothing to grumble at. The Company appoints the members of the council, and calls them together whenever it suits the pleasure of that august body. It collects a duty of four per cent. on all imports, and a shilling a gallon on liquor. And how that is spent no one knows. It gives a drawback on the duty to the traders on goods sent into the interior for buying fur, and why? Because the Hudson Bay Company is the largest trader in the country, and four per cent. is a heavy item for them to get rid of. The money collected from duties goes into the Company's pockets, and the people who pay it are never made acquainted with its disposition. Is that right? The government of the country being in direct opposition to the people under it, in trade, how can you expect that it will ever be a popular or beneficial one. Look at our settlement, do you find any life and activity in it? No! And why is it so? Because the Company will do nothing to further enterprise, and does everything in its power to prevent immigration."

"There, I cannot agree with you," interrupted Mr. Meredith, "for, take my own case, I could not have received more kindness from any one than I did from Mr. K——, the Company's agent at St. Paul; indeed he took a great deal of trouble to see me comfortably fixed. Then, notwithstanding the short acquaintance I have had with the officers in charge of Fort Garry, I can assure you they have been most considerate towards me. They state that there is an opposition existing between the trader and the Company, but at present it seems to be a healthy one; and a great deal of natural co-operation at times takes place between the free trader and the Hudson Bay Company. I look on the government as a separate affair, and the fact of the duty being deducted from those articles going into the interior, is only fair, I should say. No country charges duty on what it does not consume within its own boundaries, and you may look on the settlement as a country. The traders who go out amongst the Indians enjoy little, if any, of the advantages to be derived from the government

of Assiniboine. Why then should they be called upon to bear
a share of the expense? Although the Company in itself is a
large, rich, and powerful body, yet there is many a poor man
interested in its fur trade, who has a right to see that every
saving is made in its management. Then with regard to the
government and the prosperity of the people, the settlement
is peculiarly situated, with no means of outlet or inlet, except
by the rude ox cart. It has no resources at present except fur,
therefore the inhabitants, so far distant as they are from communication with the outside world, cannot afford to carry on
an expensive government. If therefore the Hudson Bay Company takes care of all the jurisdiction of the country for four per
cent. on imports consumed in the settlement, I think it is a
cheap bargain for the people. The settlers, to my eyes, appear
happy and contented. I don't see much wrong about the
roads and bridges. I am told the school system is excellent;
and, although many things I see are primitive in their character, yet on the whole I could live very happily in the settlement, just as it is, for many years to come. When railroads
or stages approach—when enterprise and immigration begin to
direct their course this way,—then it will be time for us to look
out for a different order of things. If I were you, Mr. Cool,
I'd not meddle in stirring up the people to desire for a thing
which they do not feel the want of. I may be wrong; but it is
my opinion, that when political changes are forced before their
time, they ultimately result in trouble to all concerned."

"These ideas, Mr. Meredith, have been picked up by you
during a few days residence here; and your observations have
consequently been limited," remarked Cool.

"Very true. But you must remember that I have come
here to settle, and you may depend upon it I have taken great
pains to enquire about things generally, for I have an interest

—a great one I may say—at stake ; and I am not likely to allow myself to be biassed one way or another. It is true, my opinions have been hurriedly formed, and I am surprised that I have been able to gain so much information in such a short time. I may change my ideas, too, after a longer residence in the country, but at present I must decline having any thing to do with a public meeting for the purposes you have already named."

"Will you attend it ?" asked Cool.

"Assuredly I will," answered Mr. Meredith.

" Strangers, when they first come to the country, are unable to determine properly how things are working," said Cool, "but I'll wager you will soon come round to my way of thinking. For my part, I will not rest until I see the Hudson Bay Company's government rooted out."

" In other countries that would be deemed treasonable language," remarked Mr. Meredith, smiling.

"Treasonable !" laughed Cool. "Why, at one time here it was treasonable for any one to be seen wearing a fur cap."

"Indeed !" said Mr. Meredith. "By the way, Mr. Cool, I have met a Mr. Whirl, who is a friend of yours, I believe."

"He's a rank Annexationist to the States," was the reply ; "beware of him."

"How is he so friendly with you then ?" asked Mr. Meredith.

" Oh, I know and understand him."

During all this time George and Grace, having been left to themselves, had enjoyed a *tete-à-tete*, Mrs. Meredith having fallen asleep in her chair with her Bible across her knees, and her spectacles down on her nose. The two boys were out in camp. A better understanding was beginning to exist between the lovers, which Mr. Meredith was very much pleased to perceive.

Cool soon after left in company with George Wade, saying, as he bade good-bye, that Mrs. Cool would call the next day.

Cool, as he wended his way to his house, felt to a certain degree disappointed and discouraged in his schemes on Mr. Meredith.

George Wade, as he walked towards the camp, felt more hope in his breast regarding his love affair; at the same time, for some reason or another, he dreaded the intimacy that had sprung up between Cool and the Merediths. Well he might.

CHAPTER XI.

HEN George Wade reached the camp, he found Mr. Barron sitting alone by the fire, the two boys being fast asleep in the tent.

"Hilloa!" cried George, somewhat surprised at the late visit. "Where have you sprung from?"

"I have been waiting here for you nearly two hours," replied Mr. Barron, "because I want to see you, particularly to-night, as I don't know the day I may have to leave for York Factory. Come and sit down beside me—have a weed?"

George accordingly threw himself on the grass, lighted his cigar, and patiently waited for Mr. Barron to speak. Little did our two friends suspect that a few feet apart from them there lay a man who, by chance found himself a listener to their conversation, and who greedily availed himself of the opportunity. This was none other than our old friend Fly-away, who had been indulging rather freely during the fore-noon. It appears, while in a state of obliviousness, he wandered out on the prairie, until, overcome by fatigue, he fell down amongst some short bushes a few feet from the Merediths' camp, and there he slept in a drunken slumber till he was aroused by George addressing Mr. Barron.

Recognizing the voice, he determined upon not making his

presence known to the two young men, but listened greedily to their conversation, hoping to be able to catch something worth while relating again.

"I owe one of you a grudge," he muttered, as he glared at them through the bushes, "and I'll pay it the first chance I get." How well he kept his word will soon be seen.

"Wade, I'm here on several errands, and as it is better to finish one before we commence another, we will begin with yourself. Have you found anything to do ? I know you do not purpose remaining idle as soon as you can find employment."

"I have not been able to obtain any work as yet," said George, "and I'm not particular, as long as I can get something honorable, and not degrading, to do."

"Then I tell you what it is," said Barron, "if you like, you can get into the Company's service, I think. They require a man for their store across the river at St. Boniface, and you would suit them exactly. You can speak a little French ?"

"Enough to make myself understood and to be able to understand," said George.

"Then I would advise you," continued Mr. Barron, "to go and see Mr. Bon, and if you can get him to stir himself in your behalf you'll get the situation. His recommendation will be sufficient, I hear, with the old Governor. I only learned of this chance for you to-day, and as soon as I could get away from the Fort I came here to tell you ; but you were away, so I waited that I might see you ; besides, I have something else to say to you."

"Are there many applicants for the berth ?" asked George.

"No," was the reply, "because few know about it. You had better, however, see Mr. Bon the first thing in the morning, and get him to go up to the Fort at once about it. He ' do it if you ask him, I'm sure."

"Barron" said George, "you have been very kind in this matter to me; I'll always remember it. There are not many who would have done as you have."

"Don't mention it," replied the other; "I suppose you'd have done the same by me."

At this moment Flyaway felt himself in a most decided predicament. Something had got up his nose, and the consequence was a very great desire on his part to sneeze, and fearing what might happen if he was discovered, he wriggled and worked his face into all sorts of ridiculous shapes endeavouring to keep it in. But his exertions were only partly successful, for after all, he allowed a smothered sort of sneeze to escape him, loud enough however to attract Mr. Barron's attention.

"What was that?" he quickly said.

Flyaway looked horrified, and cursed his nose.

"It was one of the boys," I suppose, answered George. "Tom is always restless in his sleep."

Flyaway looked relieved. "I wish you would go and see if they are asleep," suggested Barron, for I wish to tell you something which I don't want anyone else to hear."

Flyaway chuckled and opened his ears wide.

George arose, and looking into the tent, he reported both boys sound asleep. As he took his place again beside Barron, he asked him when he thought the boats would start for York Factory. "I am not sure," said Barron. "We ought to have been off by this time, but there has been delay somewhere, and now we may start any hour during the day."

"It will be a splendid trip for you," remarked George. "I wish I was going with you."

"I would like to change places with you," said Barron.

"Why?" asked George.

"I do not see," said Barron, "why I should open my mind

to you, and yet I feel a great desire to do so. The fact is
Wade, I've seen a good deal of hard life in my time, and have
been, if the truth must be told, a pretty wild young man. In
Glasgow, I came as near going to the devil as I could manage
it, and at last I came here to get away from my associates. I
was glad to get away. I got rather jolly the other night at the
Fort, and when it came to the Governor's ears, he said, 'They
send me out all their wild young bloods to tame and reform,
and I suppose this is another sample of the kind.' The old
man was not far wrong, for it is well known that sending a
young man to the Hudson Bay Territory is as good as a whaling
voyage to reform him, and I came accordingly."

"That is," interrupted George, "if they are ordered to the
interior."

"Of course," replied Barron, "for there's as much rum and
brandy in that little town of Winnipeg as would drown a regi-
ment of soldiers."

" You're about right," said George.

" And now," continued Barron, "although I have been wild,
drank heavily, and gone to the bad pretty generally, yet through
it all I can say that my heart never became hardened. I am
situated, as far as my family is concerned, very much like yourself, from what I have heard you say, except that I lost my
father when I was quite a boy. I have no mother nor sister;
if either had been alive, I never would have become as wild as
I did."

During this conversation, George observed that Barron looked
dejected and sad, not like his usual self.

" Wade," he now said, " another of my errands here is to ask
a favor from you."

" Granted already," said George, "if it is within my power."

"It is not much," replied Barron. "I am going away hundreds of miles from here, and I feel that I will never return. I have a most indescribable presentment of evil hanging over me. I cannot shake it off, and yet after all it may be what is called a diseased imagination. Be that as it may, I do not think I ever will see old Glasgow again, or that you'll ever find Barron figuring in the future about Fort Garry. Some would call this sinful. It may be so, I can't help it. If I could I would not be asking you the favor I am going to do this night."

George began to think that Barron was only recovering from a spree, and was low spirited accordingly; he therefore indulged in badinage, and endeavoured to draw his companion's thoughts from the gloomy subject, but all to no purpose.

" It is useless this sort of thing," said Barron ; "although I know you mean well."

"Listent to me! As sure as I am sitting on this box, I will never return from York Factory. · I am going away with that conviction, and I have come on that account to ask you to take charge of a small package for me,"—saying which, he drew from his coat pocket a small parcel, neatly done up in paper, and which he handed to George. " I will write a letter to you, and leave it in the office at Fort Garry, or hand it to you before I start on the trip ; and in it you will find instructions what to do with this package. Keep it safely as you would your life, and promise me, as you would a dying man, that you will do as I ask you in that letter."

"I promise," said George, "to do all in my power to meet your wishes, whatever they may be. I don't expect you'll ask impossibilities from me."

"Not I, Wade !"

Flyaway was brimful of curiosity.

George now rose, and placed the parcel in his trunk, and

while he was doing so, he noticed Barron leaning his head on his arms.

"Poor fellow," thought George, "there is something troubling him, I fear;" and as he threw himself down beside the despondent man, the latter lifted his head, and said—

"Wade, were you ever in love with two girls about the same time?" George flushed to the temples, but answered, "Not exactly!"

"You're a lucky fellow," continued Barron, "and I'm sure I wish you happiness."

"What do you mean?" asked George.

"I told you," answered Barron, "that I'd open my mind to you, and I will, although it may be bad taste my doing so to you under the circumstances; but the truth is, I have no one to whom I feel I can trust myself, except yourself; and I think I will feel better if I unburden my mind to you. But, before doing so, will you promise not to feel hard at anything I may say?"

"Heave ahead," replied George, "I never take offence unless it is intended."

"Then here's my story," said Barron. "When I lived in Glasgow, I became acquainted with a young girl, who moved in a humbler sphere of life than I did. She was very beautiful however, and captivating, and indeed she seemed worthy of a higer station in society. I became enamoured of her, and was a frequent visitor at her father's house, so much so that my guardian hearing about it, demanded an explanation from me, which I gave in my own way, and satisfied him for the time being. Thus matters stood. I continued to visit the girl, and other young men, swells of the city, to my disgust found their way to her house. I remonstrated with her, and she promised me to give them the cold shoulder, but still I heard of their continued

visits. I believe Wade, I truly loved that girl. I believe that
had I been able I would have married her; but about this
time my guardian, no doubt to break me from my fascination
towards the girl, as well as to stop me in a wild career, persuaded me to leave for this country. I have only this day received
letters stating that the girl in Glasgow has married one of the
very swells I cautioned her against."

"That was hard, Barron, I must say," said George, "but
one who could forget you so soon is not worth thinking about."

"Would you believe it," said Barron, "I had almost forgotten
her when the news of her marriage brought her back to my
memory."

George was regularly puzzled.

"And now," continued Barron, "comes the part of my story,
where I must ask you not to feel hard with me. You're a
lucky fellow Wade."

George could not think what the other was driving at.

"I confess," continued Barron, "I have felt bad since I
heard of the marriage of the Glasgow girl; but there is another
matter that has troubled me far more. Soon after we became
acquainted with the Merediths, I learned to love Grace.
Don't start. Hear me out. You are the only one who knows
it. I soon afterwards saw that another young man loved her
as well, and I saw what is more, that she returned his love.
Wade, Grace Meredith is in my thoughts, waking and sleeping.
She is my good angel. She will only know my love when I'm
gone. You are more deserving of her, and I wish you joy and
happiness. Watch over her; take care of her; you have in
her indeed a pearl without price. I thought I loved the girl
in Glasgow. I believe I did; but I never knew what real love
was till I met Grace Meredith. And what is more, I never will
love another. Oh! God, I've a lonely feeling over my heart;

haven't you something strong, Wade, somewhere handy, perhaps it will give a little life to a fellow ?"

George rose and took a flask of brandy from his trunk, which he handed to Barron. There was a long pause in the conversation ; at last George spoke.

"I do not deny, Barron, that I love Grace Meredith ; but I am not so sure as you seem to be that she returns the feeling ; and as for my being deserving, I fear you over estimate my worth, for it is that very thing which deters me from speaking my mind to her. You have been so open with me, it is fair that I should be the same to you."

George hereupon gave Barron sketches from his life while in the East India service ; amongst others, he described an incident that occurred in which he (George), innocently became involved, and which, for a time, brought disgrace upon his name, and was chiefly the reason for his leaving the service.

"Now," he said, as he finished the story, "although I was to a certain degree blameworthy in that affair, yet I got into it without any intention of wrong on my part. It has, however, been handled by my enemies to my detriment, and they may do the same again."

"I rather think they will," muttered Flyaway to himself.

"And how can I explain it to Mr. Meredith," George continued, "so that he can understand it properly ? In fact if he heard about it, I would refuse any explanation to him regarding the affair. You see everything does not run as smoothly with me as you thought. The fact is, Grace Meredith is too good for me. I have never spoken to her about love ; although one day I came 'pretty near to it ; and I cannot make out whether she really cares for me or not ; besides, that unfortunate occurrence hanging over my head prevents me from urging my suit. Barron, you have shown yourself a noble fellow towards me, and although it would almost break my heart to lose Grace Meredith, yet I would like you to speak to her about yourself."

"No," said Barron, "I have struggled and struggled against it, and now I am resolved to act like a man. I may leave to-morrow, or the next day, and when I do, I part from Grace Meredith for ever. But, Wade, the memory of her will remain in my heart as long as I live."

By this time the fire had smouldered out, and as it was too late for Mr. Barron to return to the Fort, the two young men, after a little further conversation, turned in under the same blanket. The last thing Mr. Barron did was to remind George to be careful of the package and to follow the instructions in the letter.

In the meantime Flyaway began to find his position a very unpleasant one, and he was not sorry to see the two young men lie down to sleep. When he felt perfectly sure that he could move with impunity, he made the best of his way back in the direction of the town, and there we will leave him for the present, knocking loudly at the door of Cool's house.

In the morning, Mr. Barron having returned to the Fort, George went and saw Mr. Bon about the situation in the Company's service.

"It is certainly a good chance," said Mr. Bon, "and I will only be too happy if I can be of service to you; but I fear Mr. Barron has placed too much importance on any influence I may have in the matter; however, I will do what I can. I will go and speak to the Governor about you, but the probability is he will wish to see you and judge for himself. He is not a man who places a great deal of faith in recommendations; he prefers his own judgment to anything of that sort."

J

"Shall I remain here or go to the Fort with you?" asked George.

"I think you had better remain here, and I will let you know if you are wanted," saying which, Mr. Bon left on his mission.

While George was waiting in Mr. Bon's store, he had an opportunity of observing a few of the peculiarities in the mode of carrying on trade in the North-West. At one end, and seated on the counter, were two half-breed plain hunters, busily engaged at a game of cards, over which they were very noisy in a good-humored way. In another part of the store a young man was playing on a fiddle, while a half-breed was dancing to the music. Behind the counter were two or three men and women picking out and handling the goods as they felt inclined. They seemed to have unlimited *carte-blanche* to take what they wished.

George was astonished at the freedom allowed them, and asked one of the clerks if he was not afraid of goods being stolen or taken by mistake.

"Lord, no!" answered the young man. "These are our winterers, and we can trust any thing with them. There is not one of them who will take a single article without giving us an account of it. There are a few in the settlement we would not allow behind the counter, but we know them well."

"How do you keep track of your sales when you allow them to help themselves?" asked George.

"You see, sir," was the reply, "they first of all pick out their outfit, and when they have finished doing that, they then choose what they will want for their own use, till they come back next year. As soon as they have chosen all they require, we go with our book and take an account of the articles, and charge them up. The men then bale their outfits and pack them away in their carts, and they are ready for their trip, not to return to the settlement till next summer. Many of them start without any invoice or account of their goods. When they are out on the plains they sell as they can, and get as much fur as possible for their outfit."

"You can't keep your stock very regular, for when you allow them to choose for themselves, they may pick out the very articles you require most in the store, for your every day customers."

"We take care of that," said the clerk, laughing. "We hide lots of our goods until the winterers have left for the plains."

At the back door another clerk was looking after the unloading of several carts just arrived from St. Cloud. The hides were thrown off; the half-breeds went to work with a will, and soon had all their freight piled inside the door.

During all this time there was a good deal of bustle and noise in the store, for it was a busy time. In the midst of it, however, some one announced that Pierre Gladieux was going to run his horse against that of Urban Romain. Immediately men, women and children poured out of the store. The two clerks locked up the shop; one of them asking George to accompany them, and all went out on the prairie a short distance, where the two racers were ready for the start. The distance was a mile, and the two horsemen having gone as far as Fort Garry, a stake was planted at the end of the course to be run, and then both horses started fairly together.

Pierre Gladieux came in the winner by about two lengths, but there were no high words over it. The only results were several more races got up on the strength of the one just over. As soon, however, as the first race had been run, customers and clerks returned to the store, and business was resumed again. The card-players went on with their game; the fiddler took up his fiddle; and the customers commenced overhauling the shelves where they had left off. Notwithstanding this apparent easy, careless mode of carrying on trade, which was peculiar to Red River, there was not as much loss by bad debts or theft as there would have been in any other place the same size in Canada or the United States. Shortly before the time of our story it was not customary to put locks on store doors, latches being all that were necessary. This will be hardly credited, but it is nevertheless true. Stealing at that time was almost unknown in Red River, and was considered one of the worst of crimes. The confidence that existed between customer and merchant facilitated things greatly in carrying on business; and the half-breeds in their dealings are not difficult to please, nor are they given to grumbling and fault-finding. If an article does not suit them they refuse it at once, and that is the end of it.

Although everything in Mr. Bon's store seemed to be carried on in confusion, it was far from being the case in reality, as his accounts were found to be invariably correct, and no one had a better standing abroad than he possessed.

We will have more to say about the peculiarities of the Red River trade before we finish our story; in the meantime we may say, that on Mr. Bon's return George found that he had been accepted conditionally by the Governor on a month's trial. If at the end of that time it should be to the mutual satisfaction of the Company and himself he was to remain. The salary was small, but as George said it was a beginning. His duties were to commence a week from that day. George thanked Mr. Bon for his trouble, and mentally blessed Mr. Barron; and he felt his heart light as he stepped cheerfully along in the direction of the hotel, to let the Merediths know of his good luck.

While he is doing this, we will take a look in upon Mr. Cool, who is busily engaged with Dr. Flyaway. The latter, after repeated knockings, had succeeded the night before in obtaining an entrance to the house, much to the disgust of Mrs. Cool, who could not bear the man. "A drunken, conceited rascal," she used to call him. Flyaway had retailed the conversation overheard by him between George and Mr. Barron, and, if we may use the expression, Cool's heart "jumped with joy," when he heard it. His wife was to visit the Merediths that afternoon, why should she not use this as a lever to pry Mr. George Wade out of the family? It needed caution as well as time—but the lever was in his hands, and the unscrupulous man determined to use it, for he hated George Wade from the bottom of his heart. Accordingly he laid his plans open at once before his amiable dame, who, like a good wife, concurred in them, and promised to assist him to the best of her ability. When Cool mentioned how Flyaway had overheard it, she remarked, "the cowardly, sneaking, little rascal, it's just like him, to pry about, listening to what folks say; but I'll let the Merediths know in my own way, what they may expect from this exemplary young Wade."

"You're a trump," said Cool, laughing.

"You shouldn't call me by such vulgar names," replied his his wife, affecting displeasure.

Cool now rejoined Flyaway, whom he had left in the office, and being a man who made it a rule to strike when the iron was hot, he intimated to the Doctor his desire to become free from the fur trade. "You," he continued, "are now accustomed to it, and indeed, I am only a hindrance to your operations, as my heart is not in the business. I think, as a friend,

I would advise you to carry on the trading, without any drag or trammel being on you in any way. Besides, you are really entitled to the whole profits realized on the furs,” (there had not been a shilling made in that way by them since Cool and Flyaway entered partnership.)

“ Not at all,” said Flyaway, “ if you share the profits, you also share any losses there may be.”

“ Exactly,” returned Cool. “ But,” he continued, “ I am now anxious to confine myself to the business of the settlement altogether, and I would like you to take hold of the fur trade on your own and sole account.”

“ In other words,” said Flyaway, “ you have made all the money you think you can out of me, and now you want to be rid of me. Very good. What do you propose ? ”

“ You are too hasty,” answered Cool ; “ I have no reason for wishing to get rid of you, as you call it, it is merely a matter of business. There is so much money in the concern belonging to you, together with an equal share from my capital, to be invested in fur. Now to tell you the truth, it has not been a paying affair, and as I don’t understand it, I’m anxious to quit it. Is there anything wrong in this ? ”

“ Mr. Cool,” interrupted Flyaway, “ you mentioned just now that there was an equal amount of your money with mine invested in the fur business. Allow me to remark that I have never yet obtained an outfit to come up to the sum of money you have belonging to me. I’d like to know where your capital has been all this time ! ”

“ Why,” said Cool, “ there are a hundred and one expenses connected with the business, which you never dream of.”

“ I should hope not, or else they would be sure to give me the night-mare,” replied Flyaway ruefully; “ well, what do you propose, Mr. Cool ? ”

"That you take an outfit," said the other, "for the whole amount of the balance of money belonging to you in our business. I should then advise you to start for the plains, for, from all accounts, the buffalo are expected to be plentiful."

"I would prefer," said Flyaway, "to get the amount in cash, as I can then return to St. Paul, and buy my own outfit, as I have done for you sometimes."

"No doubt you could," replied Cool, "but the fact is, I have not the cash to give you. But after all, Flyaway, it is only a matter of price, and I will see you all right in that respect. You just pick out the articles you want."

"This is what I call a dirty kick out," remarked Flyaway; "but I'll think over it, and let you know soon, as I feel now, I don't think you are treating me well. As for going to the plains, I don't understand that trade. Then, there are things I will want that you have not got in your store."

"I'll get them for you," said Cool.

Flyaway then took his departure, muttering as he left the door, "d———n him, he's made use of me, and now that he has other fish to fry he leaves me in the lurch. There's no use going to law with him; he'll beat me on that. I'm sorry I told him about the affair last night." In this mood the indignant man wended his way to the hotel, to take a drink over the matter.

In the meantime, Mrs. Cool had called on the Merediths, arriving there just as George was leaving on his return to camp. Little did Wade think of the trouble in store for him.

CHAPTER XII.

HE Harrican farm was finely situated on the bank of the Red River, and commanded a view of the town of Winnepeg, St. Boniface, with its cathedral and convents, and Fort Garry. On a rising ground it was surrounded by maple trees, which added greatly to the beauty of the spot. The house and barns were built of the same material as the generality of buildings in Red River, namely, logs. Through the carelessness, however, of Robert, the place had been allowed to go to rack and ruin ; and the Merediths, when they finally secured the farm, found that a great deal had to be done to make it at all comfortable. Mr. Meredith had met Jack Harrican and come to a proper understanding with him, so that there was no unpleasant feeling felt on either side when the family moved in to the house. Jack Harrican, as we said, was careful and plodding ; but at the same time he was obliging and kind-hearted ; and Mr. Meredith felt when he first met him, that he would prove a good neighbour.

George Wade, having a few days to himself before entering the Company's service, volunteered to assist the Merediths in arranging things about their new home. His offer was accepted, however, with a certain unusual restraint on the part of Mrs. Meredith, which puzzled him exceedingly, but thinking it all imagination, he went to work with a will, assisting the two boys. Jack and Tom were as familiar with any work pertaining to a farm, and it was astonishing how quickly fences were repaired and things generally cleaned up around the place. The walls of the house had been so neglected that wide seams gaped between the logs, and to fill this up was one of the first jobs undertaken. On the river bank they found a sort of white earth which they were told was used for the purpose of plastering, or as it is called, mudding the houses. Hay is first cut or chopped fine, and mixed with the earth, water is then added until it becomes like ordinary plaster. This preparation is then filled into the seams by means of a trowel, and afterwards the whole wall is whitewashed, giving it an appearance of smoothness and finish one would not expect to see in a log building. Jack, Tom and George Wade soon became initiated in the mudding process, and in a day or two had the house and outbuildings looking very creditable. The roof was a thatch one, and sadly in need of repair, but Mr. Meredith decided upon allowing it to remain as it was until the rest of the work around the place was completed. Several improvements had to be made on the inside of the house; and as George Wade had learned while on shipboard, to become an adept at carpenter work, he, as soon as the mudding was finished, commenced putting up some doors, shelves and such like ; Mr. Meredith having a set of tools suitable for the purpose.

The Merediths had not cumbered themselves with furniture when they left Canada, and now they felt the want of it, as it was next to impossible to get any in Red River. George and Mr. Meredith, however, succeeded in making a table and four bedsteads, and while they were discussing as to how they were to get along about chairs, Tom suggested that they should use their trunks.

" Handy things to carry with you from one room to another,"
said Mr. Meredith, laughing.

Grace, who was standing by, busily engaged in unpacking
crockery and so forth, now exclaimed that there was an Indian
woman coming towards the house with the very thing they
wanted. Sure enough when they looked out of the window they
saw an old Indian stalking along, followed by his two squaws,
one of whom carried a couple of rudely manufactured chairs on
her back, while the other had a large roll of some sort of matting. The old Indian had his blanket folded closely around
him, out of which peeped his tomahawk and pipe. He never
looked behind to see if his wives were following, but kept
steadily on until he reached the door. When he knocked, Grace
received him, and as he entered the house, she motioned him
to be seated on one of the boxes. As he accepted the proffered
seat, he made signs to his two wives to squat themselves on the
floor at his feet. He then handed one of them his " fire bag "
or tobacco pouch and pipe, and told her to fill and light it for
him. Grace felt herself flush to the temples from indignation
at this treatment of her sex ; but the two most interested
seemed to accept the position as a matter of course. What a
subject for a lecture on " Woman's Rights !"

When the old Indian received his pipe filled and lighted, he
puffed away in dignified silence, while the two squaws jab-
bered away to each other, pointing every now and again
towards Grace, as if they were speaking of her. At last Grace
finding her patience giving way at the prolonged silence of the
old Indian, and seeming indifference of his two squaws, pointed
to the two chairs in such a way as to show she wished to buy
them. The chairs themselves were rough, but strong, and instead of cane, they had used strips of buffalo hide for the seats,
twisted into a sort of network, which made it comfortable

enough, but not very elegant ; the workmanship was very rude, but durable, and as Grace afterwards remarked, "they were better than nothing."

George Wade now came in, and his services were called into action to try and find out from the Indians what they would sell the chairs for. Taking a shilling piece out of his pocket, he offered it to them, signifying at the same time that it was to be considered as purchase money ; but the old Indian shook his head and uttered a grunt ; then raising his hand he showed his five fingers twice, meaning ten shillings for the two chairs.

"Its a dreadful price," said Grace, " for these things, but what are we to do?' and, she continued, "we must strive to let them know that we require two more."

The matting was next examined and found that it would do very well for the floor of a bedroom instead of carpeting. It was made of rushes that grew in the swamp, and looked very cool and durable. The Indians around Fort Garry make a great deal of it, and sell it to the settlers. They also use it for their wigwams. The old Indian showed eight fingers this time, and the bargain was closed. The next thing was to let the savages know that two more chairs were wanted, and while George and Grace were discussing the best plan to adopt for the purpose, the old Indian astonished them by saying—

" Me understand English ; my boy make two chairs next week ; pay ten shillings for 'em, eh ?"

Here had George and Grace been perplexing themselves how to explain their ideas to the old rascal, when all the time he was quietly listening to and understanding their conversation, and could have saved them a good deal of trouble. The three Indians laughed heartily when they perceived the looks of astonishment mingled with vexation on the faces of George and Grace, and then the old fellow remarked—

" Injin very hungry—something to eat, eh?" pointing to his mouth.

Grace said there was nothing in the house of the kind, upon which the Indian scowled at her. George who perceived this, and having heard about the character of the savages, proposed giving them a little tea and sugar ; and to pave the way he took a piece of tobacco from his pocket and presented it to the Indian. Grace took the hint, and immediately procured the necessary articles, which she gave to one of the squaws.

" Thank ye !" said the Indian, "chairs next week ; good-bye, Injin glad ; good young squaw " (pointing to Grace.)

The three then left, after getting the money for the matting and chairs, and when they were gone, George remarked—

" I have been told that it is always good when an Indian comes into your house to offer him a little something, and no matter how small the gift is, he is sure to appreciate it."

" We really had nothing to give them," said Grace, " except tea and sugar, and I never thought of these."

"Well, I am glad I did," replied George, "and these Indians apparently are more industrious and handy than the generality of the tribe around here, and they may be of service to you. These chairs are very strong, and although not very elegant, are good enough for the time being."

The door leading into Mrs. Meredith's room now suddenly opened, and the old lady herself somewhat excitedly put her head out and shouted " Gracie ! Gracie !"

" Here mother," said Grace.

" Just look out of that window," exclaimed Mrs. Meredith. " I guess these pesky critters have gone daft. What on earth are they about ?"

At this moment a scream was heard, and on Grace and George going to the window, they preceived one of the squaws rushing towards the bank of the river, where she soon disappeared amongst the bushes. Immediately afterwards a dense volume of smoke was seen to ascend from the spot, which made the old Indian hasten on, and the remaining squaw to quickly follow in the footsteps of her predecessor.

The Merediths and George, when they perceived the smoke and heard the cries of the Indians, ran out to see what was the trouble; and from the brow of the hill they saw that one of the wigwams located there had caught fire and was burning furiously.

George and the two boys went down to find out how it had happened, and when they reached the spot they found the two squaws sitting a little apart, surrounded by their children and rocking themselves violently, moaning all the time. They seemed to feel the loss of their lodge as much as if it had been a large and costly building. The old Indian was seated on a fallen tree, sullenly viewing the demolition of his " house," and all it contained. It was his all, his gun being in the fire with the rest of the things. He and his family were houseless, and without property of any kind, except what was on their persons. Who can wonder, then, that these poor creatures looked upon their misfortune in the worst light.

George went forward and began to commiserate the old Indian on what had happened, but was rather startled when immediately afterwards a pair of black piercing vindictive eyes looked up into his and their possessor said, or rather hissed out—

" Lying Tongue ; bad Sioux did that ; I will have blood for it ; travel—travel—will kill bad Sioux for that." Then turning to his squaws, he spoke to them in Indian, pointing in the direction of the Assiniboine river and afterwards in the direction of the Merediths' house, then gathering his blanket closely around him, he stalked quickly away without uttering

another word or noticing George and the two boys in the least.
It will be seen hereafter how fearfully he kept his word.
Grace did all she could for the two squaws and their children,
and some of the neighboring Indian women assisted them in
erecting another wigwam, which is done by means of poles put
on end and leaning at or near the tips on each other until
they assume the form of a sort of cone. On these are placed
pieces of bark, dried hides, or anything else that will keep
out wind and rain. A hole is left at the top for allowing the
smoke to escape, the fire being always built in the middle of
the lodge.

The day succeeding the fire found the Merediths as comfortably settled in their new home as could have been expected
under the circumstances. George Wade had to begin his
duties the next day. The farm looked tidier ; the house
more comfortable; indeed, for the short time they had been at
work a wonderful change for the better was perceptible in every
way.

Jack and Tom on the day in question, were busily engaged
mending the thatch on the roof, and while they were in that
exalted position, Tom, all of a sudden, cried out, "Here's Cool,
or I'm a Dutchman, coming along by the river side." Cool it
was sure enough.

" I have heard," said George, before the expected gentleman
arrived, "that there is to be a public meeting of some sort to
take place this afternoon. I dare say Mr. Cool is coming on
that business, as I hear of his name figuring in the matter."

" I will go with him," replied Mr. Meredith ; "but I will
take no part in the proceedings."

The prediction of George proved true. Mr. Cool had come to
invite Mr. Meredith to the meeting. "What a change !" he
exclaimed, as he drew near the house, and had saluted all pres-

ent in his usual polite manner. "Here's enterprise for you. I tell you what it is, we want a few more like you in the country. The people here are not fit to possess good farms, for they don't know how to take care of them."

"I am not so sure of that," returned Mr. Meredith. "Considering everything, my opinion is, that they deserve a great deal of credit for the advanced state the country is in to-day."

"They have an able champion in you, at all events," replied Cool, laughing ; "but, notwithstanding, you will see them, ere long, giving place (especially the French) to a better, more thrifty, and more enterprising people."

"Well! well! we'll see," said Mr. Meredith. "Won't you come in, Mr. Cool? Mrs. Meredith will be glad to see you."

"I must ask to be excused," said Cool. "The meeting, of which I spoke to you some time ago, takes place this afternoon, in about half an hour, and I ran down here to ask you to come to it. We will require our time. What do you say?"

"O, I'll go, of course," answered Mr. Meredith, as he entered the house to put on his coat, and otherwise arrange his personal appearance.

While Cool was waiting, he approached George, and remarked that Mr. Barron was certainly going to leave the next day; and then he complimented Wade on obtaining a situation in the H. B. C. service, adding, however, that he might have done better.

"Perhaps," said George.

Mr. Meredith now appearing, put an end to any further conversation between the two, much to the satisfaction of George.

We will accompany the two gentlemen on the way to the meeting. As they left the House, Mr. Cool turned to Mr. Meredith, and said,

"That young man Wade seems to be a regular and constant

visitor at your house.   Do you know anything regarding his antecedents ?"

"Nothing further than his being the son of a rich gentleman of high standing in England, and his having been in the East India Company's service.   Since we met him (which was in Chicago, on our way here), we have found him a very agreeable, quiet, gentlemanly person.   In fact, I like George Wade."

"I have no desire," said Cool, "to injure the young man in your estimation ; but, at the same time, I think you should be careful how far you allow the present intimacy between Wade and your family to extend, until you know more about him."

"Mrs. Meredith was telling me some story which she heard from your wife about George, but I could not understand very well what it was.   Do you know anything of it, and how far it affects the character of the young man ?"

"It is simply this," answered Cool; and, as they walked along, the unscrupulous, unfeeling man poured into the ear of Mr. Meredith a highly coloured version of the story overheard by Flyaway, and which, for the present, we will withhold from our readers.

"This is very strange," said Mr. Meredith, "and, if true, George Wade is no fit companion for my daughter."

"Besides this," continued Cool, "he has been heard speculating with another on the chances of obtaining the hand of Miss Meredith in marriage."

"There is something very, very strange in all this," mused Mr. Meredith.   "George has never shown the slightest approach, since I've known him, of being capable of such an act."

"The best way," suggested Cool, "is to question the young man himself.   Should he deny it, you will still be able to judge by his manner whether he's hiding anything or not"

" Very true," rejoined Mr. Meredith.   " I'll speak to him."

" Just what I want," thought Cool.

The two soon after arrived at the court house, adjoining Fort Garry, and found there only five or six persons assembled, and no appearance of any more to come.

When Cool entered with Mr. Meredith, the latter was introduced to a gentleman lately from Canada, who was to give his views at the meeting on the condition of the country.   A very dandyish—sort of a positively " dem-me" individual he turned out to be—full of schemes, all of which bore a very good face in a theoretical point of view, but taken practically, they looked very uncertain.   Salt, coal and iron mines were to be worked with astonishing rapidity; railroads built; manufactories established and pushed ahead; and a hundred other undertakings started; the only thing requisite to bring all this about being annexation to Canada.

Mr. Meredith listened as well as he could to this gushing individual, who represented himself as a particular friend of all the members of Parliament in Upper and Lower Canada, and on intimate terms generally with every man of influence in the Provinces—so he said.   Finding that there seemed to be no likelihood of any addition to the number of those present, Mr. Cool, on being appointed chairman of the meeting, formally introduced the gushing individual to the audience.   A speech was the result, brimful of everything favorable to Canada and unfavorable to the Hudson Bay Company government.   The people of the North-West were called upon to repudiate and crush the monopoly, in other words to kick it aside and go in neck and heels for Canada.

Mr. Cool followed in pretty much the same strain, only a little more moderate in tone.   He represented that the people of Red River had no right to respect the laws of the Company;

K

that the charter was not valid; and that therefore any punishment inflicted on offenders by the Hudson Bay Company was an infringement on the rights of British subjects. He too, called out loudly for annexation to Canada.

Two others spoke after Mr. Cool, one of whom was very much like him in appearance, of a very determined character; cloaked outwardly, however, a good deal by an easy manner peculiar to him. This speaker said he would defy the laws of the Company; that he had made it a point to always fight against and hurt the H. B. C. to the best of his ability, and he would continue to do so. He had only that morning brought in his goods by force into the settlement without paying the 4 per cent. duty on them, and he dared the Company to collect its revenue tax from him. He, too, shouted lustily for Canada, and proposed three groans for the Honorable Hudson Bay Company.

Mr. Meredith could not be prevailed upon to speak. The reporter of the *Buster* was present, taking copious notes, in which he was very particular to say that the meeting broke up in an enthusiastic manner, with three cheers for the Queen and six for Canada. Mr. Meredith was disgusted with the whole proceedings, and told Mr. Cool so pretty plainly; but the only reply that he received was, "that things would work round better after a little."

And now that this precious meeting is at an end, we will look back on something that happened not very far from the Merediths' house.

George and Grace had gone out together to the town on an errand for Mrs. Meredith, and when they were returning home, George took the opportunity to plead his cause with Grace. It is needless here to mention all that happened during that interview. The many little endearments that generally pass on such occasions are more interesting to those directly engaged than to outsiders. It is sufficient to say that George was successful in his suit. After the two lovers had plighted their troth to each other, George said:

"We have had a long misunderstanding, Grace; but it is all over now. I began to think you almost tried to keep out of my way."

"And I," said Grace, "not understanding what was the matter, could not ask for an explanation."

"We'll not speak of it," returned George; "it is all over now, and amounted to really nothing after all. I will speak to your father to-morrow," he continued, "and ask his consent as well as your mother's to our engagement."

"I wish you would," said Grace, "for such matters ought never to be kept secret; besides I must warn you that you have enemies in the settlement, who will, I'm afraid, do all they can to injure you, especially with my parents. Already something has been said to try and lower you in their estimation. My poor mother is too ready to listen to stories, and she has been worked upon."

"I did observe a certain restraint," replied George, "when my offer of assistance to fix up the house was accepted, which I could not account for, and which I passed over as imagination on my part."

"I fear my mother did show a little coolness towards you in her manner; although she always speaks very highly of you. But an impression had been left temporarily on her mind unfavorable towards you. She cannot disguise her feelings; she, however, has forgotten all about it already. Whatever happens George, I will never desert you. You are my bethrothed, and as such, no power on earth will drive you from my heart."

George was moved almost to tears at this devotion on the

part of the noble girl by his side ; although he was puzzled to know who his enemies were, and how they were trying to injure him.   Suddenly he remembered his interview with Mr. Barron, but instantly dismissed the idea of treachery connected with it.   He, however, thought it his duty to speak to Grace about his absent friend.   Accordingly, he told her how Mr. Barron regarded her, and was about confessing his selfishness in not mentioning it to her before, when she stopped him.

" I like Mr. Barron," she said, "for his many good qualities, but I never could love him."

The two lovers had by this time reached the door of the house.   George then bade his affianced a fond good-bye, and departed for the hotel, where he was staying since they had broken camp.   He little dreamt what was in store for him on the morrow.

CHAPTER XIII.

HE old Indian, when he left his ruined lodge, passed quickly through the town in the direction of the White Horse Plains.   Looking to neither one side nor the other he pressed on, his face wearing the same vindictive look it had when he perceived his wigwam in flames.   The night was clear ; the moon shining brightly enabled the savage to keep on his way with rapid strides. and without stopping, until he reached the large Roman Catholic Church, about twenty miles up the Assiniboine. Soon afterwards he passed Lane's Fort, H. B. C., and coming in sight of a wigwam on one side of the road, he halted, and throwing off his blanket, he stripped himself of every other article of clothing.   Then, taking his long hunting knife between his teeth, he stealthily approached the lodge, until within a short distance from it, when he dropped on his hands and knees.   Cautiously he drew himself forward, listening attentively all the while ; but everything seemed to favor his purpose, so he crept along until he was at the opening of the wigwam.   Slowly and noiselessly he drew himself inside ; then regaining his feet, he stepped to one side into the gloom and there viewed his intended victims.   There were two women and three children, their male protector being absent, or not having returned from his trip to the town.   Our old Indian now took his knife in

his right hand; his features assumed an almost demoniacal
expression, while his eyes glared like those of a wild beast.
His revenge was about to be accomplished. Bending over one
of the prostrate squaws, he quickly and surely plunged his
knife into her breast, a low moan following from the lips of
the dying woman, and then all was still again. Quietly with-
drawing the weapon from the side of the first victim, the old
Indian stabbed the other woman ; but his aim had not been so
good, for a wild scream followed, which he, however, soon smothered with his left hand, while with his right he despatched the
unfortunate creature. The three children were awakened by the
scream, but before they could realize what was the matter, the
cruel monster finished their short career on earth, and threw
their dead bodies across those of their mothers.

The revenge of the old savage seemed now complete; he
carefully closed the entrance to the wigwam, and crept away
as cautiously as he came, until he reached the spot where he
had left his clothes. Wiping his knife on the grass at his feet,
he placed it in its sheath ; and having dressed himself, he drew
his blanket closely around him, and started on his return to
town. The dead bodies of the murdered women and children
were not discovered for three or four days afterwards; not
until the husband returned from his trip.

No one knew how it happened, as the old Indian had been
very careful in hiding the marks of his trail, so that it was
almost impossible to trace it to him. The bereaved Indian,
however, suspected the man who committed the act, because
there had been a long-standing feud between them, and also
because he knew how he had set fire in wanton mischief to the
old Indian's lodge. The indignation of the settlers around
Fort Garry was so great when they heard of this cold-blooded
murder, and the suspected perpetrator of it, that the old Indian

found it advisable to leave for the back country with his squaws and children; but before he went away, he punctually kept his promise to Grace regarding the two chairs.

In the forenoon of the day on which George began his duties in the Hudson Bay Company's service, and while he was busily engaged with the customers in the shop, he espied Mr. Meredith on the ferry coming across the river to St. Boniface, and rather wondered at the early visit. As Mr. Meredith left the boat, George observed that he walked in the direction of the store in a half hesitating, faltering sort of manner, and·felt a misgiving of something being wrong; the more so as he noticed an anxious, careworn, troubled look in the old gentleman's face.

Instead of going directly to the H. B. C. store, Mr. Meredith turned to the left, and walked in the direction of the Cathedral; and fully an hour elapsed before he returned and visited George Wade. When he did so, the latter offered his hand as cordially as usual, but was pained exceedingly when the act of courtesy was received on the part of Mr. Meredith with a degree of reserve quite unaccountable, but which showed plainly that something was amiss.

"I've made a start to-day," said George, without appearing to notice the change in his visitor's manner, "and I am surprised to find how easy it is to get along with the people of the country. They are far from being troublesome in dealing with them. As I have only had a few hours' experience, I hope my estimation of them will prove a correct one on a longer acquaintance."

"I am glad to find that you are so well satisfied," replied Mr. Meredith; "and I would not have interrupted you in your new duties so early, only I have something on my mind which I find myself obliged to speak to you about without delay."

"It is quite evident," returned George, "that you are troubled, for you don't look so cheerful as you usually do. I hope it is nothing serious."

" I hope so, indeed, George," was the reply, "but it is for you to decide that question. Can we go somewhere by ourselves, where we'll not be interrupted for a short time?"

"Certainly," answered Wade. "My room is behind the shop, let us go in there;" saying which, he led the way to his chamber with a sinking heart. He felt as if some calamity was about to happen.

An hour passed and still the two remained closeted together; and the clerk who assisted George in the store began to wonder what kept him away so long. At last the door opened, and as Mr. Meredith came out, he turned and addressed George, who stood behind him with a look of most intense anguish on his face that was pitiable to see on one so frank and noble as he was.

"I feel deeply, Wade!" said Mr. Meredith, so as not to be overheard in the shop, "that you will not give me some satisfactory explanation of this strange affair. Why will you not ease my mind? I look upon you already almost as one of my sons; think you then that I can easily drive you from my heart. I have my duty, however, to perform as far as my child is concerned, and yet it is like parting with one's own flesh and blood to leave you in this way! Come Wade, now be a man; confide in me. If you have sinned thoughtlessly, I am not the one to be severe, only give me some loophole to enable me to look on you as I did before this unfortunate occurrence came to my ears. If you are not the guilty one you have been represented as, why cannot you tell me the whole story, and I will be ready to make all allowances for you?"

"You are very kind," replied George. "I was in hopes that

I had suffered enough for a thoughtless deed, but it seems that my enemies are determined to rake up this old sore wherever I go. God knows," he continued bitterly, "I have paid the penalty a hundred times over for that act of mine. It is no use, sir; I cannot say more to you than I have done; some day I may be able to explain all. I told Mr. Barron a portion of the story, but not the whole; how the affair has reached your ears is a mystery to me. If you will trust me when I say that I am innocent of the charges you have heard against me, I can assure you that as far as I became connected with them, it was more by accident than any premeditated action on my part, and strong circumstantial evidence, untrue though it is, has worked a great deal of harm against me. If you will not trust me, I must bow my head to your will, and only bide my time when I will be free to show you how great a wrong has been done me."

"I do not condemn you, George; neither can I look upon you as the heartless man you have been described; but until the matter is cleared up, my duty compels me to prevent your engagement with my daughter from going any further. And to show you how I must feel in taking this course, I may tell you that I've looked forward to a union between you and Grace. There is no young man I know whom I'd sooner have as a son-in-law than yourself George; but while this unlucky affair hangs over your head, I must ask you as a man of honor, which I still think you to be, notwithstanding what I have heard, to hold no further communication with Grace, other than to break off your engagement for the present."

"I will write to her," replied George, sadly, "and tell her your wishes, and will not of course present myself at your house, where I now feel I will be unwelcome."

"It grieves me to the heart to hear you say so," said Mr,

Meredith; "but, my dear boy, think over it; do not let our friendship be interrupted in this way; for I cannot look upon it in any other light than merely an interruption. I ask you once more, George—as a favor to myself, a favor to Grace, a favor to us all—to clear up this matter; for that you can do so, I feel more and more convinced."

"Mr. Meredith," replied George, "I am at least obliged to you for thinking so; but when I tell you that I cannot explain any thing further, I tell you the truth. I am bound."

"I am sorry for it, very sorry, George," answered Mr. Meredith. "We will all miss you; but I am still hopeful that our separation will only be for a short time. Do not think me ungrateful in taking the course that is forced upon me. A father's duty ought to be above all other considerations. "Good bye George,—good bye;" and the old man wrung Wade's hand affectionately, although sorrowfully, when parting from him.

Our readers must recollect that Mr. Cool had related the story received from Flyaway in a highly coloured form, greatly to the detriment of Wade's character. He had also described it as coming from another party than the little Doctor, so as to further mislead the old gentleman. It is not to be wondered at, therefore, that the father felt a deep solicitude on the subject, and took the first opportunity of asking an explanation from the principal actor in it, especially as he knew his child's happiness rested in the scale.

George, in the conversation that took place in his bedroom, succeeded in dispelling, to a certain degree, the worst impressions left on Mr. Meredith's mind by Mr. Cool; but he had not been able to explain the matter so as to remove the stain altogether. Mr. Meredith, therefore, left, feeling very much troubled in mind, especially as he could not foresee how it might affect Grace. He was not aware yet how completely George had won her heart.

George, when the old gentleman left, went back to his room, and threw himself on his bed in a state of wretched despair. Only that morning he had commenced, as it were, a new life, with health and strength combined, and a will to rise in the world by his own exertions. The prospect of winning Grace as his wife was also an incentive to work hard in his new sphere. All that was changed now. He felt forlorn, miserable, and dejected, instead of buoyant, and, for a time, he seriously felt inclined to give up his situation, and leave the country altogether. The better counsels of his mind prevailed, however, and he rose from his bed determined to fight it out, trusting in Providence to assist him over his troubles; while, at the same time, he could not throw off the load that was on his heart, nor could he set to work with that happiness and contentment which he experienced before his late conversation with Mr. Meredith.

The Hudson Bay Company's steamer *International* was to leave that afternoon for Georgetown, and consequently George found enough to keep him busy in looking after the loading of some bales of furs for shipment. A short time before the departure of the boat, the editor of the *Buster* came down with a couple of friends, and took passage for the east. As he went on board, this "man of the quill" took from his breast pocket a packet of *Busters*, and distributed them amongst the officers and others on the steamer. The copies thus handed round gratuitously contained a long and flowing account of the late political meeting, which was represented as having been a large and influential one, and an exponent of the views of the settlers generally regarding the desire for a change of government on the part of the Red River people. The report in question was only one of the many samples of the falsities and absurdities contained from time to time in the columns of the *Buster*, they being inserted for no other reason than to mislead public opinion abroad, so as to raise a cry for the deliverance of the "Nor'-Westers" from their so-called yoke. To parties at a distance, unacquainted with the real state of affairs in the settlement, the meeting in question, *as it appeared in print,* looked to have been largely attended by the most influential people in the settlement; even the speeches delivered on the occasion were altered, or, as the editor remarked, "improved upon," to suit the purpose aimed at. The editorial commenting upon the proceedings went still further in its abuse of the Hudson Bay Company. This hash of lies was then dished by mail, to be sent far and near, proclaiming to the world what was not the case, and endeavoring to enlist the sympathies of people where no cause for any such feeling existed. The *Buster* was, in fact, the organ of a few ambitious, intriguing men in the settlement, such as Cool, who, while working for a change of government, calculated upon a large benefit to themselves personally, without taking into account the welfare and condition of the settlers at all.

These very men who controlled the newspaper, succeeded by artful scheming representations in inducing many people in Red River to sign petitions on several occasions praying for changes, when there was little need of any alteration in the state of affairs felt at the time by the mass of the people. The settlers, when questioned, would say that they were contented and happy enough; but fair promises were made to them; their lot was represented as a hard one compared with what was in store for them, so that many of them, although having little if anything to complain of, yet felt that there was no harm trying for better things, and so put their names to documents the purport of which few of them fairly understood. Their country was too far removed from the influence of the outside world for them to feel the want of the privileges and accompanying vices enjoyed by those living in more civilized parts. It was, therefore, only when designing men besought them to resist the government under which they had lived and prospered, and to wish for another, the nature and advantage of which they could not fully comprehend, that they allowed themselves to be cajoled into signing petitions, thus giving the impression abroad that they were groaning under a thraldom of oppression and misery, while in·reality a freer people did not live on the face of the earth.

Mr. Meredith when he read the *Buster's* report of the meeting, was astonished at its barefacedness, while feeling at the same time highly indignant at the fraud; and when a short time afterwards he met Mr. Cool, he remonstrated with that gentleman on permitting any such statement to go abroad without a contradiction.

"Everything is fair in war time," was the laughing reply he received, which however only tended the more to impress Mr. Meredith with the shallowness and insincerity of the party professing to work in the interests of Canada. "Nothing good can come out of it," was the mental reservation of the old gentleman at the time.

Mr. Barron having sent word that he was to start that afternoon for York Factory, George, as soon as the steamer had left, went into the Fort to see him before his departure. He found him in his room busily packing up and putting his clothes, &c., into small boxes, so that they could be handled more easily than if they were in a large trunk.

"I'm glad to see you Wade," said Mr. Barron. "I'm to be off at last. I thought we were never going to start."

"I'm sorry you are going away," replied George," for I find

that I need a friend here in the settlement more than ever, and somehow you and I have chummed together pretty well."

" I think we could get along," returned the other, " but has anything specially happened to make you require the services of a friend ?"

" Well," replied George, "you have understood my words in a too literal point of view. I did not mean that the necessity I felt for a friend at present was the cause of my regret at your departure. Your remaining at Fort Garry would be a pleasure to me at any time ; but what I mean is that something has taken place since I last saw you that makes me feel the want of some one to confide in and consult with."

" Perhaps I can be of use to you before I go," suggested Mr. Barron. " What is the trouble ?"

" You remember," said George, " the night in camp when I found you waiting for me ?"

" Of course I do," replied Mr. Barron ; "and I wished to see you particularly regarding it before I left."

" You remember also," continued George, my having told you a history of some of my doings before I came to Red River. One affair especially which I felt a great deal of anxiety about lest it should get to the ears of Mr. Meredith ?"

" Yes, I do perfectly," said Mr. Barron.

" Then that story has been heard by the old gentleman, and he has asked an explanation from me."

" The d—l !" interrupted Mr. Barron ; "how could he have heard it unless you have given your confidence to some one else beside me ? You surely don't suppose that I had a hand in letting him know about it ?"

" No," said George, " I do not ; and I have told no one in Red River of the affair but yourself; there is the mystery. How, when and where could he have heard about it ! Besides, it has been put before Mr. Meredith in the very worst form, and not at all in a truthful manner."

" Why don't you make a clean breast of it to him ? I'm sure he will believe your story."

" I have no doubt of it," replied George, " but the truth is I cannot just yet do what you propose. If you remember, I told you at the camp that if Mr. Meredith should hear of it, and ask me for an explanation, I would decline giving it. The reason is, I am bound by a sacred promise not to divulge until permitted the very portion of the story that would clear me. I did not tell you all that night, nor can I do so now ; but this I did say to Mr. Meredith, that I was not as guilty as I had been represented to him ; only he would have to accept my word for it in the meantime, and that some day I would be able to explain all."

" And what did he say to that ?" asked Barron.

" He seemed very sorry, but told me that his duty to his daughter compelled him to put a stop to any further intercourse between us, until I could clear up the affair. He said he still entertained the same kindly feelings towards me as before, and he hoped that the interruption to our friendship would only be temporary ; and ere we parted he almost begged of me to give the necessary explanation. I told him again I could not, so he left me. I am sure Mr. Meredith is a good, kind-hearted man, and, although he has forbidden me his house, I never will cease respecting and liking him."

" Did he give his authority for what he had heard ?" asked Mr. Barron.

" No, he would not, although I pressed him to do so," replied George.

" Are you sure," suggested Barron, " that the two boys were

asleep that night ?   You know I felt a little ticklish about them at the time."

"I cannot imagine," answered Wade, "that they overheard our conversation ; and even if they had done so, that they could have divulged it, for both Jack and Tom seem to be warm friends of mine."

"Then it is a puzzle," remarked Barron ; "and I only wish I could help you out of it.   Do you suppose any one could have written ?"

"There are those," replied George, "who would be very glad to write about it, so as to injure me ; but how could they be aware of my acquaintance with Mr. Meredith, or that such a person exists ?"

"Very true," said the other.   "And now, what do you propose doing ?"

"I have only one course left me to pursue," said George, "and that is to write Grace Meredith, acquainting her with what has happened, and asking her not to lose all confidence in me.   I have not yet told you, Barron, that since our conversation in camp, I found out that she returns my love, and, in fact, we are now plighted to each other.   We were out alone one afternoon, walking from the town, when I was unable to resist the temptation of telling her how I had learned to love her. To my surprise, Barron, and I say candidly, for I did not expect so much happiness, I discovered that I was not unacceptable to her.   Already rumor had been busy with the unfortunate affair which has now well nigh blasted my hopes ; for she told me that something to my disadvantage had reached the ears of her parents ; but she said that until I proved myself unworthy of her, she never would believe any evil stories about me.   At the same time, she warned me that there were enemies of mine in the settlement, who were plotting mischief against me, and it seems her words have proved only too true."

"She is a noble girl," remarked Barron; "and notwithstanding all that has occurred, I do envy you, although I do not grudge you your good fortune, for I will be very much mistaken in Grace Meredith if she deserts you for what has happened between you and her father. No! no! depend upon it she will only love you the more."

"I do not feel," said George, "that Grace will desert me, or that she will be easily influenced against me; but I would not seek to keep up an intercourse with her contrary to the wish of her father, so that she and I will be separated for a time, and how long it will last I cannot tell. During all this time I will be in a state of uncertainty, and it may lead ultimately to our engagement being broken altogether. I tell you what it is, Barron, I am miserable, and feel very like throwing up my situation and leaving the country."

"Don't think of such a course," said Barron; "keep your courage up, a good day is in store for you. You, at all events," he continued, trying to smile, "are not so hopelessly lost as I am. Work away, as if nothing had happened. Show your enemies, whoever they are, that they have no power over you. Trust in the good sense of the noble girl who has put her faith in you, and the day will come when you will get your reward. This is my advice, and in the meantime you ought to leave no stone unturned to obtain a release from your unfortunate promise—although I cannot see that one so unjust is, properly speaking, binding."

"It is so binding," interrupted George, "that I mean to keep it to my dying day, if necessary."

At this moment one of the clerks from the office entered the room, and said that the boats would soon start, and

L

advised Mr. Barron to hasten with his packing. George volunteering to assist, the boxes were soon got ready by the united exertions of the two young men.

Mr. Barron then bade good-bye to those with whom he had been associating in the Fort, and he and George walked slowly down to the river side. Bales and packages of merchandise, destined for different parts in the North, were being carried down on men's backs, and packed away in the York boats comprising the brigade. There were in all eight of these small craft, each one being about the same size—32 feet long by 8 feet beam. They were sharp at each end, both bow and stern running upwards from the centre to a peak in the form of a bow. The model was one well adapted for the purposes to which the boats were put; they being very suitable for both rowing and sailing, as well as portaging. Each of them could carry from five to six tons weight, and was manned by seven or eight oarsmen and one steersman. On the river bank were gathered numbers of women and children waiting to see their husbands, brothers and lovers off on their long trip. Now and again a stalwart half-breed could be seen, as he passed to and fro, snatching a kiss from his wife, or perhaps the girl he loved. There were no tears, no appearance outwardly of regret at leave taking: all was fun and good humor instead. The men were too much accustomed to starting away on such trips, and the women came to look upon it as an ordinary occurrence, to feel deeply parting with those they loved. Yet many a poor woman's prayer followed the boats for the safety of her loved ones on board.

In front of the main entrance to Fort Garry a number of the Hudson Bay Company officers were collected in a group, laughing and chatting, waiting to see the brigade start. Mr. Barron and George, however, walked a little apart from them arm in arm, talking over subjects in which they alone were interested.

"I have brought this letter with me," said the former, taking the epistle from his pocket, "and I wish you not to open it till I am some time on my journey, say a week or ten days, and in it you will find the instructions regarding the disposal of the packet I entrusted to your safe keeping."

"And which," replied George, "I will attend to carefully."

"I am sure you will," answered Barron ; "and now I have another favor and the last one to ask from you. You say you are going to write to Grace Meredith, and as you will not be likely to see her personally, at least for a short time, will you object to mention in your letter my regret at not being able to see her before leaving ? The truth is, I could not make up my mind to go and say good-bye to her, and I would not like her to think that I did not wish to do so at least."

"Certainly I will," answered George.

"And now, Wade, I see the men are going down to the boats. There's the guide shaking hands with the fellows at the gate, so we'd better hasten along also. I don't expect to ever see you again ; the presentiment that I never will return grows stronger every day ; but while I live I never will forget you. Next to Grace Meredith you will continue to hold a place in my heart."

George felt the parting with his friend very much.

When they reached the river side the men were all on board the boats, and Mr. Barron having shaken George warmly by the hand, sprang into the one in which he was to be a passenger. The guide then gave the signal, and the first boat pulled out into the stream. This was followed by another, and so on until the eight had started, one after the other in line. As the men bent to the large sweeps, which they handled dextrously,

they struck up a familiar boat song, the chorus being taken up
time about by the several boats' crews forming the brigade. It
was a novel and picturesque sight as they turned the point
where the Assiniboine flows into the Red River, opposite the
cathedral of St. Boniface. A large number of people followed
them a distance down the bank, waving to them and shouting
out all sorts of good wishes for their safe return.

The last seen of Mr. Barron by George, he was standing at
the stern of the boat beside the steersman, waving his handkerchief, to which George replied in the same way, and then turned his steps in the direction of the Fort. As he did so, an old
man, tottering along leaning on his stick, made the remark —

" I remember, sir, the time when one of these York boats
could hardly turn its own length in that river—pointing to
the Assiniboine—and now three of them can easily go abreast
in it, and in my early days no two boats could row side by side
even in the Red River, where you see it so wide now. Ah !
there's great changes going on in the world now-a-days," muttered the old man as he hobbled away.

We will have occasion later in our story to follow the fortunes
of Mr. Barron in his trip to York Factory ; in the meantime,
however, our old friend Dr. Flyaway commands a little of our
attention.

CHAPTER XIV.

OOL and Whirl sat in the office of the former, with a copy of the *Buster* spread before them on the table, over which they were laughing heartily. "By Jove," said Cool, "little Twaddle has made a hit this time on his own account, which is very creditable to him. Listen while I read it aloud."

"Among the passengers to Georgetown, on the *International*, was Mr. Rufus Twaddle, our indefatigable editor, who was greeted as the boat moved off by three rousing cheers, and the good wishes of those who had gone down to see him off. Mr. Twaddle has been with us for a number of years, and during the time we have had the pleasure of being connected with him in the management of this paper, he had enjoyed the unremitting hostility and persecution of the Hon. Hudson Bay Company ; but we are glad to be able to say, and assure both friends and foes, that Mr. Twaddle has not deserted the land of his adoption, but has only gone on a visit to some friends in the East, amongst whom he purposes enjoying a short holiday, in order to gain that recuperation of health which he requires so much after a long season of arduous literary labour. He will return in a few weeks to his post on the staff of the *Buster*, and will continue to oppose oppression and welcome freedom as before."

"That is the biggest stretch of imagination I have ever heard or read of," remarked Whirl. " I understand old Potts and Ames went down to the boat with him, the former to get a drink out of the brandy flask, and the latter because he had nothing else to do. Gad! Twaddle, you've done it up brown this time;" and Whirl leaned back in his chair and laughed aloud.

" There is more in it than you perhaps imagine," said Cool ; " and I give Twaddle a good deal of credit for his penetration. The *Buster* you see has gone in heavy against the Company (in fact I think it over does it a little), and of late is coming out strongly in favor of Canada. Now, when this report of the editor's popularity amongst the people is seen (shown, of course, by the rousing cheers) the statements of the *Buster* are far more likely to carry weight than if it were known abroad that its opinions are not valued a straw in the settlement. Twaddle is more clever than I took him to be."

" I doubt very much," said Whirl, "if he intended your con-struction to be put upon the paragraph in question ; he is so confoundedly conceited that I think he did it to satisfy his own vanity."

" Perhaps," returned Cool, " but it will answer our purpose all the same."

" How did you manage with Flyaway," asked Whirl.

"I had hard work to persuade him to take an outfit," answered Cool. " We had a regular battle over our account, but, after a great deal of trouble, I succeeded in convincing him that his only course lay in accepting my proposition. He has been all morning picking out the articles he requires ; and I believe he has made an agreement with Rosette to join his band."

" Had you anything to do with the latter arrangement ?" enquired Whirl with a smile.

" A little," said Cool, " I spoke to Rosette."

" I have no doubt of it; and you could not have placed Flyaway in better hands to have him fleeced and regularly done for."

" I have really no wish to injure the doctor," interrupted Cool; " but as long as he is in the country, he will be a hindrance to my plans and operations. For if he is not against them, he will be so confoundedly in favor of them, that he will spoil the effect."

" I don't believe," remarked Whirl, "that you will have much trouble with him after this, for if he doesn't come back from the plains pretty well ' strapped,' I am very much mistaken."

" I won't be surprised," added Cool, "when he does return to find that he has spent the greater portion of the proceeds of both goods and any furs he may have collected. I expect Flyaway this morning to finish up. You see (pointing out at the window) there is his tent, and there are his carts,—he has hired two of Rosette's men to go with him, one of them having a wife to do the cooking for the party."

At this moment Dr. Flyaway arrived, and, on entering the room, he addressed Cool at once, without appearing to notice the presence of Whirl.

"I've been to the Company's store," he said, "and have picked out the things. I had my cart there, ready to load them up, but the clerk told me his orders were not to deliver Mr. Cool any goods without the cash."

" Confound it all; there must be some mistake here," said Cool. " I have a running account at the Fort."

" It may have been running too long," interrupted Flyaway. "That's where the rub is, I expect."

"Nothing of the sort," answered Cool. " I have endeavored to keep my account square with the Company, more especially as in other ways I am not their particular friend. [Cool had been indebted to the Hudson Bay Company over five hundred pounds sterling for nearly two years, without any exertion on his part to pay it.]   I will go down and see about it myself," he continued.

" The sooner the better," replied Flyaway ; " for Rosette may start this afternoon, and I don't want to be left behind.   I wish to stick to him."

" The closer the better," thought Cool.

All this time Whirl had been busily engaged reading a newspaper.   He now looked up, and addressed Flyaway :

" I say, Doctor, as you will be passing the Portage on your way, will you oblige me by taking a letter as far as there, and delivering it to Dick Strong ?"

" I've no objection," said Flyaway, " as long as you say it doesn't contain money, and make me responsible afterwards if I lose it."

" I'm not so bad as all that," returned Whirl.

" Bad enough," answered Flyaway, " when you sold me that horse before I left for the States.   You declared he was a buffalo-runner, and Rosette now tells me he's nothing of the kind."

" Perhaps Rosette wants to sell you a horse himself," said Whirl.

" No, he doesn't, because I don't want to buy."

" Then," said Whirl, " wait till you have returned from the plains, and if he is not accustomed to buffalo hunting, I'll arrange with you."

" In other words," said Flyaway, " when the milk is spilt, you'll try to sup it up with a spoon."

Whirl did not reply, but, turning to the table, he hastily wrote a note, which, when sealed, he handed to Flyaway, requesting him to deliver it as directed.

The Doctor put the letter in his pocket.　It would have been better had he refused to take it.

Cool, in the meanwhile, had gone to the Fort to see about Flyaway's things, and there he found that there had been no mistake in the "non-delivery" of the goods, as he could not get them without paying for them.　This he accordingly did with a very bad grace, and vowing at the same time, vengeance on the Company, for what he looked upon as an insult, but which any ordinary merchant would have done under the same circumstances.

When Cool returned to his house, he found that Rosette had been there, and Flyaway in a great flurry to get away.　The goods from the Fort were therefore hastily packed with the rest of the outfit, and all loaded on the carts.　The horses were soon caught, the tent or lodge taken down, poles strapped together, and then all was ready for a start.　Flyaway, who was on horseback, then rode up to Cool, and said,

" When I came here three years ago I had some money, and here I am reduced to an outfit on the plains.　You have taken most of it out of me, Cool ; and now that you've something else on hand, you desert me.　I can see it all.　I am not blind altogether.　I'll go out and do the best I can ; but I'll be blessed if you and I have any further business arrangements together. I'm now free from you.　I'm pretty well singed ; but I suppose the hair will grow out again.　Remember me to my very particular friend, Mrs. Cool.　Good-bye—good-bye.　Whirl, I'll take care of your letter."

"And it will take care of you," muttered Whirl.

The Doctor then rode off at full gallop after his carts out on the prairie ; and when he reached Rosette's camp, he found that an early start in the morning had been agreed upon ; so he pitched his lodge and prepared to spend the night.

On the departure of the Doctor, Whirl turned to Cool, and said—"I've given Flyaway a letter to Dick Strong, and what do you suppose were the contents of it?"

"Give it up," replied Cool.

"Simply to get the spitfire drunk and exchange some goods with him. You see Dick and I are in together, and Flyaway has a few things in his outfit that Strong requires."

"You're the first then," returned Cool laughing, "to fleece the poor d——l."

"The second, you mean," returned Whirl. "I think you've been ahead of me in that. If Strong commences, he'll keep Flyaway drunk for a week; and Rosette will keep him company. Together they'll make a fine pair."

When the Doctor had fixed up for the night, Rosette the plain hunter, invited him over to his lodge to have supper, which was gladly accepted, the Doctor having in view a jolly night afterwards.

When he entered Rosette's tent, he found a number of men seated round on the ground crosslegs, like so many tailors, and a bottle passing freely round amongst them. A plate, tin cup and spoon lay before each of them, and as a place had been reserved for Flyaway, he squatted himself in a similar manner to the rest; and as soon as he had taken a pull at the bottle, the supper was brought in. It consisted of a large pan of what is termed "bouilli," a sort of hash made of pemmican, flour, water and any other fixings procurable to make it tasty. On a large dish were a number of boiled buffalo tongues, and near it a large kettle of tea. A bag of sugar and some baked bannocks of flour made up the balance of the "spread." Each man helped himself to a plateful of the "bouilli;" stuck his knife into a buffalo tongue; poured out a cup of tea, and then eating commenced. During the meal, jokes, laughter, and stories of adventure and trading went the rounds; and when all had partaken to their satisfaction, the dishes were removed by the women of the camp, pipes were lighted, and the men prepared to take matters easy, while the women and children were enjoying their supper round the fire. Rosette said they were going as far as "White Horse Plains" on the morrow, where they were to meet several other bands of hunters, who had agreed to form together in one large camp, for the purpose of travelling together to the hunting grounds.

The bottle began once more to circulate freely; one of the men procured his fiddle; cards were brought out; and a jolly time was evidently about to be enjoyed. Both Rosette and Flyaway indulged more than the rest, which resulted in putting the latter asleep; while the former grew more and more boisterous in his manner. The worst passions of Rosette now began to show themselves. When drunk, he was a source of terror to those residing in and around the town; and on several occasions, through his mad-like conduct, while intoxicated, he had escaped serious injury from the hands of settlers, on account of some depredations on his part.

The men that were with him feared him and disliked him at the same time. He was, however, a powerful and successful trader, and few had the hardihood to refuse joining camps with him when he asked them to do so. The more he drank the more he swore against several parties in the town, from whom he considered he had received injuries, and at last he wound up by declaring that before daybreak he would set fire to the hay-stacks of a certain person whom he hated. The men now finding him in such a state, quietly slipped away one by one, until Rosette was left with only Flyaway in the tent; that interesting individual being sound asleep in one corner of it.

The excited plain hunter now staggered to his feet, and perceiving his companions gone, he went out into the open air, and catching a stray horse, that happened to be grazing close by the camp, he mounted without saddle or bridle, and dashed away in the direction of the town.

Soon after he reached there, two shots were heard, clear and sharp on the night air. A whoop followed, and then Rosette could have been seen flying round by some bushes near the river, taking a circuitous route to his camp. Immediately afterwards a bright flame appeared in rear of one of the houses. Rosette had kept his word—the hay-stacks were on fire.

As soon as Rosette reached camp, he awoke everyone in it, and insisted on an immediate start, stating at the same time what he had done. The rest of the hunters agreed to what he so peremptorily demanded, because none of them cared about disputing the point with the excited man. Men were therefore sent out to bring in the horses, the women and children were hastily aroused and told to prepare for a start. The tents were taken down, and the poles strapped on to the sides of the carts; all the cooking and other utensils were collected, and soon there appeared nothing but the smouldering fire to indicate where the camp had stood. Flyaway was lifted into one of the carts, he being in an unfit state to ride on horseback; and while they were waiting for the men to bring in the horses, Rosette took two or three more pulls at the rum bottle.

It must not be understood, however, by our readers, that Rosette is intended to represent the generality of the Red River plain hunters. On the contrary, he was a man, as we have said before, both feared and disliked amongst them, and his many mad-like and vicious acts were condemned by those who were forced by circumstances to associate themselves with him. The plain hunters, or "winterers," as they are sometimes called, are a fine class of men, simple and honest in their dealings, quiet and peaceable in their nature, and yet the records of their deeds on the plains show them to be fearless and daring when necessary. When under the influence of liquor, some of them become noisy and boisterous at times, but it has never been known for them to commit any acts of depredation or hostility towards the settlers while in that state. There are black sheep in every flock, and Rosette was one of the blackest amongst his people.

We may mention here, also, that there is a marked distinction between the French half-breed settler and his brother on the plains. The former, by coming so much in contact with people from the outside world, through his trips to the States, and life in the settlement, has become more shrewd, wary and inclined towards settled pursuits; while the latter retains all the habits consequent upon a free and roving mode of life, such as that of a plain hunter is. A difference in their style of dress is quite perceptible. The plain hunter is lavish and careless with his money wherever he goes, while the half-breed at home is more solicitous over a few shillings than he would be over so many pounds. It is this extravagance in money matters that prevents the "winterers" from becoming rich as a rule. There are, however, some of them who are careful and saving, and these invariably become wealthy, and frequently possess investments abroad, both in England and Canada.

When Rosette's party reached "White Horse Plains" in the morning, it was deemed advisable to secrete their leader, lest he might be arrested, and thus delay the whole band; and it was well they did so, for during the day a couple of constables arrived with a warrant for his apprehension. But on their being unable to gain any information as to the whereabouts of the man they wanted to find, they soon returned to Fort Garry.

While Rosette was in his hiding place however, the arrangements for forming a large camp were entered into ; and as he was not able to attend while they were going on, he found himself in a secondary position to the one he expected to fill.

When a number of half-breeds assemble for the purpose of going in a body to the plains, they first appoint a chief, and those who are to be his advisers, during the hunting season. The camp we have to do with numbered a little over fifty men, many of whom had their families with them.   They, therefore, found it necessary to appoint twelve councillors to assist their chief, who in turn nominated six captains, and these latter picked out the men whom they wished to have in their watches. It was the duty of these captains to take turns with their men in guarding the camp at night against surprise or any approaching evil.   The chief and councillors regulated the movements of the camp, settled all disputes between the men, and punished all offenders against the established rules or laws of the plains.

Rosette, who had been expecting the chief position in the band, was very much disappointed and enraged to find himself merely a councillor.   For several days afterwards he remained sullen and moody ; and his friend, Flyaway, found him anything but a pleasant companion.

The band camped a few days at " White Horse Plains" before starting on their journey, and then they travelled as far as Portage-la-Prairie, where another halt took place.

Flyaway presented the letter to Dick Strong, as he had promised ; and, as Whirl had predicted, the consequence was a "big drunk," in which Rosette joined heartily.   The people of Portage-la-Prairie not coming within the jurisdiction of the

Governor and Council of Assiniboine, and being therefore in a helpless state, as far as law and order were concerned, determined upon setting up a petty government on their own account, and which they designated as that of Manitoba. The *Buster*, on one occasion, saw fit to poke fun at the movement, in the following paragraph, which appeared in its columns :—

" We had the honor of a visit from his Excellency the Governor of Manitoba. We learn that he was down on official business with His Excellency of Rupert's Land. We trust they came to an amicable understanding on international affairs, and that there will be no cause of coldness between the two countries. But, if it be not impertinent, we would suggest the most dignified manner of carrying on a diplomatic intercourse would be by the appointment of ambassadors accredited to reside near the respective governments. And we trust His Excellency of Rupert's Land will at once see the propriety of appointing an Ambassador Extraordinary to reside near the Government of St. Mary."

In a couple of months afterwards, however, it seems to have changed its tone, for it came out with the following, probably having forgotten its previous " jeers ":—

" We are glad to be able to announce that the Government lately formed at Portage-la-Prairie still prospers, and seems to satisfy the minds of the residents there perfectly. We learn that a court house and council chamber is in course of construction, and bridges and roads have been made. Notwithstanding the scoffs and jeers of the monopoly party here, we are glad to be able to chronicle the success of this rude attempt at giving to all men in that district individual liberty. We can only say to our neighbouring and more happily situated colonists—keep on in your course. Avoid petty jealousies,

and strive only for collective benefit, and you will earn contentment for yourselves, and the respect of all your neighbours."

Cool's hand was in that pie. The truth of the matter was
that a division existed amongst the people at Portage-la-Prairie
on the subject, some being in favor of admission under the
jurisdiction of the Governor and Council of Assiniboine, while
others supported the independent movement. The Governor
and Council of Assiniboine kept aloof from the matter altogether, and put no obstacle (as it has been said they did), in
the way of the Portage-la-Prairie people, to prevent them from
framing their own laws, and appointing their own officers for
the enforcement of them. The monopoly party, as the
Buster described it, was a mythical creation of the invincible
Twaddle's brain, as the only "party" in the settlement was
the small clique of the *Buster's* own friends,—a set of mal-
contents and opponents to law and order, who for their own
selfish ends, as we will presently see, thought proper to disturb
the public peace, and endeavour to upset the only guarantee
to life and property then existing in the settlement.

Flyaway was one of the first to feel that power of the law, as
administered by the President and Council of Manitoba. For
getting very obstreperous one evening, while under the influence
of liquor, he was taken care of for that night, being provided
with bed and bedding free gratis on the occasion.

The court house and council chamber referred to in the
Buster, consisted of a log cabin, with (as Flyaway described it) a
confoundedly dark hole as a jail. The chief offenders around
the Portage were the Indians, amongst them being a portion
of the Sioux who escaped from Minnisota, after the massacre of
1866. A rascally thieving lot, steeped in human blood, their
atrocities committed in the United States seems to have been
like a curse hanging over them, for their numbers have de-

creased ever since they entered British territory. Outcasts
they have been indeed, disowned by their own tribe, they are
looked down upon by other Indians, and hated cordially by all
whites, British or American. They fled to Red River when
driven across the line, and on their arrival at Fort Garry they
made such demands as the Hudson Bay Company were not
then in a position to refuse. Since that time they have taken
up their abode in the vicinity of Portage-la-Prairie, and have
lived by hunting, fishing, begging, and stealing, the latter
being their principal occupation. For some time after their
arrival in Red River, they were so troublesome, and their
demands so insolent, that they became a perfect scourge to the
settlement. One of the most respectable settlers therefore,
actuated by a desire to remove dangerous characters, and at
the same time with a sense of detestation at the horrible
deeds committed by the wretches, determined upon capturing
two of the leaders, Little Six and Medicine Bottle. For that
purpose he contrived means while they were on a visit to his
house to entrap them, and made his preparations accordingly.
In every room he placed a bottle of either wine or spirits, and
when the two savages made their appearance he endeavoured
to show them every hospitality which an Indian prizes. At
the request of Little Six, he showed him over all the apart-
ments, in each of which the unsuspecting chief was persuaded
to take a drink. After the inspection of the house, Little Six
sat down in one of the rooms to take a smoke, and while he
was doing this, the settler sent on horses to a point on the
river half-way between Fort Garry and Pembina, to act as a
relay on the road to hurry the captives out of the country, and
had sleds made ready with other horses harnessed in them at
the door. He then procured the assistance of two friends,
and rushing suddenly into the room where Little Six sat un-

M

prepared for such an attack, they bound him hand and foot, first disarming him of his long knife. They then tied him down on one of the sleds, and sent it slowly on, while they proceeded to capture Medicine Bottle in a neighbouring house.

The settler knowing that many of the Sioux tribe were lurking about the Fort, and fearing lest the two entrapped Indians might whoop or cry out, had given Little Six a dose of chloroform, to keep him quiet. As Medicine Bottle was leaving the house, they rushed upon him and threw him to the ground, the settler applying at the same time a handkerchief to the nostrils of the fallen man, saturated with what was supposed to be chloroform, but which was nothing else than whisky, taken by mistake from the wrong bottle.

" *Wash-tee-do ! Wash-tee-do !*" cried the savage, which in English means good ! good ! Medicine bottle being bound on the second sled, he was driven off to join his companion, Little Six ; and after some narrow escapes from being discovered by several of the Sioux Indians, who were prowling about, the two captured savages were delivered over to the United States authorities at Pembina, and were only executed about two years afterwards for their atrocities.

The United States Government are very much to blame for not punishing these monsters sooner than they did after they fell into their hands, for had either Little Six or Medicine Bottle escaped, the courageous settler and his family would have most probably met with a dreadful death from the hands of the crafty and cruel monsters, in revenge for having delivered them over to a just punishment for their deeds.

The H. B. C. Fort at Portage-la-Prairie is a small stockade, generally in charge of an officer of the Company, and one or two men under him. It is not a very important post.

Flyaway, in the course of his drunken perambulations, stumbled into this as he termed it "Hudson Bay Company Den," and, seconded by Rosette, threatened to tear the whole place down on the devoted head of the officer in charge. But that individual took the matter very cooly, by asking the excited pair into the store to take a drink. This was gladly accepted by both, and the consequence was that the next morning, when the band of plain hunters were starting, they had to call at the Fort, and lift both Flyaway and Rosette into a cart, where they lay until they became sober, the brigade jogging along the meanwhile.

This is the last we will see of Flyaway, until we again meet him on the plains, a pleasure which we hope to have ere we close our story. It is almost needless to say that the letter to Dick Strong had its effect, that worthy having fleeced the unfortunate Doctor out of some very important articles in his outfit while he was drunk, and palmed off upon him a lot of worthless stuff in place of them ; a fact, however, which Flyaway did not discover until he unpacked his goods out on the plains.

Rosette and Flyaway, in their drunken frolics at the Portage, were the indirect cause of a very serious and melancholy occurrence, which took place soon after their departure. It appears while they were in the midst of their carousal, they visited the camps of some of the Indians in the neighbourhood, and not being at the time very particular as to who their associates were, they shared the contents of their bottle with the savages. These, having experienced the excitement by the liquor, were seized with a craving for more of the fire-water, and there being only one place (a small saloon and store) in the neighbourhood where they could procure the article, five or six of the band proceeded to the house, and made a demand on the man in charge for some rum. This being refused, they at first uttered threats, and finally one of them shot the poor fellow through the side. Some of the neighbours coming up soon afterwards, the wretches fled, leaving the wounded man on the floor of the house. The unfortunate victim of the outrage was afterwards conveyed to Fort Garry for medical treatment, where he lingered in agony for a few weeks, until death at last put an end to his sufferings.

Having bid adieu to Flyaway and his worthless companion for a time, we will turn our attention to the neighbourhood of Fort Garry, and will ask our readers to accompany us to the sitting-room in the Meredith farm-house. We will there find Grace alone, with a letter spread open before her, over which she is bending her pale face. She is weeping. The letter is from George Wade, describing his late unfortunate interview with her father ; but he wrote—" I am innocent of the charge, and have done nothing to bring dishonor on my name ; only by a solemn promise extorted from me some years ago, I am prevented from giving such explanations as would free me from the imputations that have been cast upon me. I hope ere long, however, to be able to clear up everything satisfactorily, and I only ask that, until that time arrives, you will not condemn me. Can you give me hope that I will not be forgotten, my own dear Grace, and that you will think sometimes of one who will never cease to pray for your welfare and happiness ?" George then went on to say that he had been forbidden any further intercourse with her ; how deeply he felt it ; and begged for but one letter from her, to tell him that she at least did not consider him the guilty wretch he had been described. The letter was couched in the most endearing, yet sorrowful language, and brought a pang of pain to the heart of poor Grace ; the more so as she had not been prepared for it, and without warning, the hope of her life seemed dashed to the ground, perhaps never to be regained.

The poor girl sat for some time brooding over this strange turn in affairs, and, as she thought of her good, kind-hearted lover, and the cruel separation that threatened them, the tears fell fast, as a future of misery presented itself to her mind. George Wade was her first and only love, and it cannot be wondered at if the blow was a severe one to the poor girl's heart. Alas! it proved a very serious matter in the end, as we shall see.

Suddenly Grace rose to her feet. A gleam of hope passed across her features. "I will go to my father," she said, aloud ; "his good, kind heart will not refuse me. I will ask him to allow me to see George, and then I am sure I will arrange this misunderstanding."

Acting upon the impulse of the moment, she immediately went in search of Mr. Meredith, whom she found outside in the garden. Going up to him with the open letter in her hand, she said, "Father, what is the meaning of all this ?"

"Of what, my darling ?" said Mr. Meredith ; although his heart rebelled at the question. He knew full well what his daughter meant, but he almost feared to answer her.

"Of this letter," answered Grace. "What has George done, father, to be treated so harshly ? Oh ! surely you will not be so cruel as to do what he says here you have threatened ? Some wicked person has belied him to you. You cannot, father, believe anything evil of George Wade ?"

"I do not wish to, my daughter ; but he will not give me a satisfactory answer regarding the accusations made against him."

"Is it not enough that he denies them ?" asked Grace.

"My dear girl," said her father, "you are my only daughter, and my pride—the comfort of my old age. Were any evil to befall you, Grace, it would send me sorrowing to my grave. I must, therefore, watch over and guard you from any evil, and I cannot be too careful. I like George Wade; indeed, so much did I esteem him, that I looked forward with pleasure to the day when I could call him son. Think you, then, that this has not been a severe blow to me! I went to him, without telling you what I'd heard, because I did not believe it. When I asked him for an explanation, he refused at once to give any. I reasoned with him, but all to no purpose. And and now there is no course left open for me to take but to pre-vent his intimacy in our family from going any further. I could not bear a single blot upon your fair name."

"But father," interrupted Grace, "George denies having ever committed the wrong he has been accused of. Why won't you believe him?

"Because my dear girl, I must have proof in a matter of so much importance—where the happiness of my only daughter is concerned."

"Father," said Grace, "if you will permit me to visit George, I am sure he will listen to my appeal, and give you the explanation required. Do let me go, father. Oh! if you knew how miserable I am you would not refuse me."

"My dear child I cannot even do this; but you may write to him, and I pray God he will listen to you."

"Oh! Father, if you would only allow me to go and see him, I am sure he would heed me. Won't you, father? Jack could go with me."

"Do not ask me, Grace. It is very hard for me to refuse you; but I cannot give my consent to this. If you write an earnest appeal to him, surely he will answer it."

"Then I will write to him ; but I feel that I could do so much better if I saw him and spoke to him."

"I do trust," said Mr. Meredith, " that he will explain this unfortunate affair, for I cannot think him guilty."

"He has not told me in his letter what he is accused of," said Grace ; "only that he is innocent of the accusations made against him to you."

" I cannot tell you either, my daughter. You will simply ask him to give me the explanations I require."

" I will do so, father, but if he should refuse, I will never believe him guilty of any crime or dishonor ; neither can I change my great love for him."

Father and daughter then separated, the latter to write the letter on which so much depended. Before doing so, however, Grace knelt down at her bedside and poured out an earnest prayer to God for reconciliation between her lover and her father.

Alas ! even the prayers sent from the heart do not always meet with the response poor mortals most desire.

CHAPTER XV.

HEN Grace had finished her letter, she called her two brothers, Jack and Tom, and entrusted the precious epistle to their care; at the same time asking them to be sure and wait for an answer.

As soon as the two boys started on their mission, Tom said—

"What is the matter between George and Grace? There must be something when she is writing to him; she never did that before."

"I think," returned Jack, " there is something up, because, did you notice how anxious and careworn Gracie seemed when she gave us the letter ! If it's George's fault, I think you and I can lick him, eh, Tom ?"

"Yes ! and what is more, we'll do it," replied Tom ; "but, perhaps George is not to blame at all, it may be some one else ; for I never yet found George Wade doing a mean action."

"Nor I," said Jack ; "so we won't condemn him without hearing his story first."

The two boys were at a loss to conjecture the reason for what appeared to them their extraordinary mission, for they were shrewd enough to see that something unusual had occurred. So the moment they reached the Hudson Bay Company's store at St. Boniface, they bolted in upon George, and without the slightest hesitation they both blurted forth—

"What's up, George, between you and Grace?"

George was somewhat unprepared for this sudden outburst; but replied that he hoped there was nothing.

"But there must be something, for Gracie looked so pale and —and—she seemed as if she'd been crying."

Poor George's heart sank within him, and he turned away to hide his emotion.

"Come, George," said Tom, "tell us all that has happened; both Jack and I don't believe you are to blame."

"And you are right," exclaimed Wade; "for I am not to blame, but I have some wicked enemies."

"Who are they?" asked both boys at once, "and we'll fix them; just tell us who they are."

Jack and Tom now remembered for the first time that they had a letter for George. Jack, therefore, took it from his pocket, and handed it to Wade, saying that an answer was expected. George, when he received the letter, asked to be excused, and went into his bedroom to read the contents, fearing to betray any emotion before the boys. Jack and Tom looked at each other, but said nothing. George remained some time in his room; it was a trying moment for him; a fierce battle was going on in his mind. The appeal of Grace went direct to his heart, and there arose a very strong temptation to break his promise, so as to avoid the pang of separation from her at last; however, his better nature prevailed, and he sat down to write his final answer on the subject. He described the painfulness of his position, and how much he felt having to refuse the desired explanations; but he wrote, "You, my own dear Grace, would be the first to condemn me were I to sacrifice my honor in this matter, and I can assure you that I

would be doing so were I to break the promise I gave some
years ago.   More I cannot say, except to reiterate that I am
guiltless of any crime; and I ask you not to condemn me until
I am permitted to explain all, which I trust will be ere long. I
will once more ask your father not to enforce our threatened
separation, and trust to his kind heart not to be too harsh
upon me.   Whatever happens, my own sweet Grace, I will
never cease loving you, and will ever think of your great kindness to me.   I will write to your father to-day, and I do hope
for a favorable reply."   The letter then went on to describe
how he had fought with his inclinations in opposition to his
sense of what was right, and renewed his protestations of love
and constancy.   As soon as he had sealed the letter, he went
out to where Jack and Tom were waiting, and handed it to
them.

" Can't you leave the store," asked Tom, "and come over
with us and see Gracie ?   Come along, George."

" Oh ! how I wish to go," thought George ; but he replied,
" I am sorry to say, Tom, that I cannot do as you ask, for your
father has prohibited me from visiting your house until certain
matters in which my honour has been mixed up with are
cleared away."

" Then why don't you clear them away ?" asked Jack.

" The story is a long one," replied George, " and one which
I cannot fully explain to you, but in a few words I may say
that some years ago I became involved in an unfortunate
scrape, and foolishly pledged myself not to reveal certain facts,
which, although they would clear myself, would certainly impli-
cate another.   By some means I have raised enemies in Red
River, who have got hold of the circumstances of that unfortunate affair, and they have made use of them to poison the mind
of your father against me.   I am prevented by my promise

from freeing myself, and your father, until I am able to do so, has forbidden my visiting your house. I do not blame Mr. Meredith; but it is a sad blow to me who began to look upon your home almost as my own."

"Do you know who your enemies are?" asked Tom.

"I can only suspect them; for your father would not tell me who the parties are who told him."

"I'll find out," exclaimed Tom ; "you'll see if I don't."

"Well, George," said Jack, "I do think father might take your word for it; he knows you well enough by this time to believe what you say."

"These are my sentiments," chimed in Tom.

"I thought so, too, at first," said George; "but my calmer judgment taught me that a father has a right to be very careful how he risks the honor or happiness of his children."

"As for his children," said Tom, "both Jack and I will always stick up for you, and I'm sure Gracie will too."

"Thank you for that, my boys," said George; "and I hope the day is not far off when I will be able to show that I'm not altogether unworthy of your good will."

Tom now took George aside, and suggested to him that he should correspond with Grace, and that he (Tom) would act as carrier on all occasions between the two lovers, without the knowledge of Mr. Meredith.

George thanked the kind-hearted boy, but said " that he could not accept his offer, as it would be dishonorable to do so."

Tom thought him dreadfully particular, and thereupon determined in his own mind to bring little messages on his own account, between George and Grace, as long as they should be separated.

"I suppose I can come over and see you sometimes?" asked Tom.

"If your father does not forbid you to do so, I will always be glad to see you," said George.

"We won't tell him anything about it, and then he can't prevent us," said both boys at once.

George could not help smiling, and inwardly thanked his two young friends; he then told them he still hoped to prevail upon their father to allow him to visit them us usual.

"If he don't," exclaimed both boys, "it's a confounded shame, and you'll see he'll be sorry for it yet."

Jack and Tom now shook hands with George, and set out on their return home, where we will leave them for the present.

Mr. Meredith had conceived a great fancy for going into stock raising, and for some time he had been looking about for a desirable locality in which to commence operations. At last he heard of a spot which seemed to him, from its description, as a suitable place, and, therefore, determined upon paying it a visit. Accordingly, on the morning of Jack and Tom's mission to George, he started out, telling Mrs. Meredith and Grace that he would not return till the next day.

Let us follow him. After leaving the farm, he drove along as far as the parish of Kildonan, where the greater portion of the Scotch settlers live. There he was joined by a gentleman who had an interest in the place which Mr. Meredith had in view. Each carried a shot gun, as there was every chance of their having a crack at some game. Striking out upon the plains, they drove along over a rolling prairie, which already began to show signs of the approaching autumn. The grass, which was long, had a slight tinge of yellow, and the wind being strong at the time, it waved and rolled along, resembling very much the motion of a body of water agitated by the wind.

Prairie fires had not begun to commit their depredations, else, said Mr. Meredith's friend, " we might have to experience a hot time of it driving through this tall grass."

In several places, where the land was high, they found heaps of stones piled one upon the other; these had been erected by Indians years before, for some purpose peculiar to their tribe. At last they came to a small lake, and the gentleman who was with Mr. Meredith alighted from the buggy, for the purpose of having a shot at some ducks that were within range. The long grass served as a good shield for the sportsman until he reached the margin of the lake, and then the tall weeds or rushes enabled him to approach his unsuspecting victims without detection.

Mr. Meredith soon heard the sound of a couple of shots, and immediately afterwards his friend approached, having bagged five ducks.

"There," said the friend, whom we will hereafter know as Mr. Lister, "these will give us a good supper, when we reach Grosse Isle."

A brace of Prairie chickens were afterwards secured, and towards noon they reached their destination, which proved to the eyes of Mr. Meredith a very pretty spot. Grosse Isle is particularly adapted for stock raising, having a good supply of water, with every facility for collecting hay, and sufficient wood land to serve for a shelter to the cattle from the hot rays of the sun in summer, and severity of the weather in winter. Mr. Lister, who owned the place, had given particular attention to stock raising, and only resolved upon giving it up when he found it interfered with his other and more important business as a merchant.

Mr. Meredith, on the other hand, thought himself very fortunate in being able to secure such a favorable opportunity, and was delighted with the place. There were over one hundred head of cattle belonging to Mr. Lister, which he offered to Mr. Meredith, together with the buildings on the place, and a sufficiency of hay provided for the approaching winter.

Altogether it was a chance which might not occur again for some time to Mr. Meredith, and he felt very much inclined to close with Mr. Lister's offer, which was a liberal one. A complete inspection of the premises had just been finished by Mr. Meredith and Mr. Lister, when the cattle began to return from the fields to be watered, and to obtain the protection of the smudge fires, which were lighted in the evening as a preventive from mosquitoes and flies. Mr. Meredith was quite pleased and astonished to find such a fine class of animals as those which came lowing in from the pastures. The buildings were all built of stone, procured from a quarry about a mile distant, and consisted of a good-sized farm-house, dairies, stables and granary. After supper, Mr. Meredith and Mr. Lister sat down in the sitting-room of the farm-house to enjoy a smoke, which was afterwards followed by some hot brandy and water.

"There are several places in the settlement suitable for stock raising," said Mr. Lister; "but I have discovered none so good as Grosse Isle."

"I am very well pleased with the place," said Mr. Meredith, "and have no desire to look further, since we have agreed upon a price; but I would like to increase the number of cattle this fall at least one-half, and I am at a loss how it can best be done. There is the hay—from what you say, there is hardly sufficient to feed the hundred head now on hand."

" That difficulty can easily be got over. In the first place, I would advise you to take a week or so, and visit amongst the farmers along the Red and Assiniboine rivers, where, I am sure, you'll have no difficulty in picking up fifty head of cattle.

Then for hay, it often occurs that the spring crop is burned by the prairie fires, and farmers have to go out and cut the grass in the fall; of course the hay is not so good, but it will do on a pinch. There is stable room here for two hundred head, so that there is nothing to prevent your increasing your stock, if you wish."

Thus the two men chatted till late in the evening, and finally a bargain was agreed upon for the transfer of the farm to Mr. Meredith.

The next morning, on their return home, they passed a party of Indians, seated on the bank of the Red River, busily engaged in gambling. As the sight was a new one to Mr. Meredith, he and Mr. Lister stopped to witness the game, little dreaming of the serious consequences that afterwards took place.

About a dozen Indians were seated on the ground in the form of a ring, and while one of the number beat a sort of drum, the others gambled, keeping time with their motions to the sound of the rude music. The manner of the game was as follows :— One of the Indians had several small pebbles in his hand, which, as soon as the drum sounded, he hid beneath his blanket. He then chanted an Indian song, and threw his body into all sorts of wild contortions, as if to distract the attention of the other Indians. During this time, the betting was going on,—sometimes a knife, then a pipe, or perhaps a blanket was thrown into the centre of the group, to be risked on the chances of the game.

As soon as all the stakes were put up, the drum ceased suddenly ; a call was made upon the Indian with the pebbles to show his hand, and the winner, or one who had guessed correctly, took possession of the spoils. It seemed more like a game of odds and evens than anything else. Sometimes two

Indians play against each other, and then the game becomes very exciting.   As Mr. Meredith and Mr. Lister stood watching the group of gamblers in question, they observed that one Indian, a particularly evil looking personage, was losing heavily, and that another seemed to be the sole winner.   Finally the unfortunate savage threw down his blanket, as the last thing he had to stake, and that, too, was about to disappear, when he made a clutch at it, and endeavoured to prevent the winner from taking possession of his gain.   In an instant a long knife was drawn, the loser was threatened, if he would not desist.   Quick as lightning the Indian who had lost, sprang upon his more fortunate associate ; a dreadful struggle took place, in the midst of which the two Indians rolled down the river bank, and when they reached the bottom, one was dead. The winner had lost his life, and the loser had killed him.   The murderer did not return to the group, but walked quickly away in the direction of the town.   The avenger was on his track, however, in the shape of the brother of the murdered man, and next morning the murderer was found lying in his own gore, amidst the signs of a fearful struggle that had taken place during the night.   Such is Indian life.

Mr. Meredith was very much shocked at what he had witnessed ; but was assured by Mr. Lister that such scenes did not often occur in the neighborhood of the settlement.

We will now pass quickly over several days which elapsed, during which George Wade had again been refused admission to the Meredith family, without the necessary explanations. Grace felt the position of her lover very much—so much, indeed, that it began to prey upon her health.   Still Mr. Meredith held out, although his heart bled for both George and Grace.

Both Jack and Tom remained true to their word, and many

a sly visit was paid by the two boys to George Wade ; and each time they went to see him they always had a good deal to say about Grace, although not from her. In the meanwhile, Mr. Meredith had taken possession of Grosse Isle, and was preparing for his trip among the farmers. Before starting out, however, he set Jack and Tom at work to gather in as much hay as possible. This was done by means of a mower and horse-rake, both of which the boys understood how to manage. Mr. Meredith gave instructions to his sons to go on cutting until he returned from his search for cattle. And while the two boys are roving over the prairie, cutting the grass wherever they found choice spots, we will follow Mr. Meredith in his trip amongst the farmers.

By the direction of Mr. Lister, he commenced at the parish of Kildonan, and visited the several houses to which he had been directed. In this way he became acquainted with many of the Scotch settlers, and found them a thrifty, well-to-do, and intelligent set of men. During his perambulations through the settlement, Mr. Meredith collected a great deal of information regarding the earlier days of Red River, as well as a considerable insight into the manners and customs of the people. The farm houses, as a general thing, he found to be built of logs, very comfortably furnished. Indeed, he was quite surprised to find many farmers living in as good circumstances as any whom he knew in Canada. He found himself invariably treated with the greatest hospitality wherever he went, and enjoyed a chat with some of the old inhabitants of the place.

One evening he called at the house of a farmer, whose father had come to the country with the first brigade of Scotch immigrants, in 1812, under the patronage of the Earl of Selkirk. Mr. Meredith was invited to spend the night at this house, which invitation he gladly accepted. As soon, therefore, as the

N

dishes had been cleared away from the tea-table, and the pipes lighted, the following conversation took place between the old man and Mr. Meredith :—

"I believe," said the latter, that you were one of the first of the Scotch settlers who came to this country."

"Aye, indeed, was I," answered the old man ; "and a hard time we had of it. It's mighty comfortable and fine now-a-days here ; but I can remember the time when there was neither comfort or safety around these parts."

" I can easily imagine that," said Mr. Meredith.

" So you may," replied the other. "It was in the year 1812 when we arrived at Hudson Bay, and a dreadful hard time we had of it coming from York Factory to this place. We thought we had escaped our greatest danger when we left the ocean behind us, but we little dreamed what was before us. Eh, man, but we had to work hard to get along, and it was only through the mercy of Divine Providence that we got here at all."

" I suppose," suggested Mr. Meredith, " it was a great relief when you at last reached your destination."

" Not much of that after all," said the old man ; " for we had hardly set our feet in the country when a lot o' these daft deevils—the Indians—came and gave us warning to start at once out o' it. We thought they were Indians, but we were mistaken, for they were nothing more nor less than a lot o' scamps belonging to the North-West Company, dressed up for the occasion to frighten us."

" And were they so cruel as to try and drive you out of the country after your long and dangerous journey ?"

" Deed were they ; and go we had too. Oh ! it was hard ; and the miserable deevils next thing to robbed us of every thing we had ; only, I will say, that before they left us they treated us better, and I've always thought that it was'na of their free will that they used us as they did at first."

" Where did you go then ?"

" To Pembina, where we had to live all winter in tents, and had to support ourselves as best we could by hunting."

" How did you get on after that miserable winter?" asked Mr. Meredith.

" We returned to the settlement the next summer," was the reply, " and commenced preparing for farming, having procured some seed wheat from Fort Alexander. We expected some friends of ours that fall from Scotland ; but as they did'na come, we went away back to Pembina for the winter. Oh ! that was a hard time—much harder than before, for the deevils of half-breeds would'na let us hunt for a living ; so in the spring we went back to the settlement, vowing never to return to Pembina."

" I have heard a great deal about the North-West Company troubles. I suppose you were through them ?"

" Certainly, I was, and it is only a wonder that I am here to tell you," said the old man.   " It was first one thing and then another ; house burning, robbing and killing, until it was'na safe to be seen abroad. The Hudson Bay Company tried to be our friends, but they were not powerful enough ; and the consequence was when our friends arrived from Scotland, instead of a fine thriving country, they found nothing but ruins and desolation. Then came the killing of Governor Semple ; but, oh ! the story is a long one to tell you ; the end o' it a' was, however, that we spent a miserable time of it, between fighting and famine ; but I don't blame the half-breeds as much as I do the deevils that urged them on to it, for my lang experience amang the French tells me that they are not a blood-thirsty nor quarrelsome people, unless they are driven to it by wicked deevils behind the bush."

" How were those troubles ended ?" asked Mr. Meredith.

" Lord Selkirk arrived in the country," said the old man, " in 1817, and after that things began to mend. It was then that this parish got its name of Kildonan ; and, in fact, the plans of the settlement laid."

" I suppose your trials were then pretty much over ?"

" As far as fighting was concerned we had little more of that ; but we suffered a great deal from famine during the two next winters. First, because we were too late in sowing, and the next summer the grasshoppers came and destroyed every-thing in the shape of vegetables or grain in the settlement. The sufferings we then had to endure were terrible, and almost as bad as the deevilish acts of the North-West Company ; and what made it worse, some French families arrived from Can-ada about the same time, which made so many more mouths to feed. In 1819 the grasshoppers again appeared, and ever since then they have been off and on the plague of Red River Settlement, although we have never been without seed in the country."

" Well," exclaimed Mr. Meredith, " your way has certain-ly been up hill in this country."

" That it has," sighed the old man, " but it is some consola-tion for me to look around and see my children a' sae happy and comfortable. They havna had sic hard times in their life-time as their auld grandfather ; and best of all for them, they enjoy the pleasure of hearing a minister o' their ain persuasion —a blessing which I didna enjoy for many a day when I first came to the country, for they would na' give us a Scotch min-ister for a lang time."

" I have heard," said Mr. Meredith, " that the Hudson Bay

and North-West Companies amalgamated ; how did things progress after that ?"

" Aye," said the old man, " they joined hands in 1821, and from that time the settlement has been getting better and better until it is what you see it now, but it wasna a' plain sailing either ; for we suffered a deal with grasshoppers and floods and such like, but we have now no reason to complain, an' you'll find a' the people in Kildonan well to do, and most o' them have money invested in Canada and the old country."

Mr. Meredith, having spent a pleasant evening, now retired to his bed, as he had to make an early start in the morning. His conversation with the old man had shown him the hardy, persevering nature of one class of settlers in Red River, and gave him a favorable opinion of the people he had come to live amongst.

In the morning, as Mr. Meredith drove along down the settlement, he found the words of the old Scotch settler fully verified, for the houses of the farmers presented a thrifty, tidy appearance, while their farm-yards indicated a flourishing condition of affairs. About every mile he came across a wind-mill in active operation, grinding the grain for the neighbouring farmers. These mills, although rough in appearance, answer the purpose very well, and prevent the settlers from having to carry their grist a long distance.

The road leading from Fort Garry to the Stone Fort runs along the Red River, about half a mile distant from the banks. The space between the road and the river side is generally divided into fields, while beyond is open prairie, neither fenced in nor cultivated. The cattle belonging to the settlers are allowed, during the summer months, to roam at will over the prairie, undisturbed in the enjoyment of an abundance of pasture-ground.

After passing Kildonan, Mr. Meredith found himself in St. Paul, another flourishing parish, which also gave signs of prosperity and carefulness. The houses were more scattered than in Kildonan, but everywhere thrift and industry gave token of being at work. The next parish is St. Andrews, the largest in the settlement—both it and St. Paul being inhabited by English half-breeds, most of whom earn a livelihood by farming.

Mr. Meredith had now succeeded in picking up about thirty animals, principally oxen, and, after having gone as far as the Stone Fort, he resolved upon returning home, intending to take a trip up the Assiniboine to finish his complement of cattle. In his conversations with several of the farmers, both English and Scotch, Mr. Meredith found out that all kinds of vegetables flourished well in the settlement, as well as barley, oats and wheat. At several places on the road he passed large numbers of sheep grazing on the prairie, and from their appearance, he was led to believe that wool-growing would yet prove a profitable business in the settlement, a fact which is now admitted by all who are capable of judging.

Mr. Meredith on his way home drove out to Grosse Isle, to see how his two boys were getting on, and found that they had cut quite a quantity of hay, which would have to be secured immediately, so as to escape the ravages of the prairie fires. The purchase, therefore, of the remaining twenty head of cattle was left over until the hay could be collected in and properly stacked. Mr. Meredith accordingly paid a short visit to the Harrican farm, and returned to Grosse Isle, where he remained with his sons and one or two men for several days, until all the hay was hauled into the yard.

Jack and a couple of men were then left in charge of the stock, while Mr. Meredith and Tom returned home, where they found Mrs. Meredith and Grace looking anxiously for their arrival. Mr. Meredith now began to think seriously about purchasing the Harrican farm ; and on that account, before his departure up the Assiniboine river, he called on Jack Harrican to consult with him on the subject.

It appears that Cool still insisted upon his right to the property, and Jack, therefore, could do nothing more than sell the farm to Mr. Meredith, subject to the decision of the next Court. This Mr. Meredith agreed to, paying Harrican, at the same time, a small sum of money to bind the bargain.

The night on which this agreement was entered into, Mrs. Meredith gave her husband a sound rating for what she considered several delinquencies. In the first place, the trouble between George Wade and Grace was expatiated upon by the good old lady. Her heart, as we have before said, was soft, although her tongue, at times, uttered hard and unkind expressions. In this case the softness of her heart moved a feeling of pity within her towards the two lovers, and the only relief she could find was in expressing her disapprobation of the course taken by Mr. Meredith towards George. This she did in her usual style, by giving her good man a regular curtain lecture on the night of his arrival from Grosse Isle. But there were times when Mr. Meredith could listen to his wife's remarks without allowing them to influence him in the least, and unfortunately for George and Grace he received this curtain lecture without permitting it to alter his purpose in the least.

" Look you here, Mr. Meredith," his good wife said, " suppose anyone had stepped in between you and me before we were married, and our folks had listened to such nonsense, where would you have been now ?"

" In Red River all the same, I suppose," returned Mr. Meredith, " and you'd have been Mrs. Somebody else."

" You wretch !" exclaimed the excited old lady, " is that the way you speak to me after all the years we have spent together."

"Well, wife, it's only a supposition after all, and can't do a great deal of harm. We're too old to separate now."

"I've a great mind to start back to Canada to-morrow."

"I think," said her tantalizing husband, "you'd better go to sleep and dream over it."

"You will have you own way, sometimes, Mr. Meredith," continued the old lady; "but I would like you to know that you're breaking your child's heart as fast as you can. Gracie can't bear such things easily. Haven't you noticed how pale and miserable she is looking now-a-days?"

"Good wife," exclaimed Mr. Meredith, "you never found me a harsh husband nor an exacting father; but in this case I feel it my duty to forbid George Wade to enter our house until he can or will clear up the stories I have heard about him. Gracie, no doubt, feels it very much now, but her good sense will soon teach her that it is for the best."

"I don't believe any of the stories you have been told about George, for I always found him good and kind; and, in my opinion, it is that rascal, Cool, who has been trying to injure him. I can see through a millstone sometimes, should it be ever so thick. Yes, there is always a hole in the centre of it. Mr. Meredith, you are fast becoming a wretch."

"So you say; but, good wife, joking aside, all I ask of George Wade is to explain things. I like the young fellow as well as you do, and am not inclined to believe anything against him. Why won't he speak?"

"Don't he tell you, because he has given some promise long ago, which he would have to break were he to explain things to you."

"I do not think a promise of that kind should be kept, especially under the circumstances."

" George Wade does not think so," said Mrs. Meredith, " and you ought, for Gracie's sake, to take his word that he is innocent, and trust to his explaining everything hereafter."

" It is for Gracie's sake that I will not take his word, much as I like the lad."

" You needn't let them get married," suggested the old lady, " and still not forbid him the house altogether."

" Good wife, I feel I am doing everything for the best ; so there is no use talking any more about it."

" You'll yet be sorry for what you're doing, you'll see," said Mrs. Meredith as she indignantly turned her back upon her spouse.

Grace felt her separation from George Wade very much, she had learned to love him dearly, and love with her was no passing passion to be easily laid aside.   Many a silent tear did she shed over her hard lot.   Her usual buoyancy of spirits gave way to fits of melancholy ; and her mother saw with dismay her only daughter pining away before her eyes.   Mr. Meredith, who happened to be very much away from home looking after his stock farm, did not observe the change in Grace, and therefore saw no reason for altering his opinion about the wisdom of the course he was pursuing towards George Wade.

Jack (who was now at home) and Tom, however, saw the change in their sister, and paid many a visit to George, not only to try and get him to explain matters to their father, but also to bring little messages (invented for the purpose) between the lovers.   This although done with the best of intentions by the boys, worked more harm than they were aware of.

During one of these visits, while Mr. Meredith was up the Assiniboine buying cattle, George handed Tom a package and a letter which he desired the boy to give to his father first, to

be then handed to Grace.   Tom promised faithfully to perform
the service, but inwardly he resolved that his father would
never see them.

Accordingly, on his return home, Tom went immediately to
Grace and handing the package and letter to her said that they
were from George.

Grace seized the letter, and with trembling hands proceeded
to open it, hoping that at least the desired explanations were
about to be given.   Alas, what a disappointment was in store
for her.   The letter read as follows :—

"MY OWN DEAR GRACE,—In honour I was bound to first
send this to your father before you could receive it.   To think
that I am thus separated from the one who is dearest to me
upon earth, is dreadful.   I cannot stand it any longer, and have
written this to say farewell for a time.   Although I never can
forget you, yet the fact of my being so near you without being
able to see your sweet face, makes me miserable.   I have
therefore accepted an offer from the Company to take charge of
a small post in the interior.   There I will be away from the
scene of so much unhappiness to me.   I start from here in a
week, and expect to return in a few months.   I entertain the
hope by that time to be free from my unfortunate promise, and
would ask until then to believe me true to our plighted faith.
Oh! my dear Grace, although the present is hard to bear, I
hope the future will be fraught with much happiness for us.
You remember some time ago I told you of Barron's feelings
towards you.   Before leaving, he entrusted the small package
which I send you to my care, asking me to give it to you after
his departure for York Factory.   I now fulfil his wishes, and hope
there will be nothing in the package to cause you any further
misery.   Keep up your heart, my darling, in the hope that a

kind Providence will see us through our troubles, and think of me as your

    "Loving, devoted,

       " Although unhappy,

           " GEORGE."

The letter served only as another pang of sorrow to poor Grace, when she thought of her lover going so far away, to be exposed, perhaps, to dangers or sickness, with no chance of her being able to see him. It seemed but an addition to her troubles, which were already greater than she could bear.

Long and silently she sat with the letter crushed in her hand; her pale face giving token of the deep distress she was in. At last the package from Barron attracted her attention, as it lay on the table before her. "What can it be?" she thought. "I wonder if there could be anything in it to unravel this unhappy mystery that hangs over poor George's head." Had she known that the solution of the mystery then lay before her, what a world of misery it could have saved her.

Eagerly undoing the outside covering of the package, she discovered a small wooden box, inside of which she found a handsomely carved silver casket. The workmanship on it showed plainly that it was the work of no modern artificer or inexperienced workman—in fact it was a valuable little box.

Grace opened the lid, wondering what could be the meaning of the strange gift, and discovered a small note lying at the bottom of the casket. It read as follows :—

"MY DEAR MISS MEREDITH,—Mine has been a hopeless love. Your image will ever be with me; but I have a presentiment that my life will be a short one. Farewell! and think kindly of one who loved, but without hope. I have sent this as a parting gift. Guard it well—it is more valuable than you imagine. With this note, you will find in the casket a small sealed package. My earnest desire is that you do not open this until your marriage day. That God may bless both you and George, will be the last wish of

"FREDERICK BARRON."

Grace took the small sealed package from the casket. Oh ! how she longed to open it ; but the wish of Barron had to be respected, and, with a sigh, she placed it back once more in its case.

"My marriage day," thought Grace; "that seems a long way off."

Had she known the great value of the casket to her and her happiness, would she have obeyed the wish of Mr. Barron? Who can tell?

CHAPTER XVI.

E will now turn our attention to Mr. Barron, during his trip to York Factory. The last we saw of him, he was turning the bend of the river opposite St. Boniface, where the Assiniboine enters the Red River.

As soon as he lost sight of George Wade, Mr. Barron sat down, and watched the men as they rowed and sang in concert, keeping time to the motion of the oars. As one boat's crew would cease singing, another in the brigade would take it up, and so on they went, making good time with the current. As they passed along, Mr. Barron observed the tidy-looking farm houses lining each bank of the river. The crops looked promising, as they turned out afterwards ; and it was well they did, for the next year the grasshoppers came, and brought utter desolation amongst the grain fields.

Each house possessed a sort of landing by the river side, for the purpose of obtaining water, there being few wells in the settlement. In many places they saw nets floating in the river, belonging to the people living along the banks, and numerous dug-out canoes drawn up on the land near by. Nothing of importance occurred to the brigade until they reached the Stone Fort, where they halted to take in a further supply of provisions, and some bales of merchandise. Mr. Barron could not rouse his spirits; his thoughts were with the friends he had left behind, and the image of Grace Meredith was continually before him.

Several of the boatmen got drunk at the Stone Fort, and a couple deserted. The guide, therefore, pushed off as quickly as possible, after everything had been received on board. Accordingly Mr. Barron had not a great deal of time to look about him; a pleasure, however, which he did not regret, as he felt little inclination for the society of any one. A deep-rooted melancholy seemed to have taken possession of his mind, and all the efforts of the old steersman beside him to rouse him from his lethargy were unavailing.

The Stone Fort, and surrounding country is, perhaps, the most beautiful part of the Red River settlement. The Fort itself is far before Fort Garry, both in point of appearance and accommodation; in fact, it was at first designed to serve as the seat of government for the colony, although Fort Garry afterwards superseded it in that respect. Still the Governor of Rupert's Land used to make it his headquarters while in the settlement, on account of its retired and pleasant situation. The Fort is built on high land, and the neighbourhood abounds with small trees, which are used principally for firewood.

We will now follow the brigade in its course towards Lake Winnipeg; but, before doing so, we will take a look at some of the principal characters in it, namely, the guide and steersman.

The man who occupied the latter position in Mr. Barron's boat was a fair specimen of his class. He was short in stature, very broad and powerfully built; his brown and furrowed features showed plainly that he had weathered many a storm. He was full of fun; a joke seemed ever resting upon his lips; and his hearty laugh did more than anything else to encourage the men in their arduous labours at the oars. His eye was sharp and keen, while his strong arm showed great dexterity in wielding the heavy sweep that served as a rudder for the boat. One, to look at his easy, confident manner, as he stood at the stern of the small vessel, felt little fear in trusting to his management.

The guide who had charge of the brigade on this occasion, was a tall, muscular man, who evidently had spent the greater portion of his life at the work he was engaged in. Unlike the steersman we have described, he was a man of few words, of a kindly disposition however; well liked by the men, and, therefore, having great influence over them. It is a noticeable fact that the French half-breed can be led by kindness to do what you want than by severity or roughness; they will not be driven, but are easily led. The guide in a brigade generally has a tent for himself, although he does not always make use of it; and when there are any Company officers on board, they generally eat first, then the guide and steersman, and the boatmen by themselves. Like the bands who go to the buffalo-hunt, the brigades engaged in freighting goods have their own customs, laws, and a certain kind of discipline peculiar to themselves.

On this occasion, the guide and Mr. Barron occupied the same tent, and ate together, and, through the request of Mr. Barron, Cadotte, the old steersman, formed one of their party. This made matters more pleasant and comfortable on the journey; and old Cadotte, who saw that Mr. Barron was low-spirited, did all in his power to enliven him with anecdotes, descriptions, and jokes. Mr. Barron, however, could not rouse himself, and gradually grew worse and worse, until at last he would start with nervousness on the slightest occasion.

As soon as they entered Lake Winnipeg, the wind being fair, they hoisted their large square sail. The rowers ceased their labours, and lounged about the boat in all sorts of attitudes. Old Cadotte, with his long sweep, seemed in his element, and even Mr. Barron roused himself for a while under the invigorating breeze and excitement of the boat plunging along over the waves. The wind, however, began to increase, until it blew a perfect hurricane; but, fortunately for them, it was a fair one, and Cadotte decided upon keeping on their course, although usually, when it blows very hard, the York boats put into some of the harbours, generally to be found close to the islands that dot the lake. Thus they flew before the wind; no jokes now escaped from the lips of the old steersman; he became all attention to his duty, and nobly did he perform his task.

Now and again, however, he turned his eyes in the direction of the heavens, as if to see whether the storm was abating or likely to become worse. Towards evening the sky became completely overcast. A peal of thunder, followed by a bright flash of lightning, told those in the boat that they had to prepare for danger. The sail was shortened as well as it could be. Old Cadotte stood on the stern of the small vessel, his lips compressed, and his dark eyes with quick rapid glances taking in as it were the whole position of affairs. "It can't be helped," he muttered, "we've got to run before it now; but," turning to Mr. Barron, he said, "I'm glad, sir, the other boats have found shelter."

Poor Barron did not seem to realize their danger, for he remained sitting beside the steersman, his head resting on the side of the boat. Not a word did he utter in reply to old Cadotte. He seemed perfectly careless whether they sank or not. The rain now fell in torrents, but fortunately the thunder storm soon passed over, leaving the sky quite clear, although the wind continued to blow as hard as ever.

Night now came on—the stars glimmered in myriads over-head as they scudded along over the rolling waves. The worst was past, yet still Cadotte felt that all his attention was neces-sary to keep the boat from being swamped. At this juncture Mr. Barron suddenly raised his face, his eyes became riveted as if on some object. Slowly rising from his stooping position, his head thrown forward, he hoarsely whispered to Cadotte—"Do you see her? There! there!—away ahead. Look, she is beckoning to us to come on. Oh! Cadotte can't you make this boat go faster. Grace! Grace! we're coming—we're coming. My God, Cadotte, shake out that sail and let us go faster." At this moment he gave a loud scream. "She's gone—she's gone," he exclaimed, and then fell back at the feet of Cadotte.

The latter, greatly surprised as well as alarmed, now called out to Deschambault, the guide, who was at the bow of the boat—"Deschambault, come here, there is something the mat-ter with Mr. Barron."

The guide immediately came to where Mr. Barron lay, and taking his hat he dipped it into the lake and sprinkled water over the face and head of the unconscious man.

Mr. Barron slowly opened his eyes on being thus revived, and the first question he asked was—

"Did you see her, and has she really gone?"

"We didn't see anything, sir," answered Cadotte. "You've not been well since you started. It was all fancy, sir, there was no one near the boat."

"There was I tell you," querulously answered Barron. Surely I'm not blind, and I saw her as plainly as I see you."

"Saw who?" asked Deschambault.

"Never mind," replied Barron, sinking back again. "What's the use; if it was a vision, it only proves that my presentiment will come true. I won't be a long liver."

O

Both Deschambault and Cadotte looked at each other and shook their heads. They had learned to both admire and like Barron, and they felt very much pained to see him in the condition he was. They knew, from there being no liquor in the boat, that he could not be intoxicated, and the only other version they could place upon his strange conduct was that he must be very ill and delirious; they therefore paid every attention to him, and as soon as they reached Norway House they reported the matter to the doctor in charge.

To their surprise, however, they saw Mr. Barron apparently in perfect health walking about, and the doctor told them that he could find nothing the matter with him. The vision on the lake therefore remained a mystery to the two men.

Norway House is an important post belonging to the Hudson Bay Company. The annual council of chief factors and chief traders is held there, and all the business of the Company in the North-West discussed, and such changes made as are deemed necessary. Norway House is built upon an island at the mouth of one of the tributaries to Lake Winnipeg, called Jack River. Opposite, on another island, is a small Indian village of two hundred inhabitants. A Catholic priest resides there; and the Hudson Bay Company has a small store for the accommodation of the villagers, and still more so of the Company, who collect a large quantity of furs through it.

Mr. Barron's boat remained at Norway House for a day and a night, to await the coming of the rest of the brigade that had stayed behind on account of the storm.

During the evening of the night they thus lay over at Norway House, Mr. Barron had another mental visitation that started all the inmates of the Fort. It appears while the Company's officers were sitting chatting with Mr. Barron after tea, he suddenly rose to his feet, exclaiming, " Hist ! hist !

didn't you hear that? There! there! (pointing round the room) don't you hear the rustling of a silk dress ; but I can see no one. There," sinking back upon his chair, the perspiration streaming down his pale face, he exclaimed, "My God what can it mean ; this is dreadful."

All those present stood aghast at this strange freak, and a deep gloom seemed to rest upon the people of the Fort, as the story was retailed from one to the other. Nor were they sorry when the missing boats arrived. And the whole brigade started on its journey the next day. The boatmen began to whisper amongst themselves regarding the strange things that had occurred, and several of them began to look suspiciously on Mr. Barron. Both Cadotte and Deschambault, however, stood by him, and as there was no repetition of the supernatural visitations during the trip, the feelings of the men gradually calmed down, until the matter became almost forgotten.

Soon after leaving Norway House the portaging began, which consists in hauling the boat alongside the shore, when practicable, and unloading it whenever they come to rapids, of which there are a large number, between Lake Winnipeg and York Factory. As soon as the boat is made fast at the head or foot of the rapids, the men take out the packages of goods and commence carrying them on their backs to the point below or above. The boat is then hauled across on land, or run down the swift current, light. Voyageurs, in carrying their loads, use a broad strap of leather, which they pass across their brows and round the package or packages on their backs. By this means, strange to say, they can carry much larger and heavier loads than by passing the strap across their breasts. It is a very rare sight to see one of these voyageurs walking across a portage with his load ; you will generally find him on what is called a "jog trot," consequently little time is lost at a portage.   This sort of work has sometimes to be done half a dozen or a dozen times during the day, and, therefore, the travelling is often slow; but, taking everything into consideration, the difficulties of the route, &c., the trip from Fort Garry is not so tiresome as might be supposed.   Nothing occurred to our party of voyageurs until they came to what is called " White Fall Portage," which derives its name from the peculiar color of the stone in its vicinity.

Shortly after they left this place, old Cadotte went up to Mr. Barron, and asked him " whether he would like to have a lob-stick cut ? "

" A lob-stick," replied Barron, " what on earth is that ? "

Old Cadotte pointed to a large tree, standing at a bend in the river, with nothing but a few branches at the top, all the rest having been cut off.   " There," he said, " that is a lob-stick.   Every officer of the Company going up or down the first time always has one cut, and it is then named after him. That one there is Dr. Rae's lob-stick."

" How do you manage to do it ? " asked Mr. Barron.

" Why," replied the steersman, " you climb up nearly to the top, and then bob off the branches as you come down. You had better get me to make one for you."

" All right," said Mr. Barron.

The boat was put ashore, and old Cadotte was soon lost sight of in the branches of a splendid tree.   Presently the sound of his axe was heard, and then the branches began to tumble down one after the other.   In a short time the trunk was clear, except the few branches left at the top.

" There," said Cadotte, " you'd better cut your name upon it now.   No one will ever touch it after that."

Mr. Barron then took out his pen-knife, and cut out the letters—

"GRACE MEREDITH."

The old steersman looked on with surprise as each letter made its appearance. At last he remarked as the word " Grace " was finished—" you're not cutting your own name, sir ! "

" I am aware of that," replied Barron, " But, Cadotte, I want you to christen that tree 'GRACE DARLING,' and point it out as such to all your friends."

And there to this day the " Grace Darling " can be seen by any one in the neighbourhood of White Fall Portage.

About ten miles further on, the brigade came in view of " Hell's Gates." These consist of three passages in the solid rock, through which the river rushes at the rate of five miles an hour. The passages are not much wider than sufficient to allow a York boat to pass through, and on each side the rock rises in a perpendicular wall about thirty feet high.

The boats are steered for the opening of the deepest passage, and the greatest dexterity is required on the part of the steersman, to prevent a serious accident. In ascending these rapids the men use poles, which they insert into clefts or steps, made for the purpose, on each side of the rock. It requires a great deal of hardy perseverance on the part of the boatmen to to ascend these rapids, as the slightest giving way on their part would assuredly result in utter destruction.

It was while running through Hell's Gates that Mr. Barron roused himself for the first and last time from his melancholy, and seemed to interest himself in the movements of the boat's crew.

" I think," he remarked, when they had descended in safety, " that Hell's Gates is an appropriate name for that place, for it is a d——h ticklish spot to go through."

After Hell's Gates, the party passed through Rabbit Lake and Windy Lake; then they came to Simpson's Opening, and afterwards stopped a day at Oxford House, another Hudson Bay Company's post.

Oxford House is situated on the lake of the same name. The boats discharged some bales at this place, and Mr. Barron had an opportunity of once more sleeping under a roof, as Deschambault decided upon not starting on their way till morning.

About half a mile from the shore, on Oxford Lake, opposite the Fort, there is a hole which it is said has never been fathomed. The Indians have a superstitious fear of passing over the spot at any time, and on no account can they be induced to do so during the night. The next lake on the route is Knee Lake, a sheet of water nearly one hundred miles long, and thickly studded with small islands. Here the voyageurs caught a number of white and jack fish, and in the evening, having landed on one of the islands, a hearty supper was made.

The next day they passed a large rock in Swampy Lake, rising high out of the water. This is called "Dram Stone," from it being the custom for the men to expect a glass of liquor at this point, from the officer in charge of the boats.

Mr. Barron, however, was unable to keep up the custom, for, as we have said before, there was no grog on board of the boat. He had, however, to promise the expected dram to the men whenever they reached York Factory. Numerous portages were then passed without anything of importance happening, until they reached Black Water Creek. Here the trout, averaging from three to four pounds weight, are so thick that at times one can kick them out of the water; a great deal less trouble than fishing for them. We wonder what "Walton" would say to that.

When the brigade reached a place called Mill Sand, about

three-quarters of a mile from York Factory, Mr. Barron and Deschambault perceiving a large white bear on the land, had the boat put ashore and immediately gave chase. Deschambault being a crack shot, bruin easily fell a prey to the sportsmen, and when killed, was found to measure about the size of an ordinary ox. These white bears are very ferocious and dangerous customers to meet; it is, therefore, no small undertaking to go out hunting such game. The carcase of the animal was left where it was killed, until they could send out from the Fort to bring it in.

York Factory was at last reached, the brigade having been sixteen days on the trip—a distance of over 800 miles. Mr. Barron throughout the whole of that time had appeared to be suffering in mind, and both Deschambault and Cadotte were very glad that he had reached York Factory without any serious illness.

York Factory is the largest Fort belonging to the Hudson Bay Company, as well as being the most important one. To give our readers some idea of its extent, we may mention that there are some twenty-five buildings inside the walls, as well as about ten outside. These consist of stores, dwelling-houses, workshops, offices, a school, church and powder magazine, as well as a lookout house 90 feet high.

The number of employees about the place, ranges as follows : 60 men; 6 officers; 1 officer in charge; 1 minister; 1 doctor. To this point, the Hudson Bay Company's ship pays an annual visit, loaded with wares for the trade, and goes back bringing the furs from the previous year's catch. The ground on which the Fort is built, was originally a swamp, which has since been filled up, an undertaking which must have cost a very large sum of money.

There are from fifty to sixty trained dogs kept continually

about York Factory, for the use of the fur traders in winter. During the summer, these animals are allowed to roam at large, where they feed themselves along the shores of Hudson Bay on the whales and fish that are thrown by the waves upon the beach. In winter, however, they are kept locked up, and on that account become very ferocious ; as an instance of which we may mention a case, where they devoured a woman and child, the scull of the latter being the only part left to show how they had perished.

On the night of Mr. Barron's arrival, he had a repetition of the mysterious vision. This time, it appeared outside his window. He had hardly lain down on his bed, when he distinctly heard three taps upon the glass. Immediately he sprang from his bed and looking out, he saw to his astonishment the form of Grace Meredith beckoning to him in the bright moonlight. As he endeavoured to open the window, however, the vision disappeared, and poor Barron, uttering a loud cry, fell back on the floor of his room. The noise roused several of the clerks, whose rooms adjoined his, and they rushing in, found Mr. Barron lying insensible on the floor, and a small stream of blood trickling from his mouth and nostrils.

CHAPTER XVII.

OURT day had come at last, and the Harrican-Cool trial was about to take place. Before describing, however, how the matter became settled between the two parties, let us take a look at the Court itself, and how it was managed, during the Hudson Bay Company's rule.

Within a picket enclosure, outside the walls of Fort Garry, stood the court house and jail—the latter consisting of two or three cells, while the former was little more than an ordinary-sized room, with a railing dividing it in two. On one side of this stood the judge's bench, a table for the clerk of the court, and a couple of long forms for the accommodation of the jury. The rest of the room was furnished with seats sufficient for about one hundred persons.

Long before the hour for opening the court, a crowd of people could generally be seen loitering about the door in small knots, some discussing passing events of the day ; others, the merits of the several cases on the list ; while some were holding independent courts on their own behalf. These latter frequently settled cases without the necessities for judge or jury, and thus did away with unnecessary expense and a great deal of hard feeling. In fact, it often happened that not one-half of the cases on the docket ever found their way into Court, the parties, through the instrumentality of their friends, agreeing between themselves beforehand.

We may mention here that the law, as administered in Red River, under the H. B. C. rule, savored more of equity than a mere regard for legal technicalities. It was, in fact, little more than a form of arbitration, where the rights of both contending parties were heard, and justice done as far as possible on the actual merits of the case.

About ten o'clock, his Honour usually appeared, walking from the Fort to the court house, and immediately all parties hastened in to secure their seats. On the bench were three magistrates, as well as the sheriff, to assist his Honor; and generally the first act of the judge, on entering the court room, was to wish the magistrates all a very good morning. The next, to arrange his books and papers; after which he desired the sheriff to call out the names of the constables, and, silence being then proclaimed, the Court was duly declared open for business.

The judge was a mild, pleasant looking old gentleman, with snow-white hair and whiskers. There was nothing very formidable in his appearance to frighten offenders; indeed his mildness of disposition, and great desire for fairness, often made him the victim of men in the heat of argument, who, in any other court, would have been committed for contempt.

On the morning we speak of, before any case was called, a long, thin man stood up, and addressed the judge, to the effect that one of the magistrates on the bench before him had charged him six shillings for issuing a warrant in a criminal case, and contended that "he had no right to do so."

The judge thereupon remonstrated with the magistrate, but the latter thought, as he had possession of the six shillings, he would keep them. His Honour, therefore, turned to the long, thin man, and delivered judgment as follows;

" The Court believes you will get back your six shillings."

" Seeing's believing," muttered the unhappy loser of the money, as he walked away.

And now, when the Court is going on with the cases before it, let us take a look at one outside, in which we are more interested.

A group of persons, consisting of Mr. Meredith, Jack and Robert Harrican, Cool and Whirl, stood together, and the substance of their conversation referred to the late transaction concerning the Harrican Farm. It appears that Cool and Whirl had begun to disagree, and that the latter threatened to "split" on the former. Cool, therefore, thought his best course would be to settle the matter without going into Court, especially as he began to find out that his claim on the farm in any case would be a very doubtful one. As we have said in a former part of our story, Robert Harrican was indebted to Cool for a certain sum of money. Cool consequently offered to hand over to Jack the paper which Robert had signed, provided the debt which the latter owed him was paid beforehand.

Jack had every desire to see his brother free from Cool; and, although he could not well afford the money at the time, he agreed to the peremptory demand.

The party then adjourned to Cool's house, and the business was finally settled, without the necessity for any legal expenses.

Whirl accompanied Mr. Meredith from the house, after the completion of the bargain, and as they walked away together he said :—

" I very much regret having mixed myself up in this affair at all, but the fact is I did not at the time understand the real features of the case. It now appears to me as a rascally transaction altogether."

" Very much that way," returned Mr. Meredith.

"I hope you will exculpate me from having had any share
in it, after I became aware how matters stood ?"

"I really have nothing to do with it," coldly returned Mr.
Meredith.

Very little more was said between the two men until they
separated.   Mr. Meredith, however, saw through the dirty
transaction, and his faith in both Cool and Whirl was wholly
destroyed.

We will now return to the Court, and watch the proceedings
there.   A hard case was being tried, the circumstances of which
were as follow :—

A trader in the settlement, by the name of Sharp, had
purchased a quantity of buffalo robes from a plain hunter, for
which he had given his note, payable in three months.   The
buffalo robes were sent to St. Paul for sale, and on their way
they got damaged by water, so much so that their value de-
teriorated considerably.

When the plain hunter called on Sharp for payment of the
note, he was coolly told that he would have to make a deduction, as the robes did not bring the price in St. Paul which
they ought to have done.   The plain hunter expostulated, but
all to no purpose ; either the deduction had to be made, or the
note would not be paid.   The result of all this was that the
case came before the Court which we are at present describing,
and judgment was delivered against Sharp.

It was generally the custom for the party against whom a
judgment was delivered, to state the day on which he would be
able to pay the amount, and if the length of time was too
great, the prosecutor had the right to object to it.   In this
case the plain hunter insisted that the amount of the note, as
well as the costs, should be paid that afternoon.

During the day, therefore, the sheriff visited Mr. Sharp,

prepared to execute the judgment, in case he did not receive the amount claimed by it. Mr. Sharp could not pay the sum required, and the sheriff thereupon proceeded to seize his goods and chattels, when, to his surprise, Mr. Sharp set upon him, vowing that he would resist any such action, and dared the Hudson Bay Company to do their worst. The sheriff, not expecting any such resistance, immediately withdrew, but afterwards returned with two constables, by whom the invincible Mr. Sharp was tied hand and foot, and quickly carried to the jail.

Now it happened that Sharp was a mutual friend of the two worthies, Cool and Whirl, and they therefore felt very disconsolate over his trying position. On the night of the imprisonment, therefore, Whirl paid a visit to his friend Cool. The latter sat ruminating over the events of the day when the former entered the room.

"Good evening, Whirl."

"Good evening, Cool."

"You played me a dirty trick to-day, Whirl."

"You played me a dirtier one a week ago."

"How so?" asked Cool.

"I suppose you are aware of having secured all Morin's furs without giving me the slightest chance on my debt. I wouldn't think anything of that, had we not an agreement on such matters existing between us; but are you also aware that you gave him a lot of old mink and marten of your own, which you advised him to mix in with some of his good furs, and offer the whole thing to me, you making up the difference on his part of the transaction? That was sharp of you, wasn't it? But you overlooked the fact that I'm as old a trader as yourself, and that I could 'spot' your furs the moment I saw them. However, the only one who really suffered in the affair

was Morin ; for, as sure as fate, I'll put him through a course
of sprouts the moment I have the chance."

Cool laughed aloud.

" Whirl," he said, " it's a common thing, and you ought to be
proud of your sharpsightedness."

" Oh, I do not care about it," said Whirl, " only I didn't
expect it from you exactly ; honor amongst thieves, you know
—eh, Cool ? "

" 'Pshaw !" said the latter, "I only did it as a trick to try you."

" One, however, which I did not appreciate, you see ; but we
won't say anything more about it—I came to see you about
something else."

" Sharp, I suppose," interrupted Cool.

" Exactly," returned Whirl, " what's to be done about him ? "

" One thing is certain," said Cool, " I can't help him in a
pecuniary shape."

" I don't suppose you can," replied Whirl ; " but is there no
other way by which we can get him out of the scrape ? "'

" The only way I see," said Cool, " is by getting him out of
jail. What is to prevent our taking him out ? The Hudson
Bay Company could not help themselves. A few stout men
can put them at defiance ; and I know where these same men
can be found. I have just been waiting for a chance of this
kind to give the authorities at Fort Garry some trouble. Depend upon it, were we to take Sharp out of jail to-night, they
durst not put him in again ; and it will be only an opportunity
to weaken them still more in the eyes of the people. What
say you, Whirl ? "

" It's a bold attempt," said the latter, " and I fear will not
bring much credit to the actors in it. Still, anything is better
than to allow poor Sharp to remain in jail."

"We have not much time to lose, then, so we had better make up our minds as quickly as possible. Are you game?"

"As for being game," said Whirl, "it does not require a great deal of courage to undertake the thing, since there are only a couple of men on guard at the jail; and these will have no opportunity to sound an alarm, as they are unarmed, and at some distance from the other buildings adjoining the Fort."

"Will you join, then, in the attempt to-night?" asked Cool, "for if so, I'll have the men ready by ten o'clock."

"I'll join!" at length Whirl exclaimed, after a long pause, during which he seemed to have been deep in thought; "although," he added, "my opinion is that the whole affair will do us more harm than the Hudson Bay Company, or Sharp will suffer for it in the long run."

"I don't care," said Cool, "so long as we can have a slap at the Hudson Bay Company."

The two conspirators now separated, one to collect the men necessary for the undertaking, the other to think over the fix he had got himself into.

About half-past nine o'clock, in one of the rooms of Cool's house, might have been seen a number of armed men collected together, speaking in excited tones, and apparently eager to start out on their expedition. Whirl had not arrived, and Cool kept anxiously looking for his appearance. There was little confidence between these two men, and Cool felt it just possible that Whirl might betray them. It was, therefore, a great relief to him when the suspected man entered the room.

"What has kept you?" asked Cool.

"Nothing," replied the other; "it isn't ten o'clock yet."

"We've decided upon going down to the jail one by one, so as not to attract attention, and we'll all meet together just behind the building. As soon as we are all there, we will

creep silently round to the door and knock at it. The keeper,
not suspecting trouble, will open it, and the moment he does so
we will all rush in, and in the hubbub will release Sharp. I
don't expect the whole thing will last over ten minutes. Each
man has a piece of black crape to put over his eyes, and we
have all agreed that not a word is to be spoken by any one in
the party. Sharp expects us, so he will not be astonished at
our visit."

"You've planned everything to a nicety," said Whirl. "One
would almost think that you've had this sort of thing in view
for some time."

"So I have," answered Cool, winking.

All the men had now left the house, so the two worthies
followed their example, and in a short time the whole party of
jail breakers were collected together beneath the court house
walls. Cool then crept round the picket wall, followed by the
rest of the men, and knocked at the front door of the jail.
All held their breath in readiness for the rush. Presently the
bolt was drawn, and a light appeared, and before the unfortunate keeper had time to ask who was there, he found himself
thrown down and trampled upon by a number of men. His
comrade, hearing the noise, rushed out, but was immediately
met with a blow on the head, which knocked him senseless to
the floor. The lights by this time had been extinguished, so
that the jail-breakers found some difficulty in finding the room
in which their friend Sharp was confined. The first door they
burst in belonged to a cell in which a noted woman of bad
character was a prisoner. She, not knowing what was the
matter, began to scream at the top of her voice, which made
the hubbub still greater. In the next cell, however, they found
Sharp, and, fearing discovery through the noise of the woman,

they hastened away with their liberated prisoner as quickly as possible.

The woman, finding everything quiet, and the door of her cell open, began to think it high time for her to take advantage of the unusual circumstance. She, therefore, slowly felt her way along the passage, until, near the front door, she stumbled over the prostrate keeper, who immediately caught her by the leg.

" Lord a' mercy !" she exclaimed, as she made a dive for the open air, followed by a little dog belonging to the keeper, which pursued her quite a distance up the road, barking at her heels as she rushed along.

Sharp was conducted to his house by his friends, where a supper was prepared for them by Mrs. Sharp ; and several of the men remained on guard all night, lest an attempt should be made by the authorities to retake their prisoner.

In the morning there was a good deal of excitement amongst the people as soon as the news of the escape became known. All right thinking persons condemned the act ; and Whirl was correct in his supposition that it would do them no good ; for although it was not generally known who were the actors in the affair, it was supposed by most of the settlers that both Cool and Whirl had a great deal to do with it.

They were consequently regarded with coldness by many who had previously been on intimate terms with them ; indeed it was the first step in the great fall they afterwards experienced in the estimation of most of the people of Red River. We have already said that the settlers, as a rule, were law-abiding and quiet; in fact it was to this characteristic in the people that the Hudson Bay Company managed to get on as they did, for had the settlers been troublesome, they could not have governed the country as long as they did.

P

As soon as the escape of the prisoner became known to the Governor, he, as a precautionary measure, had a number of special constables sworn in to guard against a repetition of such an outrage on the public peace and safety. To avoid any unnecessary trouble, the Governor, who was in every way a good man, averse to anything like severity, saw fit to call upon Sharp and demand personally what he intended to do in the matter. The interview was a long one, and resulted in the Governor paying out of his own pocket the sum due the plain hunter. This was done so that a poor man should not suffer. Because the Government happened to be weak at the time, the Governor therefore, desirous of allowing the public mind to remain undisturbed, paid out of his own private fund a large sum of money.

Sharp looked upon the matter as a happy hit on his part, never taking into consideration the meanness and unfairness of of the whole proceeding. Cool thought it a grand success, and a great victory over the Company. Whirl actually felt ashamed of the part he had played in it.

Twaddle had just returned from his trip, and the next issue of the *Buster* came out with a long article upon the popular feeling against the injustice of the Hudson Bay Company rule, as exemplified by the late attack upon the jail, and release from prison of one of their most respectable citizens. No mention was made of the reason why that respectable citizen was imprisoned; it was enough that he had been put in durance vile by the H. B. C. authorities. Jail breaking was held up as a virtue, and the settlers were encouraged to set the laws at defiance, and thus destroy their only safeguard to peace and safety. The whole article was dished up in the endeavor to show the outside world that the settlers of Red River were groaning under an oppressive, tyrannical government. But, unfortunately, Twaddle did not sufficiently understand the people he was living amongst; he had gone too far, as he found to his cost; for soon after a deputation of respectable citizens called on him with the following document, and requested him to publish it. He at first refused to do so, but at last he was compelled to swallow the bitter pill. Here is the document:—

"BUSTER EXTRA.

"_To the Governor, Deputy Governor, and Committee of the Honourable Hudson's Bay Company_:

"HONOURABLE GENTLEMEN,—We, the undersigned inhabitants of the Red River Settlement, in the Hudson's Bay Terri tory, beg to submit to your Honors the following remarks:—

"1st. A deplorable occurrence took place last week; the law was put at defiance; the doors of the prison forced open during the night, and a prisoner rescued. The editor of the only newspaper in the settlement published an account of this fact in such a way as to give a very false impression, and throw discredit on the peaceful members of this little community. The base act was represented as a public demonstration, while on the contrary it was the deed of but a few individuals, and met with the disapproval and scorn of the population.

"2nd. The same sheet has for several months in almost every issue thrown blame and contempt on the Honourable Hudson's Bay Company, and especially on those entrusted by this Honourable Body with the charge of governing the settlement. Far from approving this course, we, on the contrary, readily embrace this opportunity to express our respect and gratitude towards our worthy Governor, who in the management of our public affairs has gained universal confidence and esteem. In the meantime the different members of the administration as well as the legal officers being as a general rule in perfect accordance with their honourable and distinguished Head, are far from deserving the insults lavished upon them by the editor of the *Buster*.

" 3rd. Changes are anticipated in the country. We cannot forsee the result of the negotiations pending between the Imperial Government and your Honourable Body, but we are confident that you will not lose sight of our condition, and we humbly entreat your Honours to take measures in the said transactions to secure the welfare of the natives and inhabitants of this settlement, and to guard them against the preponderance and undue influence of new-comers. *And your petitioners will ever pray.*"

Then followed over eight hundred names of the principal settlers in Red River.

This was a terrible blow to poor Twaddle, and a crusher on any influence the *Buster* might have hoped to obtain over the people.

We cannot allow this jail-breaking propensity on the part of a few lawless men to pass over without a few comments. Taking advantage of the weakness of the government then existing, a few men, to further their own interests, took up the cudgels in favour of annexation to Canada. Unfortunately for their cause, which in itself was a good one, they resorted to lawless and unprincipled means to carry out their project, which, instead of giving the settlers a good idea of what Canadians were really like, actually obliged people to dread and fear having anything to do with them. And it was for this reason, because such men as Sharp and Cool were connected with the movement, and because they resorted to such base and barefaced means, that the very idea of annexation to Canada became to be looked upon by the settlers with suspicion, if not aversion. And what made the matter still worse, these same men put themselves forward as the representative party of Canada. But we will have occasion to refer to this matter again before the close of our story.

In the meantime, let us take a look at certain of our characters after the appearance in public of the *Buster Extra*. Cool and Whirl sat together in the former's private room.

"Well," said Whirl, "here's a pretty kettle of fish. Where's your slap at the Hudson Bay Company ? I'm afraid the tables are turned."

"They look as if they were at present," said Cool, "but the game is not up yet. If that d——n little Twaddle had stuck out as he ought to have done, the *Extra* never would have been printed."

"I think," returned Whirl, "eight hundred signatures to a document is enough to make any man print it."

"They never could have obliged me to do it."

"What are you going to do now?" asked Whirl. "I'm afraid Canada will suffer by its champion," he added.

"I don't care a row of pins for Canada," returned Cool, "but I can't afford to let Canada drop now, so I'll fight it out, and I'll get Twaddle to write an article saying that the *Extra* was forced out of him. That will ease the feeling abroad, if it does no more good."

"I think," remarked Whirl, "that after all my advocacy of annexation to the United States will stand me more good than that of Union with Canada, if you go on much longer as you are doing."

"Hilloah !" exclaimed Cool, "who helped to break open the jail, eh ?"

While our two worthies are thus discussing their own peculiarities, we will take a look at Mr. Meredith, as he sat reading the *Buster Extra.* Surprise as well as indignation were both reflected in his countenance. "What a disgraceful affair. I should think this will be a lesson to Cool."

"I'm afraid," replied Grace, who sat near him, "that nothing can teach that man to do right. I wish, father, you had not listened to what he said about George."

"Hush, my girl, do not let us speak of that unhappy event."

"Oh! father, how can I help it. George will never be out of my thoughts; do you suppose I can forget him?"

"Well! well! my dear girl, we can only hope for the best, and that George will once more be the same as ever to us."

"Father, George can never alter in my estimation."

Mr. Meredith bowed his head over the paper; he felt the absence of George very deeply, much more so indeed than Grace was aware of. He had also begun to observe a marked change in Grace from her usual buoyant, happy manner. He, therefore, to change the subject, spoke of the doings of Cool and his friends. "I wonder," he said, "that Canadians allow themselves to be linked in with such men; it is a disgrace and a shame to countenance acts that jeopardise the public safety. Why, if matters go on in this way, we will have nothing but mob law, and then good-bye to the settlement. Upon my word, I'm almost sorry that I have invested in the stock farm; there's a want of security to property holders while such doings are going on."

"They wouldn't be allowed in Canada," remarked Mrs. Meredith; "and I always said you were crazy to come to such a country."

"There is one satisfaction however, the mass of the settlers do not approve of those lawless acts. I am very glad to see this," (pointing to the *Extra*).

“ It's an ill wind that blows no one good,” said Tom.   “ Old Bet got out of jug by it, anyway.”

“ You had better go to bed, you scamp,” exclaimed Mrs. Meredith.   “ What have you to do with old Bet?”

CHAPTER XVIII.

BEFORE leaving for his post in the interior, George Wade received a visit from Jack and Tom, when the latter told him how he had delivered the letter and package to Grace, without the knowledge of Mr. Meredith.

"I am sorry you did that," said George, "for I fear he will think that I have broken faith with him."

"You needn't fear," replied Tom, "for father will never know anything about it."

Grace, when she learned from Tom that her father had not seen the letter from George, immediately went and told Mr. Meredith that she had received the communication from her lover, accompanying the parcel from Mr. Barron, begging, at the same time, that nothing should be said to Tom on the subject. Grace also obtained permission to answer Wade's letter, and this was the last correspondence that ever passed between them. George started a few days afterwards for the post in the interior.

We will now look a little ahead of our story, and visit the spot where Wade was sent to, namely, Fort à la Corne. The fall had passed, and winter had thrown its snowy robe over the country. George, who had been some time at the post, was preparing for an expedition in search of furs. He and his two men were, therefore, busy at work mending both harness and sleds, &c., &c.

A short distance from the post there lived a free trader, who was running opposition to the Company. George mistrusted that this opponent had some scheme in view to gain an advantage over him. He, therefore, sent one of his men to reconnoitre, and, if possible, find out the movements of the free trader. This happened at night. Cautiously the man crept towards the log cabin in which Wade's opponent lived, and when he reached the small window, he peered in, and found there reason for suspicion. The free trader and his men were sitting before their large fire, apparently engaged in earnest conversation. The spy sent to watch their proceedings put his ear close to the door, and listened. The following is what he heard :—

"I want to fool that new chap at the Company's post," said the free trader.

"I think we can easily do that," said one of the men; "he's green."

"He may be green," answered the free trader; "but sometimes these green hands give us a good deal of trouble. Are you sure, Louis, that those Indians will be at the place when we reach there ?"

"I am certain, sure, for I saw one of them this very day, and he told me to come and see them."

"Perhaps he said they had a lot of furs," replied the trader, sneeringly.

"You needn't sneer," retorted the other, "and you needn't go unless you like; but I can tell you, you will be sorry for it. The Indian I saw said they hadn't many furs; but did you ever hear one of them confess how many skins he had in his lodge ?"

"Of course not; but one can generally tell if they have any or not by speaking to them."

"Well, I tell you, my opinion is, you'll make a good haul if you go."

"Then we'll go," replied the trader. "But how will we manage to get away without being seen by Wade at the post?"

"I'll tell you," said the trader's man who had not as yet spoken; "I'll go over and pay a visit at the post. While I am there, you can be getting the sleds ready, and have the dogs harnessed, so that we can leave at a minute's warning. The moment the lights are out at Wade's, we'll start."

"Just the thing," said the trader. "You had better go on your visit at once, then."

The listener was preparing to leave, when his ears caught a very important question, put by the trader to his man : "How far is it, and which way will we go?" Hereupon the man gave a minute description of the place, and the best road to it. The listener had heard enough ; he bolted, and in five minutes afterwards Wade received the whole story.

George immediately sent one of his men to an adjoining store, to collect such articles as he required for the trip. The sleds were put into the same house, to be loaded up and corded. Eight of the best dogs were picked out and harnessed ; everything, indeed, was pretty well in readiness, when a knock came to the door of Wade's house, and soon the emissary from the trader's establishment walked in, and sat down.

"Dark night," he said.

"Yes, it is," replied George ; "too dark for me. I wish the moonlight would come soon, so that we could go on long trips. There's no furs to be had for any price just now. Have you heard of any Indians around anywhere? But I suppose I needn't ask you," continued George, "for you wouldn't tell me?"

"You don't know me," replied the man. "I'm not over fond

of La Ronde (the trader's name), and, if you wouldn't betray me, perhaps I might tell you something to your advantage."

George pricked his ears. Treachery, he thought; and he prepared to receive the information, astonished, however, to find so much falseness where he expected nothing but faithfulness. He did not know his man, however, for he was still more surprised to find the man describing a place in altogether an opposite direction from the spot where the Indians really were. The trader's man chuckled at having, as he thought, completely blinded the Company's man, and George Wade laughed in his sleeve at what had happened. He, however, thanked the man for his information, and promised faithfully to keep the secret.

Soon after this, the trader's man left, and returned to his cabin, where both he and his master, as well as Louis, had a good laugh over what they thought such a good sell on George Wade. They laughed on the wrong side, however, the following day. The free trader and his men, as soon as the time arrived, quietly left the house, and, with two dog trains, set off as fast as they could go. They had not gone far, however, when George Wade and his men left the post in hot pursuit.

Now it happened that the Company's dogs were far superior to those owned by the free trader. It was not long, therefore, until the latter were overtaken by the former, and as they came up alongside of each other, George shouted out,—

"Where are you off to so early in the morning? You seem to be in a hurry."

"So do you," replied the free trader, trying to laugh.

"Well, good bye, old chap; I hope you'll get along soon; I'm sorry I can't wait for you." So saying, George and his men rushed past.

The free trader whipped his dogs until the poor brutes

nearly gave in altogether; but all to no purpose. George had the best dogs, so the free trader, cursing his fate, resolved to follow on and take his chances.

And now a word or two about dog driving. In the first place, the generality of the dogs used for drawing loads during the winter in the North-West, are a species of cross between the dog and the wolf, and are usually called "huskies." There are generally four of these brutes harnessed to a sled, one in front of the other; the harness consisting of saddles, collars, and traces. Each of the dogs has its own peculiar name, such as "Pomp," "Black," "White," "Grey," and such like; and if any one of those in the train show signs of lagging, the driver will call out "Black, marche!" and the brute, having a wholesome dread of the whip, will turn its head, and, with a yelp, bound forward. Dog driving necessarily entails a great deal of cruelty. We say necessarily so, because without a severe application of the lash at times, one could not drive dogs at all.

The sleds are made of a flat board turned up at one end, and sometimes a cariole is used; the latter being made of parchment skin very much in the form of a large shoe. These are very comfortable indeed, as most of the body is covered up from exposure. Attached to each sled is a long line or cord, which is allowed to trail behind. This is used in case the dogs should try to run away, as they often do. The driver, in that case, siezes the line, and by that means is enabled to bring the dogs up sharp. Were it not for this, the dogs would often get away from their drivers.

A dog train is driven by certain calls. There are no reins used; four words do the whole business. When you wish the leader to go to the left, you call out "chuck;" to the the right, "yeu;" to go ahead, "marche;" and to stop, "whoa."

It often happens that a dog will become sulky or stubborn,

and in that case the driver has to beat the brute into subjection. Sometimes there is more cruelty practised in this way than necessary, as the dogs are often knocked motionless, the blows invariably being directed against the head.

The "huskies" are very much of the "Indian" in their nature, and will gorge themselves whenever they get a chance; it is therefore necessary to keep food hid from them; and when on the road they are never fed except at night. If train dogs are allowed to eat in the morning, or during the day, they will not travel far before they will lie down, and nothing will rouse them; indeed, dogs have frequently to be let loose or abandoned on account of their having gorged themselves on the provisions of their masters during the night. A dog driver usually runs behind his train, jumping on now and then to rest.

We will now turn our attention to George in his trip to visit the Indians. He soon lost sight of the free trader, and continued on his course till he came in view of the lodges. On reaching them his first act was to shake hands all round with the savages; he then went into the principal wigwam and had a long smoke and big talk, and to ingratiate himself with the Indians he produced a few presents. All this time no signs of furs appeared to exist.

George began to lose patience, but his men smoked and chatted, and at last one poor miserable mink skin was pulled out by one of the Indians from beneath the matting on which he sat. This was offered to George for purchase, and he, being under the guidance of one of his men, offered a little tea and tobacco for it. Some further talking and smoking ensued, and another mink skin made its appearance, which was bartered off, and then trade began to get a little more lively. Furs now were produced from all sorts of imaginable hiding places, and

George at last found out that the Indians, instead of being poor, as he had first supposed, were in reality rich.

One of his men had remained outside the lodge to guard the goods on the sleds from being stolen by the Indians; and while he thus kept watch, he thought he might be employing himself to some purpose. He therefore went to the door of the lodge, and made a sign to his comrade inside. This was immediately understood by the latter, and as we will presently see, acted upon at once. In the first place, the man inside placed himself near the matting from under which so many furs had already been pulled; and Wade attracting attention in another way, he managed to draw one skin from beneath the matting; then by degrees he succeeded in pushing a part of it under the edge of the wigwam, and the man outside being on the lookout, immediately drew it out altogether, and stowed it away with the furs they had bought. In this way six or seven skins were secured without the knowledge of George however, who would not have permitted such a thing; but most men engaged in fur trading do not consider it a sin to steal from an Indian. The trading had gone on in this way for sometime, and at ast George found his stock of goods nearly at an end.

About this time the free trader made his appearance, so Wade and his men took their departure in the direction of home, leaving very few furs to be collected by their opponents.

It happened soon after George left, that the loss of the mink stolen by the Company's men was discovered by the Indians, and the free trader came in for the blame of it. He protested his innocence, but all to no purpose. The savages would not believe him, and further trading was out of the question; and, indeed, the unfortunate victims began to think it high time to leave the camp, as their presence seemed to be viewed with a good deal of suspicion by the Indians.

This short sketch of fur trading will give our readers some idea of the means used for obtaining the furs, which to many of them prove so comfortable and warm during the cold winter months. The Indian suffers all the privations of the chase to secure the skins of the different fur-bearing animals, and the trader steps in to rob and cheat him out of his hard earnings.

The free trader returned to his log cabin greatly disgusted with the result of his expedition, and very much puzzled to know how George Wade could have discovered the whereabouts of the Indians. He had no reason to doubt his two men, as they were well tried, trusty servants. George Wade in the meantime returned to the post, highly pleased with his success, the more so as he had gained a complete victory over his opponent, the free trader. It very often happens, however, that the free traders are more successful than the Company's servants. The strife between the two is a bitter one, and every means are used on both sides to defeat each other. George liked this rivalry, and although he took every opportunity to get the better of the free traders, he invariably endeavoured to keep on a friendly footing with them. He, therefore, became a favourite in the interior ; at the same time he was feared and respected. George had every reason to believe that he would receive promotion in the service, and he did everything in his power to make his post a satisfactory one to the Company. The only drawback he felt to the mode of life he was leading was the utter loneliness of his position at times ; then the thoughts of the past would crowd upon him ; and the image of Grace Meredith was constantly before him. He never doubted her love for him, but his separation from her preyed upon him, and often when alone he would bemoan his hard fate. Then the circumstances of previous years would crowd themselves upon him, until at times he almost wished to remain shut out from the world, and blessed the very isolation of his position. Then again he would look forward to the day when he would be able to visit Fort Garry again; and it may be said he entertained the hope that he might then be able to clear the stain from his name, and claim Grace once more as his own, with the full consent of her parents. How the thought of such happiness gladdened the heart of the poor fellow in his lonely position!

The life of a Hudson Bay Company officer in the interior is a very varied one. Sometimes possessed of comforts, sometimes deprived of them, he often is cursed with idleness; and at other times he is blessed with too much to do. George was no exception to the rule; he, therefore, whenever an opportunity occurred, took advantage of it to make a trip away from the post. On several occasions he went off for wood, but generally his expeditions were in search of furs, in which he fortunately proved successful. We will, however, leave him in his lonely position for the present, while we look back upon other scenes connected with our story.

CHAPTER XIX.

R. MEREDITH, as soon as he obtained a clear title to the Harrican Farm from Jack, began to improve the place; and the first thing he did in that way was to put it in order for the approaching winter. The hay-yard was well fenced in, and house and stables mudded and whitewashed. The fences nearest the road were pulled down, so as to prevent the snow from drifting, and thus causing an obstruction in front of the farm stables. Pigsties, and so forth, were made warm against the severity of the weather. A supply of vegetables was stored away, and everything done to make home comfortable. He and the boys were, therefore, kept busy for several weeks. The stock farm, also, required a good deal of attention as he was determined to make it a model establishment. Jack, as soon as the work at home was finished, went out to take charge of Grosse Isle, and a couple of men were hired to assist him.

Mrs. Meredith, now that things looked settled around her, became more reconciled to her new home; and Mr. Meredith would have felt perfectly easy about his prospects were it not for a blight that rested on his family circle.

We have reference to Grace. Ever since the unfortunate turn in affairs with George Wade she had not been herself, and

Q

her father saw, with dismay, a great change coming over his favourite child. Her manner, which naturally was buoyant and cheerful, became quiet and reserved. The healthy colour left her cheeks, and gave place to an unnatural paleness. Had George Wade been in the settlement, we believe that Mr. Meredith would have gone and beseeched him to come and visit them as of wont; but the lover was far away beyond communication, and the unhappy girl could only pine for his presence. Mrs. Meredith did not fail to reproach her husband for his conduct. to Grace; and, taking it altogether, the poor man felt very miserable as well as anxious. Since the affair of the Court, he had paid very few visits to Mr. Cool, as that gentleman had on several occasions shown his true character. Moreover, Mr. Meredith did not wish to mix himself up with the so-called Canadian party, especially as he plainly foresaw that nothing but dishonour was to be gained by it, so long as they followed the course they had adopted.

Mr. Meredith, having once lost faith in Cool, began to regret having placed any confidence in his statements regarding George Wade. This feeling, added to his misery at home, brought a great deal of unhappiness to the poor man. Mr. Whirl had, true to his agreement with Cool, formed his American party, and, therefore, did not trouble Mr. Meredith very much. Sharp never got over his escape from jail; and when it became known that the Governor had paid the debt out of his own pocket, Sharp descended very low in the estimation of most people in the settlement. The Merediths did not care for many acquaintances; they preferred a few chosen ones whom they could depend upon; the loss, therefore, of Cool and Whirl was not felt very much by the family. Grace could not bear the sight of either of the two men.

About this time a theaatrical company was formed, and an

advertisement appeared in the *Buster*, announcing a play for a certain evening. Mr. Meredith took tickets for himself and the rest of the family, hoping that the change might be beneficial to Grace.

Let us attempt a description of this rude attempt at the drama in the North-West. In the first place, the hall was about forty feet long, twenty wide, and not over eight in height. Rough boards nailed together in the form of benches served as the seats, and the stage was so small that not over three or four could act at one time on the boards. The stage lights consisted of a row of tallow candles; altogether the place was roughly got up, but served its purpose for the time being.

When the Merediths arrived, they found the people crowding in already, although it was long before the hour advertised. They, therefore, had some difficulty in procuring seats. At last, however, they succeeded after some trouble, and soon afterwards the curtain rose and the play commenced. Most of the actors looked as if they were frightened at the scrape they had got themselves into; and a great deal of stammering ensued, which was made still more ridiculous by the stern tones of the excited prompter behind the scenes. The whole affair went off very well for a first attempt, and the worthy manager, at the end of the entertainment, stepped forward and announced another performance the following week. The *Buster* had a glowing account of the whole affair, and Twaddle actually had the temerity to attempt a dramatic criticism, the result of which was, that several of the actors declared openly that if ever Twaddle showed himself in the theatre again, they would kick him out. Poor Twaddle, he was a much abused man.

During the performance a couple of strangers stepped in, and their unexpected appearance produced such a sensation, that people allowed them to procure good seats in front, although, when they came in the play was about over. Both of the new comers wore long cloaks, and had an air of importance about them that said plainly, "We know what we're about;" "Who are you?" One was a tall, slim man, with rather pleasant features; the other, a stout dumpy little fellow, who appeared to think himself of more importance than the whole of those in the room put together. Twaddle, who sat near them, immediately managed to edge closer, until, at last, his curiosity obtaining the mastery over him, he ventured a remark :—

"Haw!" said the little man, "deuced rum little hole, this."

"Very," replied Twaddle.

"It's a wonder the place doesn't break down; see how they are crowded in the back part of the room."

"It may break down yet," said Twaddle. "In fact, I think it probably will."

"The devil?" exclaimed both strangers.

"Dot it down," whispered the taller of the two to the short dumpy one.

"Haw; yes, of course," and taking out a memorandum book, the necessary item was noted.

"A newspaper man, if I'm not mistaken," said the Editor of the *Buster*, "if so, I'm Twaddle."

"Haw, and who the deuce is Twaddle?"

"The Editor of the *Buster*," was the reply, "who will be happy to see you at his office in the morning."

"Dot it down," again said the tall stranger to his companion.

"Haw!" will be glad to see you as requested. Hilloa! deuced pretty girl that, eh?" referring to Grace. "What's her name, Twaddle?"

"That is Miss Meredith," was the reply.

"Haw !" said the stumpy individual, whom we will know hereafter as 'Dot it Down ;' " a native ?"

"No," said Twaddle ; "she came from Canada."

"Haw ! indeed ! Any pretty girls here, Twaddle ?"

"Heaps of them," replied the latter.

"You don't mean," exclaimed "Dot" ; " I never heard that before."

"You'll see," remarked Twaddle.

"Hope so," replied that gentleman; and, as the curtain now rose, he added : "Haw! now for some Indian lingo, I suppose."

The piece happened, however, to be a pantomime, much to the disgust of "Dot," who evidently expected an Indian war dance, or something of the kind.

One thing was very noticeable in this rude attempt at a public performance, namely, the general orderly conduct of the audience. The performers, instead of being laughed at when a mistake happened, were encouraged to proceed, and thus the affair passed off pleasantly enough.

"Dot it Down," however, was an exception to the general rule, and by his loud remarks, and sometimes sneers, he made himself so disagreeable, that at last the door keeper was obliged to admonish him to keep a little more quiet, else ——

"Dot" did not allow him to finish, but rose to resent the impertinence, as he called it, when his companion pulled him down again with the simple advice to " dot it down."

"That I will," said the invincible "Dot ;" "the people in Canada will know how strangers are used here."

Twaddle, who felt himself in honor bound to pay attention to anyone connected with the press, now hastened to apologise for the door keeper's rudeness, and invited both "Dot" and his friend to a little oyster supper after the theatricals were over. "Dot it Down" happened to be an individual very fond of luxurious living, and, without hesitation, accepted the invitation.

"You'll meet a lot of the fellows connected with the theatre."

"Haw!" indeed, most happy, said the now perfectly reconciled "Dot."

Grace Meredith seemed to enjoy the entertainment, and it afforded her father real pleasure to see her smile at several comicalities in the performance. As they were leaving the theatre, at the close of the play, Mr. Meredith, happening to cast his eyes towards the Fort, discovered a bright light burning on the roof of the jail, which rather startled him. At first he could not distinguish what it was, but soon made up his mind that the building was on fire. The old gentleman called the attention of several around him to the bright light, and then the cry of "Fire!" was passed from lip to lip. Several (Mr. Meredith amongst the rest) mounted their horses and hastened away towards the Fort, but before they reached there the fire had been extinguished by the jail-keeper, he having perceived it in time.

It was observed by several that Twaddle seemed in rather good spirits than otherwise about the affair; and, in fact, he was heard to say that it was a pity the place was not allowed to burn down. This, in connection with the late jail breaking, looked very dubious, and seemed to throw greater odium on the parties suspected of having participated in the outrage.

When the Merediths reached home they discussed the state of affairs in the settlement, all agreeing that the proceedings of a few men were a disgrace to the settlement at large; and all felt ashamed that the term "Canadian" was applied to anyone connected with such lawless acts.

The theatrical supper took place as intended, however; the attempted incendiarism forming one of the principal topics of conversation at the table. Twaddle said very little on the subject, especially as he found nearly all against such a state of affairs. "Dot" paid very little attention to anything except the oysters, to which he did justice, and when called upon to make a speech, he excused himself, upon the plea that the deliciousness of the oyster-soup had driven every other idea out of his head. The proprietor of the house in which the supper took place hereupon thought that such a nice little speech deserved an appropriate answer. He therefore rose, and said that "Dot possessed the faculty of expressing himself better than any stranger who had ever come to the country."

"Dot" was overpowered by this flattering testimonial to his ability, and consequently proposed that the party should immediately repair to the Everling Hotel, where he would have much pleasure in standing drinks to the crowd.

This was an offer too good to be refused, so it was at once accepted.

Everling, the hotel-keeper, happened to be away from home, and had left a person to look after his house. The individual who filled this important position went by the nickname of "Fluke," originating, it is said, through his managing to always come out right in any undertaking, without any apparent exertion on his part. No one in the settlement took things easier than our new friend "Fluke"—nothing disturbed his equanimity —always good natured, and never prone to take offence at anything that was said to him. "Fluke" made a good barkeeper, and never refused to join his customers in a social glass whenever he was asked, or when he thought it safe to ask himself. He used to boast that he had two pockets in his trousers—one for the use of Everling, the other for himself. If one happened to be empty it invariably borrowed from the other, the balance being generally against "Fluke." He was, however, honest enough to render an account of these two wonderful pockets to Everling on his return ; the result being, however, that the latter found himself a considerable creditor where he didn't wish to be.

When the party, headed by " Dot," entered the bar-room, they found no one there except " Fluke," and that individual sound asleep, stretched at full length on one of the benches. Twaddle thereupon undertook to tickle the nose of the slumbering man with a straw, when the sleeper awoke, and the tickler found every reason for rubbing a certain part of his body.

" Dot" now called for the drinks, and then proposed saying a few words regarding his arrival among them.

" A speech ! a speech !" was the cry ; and then "Dot," steadying himself with another " cooler," as he called it, commenced to launch forth in the most approved manner.

He spoke of the dramatic treat he had enjoyed. Spoke feelingly on oysters in general, and those at the supper in particular. He spoke in terms of the highest praise regarding the fair sex, whom he had seen in the audience that evening. He was going on to expatiate on the excellency of the Everling Hotel and of everything else in Red River, when "Fluke," who could not stand so much blarney, quickly knocked the stool from under the orator, and the indignant " Dot " found himself sprawling on the floor.

The shouting then commenced, until at last " Fluke " interfered by throwing Twaddle out of the door, and following it up by pitching "Dot " on top of him. The little editor of the *Buster* finding himself underneath, and in the dark, supposing that " Dot " was " Fluke " gave the unfortunate " Dot " a dot on the eye which dotted it for some days afterwards.

The party finding " Fluke " upon his muscle, and not wishing to get into his bad books, left the house, but before their departure, they struck up the song "We won't go home till morning." "Fluke," who really enjoyed a joke, immediately went and opened one of the upper windows of the house and there constituted himself the audience to this midnight concert.

"Dot" thinking it high time to be heard, now struck up a solo on his own account, as follows :

"Oh ! my eye Betty Martin, oh !"

Some of our readers may ask the question—"Where were the police all this time ?"

The reply is a simple one : In bed, of course, where all policemen generally are when they're wanted.

On the evening of the performance at the theatre, Tom Meredith took a short cut home, preferring to walk than drive. As he hastened along the bank of the river, he heard voices near him, one of which he at once recognized as belonging to Cool. Now, Tom had no great love for Cool, and feeling sure that some mischief was being hatched, or hoping to find out something about the George Wade affair, he stopped and cautiously approached the spot without being discovered. As soon as he could distinctly overhear what was being said, Tom found that the other speaker was Whirl. This fact confirmed the boy in his previous opinion that something bad was going on. It may seem strange that Tom entertained so much suspicion regarding those two men ; but it must be remembered that he had heard about the Harrican Farm business, and also he suspected that Cool was a secret enemy to George Wade.

" I tell you what it is," Tom overheard Whirl say, " I mean to wash my hands clean of this sort of business if you go on as you are doing. Suppose that man had been caught in the act, what would have been the consequence ? No ! no ! Cool, this sort of thing won't do."

" 'Pshaw !" said Cool.   " Things will turn out all right yet."

" I should like to see it a little more plainly than I do at present.   What have you gained by the Wade business?   Have you made anything out of the Merediths?   Then the Sharp affair ; have you done yourself or Sharp any good by it?   Then here's that last affair.   I tell you what it is, Cool, things won't work.   Already the 'Canadian' cry is looked upon with suspicion.   In fact, if you want me to win on the American dodge you are going the right way to work."

" I don't care a d——n," replied Cool, "so long as I hurt the Hudson Bay Company.   They've mistrusted me, and run me down, and hurt me in every way.   I will be revenged on them."

" You're doing them more good than harm," said Whirl, "by the course you are pursuing."

" Perhaps, amongst a few of the fools here ; but depend upon it, the influence of the *Buster* has great weight in Canada.   It is there I want to hurt the Company.   If the *Buster* was known abroad in the same light that it is here, it wouldn't be worth much ; but you see it isn't," said Cool ; " and, as long as I have any influence over Twaddle, I'm strong enough through the press."

" By the way," interrupted Whirl, " talking about the press, I see there is a bright representative of it lately arrived in the settlement."

" Oh yes," said Cool, " that fellow who is continually dotting everything down.   Both he and his companion seem asses of the first water.   But I must get hold of them—fool them—and make use of them ; and, by the way, I'm going to see old Mr. Meredith to-morrow, and try my hand with him again.   I can't afford to quarrel with him.   He'll be of use to me yet in Canada amongst his friends."

Here Tom suddenly rose from his hiding-place, and bawled out—"No, he won't; for I've heard all you said to-night, and I'll tell him when I get home."

With this the boy scampered away as fast as his legs could carry him; and true to his word, he immediately recounted all he had heard to his father.

"The scamp," muttered Mr. Meredith.   "Poor George!"

"The deuce take the brat; everything is up now between Meredith and me."

"Ha! ha! ha!" laughed Whirl.

"What are you laughing at?" asked Cool.

"Well, to tell you the truth, I was just thinking that I may be riding on the right horse and you on the wrong one."

"How so?" said Cool.

"Don't you remember having said to me that I was to go in strong for the American, while you were to act the Canadian champion.   Now you see every one of your schemes and plans seem to prove unsuccessful; and your Canadian cause, instead of gaining ground, is rapidly becoming more and more distaste-ful to people.   On the other hand, I am working along quietly, and I find a number of the settlers favor a union with the United States.   Would it not be very strange if Red River, af-ter all, would seek to join hands with Uncle Sam?"

"It isn't possible," exclaimed Cool, "for Canada would never permit it.   I tell you what it is, we are bound to become a part of the Dominion."

"That may be; but suppose the people of this country peti-tion to the contrary."

"They wouldn't be heard," said Cool.

"Perhaps so; but this I do know, that many of the old settlers think that annexation to the States would prove in the long run most beneficial to Red River.   However, a bargain is a bargain. Whoever wins is to divide the spoils with the other. I'm open to fat contracts, let them come from Uncle Sam or Canada, I don't care which. It seems to me very doubtful at present who is on the right horse."

"Deuce take that boy," thought Cool, as he and Whirl walked away. "I've lost the Merediths, anyway, and they could have been very useful to me."

CHAPTER XX.

E will now pay a visit to our old friend Flyaway, and see how he is getting on. The hunt on the plains up to the time we again meet Flyaway had not been very successful; but this was owing a good deal to the party not having reached their regular hunting ground. Flyaway depended more on his trading than on his hunting qualities; for, as we will presently see, he was not much of a hand at the chase.

After leaving Portage-la-Prairie, the regular rules of the camp were established; each captain had about ten men under him, and these took turn about in watching the camp at night. While the plain hunters are in motion, they are under the control of their guide, who carries a small flag. As soon as this emblem is lowered, the party immediately prepares to camp for the night. This is done by the carts being formed in a ring with the trams pointing outwards. Inside this ring or circular barrier, all the animals are driven for the night, and the tents are pitched outside, unless there is danger of an attack from Indians. As soon as camp is made, the chief holds his council, and the events of the past day discussed, as well as the programme for the morrow. Any crime or misdemeanour according to the regulations of the plains is tried, and the offender

punished, if found guilty. As soon as this is over and supper
finished, fun and frolic commences: the sound of fiddles can be
heard in almost every part of the camp. The hunter's life is
one composed altogether of extremes ; either he is full of ease
and gaiety, or subject to the greatest hardships. He is either
very rich or very poor ; indeed, it often happens that he is
reduced to utter starvation, and this arises solely from the im-
providence of his nature. About daylight in the morning, the
horses are let out from the corral to graze on the open prairie,
and about nine o'clock the flag is raised and the hunters start
on their journey. From the time that the flag is raised the
guides have sole control over the band ; but as soon as camp is
reached, the chief and his councillors assume the reins of government. The plain hunters know the route perfectly, and
although they submit altogether to the directions of their guide,
each man has a perfect knowledge of the locality he is in.
They generally manage to camp for the night near some lake,
river or pond, for the purpose of obtaining water for their animals as well as for themselves. As we have said before, the
band of which Flyaway was a member, had not reached their
regular hunting ground at the time we meet them. They had,
however, encountered buffalo, and enjoyed two or three successful runs after them. Flyaway had every reason to remember
his first buffalo hunt, as it was very nearly proving his last one.

It happened that the band came unexpectedly upon a herd
while *en route* ; immediately the cavalcade was stopped ; the
best runners were selected from amongst the horses, and the
hunters mounted. The chief now took charge of the band, and
directed their movements. First they approached the buffalo
at a slow trot, increasing their speed however as they came
nearer to the herd.

The latter, in the meantime, had faced round, and remained

watching the approach of the horsemen, as if in surprise at their appearance. A band of plain hunters usually keep together until the buffalo turn and take flight, then the word to start is given, and each rider makes a dash wherever he sees the best chance of obtaining shots that will pay. It was so in this instance ; the band had approached to within three or four hundred yards, when the bulls were observed to paw the ground and curve their tails. Immediately afterwards the whole herd took flight, and the hunters dashed away in hot pursuit. It was like the shock of an earthquake ; the ground literally trembled ; and the clouds of dust that arose, hid both riders and game from view ; but loud above the din could be heard shots in every direction in quick succession, showing that the slaughter was going on. As the dust cleared away, in the rear of the merciless hunters, the plain was strewn with the carcases of the buffalo killed in the chase.

The women and children left in charge of the train, now prepared to secure as much of the meat as could be saved before night fall ; as any left after dark becomes the prey of the wolves. The hunters, therefore, as soon as they had pursued the herd far enough for one day, halted and slowly returned in the direction of the carts.

Each man had now to pick out the carcases he had been fortunate enough to bring down, and this would appear to those unaccustomed to the plains, as next thing to an impossibility ; but so great is the experience amongst the hunters, that mistakes seldom occur in this way amongst them. Sometimes a novice will, as soon as he shoots his buffalo, throw some article beside it as a mark, but this is seldom or ever done amongst old plain hunters.

Immediately after the hunt, the skinning and cutting up process commences, and afterwards the women and children do the rest. The meat, when brought into camp, is cut into strips, and dried in the sun. It is then pounded into fine bits or crumbs by the women ; the tallow is melted down,—and meat and fat mixed up together. It is then packed away into bags made of buffalo hide, and allowed to harden. Each bag holds from 90 to 100 pounds of this preparation, known by the name of *pemmican* in the North-West. The dried meat is simply large slices cut from the buffalo, and dried in the sun.

Fine pemmican is made from the choice parts of the animal, and instead of the tallow, only the marrow from the bones is used. Sometimes a very fine article is made by mixing in a species of fruit known as the Pembina berry, with the marrow and meat. This is packed away in small bags, holding about ten or fifteen pounds each, and is called berry pemmican. When all the meat saved from a hunt is prepared in the way described above, the hunters continue on their journey until they once more encounter the buffalo, when the same routine again occurs.

One word more about the plain-hunters and their habits, before we relate the accident that befel poor Flyaway. The plain-hunters carry what is called the Nor'-West trading gun, which is nothing more nor less than the old flint-lock. A few -possess breech-loading rifles, but the generality of them are unable or unwilling to use them. When in full pursuit of the chase, the half-breed carries the balls in his mouth, and as he rides along, he pours into the barrel sufficient powder, and then, as he is prepared to fire, he drops in a ball without making use of any priming in the loading. Accidents sometimes occur from this mode of using firearms, as it happens occasionally that before the ball reaches half way down the barrel, it is pointed at and fired off. The consequence in such cases being an explosion, which not unfrequently maims the hunter for life. The half-breed is very quick, however, in handling his gun, and he seldom misses his mark, especially in the buffalo hunt.

The greatest snare in the path of the hunter, when he is in pursuit of the chase, is a badger-hole. It often happens that a rider will find himself thrown head formost to the ground, and his horse lying behind him, with perhaps a broken leg. These holes are not easily distinguished, especially when at full galop after a herd of buffalo, consequently the fall, when one does occur, is felt much more than if the danger could be foreseen.

Our readers can imagine how quick the hunter must be in his movements, when we tell them that he does not fire at the buffalo until within three or four yards from it ; and this when he is aware that the slightest error may draw upon him an attack from the infuriated animal, as the buffalo can see better sideways than straight forward, and therefore is prepared to take advantage of any mishap on the part of his pursuer, and frequently will make a sudden thrust at the horse, goring it, and very often killing the rider. A buffalo will seldom turn on its pursuer unless it is wounded or pressed too hard ; but when it does, let the hunter beware.

The horses used on the plains are generally trained for the purpose, and require no bridle to guide them in the chase, as they will invariably turn with the buffalo ; and it seldom happens that they are surprised. The hunter has only to attend to his gun, for his horse takes care of itself. These useful animals are called buffalo runners, and sometimes command a high price.

We have before stated that any meat left on the plains over night, becomes a prey to the wolves, which invariably follow the herd in large numbers. They are the sharks of the plains, always on the look out for a death to occur. A hunter there-

R

fore to them is like what a pestilence on board of a ship would be to the numerous sharks following in her wake.

The excitement of the chase often induces the hunters to extend their pursuit of the buffalo to a greater distance than there is any necessity for, and thus a great deal of good meat is lost. Had hunters restrained themselves, and only killed what they could take care of, the buffalo would not have become so scarce as they are now. We have heard, indeed, of some going out and killing animals merely for the sake of securing the tongues, leaving the rest of the carcase to rot or be devoured. It is a pity that some check has not been put upon this wanton waste, as we may expect to find buffalo meat a great rarity ere many years have passed ; and robes not to be had for love or money.

We must ask pardon of our readers for having kept them so long in the dark as to the fate of poor Flyaway, whom we left on the eve of his first buffalo hunt. When the riders mounted their horses, the doctor straddled the back of the nag purchased from Whirl. "Now," thought Flyaway, "I will try the mettle of the beast." While the band kept on a trot, the doctor got along finely, but as they began to go faster, he found himself gradually being left behind. The more the unfortunate Flyaway kicked at the ribs of his horse, the slower the animal seemed to go ; and finally, when the start was made, he found himself left all alone on the prairie, while his comrades were far away rushing along like mad.

"D—n you, Zerubabel ; get up." Zerubabel pricked up his ears and wagged his stump of a tail, that was all. At last a bright thought struck Flyaway ; pulling out a large pin from his coat, he managed to bury it nearly to the head in the side of poor Zerubabel. The consequence was a sudden increase of speed, which nearly left the doctor sitting on the grass.

Away went Zerubabel until Flyaway found himself in close proximity to the buffalo. Guiding his horse to the side of an old bull, which was leisurely galloping along, the doctor was in the act of lodging the contents of his gun into its side, when Zerubabel suddenly stumbled, his foot having caught in a badger-hole.

Away went the Doctor, and, unfortunately for him, he found himself lodged between the horns of the mad old bull. A second more, and the astonished man was turning a somersault in the air; the next, he was sitting on the grass, his legs at right angles, and his hair nearly on end; the buffalo in the meantime scampering off as if in great glee at what it had done.

"Oh, L—d!" muttered the terrified man, "what a bump."

Zerubabel in the meantime had risen to his feet, and stood watching his master from a distance.

"You're a horse, aint you?" said Flyaway; "you're an ass! I guess I'll trade; no more hunting for me," thought the satisfied sportsman; then taking a drink from his flask, which he invariably carried with him, he mounted his horse and slowly made his way back in the direction of the carts. When he arrived there he was met with a titter from the women and the jests of the young boys.

The plain hunters, on their return, had a good laugh at Flyaway's expense, and kept the joke up to such an extent, that at last the poor man resolved within himself to show them that he could hunt as well as them, the very next opportunity. Now we may mention here to our readers that one of the rules on the plains is, "That no person or party shall run buffalo before the general order;" and any infringement of this regulation is severely dealt with. The reason for this is that, were one or two to go out ahead of the rest, they would be the means of scattering the herd before the main body of hunters could come by, and thus spoil the hunt altogether, or make the chances of the main body very poor indeed. Were the buffalo to scatter before the hunters could reach within four or five hundred yards of them, there would be comparatively very few killed.

Flyaway, who felt nettled at the jokes and sneers of his comrades, made up his mind to break through the rules of the camp in this respect, and determined, the very first opportunity, to get ahead of the rest. Unfortunately, however, for him, he confided this resolution of his to our old friend Rossette, who, not to be outdone by the Doctor, went immediately to the chief and councillors and made known to them the plans of the unfortunate man.

Nothing was said, however, to Flyaway on the subject, until the next time they espied buffalo ahead. Then a council was held, and it was resolved that the Doctor should be taken and bound to one of the wheels of a cart, in full view of the chase. Accordingly Flyaway was waited upon by a couple of the plain hunters, who made known to him the decision of the council regarding him. The poor man expostulated, and vowed that it was all a joke of his ; that he never intended to carry his plan into operation ; but his protestations were unattended to, and he was dragged to the cart, where he was bound securely, as the council had determined.

Rosette was in high glee, and capered round the unfortunate man ; at times threatening to run away with the cart, and thus lead poor Flyaway a nice dance up and down. Then he would put his fingers up to his nose and laugh in Flyaway's face. These antics, however, on the part of Rosette disgusted the other hunters, and it was decided to let the doctor loose, which was immediately done. The liberated man vowing vengeance on Rosette, managed to mix a powerful emetic in his tea. Rosette was awfully sick. Flyaway had the laugh on his side now.

By the time that the band arrived at their regular hunting ground, or where they had resolved upon wintering, several of the hunters, Rosette amongst the rest, determined upon paying a visit to the settlement ; and after leaving their families housed for the winter, they started out on their return trip. Rosette was chosen chief of this party, and he having an object in view, induced an Indian from one of the tribes in the neighborhood to accompany him to Fort Garry.

" I will show you," he said to the savage, "how great a father I am, and how my children love me."

The Indian, who had a great respect for Rosette, therefore consented to go with the party.

Flyaway had made up his mind to pass the winter where he was, and could not therefore be induced to leave. Collecting as much pemmican, dried meat, tongues and sinews as they could, Rosette and his party set out on their return.

We have mentioned about pemmican and dried meat, but there are two other important parts of the buffalo preserved for market, and these are the tongue and sinews. Both are dried in the sun, the former being one of the delicacies of the North-West ; the latter being used when split up for sewing moccasins. It is the thread of the plains. The most delicious parts of the buffalo and those most prized by the hunters are the tongue and the hunch or lump above the shoulders.

There are what may be called two hunts on the plains, the summer and the winter one. At the former the meat only of the animals is preserved, the skins being useless on account of the scabby and short nature of the hair. Any robes caught then are rated out of season, and are next thing to worthless.

In the winter, the robes are collected and dressed for market, the fur being then long and thick.

Rosette's party, therefore, had no opportunity of bringing in any furs to the settlement ; but they brought in an abundance of provisions.   Pemmican sold at that time for 6d. per lb., and dried meat for 4d., in Fort Garry.

We will now say good-bye to Flyaway for a time, merely mentioning that true to the prediction of Cool and Whirl, he was running through his property as fast as he could—the cause being his old enemy, drunkenness.   We will therefore follow Rosette in his visit to the settlement.

Nothing of importance occurred on the way, until they reached the neighborhood of Fort Garry.   It happened that Rosette was fortunate enough in his plans regarding the Indian to reach the settlement about Christmas time.   He therefore timed himself so that he and his dusky companion should arrive at Fort Garry on the night of the 25th.   As the cunning hunter and his uncivilized dupe strode along past the houses of the settlers, he would say—

" There ! these are my children ; all these are my lodges.   I am a great chief," and the Indian would wonder.   As they came to the Red River, opposite St. Boniface, the bells of the cathedral commenced chiming.

" There," said Rosette, " my children know that I am coming, and they are glad.   Come with me, and I will show you how they honour their father."

They then crossed over upon the ice, and approached the church just as the organ pealed forth its grand tones, preparatory to the celebration of the midnight mass.

Rosette watched his opportunity, and entered the church just as the people were kneeling at prayer, and, pointing out this to the Indian at his side, he whispered,—

" There, my son, you see how my children honour their father."

The poor untutored savage was awe-stricken at the sight before him. The brilliancy of the altar dazzled his senses, while the deep tones of the organ thrilled through his very soul. Rosette was cunning enough, however, not to remain too long in the church, and therefore soon left, accompanied by the Indian ; and, fearing lest the truth might leak out, he hurried his dusky friend away from the neighbourbood of Fort Garry that very night.

" Go back," he said, " to your lodges, and tell your chief and your great men how big a father I am, and how my children honour and respect me. Many suns will not pass ere I will be with you, and my hands will not be empty."

He then presented the Indians with some food and tobacco, and sent him back the way he came.

" There," he thought, " they will say what a great chief Rosette is, and I'll make a good trade when I go back to the plains."

It was well for the cunning hunter that the savage did return immediately, for had he waited another day, he would have had the opportunity of seeing Rosette in anything but an honorable position, as we will presently see.

It may seem strange that the Indian would consent to start on his return during the night ; but it is characteristic of the race to prefer being abroad at night to the daytime.

Rosette, as soon as the Indian had started on his journey, returned to the cathedral, and remained there till the end of the service. This was somewhat unfortunate for him, as he happened to meet the son of the man whose haystacks he had set fire to. But of this hereafter.

St. Boniface Cathedral is a large stone building, which, at

the time of our story, was in an unfinished state. Adjoining were the Bishop's Palace, the Nunnery, and the College, all good substantial buildings ; indeed the church property at St. Boniface is a very valuable one, and creditable to the settlement.

Rosette, the next morning, found himself in rather a bad box, for he fell into the clutches of the law. It appears that the son of the man whose haystacks had been fired by Rosette, informed his father that he had seen the hunter at church. A warrant was therefore issued for his arrest, and Rosette was lodged in jail to answer to the charge.

On being taken before the magistrate for examination, the plain hunter pleaded his sorrow for his crime, and promised, if allowed to go at liberty, to leave the settlement. The magistrate being very glad to get rid of a troublesome as well as a dangerous character, agreed to accept bail ; and it being found in the persons of two men who feared Rosette, the cunning hunter was set at liberty, on the understanding that he should start for the plains the next day.

This Rosette managed to do, after obtaining a small outfit from one of the merchants, who gave it so as to get rid of the man.

It would have been well for poor Flyaway, had this unscrupulous man been kept a prisoner during the rest of the winter.

CHAPTER XXI.

HILE "Dot it Down" was confined to his room from the effects of his debauch at the Everling Hotel, he being too much of a dandy to be seen outside with a couple of black eyes, he received a visit from our friend Cool.

"Dot" was lying on his bed, smoking a short clay pipe, and reading the latest *Buster*, when Cool walked in and introduced himself.

"I heard you had arrived," he said "so I have taken the liberty, as well as of doing myself the pleasure, of calling and making your acquaintance."

"Haw! thank you; I'm hardly in proper shape to receive a stranger. You see a confounded fool of a fellow dropped upon me last night."

"Drop black, I should say," laughingly replied Cool.

"Haw! very good—yes! but it is too bad, is'nt it? My first appearance in Red River."

"Oh! that is nothing," said Cool; "I'll soon get your eyes painted, and nobody will know that anything is the matter with you. You come direct from Canada, I believe? Anything new going on there?"

"Very little; same old humdrum way as usual."

"It is a paradise to this place, my dear sir," interrupted Cool.

"Haw! I dare say," said "Dot."

"We are working hard here, you see," remarked Cool, pointing at the same time to the *Buster*. "Canada has many friends in Red River."

I have come up here," said "Dot," "as a very great friend of Canada."

"Indeed!" exclaimed Cool; "then allow me to shake hands with you on that. You are connected with the press, I believe?"

"Haw! yes, somewhat," replied "Dot;" "scribble a little, you see, sometimes; not much of a hand though."

"Too modest," said Cool; "your appearance belies that statement. To tell you the truth, you are exactly the man we want."

"Haw! indeed."

"Yes," said Cool, "we want some one of influence to strike a death blow at that great monopoly, the Hudson Bay Company."

"Then I am the man," exclaimed "Dot;" "for I know all about that from the time of the charter down to the present day. I've made it a study."

"Capital! capital!" said Cool, "just the man for us. Do you know Twaddle?"

"A little," replied "Dot;" "it was he who gave me these black eyes."

"Impossible, surely."

"You see the proof before you. Twaddle is the little fellow who does this, eh? (holding up the *Buster*.) Well, it was he who fell upon me."

Cool laughed. "Surely," he said, "there must be some mistake somewhere, Twaddle couldn't hurt a fly."

"He weighs over a hundred pounds," remarked "Dot,"
"and he fell upon me."

"Well, we'll not say anything more about it. I'm sure
Twaddle is sorry for it. But what do you intend to do with
yourself this winter ?"

"Haw ! take it easy of course. See the country and people, and then dot them down."

"Well, sir, I hope you will command me whenever you see
fit. I'm at your service ; I'll do anything for the sake of Canada."

"Generous man," thought "Dot."

Cool now rose to take his leave, after pressing a very urgent
invitation upon "Dot" to come over and spend a quiet evening with him.

"Dot" and Cool became fast friends from that day forward.

During the winter in Red River, gaiety is the order of the
day. There is so little going on in the way of business, that
the settlers, to pass the time, enjoy themselves to the best of
their ability. Dancing parties are of nightly occurrence, and
all the weddings take place during the winter months. Indeed,
a marriage is generally delayed until a large hop can be given
at the same time. Weddings in Red River are no trifling affairs. We have known them to be kept up for three successive
days and nights. The dances peculiar to Red River, are so
spirited as a general thing, that they make the parties, as a
usual thing, very pleasant and agreeable.

A few nights after the visit of Cool to "Dot," the latter received an invitation for himself and friend, to a dance, to be
given in the house of one of the most respectable settlers.
"Dot" took the liberty of accepting, not only for himself, but
also for his friend whom we met with him at the theatre.
"Dot" promised himself a great deal of fun at this party, as

we can judge from a conversation overheard between him and his friend.

"We're in luck," said "Dot," "and will have a good chance to see the natives in their social relations towards each other. I wonder what the girls are like ?"

" You're always raving about the opposite sex," said the other; " you'll some day or other get yourself into trouble with them."

"Haw ! not I, my dear fellow ; they adore me, the dear creatures. I have such a sweet manner about me, they say."

"Come ! come ! "Dot," none of that ; you're going ahead too fast altogether."

"Haw ! do you think so ? Well, I've no doubt I'll have little trouble in captivating some fair descendant of the redman. There, that is'nt a bad way of describing a half-breed. Very good ; sending me an invitation, eh ? Never saw my would-be-entertainers ; heard about me, I've no doubt ; but, my dear fellow, I'm sure we'll enjoy ourselves—lots to look at—lots to laugh at,—and lots to dot down."

The dancing party was given by one of the most respectable settlers in Red River, and he had invited " Dot" and his friend from a feeling of consideration toward a couple of strangers coming to a new country. Had it been known how lightly " Dot" valued the kindness, it is very doubtful whether he or his friend would have been included amongst the guests of the evening. However, " Dot" and his friend went, and we will endeavour to describe their behaviour on this occasion.

About six o'clock in the evening, a party of pleasure seekers, " Dot" amongst the rest, assembled at the residence of Mr. Bon, preparatory to starting for the house where the dance was to take piace. " Dot" was in his element, and without much ceremony, introduced himself right and left amongst the ladies, in the hope of obtaining a partner for the drive.

But alas ! he found that the fair ones did not value him as much as he valued himself.   They were neither impressed with the fact of his being a newspaper correspondent, ncr with the idea of leaving their friends for the sake of driving with a perfect stranger.

" Dot" thought this very hard, and began to form the opinion that the ladies of Red River were not too susceptible as he had imagined them to be.   He, thereferc resigned himself to his fate, and instead of a lady, he drove his friend to the party.

The gentleman who was giving the dance lived about ten miles from Fort Garry, so that some of the invited guests had to drive quite a long distance.   "Dot," unfortunately, had a very poor horse, and was consequently left far behind ; and as it began to snow, he at last lost the proper road altogether, and found himself in rather an awkward predicament.

" Dot this down," groaned his friend, from beneath the robes.   " We'll never see daylight again."

" What a heathenish country," muttered " Dot," " going ten miles to a dancing party in a night like this.   Oh ! L—d, I wish I was at home.   Whoa ! you beast, can't you find the road ?   There we go ! "

And away they went at that moment, all in a heap, to the bottom of a ditch.

" Where are you ?" cried " Dot," to his friend, as he regained his feet.

" Here, what there is left of me," came in smothered tones from beneath the overturned sleigh.

" Dot " immediately righted their conveyance, and discovered his friend, all in a heap amongst the robes.   The horse, fortunately, had not moved after he fell, and no scrious accident had occurred.   " Dot's " friend, however, insisted upon returning home.

"I wish you would show me the way." This was a puzzler, and both the discomforted men were giving up in despair, when they heard the sound of sleigh bells rapidly approaching them.

"Hist !" said "Dot."

"Do you think they will run into us ?" whispered his friend.

"Keep quiet," said "Dot," "they'll hear you."

"I wish they would," was the reply.

"I mean," returned "Dot," "I want to hear them."

"I'll make them hear us," said his friend, and with that he shouted out at the top of his voice.

Nearer and nearer came the approaching sleigh ; and, at last, when it was about passing them, "Dot" roared out, "Help ! for God's sake."

The stranger, who turned out to be none other than Cool, pulled up and replied, "Who are you ? and where are you ?"

"Stranger in a strange land," shouted "Dot." "We're in a quandary."

"You're more likely to be in a ditch."

"You're right this time," cried "Dot's" friend ; "but can't you help us out ? We're going to a dance, and a pretty dance we've had of it already."

Cool now alighted, and, coming up to our unfortunate party-goers, he recognized "Dot" at once.

"Hilloa, here's where you are."

"Yes !" said "Dot," "we've been here some time."

"Very unlucky," said Cool ; "but we'll soon put you all right. There," he continued, after arranging matters for them, "follow me, I know the road, and we have not far to go."

Thanks to Cool's guidance, our two friends at last found themselves at the party, where they both soon forgot their adventure in the hilarity of the evening.

In one apartment, in front of a large, open log fire, sat a number of gentlemen, old fogies chiefly, talking over the events of the day. This was the refreshment and smoking room, and to it Cool conducted "Dot" and his friend. A glass of what was thought to be wine was poured out for "Dot," which he immediately swallowed at one mouthful; but, alas, it turned out to be raw brandy, and the unfortunate man sputtered and gasped in an agony of torture. The old fogies started to their feet, thinking the man had taken a fit, until it was explained that he had taken brandy, supposing it to be wine. The tears streamed down "Dot's" cheeks. "Do—do—do you call—call that wine?" he managed to say. "If so its—its dev—d——h strong."

Cool laughed heartily; but it was no joke for poor "Dot," and, as it turned out afterwards, was the means of getting him into serious trouble; the fact of the matter being, that the liquor went to his head.

The host now presented himself, and led the way into the dancing room, when "Dot," who had partly recovered from his unfortunate mistake, began to ingratiate himself with the ladies. It was noticed, however, that his manner became very strange, and at last it became quite plain that he was slightly elevated.

Now there is a dance in the North-West, peculiar to the country, called the Red River jig, which is as follows: A gentleman leads a lady to the middle of the floor, and at the sound of the fiddle the pair begin to dance to each other, in a regular break-down manner. This lasts until either the gentleman or the lady is relieved by one of their own sex. The second couple continue until they also give place for others, and so on this almost endless dance continues until the fiddler gives in.

"Dot," ever ready to undertake anything that offered, managed to get a partner for this description of dance, and the gentlemen, for mischief, determined to allow him full scope for his legs. The fiddler, entering into the spirit of the joke, played his liveliest tunes. When his lady partner became tired, her place was taken by another, and so on; still no gentleman offered to relieve "Dot." The unfortunate man danced away in utter desparation, while the perspiration streamed down his face, until at last his legs began to bend under him; but to his credit, be it said, he did not give in, although towards the end of the jig he could hardly shuffle along the floor. Finally the fiddler, out of pity for the poor fellow, stopped, and "Dot" sank back exhausted to a seat. He was, however, highly complimented for his pluck, and the fair ones began to form a very favourable opinion of him; but, as we will presently see, his laurels were of short duration, as he got himself into serious trouble and disgrace before the end of the party.

It happened, unfortunately for "Dot," that he held a very high opinion of himself, especially so far as it concerned his literary powers; and he was not at all backward in fishing for compliments. Finding himself, therefore, something in the light of a hero, after his jig, he took advantage of the impression he had made, by showing several ladies a good deal of attention; one in particular attracted his particular notice, so much so, that the lady in question felt annoyed at him. Unfortunately "Dot" had partaken of several glasses of wine since the mishap with the brandy, and the consequence was that he began at last to feel muddled. About this time he happened to be sitting in a corner of the room in close conversation with the young lady to whom he had taken such a violent fancy.

"Haw!" (hic) he said, "what a lucky dog am I, to be in

such an (hic) enviable position. What pleasure it gives me to be able to sing the praises of the Red River belles in their primitive (hic) loveliness! Ah me! I will represent them on the banks of the winding streams—their wigwams beautifully (hic) sit-situated beneath the noble, spreading branches (hic) of the stately oak; their (hic) flowing tresses will (hic) —— Haw! my dear!" Here followed a huge wink, and then the loud report of a hard slap could have been heard across the room, and "Dot" realized, as well as he could at the time, that it was no joke making fun of the Red River ladies, for his cheeks burned and his eyes blinked from the effects of the blow administered by the indignant girl.

"There," she said, as she rose from her seat, "take that for your pains. It may not be very lady-like of me to do it, but it is thoroughly deserved by you."

"Dot" was amazed; he had not bargained for anything of the sort, and as he slunk away from the room he muttered, "Haw! sharp that (hic)."

One of the greatest drawbacks to Red River parties are the smoking rooms; there the gentlemen congregate together, cards are indulged in, and drinking is kept up continually. The consequence is that the ladies very frequently find themselves neglected, and the gentlemen become more or less unable to attend to their duties as the protectors of the fair sex.

"Dot it down," on being repulsed in the dancing room, immediately repaired to the smoking room, and there endeavoured to hide his injured feelings in the flowing bowl. He succeeded admirably, so much so that he persisted in talking a vast amount of rubbish, to the utter disgust of those present. His friend, therefore, finding him in this state, endeavoured to induce him to start for home, but all to no purpose. "Dot" was now resolved upon having "a bully time," as he expressed

S

it. He therefore insisted upon giving the company a few choice songs, and wound up by endeavouring to show his activity in athletic sports. The latter, however, proved the finishing touch to his evening's performance, for in trying to stand upon his head, his heels came in contact with the table, overturning it, and dashing wine glasses, tumblers and decanters in a heap upon the floor. This was too much for even Cool, and before "Dot" could recover from his surprise at what had happened, he found himself in his sleigh, on his road home, his friend, however, acting the part of Jehu this time.

The next day Cool and Whirl met, and the former related to the latter the events of the previous evening. "That "Dot" is a deuce of a fellow," he said, in great glee. "He kept the party in an uproar during the whole of the evening. If you look upon him as an acquisition to your cause, then I don't envy you."

"Just the man," said Cool. "He'll get himself into such disgrace with the people, before long, that he'll in self-defence cry them down abroad, and go in heavy for new-comers. That is one part of my game, to advocate immigration to this country, and swamp the settlers by it. We don't want Canadians and half-breeds to go together; one must fall behind; and if I can help to do it, the people here must be the ones to give way."

"Well," said Whirl, "you are on dangerous ground ; but you know your own plans best. We're on different tacks ; but its no matter who wins after all."

"Not a bit ; we'll make money out of it anyway."

Whirl felt very much inclined to be disgusted at Cool, and inwardly resolved to part company with him the first opportunity. He had some little respect for himself ; besides which, he did not see anything to be gained by Cool's wild schemes.

We will now turn our attention to Twaddle's "Den," as he called his office. There we will find "Dot it Down" in close confab with the little editor.

"Haw," said Dot; "hard at work, my dear Twaddle. Anything fresh for the *Buster*, this time? What are you up to this week? The old story, eh? Hudson Bay Company?"

"There's nothing else to talk about," said Twaddle.

"Why don't you write up annexation?" asked "Dot."

"So I do," replied Twaddle; "but I haven't made up my mind altogether whether it is to be in favor of Canada or the States. I favor the former somewhat, but you see it is well to have two strings to your bow."

"Haw! yes, of course; but you see I'm here to do all I can to upset the Hudson Bay Company, and bring in Canada; so you must, if you wish to be friends with me, renounce all ideas regarding Americanism, and go hand and glove with the Canadians."

"Well, you see," replied Twaddle, "it is a very difficult thing to edit a paper in Red River at present, especially when you depend upon it for your bread and butter; for if a fellow says too much against the Company, he offends the greater portion of his subscribers, and the trouble is, one has nothing else to write about in this blessed country. Then at the present time Canadians are not viewed with any great amount of respect in the settlement, so it is uphill work advocating their cause. It is also a useless thing preaching Americanism; so what is a fellow to do? If he were to praise up the Hudson Bay Company, people would be sure to find fault with the great monoply."

"Haw! then why the d——l don't you praise up the Company?"

"I could'nt do it, for I hate all connected with it."

"My dear Twaddle," said "Dot," "you are not made for an editor. Now, you see, instead of firing away helter-skelter at the Company, you ought to butter them up, now and again, until you find them out ; then come down on them sharp. It will have an effect ; but when you keep pegging away at the same old thing, people get tired of hearing you. You will see how I will manage them. In the first place, I mean to go down and try to get on good terms with all the officers at the Fort, from the Governor downwards. Of course, at the same time I will show them that I know a great deal about them, and thus I will learn more. When I have got all out of them that I can, I will turn round and show them up. You'll see how I'll get along. Haw! Twaddle, you've got to learn ; but I'll help you sometimes.   You'll improve after a while."

In this complacent way "Dot" talked Twaddle into the idea that the *Buster* was going altogether the wrong way, and very likely to "bust" indeed ; and still the poor little editor could not see his way towards any change for the better. The truth was, his inveterate enmity to the Hudson Bay Company stood in his way ; and "Dot" was so far right in saying that he allowed this animosity to be too apparent, and the settlers therefore could not look upon it except as a personal affair between Twaddle and the H. B. C., and not as a matter that interested the settlement at large.

"Dot it Down," after leaving the *Buster* office, repaired to his room, and there he concocted a letter for his newspaper in Canada, running down the Red River people, socially, morally, and politically speaking ; this, too, at the very time when he was receiving attentions and kindness at their hands, Such is gratitude ; but we will have more to say regarding "Dot's" correspondence ere we close our story ; and, in the meantime, we will turn our attention to another scene.

Cool, having made up his mind to make a friend of "Dot," extended to that personage the hospitality of his house whenever he choose to accept of it.

"Dot," on an occasion, having imbibed a little more than was good for him, presented himself at the door of Cool's house, and rapped loudly for admittance. Mrs. Cool, who happened to be alone in the house, answered the summons herself.

"Dot," who was in a very jolly humor indeed, expressed the great pleasnre he felt at seeing her,—

"Haw ! my dear Mrs. Cool, I did not expect (hic) to have this (hic) pleasure."

" I cannot say that I am very glad to see you in you present state," replied the good lady. "You ought to be ashamed of yourself."

"Not at all, my dear Mrs. Cool. All great men (hic) enjoy the pleasures of the (hic) flowing bowl."

" I hope you do not include yourself in the same category ?"

" Of course," said the indomitable "Dot," " special cor-cor-correspondent ? Why not, eh ? (hic.)"

" I think, sir, you had better return the way you came, for on no account can you enter here."

" My dear Mrs. Cool, think of the sorrows of a poor young man. Just a few moments' delightful (hic) intercourse with your delightful self, and—haw, (hic) dem me."

The latter exclamation was caused by finding the door quickly shut in his face by the indignant Mrs. Cool.

" The beast," she muttered, " if Cool insists upon bringing such wretches to the house I'll leave. I want to see my husband get along, but why does'nt he gather some decent people around him, instead of such characters as generally come here."

Ah ! Mrs. Cool, birds of a feather flock together.

Notwithstanding the behaviour of "Dot" at the party in

Red River, he continued to receive invitations from the hospitable settlers, who did everything in their power to make his stay amongst them pleasant and comfortable. We find him therefore one evening at a dinner party in a gentleman's house. Great pains had been taken by the host to prepare a creditable repast on the occasion. Several of the prominent men in the settlement were invited to meet the correspondent and his friend, and there was every reason to expect a pleasant evening.

The dinner passed off very well, "Dot," however, carrying on the principal part of the conversation, chiefly in sounding his own praise, &c., &c. "Dot's" friend said very little, being a man of few words, with, moreover, a great respect for "Dot's" fund of learning ; he consequently felt somewhat fluttered in expressing himself before the great correspondent. After dinner a quiet rubber of euchre was proposed, and a couple of sets were immediately formed. "Dot" insisted on playing for stakes, although it was objected to by several in the room.

The Nor-Wester's are generally ready and willing to risk at cards when an opportunity occurs ; not that we mean to say that they are all a set of gamblers, but cards when money is at stake seem to have a peculiar charm for them. "Dot," therefore, found that he had old hands to deal with, and when he rose from the table he was several pounds sterling poorer than when he commenced. After the game of euchre, "Dot" nearly got himself into serious trouble, for he was discovered by the hostess in the kitchen making violent love to one of the domestics belonging to the house ; a pretty girl be it said, to "Dot's" credit as a connoisseur.

"I fear you have made a mistake, sir," said the lady of the house. "This is the kitchen."

" Haw ! yes, deuce take it ; but what's the odds. I am travelling for information."

"Surely not in the culinary way," replied the hostess, smiling.

" Not particular, my dear madam, anything now-a-days will satisfy the public taste in Canada. I should like to describe how you people live ; that will be interesting I am sure ; besides," he continued, "this little dear," (chucking the girl under the chin.

" If you have no more respect, sir, for me in my own house than to make love to one of my servants before my face, I will call my husband. You had better, I think, join your friends in the sitting room."

" Deuce take the people in Red River," muttered "Dot," " they are confoundly particular about trifles." With this he left the kitchen.

" Dear me," said the lady, " if this is the way new-comers are going to behave themselves, I don't want to see any of them here again."

The party soon afterwards broke up, and " Dot " repairing to the hotel, found there a jovial set of fellows ready for any sort of fun. "Fluke" still reigned in Earling's place, and on this occasion he appeared for the first time in his life overcome by the spirits which it was his duty to serve out to the public. In one corner of the billiard room sat a party of " jolly dogs " round a table, intent over a game of poker. " Dot," rankling over his recent loss at euchre, resolved upon joining in the game, hoping thereby to improve his fortunes. But, alas ! there seemed to be nothing but ill-luck in store for him; the more he played the more he lost, until at last he was what is called " dead broke."

By the time he had reached this stage he was in a state of reckless indifference, and had he not been prevented by his

friend, would have borrowed from anyone willing to lend. The
end of all this was that "Dot" hid his affliction in the wine
cup, until at last he was carried up to bed in a helpless state of
drunkenness.

The next day, as soon as his headache would permit, he concocted his second letter to Canada, in which he gave a minute
description of the dinner party of the previous evening; what
was on the table ; who were there ; and it is a wonder he did
not state how much they ate. He, however, neglected to give
the scene in the kitchen, and also the one in the Everling
Hotel ; and concluded his letter by stating to the people of
Canada that the people of Red River lived pretty well after all ;
that in fact they could boast of other luxuries besides pemmican and dried meat ; a thing, of course, to be wondered at in the
opinion of " Dot." Those who happened to be at the dinner
party were described minutely, and it was shown as an extraordinary fact, that they could talk on many subjects with ease
and fluency, hardly to be expected from Red River people.
All this was meant, no doubt, by " Dot " as a compliment to
the settlers ; but it was given in such a left-hand manner, that
it was regarded more in the light of an insult than anything
else.

The gentleman who had shown the hospitality to " Dot " on
that particular occasion, when he afterwards read in the public
papers of Canada a description of his household affairs, felt
highly indignant at the outrage, and resolved to be more careful in the future when asking strangers to dine with him.

CHAPTER XXII.

HE great disadvantage under which many farmers in Red River labor, is the want of proper firewood. It frequently happens that a settler has to go a distance of fifteen or twenty miles to procure wood enough for the ordinary use of the house. As immigrants begin to take up the land this want will be more and more felt. So far, the great desire on the part of the settlers seems to have been to take their farms along the river side ; this gives them a better chance to obtain wood and water, than if they were out on the plains. But as the country becomes more settled, it will have to be divided into townships or counties, and what is open prairie now, will then be cut up into roads, farms, and so forth. The great want then will be wood, not only for burning, but also for fencing ; and it will happen that farmers, to supply themselves, will have to go to great distances from home.

It is our opinion that a great deal of fine land can be had away from the river side ; and we are aware that thousands of acres are lying waste for want of cultivation ; we say, therefore, to our readers, come ; never mind if you cannot get a farm near the river, take it out on the prairie. Dig your wells for water, and by a little extra exertion, you can obtain your firewood by drawing it from a distance. This will be about the only drawback that we are aware of; and what is it, after all, in comparison to the rich land you will possess, and the little trouble you will have in cultivating it.

We would here suggest a plan to be adopted on prairie farms, which we think might answer very well in place of fence rails. First, put in posts round your field, fifteen feet apart, then take strong wire and stretch it in say four or five rows, passing it through holes made in the posts for the purpose. This would make a more durable, neat, and less expensive fence than by using rails, when the latter are so scarce as they are in Red River.

But to return to our story, Mr. Meredith found that the Harrican Farm had little timber or woodland on it, and he therefore was obliged to send about fifteen miles to obtain the necessary fuel for the house. One cold morning, therefore, Jack and Tom (the former being on a visit from Grosse Isle), started about three o'clock, with four oxen and sleds, for the purpose of procuring a supply of wood. It was a cold trip for the two boys; but they were hardy lads and did not think much about it.

As soon as they reached the spot where they were to take the wood from, they commenced cutting down the small trees, none of which were over a foot in diameter. They were just about finishing their last sled load, when Tom, hearing the sound of bells, turned his head and saw a couple of dog trains coming along at full speed toward where he stood. Both boys stood looking at this, to them, novel sight, when the man who was driving the foremost train shouted out,—

"Hillo Jack! hillo Tom! what on earth brings you here? Don't you know me, boys?"

At first neither Jack nor Tom recognized the person who thus addressed them; but when they heard the voice they knew it to belong to George Wade.

"Hillo! George," they shouted back, "is that you? We're right glad to see you. We're out cutting wood for the house."

"How are all at home?" asked George, a shade of anxiety passing across his features.

"Father and mother are well," replied Jack, "and Grace, she's not been very well of late, George. I am so glad you've come back."

"Yes," and said Tom, "you've got to go right home with us. Father's a different man now, and he's sorry that he used you as he did. That Cool has turned out a regular rogue."

"I thought he would," returned George; "but," he continued, "what has caused your father to change his mind about me? Has he found out anything regarding that unfortunate affair?"

"No," said Jack, "not that I am aware of; but he sees now that Cool is a rogue, and he begins to think that he was too ready believing him about you."

"And then, George, Gracie has never been herself since then. Poor Gracie!" and the boys' eyes filled with tears.

"I tell you what it is, George," said Tom, "if anything happens to our Gracie, I think I'll kill that Cool."

"Hush!" said Jack, "it won't be as bad as that."

"What do you mean," exclaimed George. "You are speaking in riddles; surely nothing has happened to Gracie, tell me boys?"

"She hasn't been well of late, George, and—and you'll find her very much changed. Oh! I'm so glad you've come back."

"So am I, George," added Tom, "if it isn't too late."

"Too late," almost gasped George. "Why boys tell me the truth. Is she in danger?"

"We won't say that yet," said Jack. "She is very low, but I have not given up hope."

"Oh ! my God, this is hard ! hard !" and George Wade sobbed like a child.   Heaven forgive me I did what I thought was right."

"So you did, George," said both boys at once.   " We don't blame you at all."

"You see," continued Jack, "your being away worried Gracie ; and then she took a severe cold which caused a fever ; so what with sickness and low spirits, she has wasted away a good deal.   She's so quiet now ; she was always good, George, but now she's just like an angel, and then she speaks so often about you.   I'm sure now that you've come back she'll get better.

" I pray God she may," added George.

The boys now proposed that Wade should accompany them, and send his man ahead with the two trains of dogs.   This he agreed to do, having a deep anxiety to see Grace.

"You'd better not come right to the house," suggested Tom. " You can stay at Jack Harrican's till we break the news at home.   It might be too much for Gracie."

The trains now went on ahead, while George remained with the boys ; who, as soon as the last load of wood was finished, started on their return home.   As they walked slowly along, George and the two boys continued their conversation.

"You would have been sorry for poor mother, she's had so much of worry," said Jack.

" I am sure from what you tell me about Grace that Mrs. Meredith has had a great deal of trouble."

"And father," added Tom, " I am sure he would have given worlds to have had you back again soon after you left."

" He did everything for the best.   Are you sure he's never heard anything more about the affair ?"

"I am sure of it, for I have heard him say that although

there is as much mystery about you as ever, he is sorry that he ever believed anything against you."

In this way they talked as they walked along, and when they reached Jack Harrican's house, George remained there.

At the same time he sent a request by the boys to Mr. Meredith to come and see him.

When Jack and Tom reached home, it was late in the evening, and they found their father anxiously looking for their return. As soon as they entered the house, they called Mr. Meredith out, under the pretext of showing him their loads, and the first words they uttered, were—

"Father we've seen George Wade."

"Thank Heaven," was the reply. "Where is he ? Why did you not bring him to the house ?"

"We did'nt like to," said Jack; "for we thought it might be too great a surprise for Gracie."

"You are right," replied Mr. Meredith, " but I thank God that George has come. Where is he now ? Do you know?"

"Yes; we left him at Jack Harrican's place ; and he sent word by us that he wishes to see you."

"I'll go immediately, and you can say in the house that I have gone over to Harrican's on business."

As Mr. Meredith walked over to see George Wade, he recalled the time when he went to St. Boniface to demand the explanations. How deeply he regretted the course he had taken at that time, and how he almost cursed Cool for having thrown so much unhappiness into his family. The more he thought of George Wade's conduct from the first time he met him, the more he respected the young man, for he could not bring to remembrance one single act on Wade's part in the slightest way dishonourable. He could not but feel puzzled at the stories he had heard about him, for George never denied

them.   He only said that he was not guilty of the acts imputed
to him, but was prevented from giving any further explanation
regarding them.   It was, therefore, with a strange feeling of
doubt and uncertainty as to the reception he would receive
from George, that Mr. Meredith went over to see him.

George, in the meantime, felt very anxious, after what he
had heard from the boys, and waited for the appearance of Mr.
Meredith with impatience.   When, therefore, the old gentleman
knocked at the door, George hastened to open it, and immediately extended his hand.   Mr. Meredith was very much
overcome by this act, as well as by the sight of George.

"God bless you, Wade," he exclaimed ; " can you forgive a
poor old man ?"

" I have nothing to forgive," replied George ; " indeed I
have been the cause of much trouble to you.   But won't you
come in ? Mr. Harrican has placed his sitting room at our disposal, and we can talk there much better than here."

Mr. Meredith then entered, and as soon as he found himself alone with George, he said, " I have come over to ask you
to forget, if you can, all that has happened between us.   I was
too hasty, too unfeeling, but I thought I was doing my duty.
Alas ! I have discovered, to my cost, that one should not be
too ready to condemn the faults of others."

" Mr. Meredith," said George, " it was very hard for me to
refuse your request when you visited me at St. Boniface.   I
knew or felt that I was sealing my own doom, but I could not
do otherwise.   I have always been taught to respect a promise
once made ; and although I could have given you a perfectly
satisfactory explanation of what you heard about me, yet by
doing so I would have been obliged to sacrifice an old and good
friend of mine.   The consequences of all this, however, is
dreadful.   Poor Grace ; the boys have told me all."

Mr. Meredith bowed his head upon his arms. "Do not speak of it," he sobbed ; "may God grant that your return is not too late."

"Can I see her to-night," eagerly asked George.

"I think," said Mr. Meredith, "that you had better allow me to break the news to her gently at first, and in the morning I will come over for you. She is not strong now, George. You will see a great change in her."

"Oh ! Mr. Meredith," said George, "if you only knew what a miserable time I have spent since I left for the interior, you would pity me. The thought of Grace has been ever in my mind, and I have been haunted with a presentiment of evil happening to her ; this, too, with no chance of obtaining any news from the settlement."

"My poor boy ! my poor Grace ! Indeed, George, I am a miserable old man."

Wade now sought to turn Mr. Meredith from his sad thoughts ; but he could not succeed, and at last they separated.

We will follow Mr. Meredith, and leave George to pass a sleepless night of extreme anxiety and anguish of mind.

Grace Meredith was sitting in bed, propped up with pillows, when her father entered the room.

"Well, my girl, how do you feel to-night ?"

"I think I am a little better, father ; my spirits feel lighter. I am sure there is some good news in store for me coming very soon. Do you know I believe God often grants us a foreshadowing of either good or evil as it may be. I wonder if my prayers will be answered ? I have prayed so earnestly, father."

"God has promised to give to those who ask and believe," said Mr. Meredith.

"Then surely he will grant my prayer. Oh ! father, if

George should return, wouldn't you allow him to come and see me ?"

"Gracie, I would give worlds if he were here at this moment. Will you ever forgive me for my cruelty towards you?"

" Do not speak in that way, father ; I never blamed you. Bad men poisoned your mind against my George. Do you think he ever will come back. I know this is foolish, and perhaps wrong, but he is so dear to me. You know, father, I love you all at home as much as ever, but I have you with me. George seems lost to me ; and oh ! it is dreadful to lose one whom you love."

"But he is not lost," said Mr. Meredith, " he may return any day."

"Alas! father, I have hoped against hope, and now whenever I think of seeing him again, it seems like a dream never to be realized."

"Do you think, my dear, were he to return suddenly, would you be able to meet him without injuring yourself in your weak state?"

" Oh ! father, it would make me strong," and the poor girl's face flushed at the thought ; but she added eagerly, " have you any reason for asking that question ? Tell me, father, do you expect him ?"

Mr. Meredith hardly knew how to answer his daughter ; he feared the effect of a surprise; he however replied, " there is every reason to expect him at any moment, for it is very probable that he may be sent in from his post in charge of the packet or some of the trains from the trading posts."

" There again ! there again ! nothing but disappointment. I wonder if he ever will come back ?"

"Well, Gracie, of course, I do not wish you to raise your

hopes too high, but I have heard that George is likely to be here soon."

"Oh! father, do you think it is true? Surely you would not say this unless you had good reason to expect him. When do you think he will be here?"

"Suppose he were to be here in a day or two," replied Mr. Meredith, venturing a little more, "do you think you would be strong enough to see him?"

"Father, if I knew that George Wade would be here in the time you say, the very hope of looking on his dear face, would give new life to me. It is this weary waiting for his coming that is killing me."

"Then, Grace, my dear girl, he is hourly expected. It was intended when he started, that he should return about this time."

"My dear father, I do not think that you would tell me this unless you had good reason to believe it true; but it will be a dreadful blow to me if he does not come after all."

"Now suppose, Gracie," said Mr. Meredith, "that George should come to-morrow."

"To-morrow? whispered Grace.

"Yes, to-morrow," replied her father.

"Do you think he will?" asked Grace.

"I think he will," said Mr. Meredith.

"Oh! father you are not deceiving me, are you?" said Grace as she sank back on her pillows.

"I am not," replied her father as he rose and took her thin white hands in his; "George Wade will be here to-morrow."

Grace Meredith pressed her father's hands as she whispered, "Oh! how I have waited and longed for this moment."

The next morning Mr. Meredith walked over to Jack Harrican's house, and told George that Grace expected him.

T

"Are you sure that she is strong enough to see me?" asked Wade.

"She seems much better this morning, and I think your return will do much towards her recovery, if she is not too far gone already," he sadly added.

Mr. Meredith and George now walked over, and when they reached the farm house, Mrs. Meredith met them at the door.

"I am right glad to see you back, and if my good man had listened to me you would never have gone away; but come in, come in, and I'll go and tell Gracie you've come."

George felt a strange excitement creeping over him; an intense eagerness to see Grace; and it was with the utmost impatience that he awaited the summons to attend the sick room of her he loved so dearly. At last it came, and he was ushered in by Mrs. Meredith to where Grace lay propped up as usual with pillows. George could not prevent a start as he gazed on the wasted loveliness before him;—he could hardly realize that Grace Meredith was before him.

"George!"

"Grace!"

And Wade threw himself on his knees by the bedside and sobbed like a child. Grace drew her thin white hand across his brow and said, "My poor George, calm yourself; do not grieve in that way. Oh! look up and speak to me. How I have longed for this hour."

"Oh Grace!" Wade answered, "had I known this, no power on earth would have kept me from you."

"Do not blame my poor father," said Grace.

"I do not, Grace; he was made the tool of bad men; but it is hard, hard to bear."

"You won't go away again, George, will you?"

"No, Grace ; not at least until you are like your former self once more."

"Alas !" she sadly replied, "I do'nt know if that will ever be."

"Don't say that. I will nurse you now, my love, and you will soon get better."

"God's will be done, George ; but I fear I have not long to live."

"Cheer up, my darling ; there is many a happy day in store for us ;" but his words belied what he inwardly felt, for his heart died away within him when he looked upon the wasted features of the girl he loved so dearly.

Mr. and Mrs. Meredith, and the two boys, allowed the two lovers an undisturbed meeting, and during that eventful forenoon both George and Grace recounted to each other how much each had suffered during their cruel separation. Not a word was spoken, however, regarding the unfortunate affair that had been the cause of it.

Mr. Meredith having asked George to make their house his home, while he was in the settlement, he gladly accepted the proposition, as it would allow him to be continually near Grace to nurse and cheer her up.

A mother could not have shown more gentleness nor fondness than did George towards Grace Meredith, as he sat hour after hour by her bedside, either reading, talking, or attending to her many wants. The hopes of the lover and family were not to be realized, however, for Grace became weaker and weaker. For the first few days after George's return she appeared to improve, but after that she gradually sank lower and lower, until all hopes of her recovery seemed to die away amongst those who watched over her. Even George was obliged to despair of ever seeing her leave her sick-room. About this time Grace called her mother into her room one day, and the two remained closeted together for sometime. Mrs. Meredith was then observed to go to her husband and talk earnestly with him. Jack and Tom, who noticed all this, wondered what could be the matter, for both boys felt that something unusual had occurred.

"I wonder if Gracie is worse," said Tom. "Oh, Jack, if she dies, what will we do without her? It is dreadful to think about."

"It is no use, Tom. I'm afraid our poor sister cannot live, for the doctor next thing to told me so yesterday. I am miserable ; but while there is life there is hope. I wonder, though, what can be the matter ?"

"George has been away all morning, and that is another strange thing," added Tom.

We will leave the two boys, however, and listen to the conversation, or a part of it, between Mr. and Mrs. Meredith, which may throw some light on the mystery.

"She seems to have set her heart on it," said the old lady ; "and what harm can there be in letting her have her own way. She's not long for this world, I fear, good man."

"What does George say about it ?" asked Mr. Meredith.

"They seem to have made it up between them, and George is as anxious for it as Grace, only he fears that you won't allow it."

"It seems a strange idea," said Mr. Meredith ; "but I have suffered so much already by separating them from each other that I will never interfere with their happiness again. But I think I will see Grace herself about it."

"I fear it will be a death-bed marriage, if it does take place," said Mrs. Meredith, and her eyes filled with tears as she parted from her husband.

The latter went immediately to the bedside of Grace, and taking her hand in his, he kindly asked,—

"This is a strange wish of yours, is'nt it, my dear girl?"

"Why do you think so, father? Oh we've been separated so long, why should we not be united now? I feel, my dear father, that I have not long to live, perhaps not many days. Do not weep, father; it is time now to look the truth in the face. It will not be many days ere I will be far away from you, but it will not be for long. You will join me in heaven. And now, before I go, I want to be united to George. Oh, father, do not deny me the last request perhaps I will ever make on this earth. George and I have spoken often about it, but he feared to ask you, lest it might be the cause of another separation between us. Poor George, he has left me this morning, because I wished him to do so in order that I might speak to you myself. You won't deny me this, will you, father?"

"God forbid that I should do anything to mar your happiness, my poor child."

George at this moment came to the door of the room, and when he saw Mr. Meredith by the bedside of Grace, he drew back, but the old gentleman, when he saw him, beckoned to him to enter, which he did.

"George," said Mr. Meredith, "Grace has told me all. Why, my lad, did you not come to me and speak to me about it? But I can't blame you after what has happened. My poor children."

"Mr. Meredith, do not think of that unfortunate affair. You have been very good. Remember the explanations you required have never been given, and—

"Never mention them, my dear boy, never mention them. That is all past; I want no explanations; I ought never to have doubted you, never! never! I have acted like a fool and a madman."

" Don't speak that way, Mr. Meredith; it was quite right and natural for you to do as you did; and I thought, perhaps, that without the explanations, although you had kindly allowed me to again visit your house, still you would not consent to a union between Grace and me."

" Well, well, my dear children, we'll try and forget the past. I will not stand in the way of your union, only I wish God had willed it to be under happier circumstances; my poor girl," and the kind old gentleman bent over and kissed his daughter. "I will leave you now to yourselves."

As soon as Mr. Meredith left them, George and Grace spoke long and earnestly about their approaching marriage, indeed so engrossed did they become in the subject that Grace overtasked herself, and George was alarmed to see her sink back on her pillows in a fainting condition. George, with the assistance of Mrs. Meredith, however, managed to revive her, and had the pleasure of seeing her drop off into a slumber. George sat for hours watching the frail being before him, and the tears coursed down his cheeks as he thought of the true love she had shown for him, and how much she had suffered by it.

The marriage was agreed upon to take place the next day, as it was the desire of Grace to have the ceremony over as soon as possible. Accordingly, George had the preliminaries arranged, and the clergyman of the Church of England, who was to unite the two lovers, promised to be in attendance at the time appointed. On the morning of her marriage-day Grace seemed flushed and somewhat excited, but as the hour approached at which the ceremony was to take place she became more calm.

Mrs. Meredith did all in her power to cheer her daughter. She busied herself about the sick-room, preparing it for the coming event, and making everything around the invalid look pleasant and bright. At last the clergyman arrived, and was ushered into the room ; Mr. and Mrs. Meredith and the two boys being the only persons present, besides George and the minister. The latter spoke feelingly on the subject, and asked all present to join him in a prayer for the sick girl before them. He then in a solemn and impressive manner read the marriage service ; the hands of the weak woman and the strong man being joined together, the minister pronounced the solemn words,—" Those whom God hath joined together, let no man put asunder."

At this moment Grace seemed to give way altogether, and sank back exhausted ; and the clergyman, on this account, did not proceed with the rest of the service.

As soon, however, as Grace revived sufficiently, the communion was administered at her request to the newly married couple. When this was over, Grace drew from beneath her pillow a parcel which she requested George to unfasten. When this was done, the casket from Mr. Barron was discovered. "This is my marriage day," said Grace, "and at Mr. Barron's request, I have kept this gem sacred, without trying to unravel the mystery attached to it. George will you please open the lid, and inside the box you will find a small sealed package. This you will please undo, and probably the mystery will be solved."

George obeyed the instructions, and on opening the sealed package, he found within it a small ring studded with pearls ; attached to this, was a note in Mr. Barron's handwriting, which read as follows :—

" To GRACE.

"When you read this, I will probably be no more. You will have entered upon a new life. May God bless you, and may your future be full of happiness. May he who has won your love, prove a good guardian of the jewel above all price which he has obtained this day. The ring herewith belonged to my mother, and was her last gift to me. Keep it for my sake. I would not have it fall into any but pure hands. On one end of this casket, you will, by looking closely for it, discover a very small hole, into this press the point of a fine needle, and a secret drawer will spring out. In this you will find a paper which will tell you its own tale.

" FREDERICK BARRON."

George hunted closely for the small hole described in Barron's note, and after some considerable delay, he at last found it. When he had pressed the needle into it, the secret drawer flew out, as had been foretold, and a crumpled paper fell upon the floor. George handed this to Grace, who having opened it, read it. As she did so, her manner became excited, and finally with tears in her eyes, she handed the paper to George. The latter, on reading a few lines, started and looked wonderingly at Grace.

CHAPTER XXIII.

AT the time of our story, the church of England, in the settlement, was in a very flourishing condition, and possessed amongst it clergymen a good deal of talent and christian perseverance. Indeed, from the time of its establishment under the Rev. John West, in 1821, it has continued to increase gradually until it can now boast of many fine churches with large congregations. This has been owing chiefly to the efforts of the first missionaries who came to Red River.

The Rev. John West was succeeded by the Rev. D. T. Jones, a man who, before the end of his ministry, endeared himself to all classes in the settlement.

During the early days in the Red River colony, the Scotch settlers were for a long time without a minister of their own denomination ; a fact which caused a good deal of trouble and discontent amongst them ; and, indeed, they were not really satisfied until the Rev. John Black, in September, 1851, arrived and took charge of the Presbyterian church. The arrival of Mr. Black, was the signal for over three hundred Scotch settlers leaving the Church of England, to follow the pastor of their own familiar denomination. Ever since then the Presbyterian church has continued to increase, and is becoming larger every year, on account of the advent of strangers to the country.

The Rev. Mr. Jones was followed by the Rev. Mr. Cockran, and he in turn, was succeeded by others, until the Bishop of Rupert's Land arrived to take charge of the whole Church of England in the North-West.

At the time of our story, there were over twenty Episcopalian ministers in Rupert's Land, under the charge of Bishop Machray; a man universally respected for his christian character, and also for his fair and impartial mode of dealing with all matters connected with the church and the several flocks under his care.

Mr. Meredith, having belonged to the Church of England in Canada, had immediately on his arrival, secured a pew in the Cathedral for himself and family; and the assistant minister became a regular visitor at the house, during the illness of Grace. It was he, therefore, who performed the marriage ceremony between the two lovers.

While George was endeavouring to open the casket, the minister, who was obliged on account of other duties to leave, took his departure, and Mr. Meredith walked as far as the gate with him.

"I am afraid," said Mr. Meredith to the minister, "that the next duty you will have to perform in my family will be a very sad one. I have serious doubts regarding my daughter's recovery."

"Let us hope for the best," answered the clergyman; "God is good."

"Yes," replied Mr. Meredith, "but it is a great trial to lose a child who is the comfort of your life. It is wrong, I know, but I fairly dote over Grace. She has been a kind, good daughter to me, sir."

" She is a christian girl, Mr. Meredith, which ought to be a comfort to you, should God, in his providence, take her to Himself."

Mr. Meredith now shook hands with his pastor, and slowly returned to the house. A messenger from the Fort at this moment handed in a letter addressed to George Wade, saying that it had come by the packet from the north.

To give our readers some idea of the difficulties attending the transmission of letters to and from the interior, we will attempt a slight description of the packet during a winter trip. The mail is carried on dog sleds, either one or two being generally necessary for the duty. After they once start, they do not stop, except for camping, until they reach the end of their journey. They travel with orders to obtain fresh dogs and provisions at the several posts which they may have to pass on their trip. Only a couple of hours, and sometimes not even that, are spent at each post ; in fact only sufficient time is, as a usual thing, consumed to allow of the dogs being changed, and the letters from the post collected, until the packet once more starts upon its long journey. So regular are these dog-train mail carriers, that the time of their arrival at the several Forts along the route can generally be calculated upon to a day, and therefore the dogs are kept in readiness, so as to delay the packet when it arrives as short a time as possible. One would suppose that those travelling on such a long and wearisome a journey would only be too glad to take advantage of shelter under a roof whenever an opportunity occurred ; but such is not the case. A person travelling in the North-West during winter, will hardly if ever prefer to sleep in a house, to camping in the open air. Once on the road one becomes accustomed to open air living, although, at times, the hardships to be endured are very severe. The mode of making camp is as follows : Whenever there are woods near at hand, they generally make for their shelter during the night. As soon as a proper place is chosen, the dogs are unharnessed, and the sleds drawn up on the side from which the wind is blowing. The next thing done is to clear a sufficient space of snow, throwing it up in a bank all round the camp. This is accomplished by the means of the snow shoes, which take the place of shovels. A large fire is then built on the side farthest from the wind. Supper is next cooked, and then a smoke enjoyed. After this the buffalo-robes are stretched on the ground, and the travellers lie down to rest. The mode of sleeping in a winter camp is by all huddling together, as near as possible to each other, with their feet to the fire. The best bedfellow one can have on such an occasion is he who will stir the least in his sleep, as a restless individual will gradually manage to drag the covering from the others, and it is no joke to waken up and find yourself exposed to the keen, sharp air of a winter's night in the North West.

When Mr. Meredith entered Grace's room with the letter for George in his hand, the paper in the secret drawer had just been discovered.

When George had read the document, he exclaimed. "This is very strange ; it seems as if I now stood on the very threshold of freedom from my unfortunate promise, and yet I cannot see my way clearly before me."

"What does it all mean now ?" asked Mr. Meredith.

"Perhaps," replied George, "I had better read this strange letter ; it is from Mr. Barron."

"Read it," said Mr. Meredith.

All were attentive listeners as George read the following :—

"To Grace.

" I have already declared the hopeless love I entertained for you, and also the strange presentiment I have before me of an early death.   This latter feeling has grown more and more intense, and I cannot succeed in shaking it off.   The casket which contains this was given to me by an old and dear friend, who obtained it from a companion of his, named Ralph Loving, who was on his death-bed at the time.   There is some strange story connected with the casket, which I cannot remember altogether at this time.   I have used it for its present purpose (that of bequeathing to you by my last will and testament all my property in Scotland), because it possesses a secret drawer, which is very difficult to find, unless its exact description is given.   I have willed my property to you, first, because you are the one on earth who has the greatest hold upon my affections.

"Early in life I lost both father and mother; sisters nor brothers I have none; and not one of my relatives have ever given me any reason for loving them.   I came to this country, because I felt that the wild life I was leading in Scotland would sooner or later ruin my body as well as my soul.   Do not refuse to accept the only offering I can make.   Live on the property sometimes, for the sake of the tenants on it; and as I hope George Wade will be your husband, so I hope that neither you nor he will forget one who loved you both so well that he could have given his life for either.

"FREDERICK BARRON."

Accompanying this remarkable document, was the will of the writer, bequeathing to Grace Meredith the fine property situated near the City of Glasgow, Scotland.

"This is very strange," said Mr. Meredith; "but what is there in Barron's letter that throws any light on your troubles?"

"It is a name mentioned in it, that of Ralph Loving.   It

was he who —— ;" but here George stopped. "I am more perplexed than ever," he went on to say ; "if I was only sure that he was dead."

"Who?" asked Mr. Meredith.   "Barron?"

"No," replied George, "Ralph Loving."

At this moment Mr. Meredith remembered the letter he had for George Wade, and immediately handed it to him.

"Why the packet must be in," said George, as he broke the seal. "This is from the North."

"It was handed to me by a man from the Fort."

George started as he looked at the letter.   "Poor Barron," he exclaimed, "your words have proved too true."

"What is the matter?" eagerly asked Grace.

"Barron is dead," replied George ; "here is a letter from the officer in charge of York Factory."

"MY DEAR SIR,—I am pained to write you the sad news that your friend Barron was drowned while bathing near the Fort, a few nights since. He had been unwell for some time, and seemed very weak the morning on which he went out for a swim. He had been troubled ever since his arrival at York Factory with a most unaccountable and mysterious visitation. He used to dread some ghostly apparation, which he declared visited his room during the night at stated intervals ; and at last he became so nervous that he would start and grow pale on hearing the slightest noise behind him. I have sat in the same room with him when he has suddenly risen from his seat terror-stricken at some unseen object near him. He, on these occasions, would declare that some one (generally a lady) had passed behind him. This extreme nervousness at last prayed so much upon his mind that his body wasted away—a melancholy took possession of him,—and he continually foretold his early death—and at last his words came true. He went out one evening for a swim, and must have gone too far out. It is the opinion of the people here that his strength gave way, as he suddenly disappeared, and was not again seen until his body was recovered a couple of days afterwards. He always spoke of you, and repeatedly made me promise to write to you should anything happen to him and let you know about it. I now fulfil what I consider his dying wish. There is one who must have been ever in his thoughts, for I have heard him while asleep, time after time, distinctly utter the name "Grace." If you know her or who the lady is, tell her Barron never ceased to think of her. I will forward his effects to Fort Garry at the first opportunity.

"I am yours very truly,

" DONALD SINCLAIR.

"To George Wade, Esq.,

     "Fort Garry."

The tears stood in the eyes of every one present as George finished the above letter.[*]

"Poor fellow," said Grace ; "he deserved a better end."

"He did indeed," added George, "for I never in my life met a nobler fellow than he was ; so unselfish and kind in all his feelings. We must acquaint his friends in Scotland with his sad fate, although the Governor will no doubt do it as soon as he hears about it. There is one thing I cannot understand, and that is how he became possessed of that casket. The whole thing is inexplicable."

---

[*] The letter describing Barron's death must have been written in summer, but on account of the very few opportunities for forwarding letters to Fort Garry from York Factory, it does not appear to have reached its destination till the following winter. It is probable that it was written soon after the death of Barron, and remained in York Factory till the packet left for the Settlement.

"There is another thing I cannot understand," said Mrs. Meredith, "and that is why you allow that boy Tom there to handle and work with the silver box in the way he is doing ;—just look at him."

At this moment an exlamation from the youth himself caused all eyes to be turned towards him.

"Hi! George here's a go," said the boy excitedly.

"What is the matter now," said Mr. Meredith, somewhat sternly, for he began to feel that so many surprises would have a bad effect on Grace.

"Why father," said Tom, "here is another secret drawer,—and here's another paper.   What's up now I wonder?"

George started to his feet.   "Let me see it Tom," he said ; and then observing that Grace seemed worn out, he added in a whisper to Mr. Meredith, "let us retire to another room to investigate this fresh mystery.   Grace seems very much fatigued."   Mr. Meredith rose immediately, and told both Jack and Tom to go to their work.   He then led the way to the sitting room.

As George left the bedside of Grace, he stooped down and kissed her, and she faintly murmured—

"Come back soon, will you not ? and let me know what it is all about.   I will feel anxious till you return."

When Mr. Meredith and George reached the sitting room, they examined the casket, and found that both ends of the box resembled each other ; there being two holes exactly alike with two secret drawers instead of one.   George took the last paper discovered by Tom, and opening it, began to read.

"Thank God!" he exclaimed when he had perused a portion of it.   "Free at last.   This is indeed an unaccountable affair —it is quite evident that Barron never was aware of the existence of this paper, and how it came into his possession is most extraordinary."

"I am yet at a loss to understand what the paper has reference to."

"It contains the explanations you asked from me at St. Boniface."

CHAPTER XXIV.

EORGE WADE was on the point of unravelling the mystery which had caused so much anxiety and trouble to both himself and others, when Mrs. Meredith burst into the room crying—"Oh ! good man, our girl is worse. To-day's doings have been too much for her ; come and see her. I'm afraid she is dying."

Both George and Mr. Meredith stood aghast at this news; and without thinking more about the strange papers so unaccountably discovered, they hastened at once to the sick room. A great change had, indeed, suddenly come over Grace ; her pale features seemed more pinched in their expression, and her breathing appeared to be more laboured.

George sank on his knees by the bedside, and taking the hand of the sick girl in his, he tenderly asked her if she felt much worse. I'm afraid, he added, we have not been very considerate towards you in your weak state.

Grace turned her wan face towards him, and smiling lovingly, whispered—"George, I have been looking forward to this. I have not many hours to live. I feel my strength passing away ; but my dear George I am happy now that I am yours. It is God's will to take me ; do not grieve."

"Oh ! my own Grace do not speak in this way," said the disconsolate man. " You are wearied and worn out by the fatigue of to-day."

" My poor George," replied the dying girl, (for dying she was assuredly) " do not deceive yourself. I know that I have not long to live."

George Wade covered his face, and the hot tears moistened the poor thin hand which he clasped in his. " Oh ! this is hard to bear," he murmured. " Grace, my darling, I am free this day. I hold the proof now that I am innocent of having done the deeds that were imputed to me. They have caused a sad blank in our lives, but all is cleared up now. Oh ! Grace tell me that you will live for my sake."

" Alas !" whispered Grace ; " it is not my will but the will of God be done. I never thought you guilty. Say no more about that unhappy affair."

The exertions of speaking was too much for Grace. She closed her eyes, and for some moments she appeared unconscious of the presence of those around her. At last her eyes slowly opened ; they seemed brighter than ever they had been during her illness. Holding out her hand to Mr. Meredith, she faintly said, " My dear, dear father, call Jack and Tom, I wish so much to see them."

Mr. Meredith, utterly heart broken, silently left the room, for his two sons, and while he was away Grace stretched out her hand and smoothed the gray tresses of her weeping mother, who had lain herself on the bed beside her. "My own darling mother," she slowly said, " do not mourn for me in this way ; it will not be long ere we'll meet again."

" It will not be long, my dear child. Oh, Gracie, do not leave us. Oh ! God, save her, and pity a poor mother. She's my only comfort. Heaven, hear me," and Mrs. Meredith sobbed bitterly.

It was a sad moment. Jack and Tom now came in and stood by the bedside. The tears coursed down the cheeks of the hardy boys as they looked upon the sister they were so fond of. They could not realize that they were going to lose her so soon. Grace became so weak and her voice so low, that it was with difficulty that her words could be understood. She however motioned the two boys to her side, and kissed them. She then whispered so that George only heard her. " Father, mother, kiss me for the last time."

Mr. and Mrs. Meredith then knelt down beside her, and Grace soon after passed quietly away ; her head resting on the arm of her husband, who appeared utterly prostrated at his great loss.

" My poor George, good-bye till we meet again," were the last words slowly and with difficulty uttered by the dying girl.

The doctor, who had been hastily summoned, now arrived, but too late. The soul of Grace Meredith had winged its way to that home where there is perfect rest, and from which there is no returning.

The blow was a dreadful one to the family, although it had not been unexpected for some time previous. Long and silently they sat round the bed of death, each one loth to part from her they had all loved so well in life. It was with the greatest difficulty that George could be persuaded to leave the room.

Kind neighbors offered their services in the arrangement of the dead, which were thankfully accepted by the disconsolate parents. George, however, sat up all that night by the side of his lost bride, and as he watched, his thoughts went back to the days when he first learned to love the one so still and motionless before him. Then he traced in his mind the unfortunate course of his love ; and is it to be wondered at if he mentally prayed to God for just vengeance on the murderers of his happiness, as well as that of the loved one by his side, now so cold in the embrace of death.

Did he not during his long vigil reproach himself for acts committed in a hasty moment ; acts, which indeed were the prime causes of the sorrowful and untimely end of a lovely and gentle girl ! Who can tell ? We will presently see whether he had cause to blame himself.

As soon as it became known amongst the friends and neighbours of the Merediths that Grace was dead, a general feeling of pity and compassion was felt for the family ; and on the day of the funeral a large number attended to show their respect for the dead. It was some distance to the church-yard, and the coffin had to carried on the shoulders of those who volunteered for the purpose. This was done in the following manner, when the four men who acted as pall-bearers became tired four others from amongst those attending the funeral stepped forward and relieved them. In order to have no confusion, it was customary for four others to step forward at the same time and walk immediately behind those who were carrying the coffin, so that the moment they became tired they could quietly change places. In this way there were always eight men acting as pall-bearers. And before the procession reached the grave-yard almost every one attending the funeral had taken part in carrying the coffin.

This custom is a very beautiful one, as it shows a desire on the part of the mourners to take a real interest in paying respect to the dead.

When the Cathedral was reached, a touching sermon was delivered by the Archdeacon, who dwelt feelingly upon the affliction to the parents, relatives and bereaved husband.

Mrs. Meredith, who had followed, and as the cold hard earth

was thrown upon the remains of her only daughter, each dull thump upon the coffin brought a sharp pang to her motherly heart.

It was a mournful sight to see this family bereaved of their pride, return slowly to their desolate home, for such it now appeared to all of them. It was strange to observe George during the trying ceremony. How calm he looked ; not a tear moistened his cheek, but his face wore a haggard appearance. There were the signs of utter agony upon his features. He was too much stricken down to weep. Poor George, his sorrow was unlike any other sorrow, as he went home to the Merediths' house,—all his hopes blasted, with his young life nipped in the bud ; for he never felt young again from the moment he realized that Grace was dead—dead, his love lost to him for ever. The only comfort he felt was that it might not be for-ever ; that there was a future—a heaven where he would try to meet her once more.

CHAPTER XXV.

OR several days, George Wade refused to be comforted. His manner became absent and careless of the presence of others. His health also appeared to be giving way, and the Merediths feared least he should be laid on a bed of sickness. They had learned to love George very dearly, and felt a great deal of anxiety at the continued depression of the young man's spirits. One day, therefore, Mr. Meredith prevailed on him to take a ride out on horseback, thinking that the air and the exercise would benefit him.

George, strange to say, insisted upon mounting a very restive and vicious horse, and it was with some misgiving that the Merediths saw him start for his ride. He had not gone far before the horse became very unmanageable, and at last, taking the bit between his teeth, he bolted, and George found that he was beyond control.

Wade was a good horseman, and kept his seat in gallant style, but, unfortunately for him, the horse suddenly shied at some object on the road, and threw him headlong upon the hard, icy ground. George was found a few minutes afterwards lying senseless where he had been thrown, and on being carried into a house close at hand, it was discovered that his leg was broken above the knee. As soon as it was known who he was, word was sent to the Merediths, stating what had occurred; but the doctor forbade his removal from where he lay.

When Mrs. Meredith heard of this accident to George, it was like a death-blow to her. The poor old lady indeed felt this new calamity so deeply, that it prostrated her completely. She had begun to look on George as one of the family.

Mr. Meredith and the two boys tried to comfort her, but the only answer they could obtain was, " Oh! why did we come to this country; there has been nothing but trouble ever since we left our home in Canada. Gracie is gone. My comfort and pride has been taken from me; and now that George had begun to be like a son to me, he is laid on his bed perhaps never to rise again. Oh! dear, my gray hairs will surely go sorrowing to the grave."

" Don't say that, good wife," Mr. Meredith would say, " let us be patient, it may not be so bad as you say with George. He's young and strong, and will get over it with care. We'll go up and see him to-morrow."

Jack and Tom felt the accident very much, for they, too, had learned to look upon him as a brother.

The people, into whose house George was carried, were very kind and attentive, and spared no means in their power to make the injured man as comfortable as possible.

We will now leave the unfortunate man for a short time, until we pay a visit to other scenes. Cool, notwithstanding the rebuff given by his wife to " Dot," continued to cultivate the acquaintance of that interesting individual. Many were the ideas obtained by the correspondent from Cool, and sent to the newspapers in Canada, as coming direct from " Dot." But while the latter became more and more intimate, another person became less friendly with Cool, and that individual was our old friend Whirl.

The latter was a shrewd, calculating man, and he plainly foresaw that the Canadian party in the settlement, even should they be successful, would bring little credit to the members connected with it, as the acts already committed and ascribed to Canadians were being condemned by most of the people in the settlement.

Whirl was one whose main object in Red River was money-making, and he took part in politics only so far as they might prove conducive to the main chance—money. Now he formed the opinion that Cool was taking a very roundabout way to make money out of politics, and at the same time he felt that although the acts of the Canadian party in Red River might tend to agitate the question of annexation of the North-West in Canada, yet they would not at the same time do any good to the actors in the settlement. He, therefore, made up his mind to withdraw altogether, feeling that neither the Canadians nor Americans would prove successful in any of their schemes, on the plan that Cool seemed desirous of adopting—namely, " rebellion against the constituted government of the country." It was easily to be seen that neither Canada nor the United States would sanction the attempted overthrow of a government so as to allow either of them to step into its place.

Had Cool and his party endeavoured to lead the settlers to demand in a proper way annexation to Canada, without trying at the same time to blacken the character of the Hudson Bay Company, it is very probably that Canada would have found more friends than it did in Red River. There was no objection to a union with Canada amongst the people, but when men who represented themselves as champions of Canada defied the laws and endeavoured to bring mob violence into existence, then the settlers took fright, and without waiting to judge properly, they denounced all Canadians on account of the acts done by a few lawless men.

Whirl saw that all this was not going to pay in the end.   It was too risky a piece of business for him to engage in, for, thought he, I cannot afford to quarrel with all my neighbours for a mere uncertain prospect of " pap," to come from a government whose advent seemed not at all sure.   He, therefore, took every opportunity to let Cool know that he did not intend taking any further part in the grand scheme of anti Hudson Bay Company.   The fact was that the people of Red River felt that although the Hudson Bay Company government was weak and unsuitable to the wants of the country, still it was the only one in exisience at the time in the North-West, and therefore the sole protection to life and property.   They consequently had no desire to see it overthrown in the way Cool and his friends appeared to wish for, until another and better one was substituted in its place.

There was no anti-Canadian feeling dominant amongst the settlers ; but there was a fear that if the generality of Canadians should prove to be like the party who put themselves forward as the representatives of Canada in Red River, they would not be a good or safe people to become allied to.   Our readers must remember that all the Canadians in Red River, at the time of our story, are not to be included in the same category, as there were many fine men hailing from Canada in the North-West, who looked upon the deeds done by their countrymen as a disgrace to their nationality.   Mr. Meredith was one of this latter class.

Whirl could see, therefore, that Cool's party were not destined to succeed, and he, on that account, determined to renounce them.   The Americans, to whom he had allied himself, were few in number, and did not possess much influence; still he resolved to remain one of them from the very fact that they did not meddle with the affairs of the country, and were consequently respected by the settlers. Neither did Whirl expect that annexation to the United States would happen, but as both Canada and the United States appeared to run an equally poor chance in Red River, he made up his mind to stick to the party likely to cause him the least amount of enmity amongst his neighbours.

When Cool observed that his friend Whirl was, to use a vulgar term, "going back upon him," he at once demanded an explanation. This was the signal for a rupture, and Whirl immediately took advantage of it, and from that day the two cronies trod a separate path.

"Dot" in the meantime, however, had gone in hand and glove with Cool. This proved a poor exchange for the latter, as the correspondent about this time brought down upon his devoted head the just indignation of the Red River people, on account of the scandalous letters he had written to Canada about them. He was welcomed by few as a visitor to their houses, and at last poor "Dot" having quarreled with the several hotel keepers in the place, found it a hard matter to find a spot on which to rest his weary head.

Even Cool found some difficulty in providing a refuge for him, as Mrs. Cool had not forgotten the free and easy way in which he had addressed her at the door. These were hard times for "Dot," and he began to wish himself well out of the country. To think that he, the irrepressible "Dot" should come down from being the invited guest of dinner parties and balls to the social position of an outcast! "Dear me," he muttered "this is really too bad;" but he ought to have remembered the old proverb which says "the way of transgressors is hard." Cool evidently cared more for the opinion of people abroad, especially in Canada, than he did of those at home; and it was on this account therefore that he cultivated the friendship of "Dot" to such an extent. He knew perfectly well that by a little flattery he could weld the little correspondent's ideas to suit his own ; and he spared no means to effect this object.

When " Dot" was shown the cold shoulder by the neighbours, Cool stepped in with an overflowing amount of friendly protestations. When " Dot" could not get a dinner elsewhere, Cool immediately asked him to dine. When ".Dot" could not even get a stone upon which to rest his weary head, Cool produced a soft feather bed.

Thus matters stood when word came from Canada, that a deputation had gone to England for the purpose of making arrangements with the Home Government and the Hudson Bay Company for the transfer of the North-West to the Dominion. Cool's spirits rose apace, and " Dot" strutted about as much as to say, " there you see what I've done."

People in Red River, however, took little if any interest in the matter. The *Buster* not having altogether quarrelled with Whirl, mentioned in an editorial that while Cartier and Mc-Dougall had gone to England, with a view of uniting the North-West to Canada, Senator Ramsey was presenting a series of resolutions at Washington, for the purpose of annexing Red River under Uncle Sam's jurisdiction, winding up the article by saying, which ever way the cat jumped, the North-West was bound to be a great country.

Very cautious on the part of Mr. Twaddle, who not being at the time very sure of the direction to be taken by the cat, felt it to be the best plan to " straddle the fence," as it is called, until the jump was taken.

It was very plain, however, to most persons in the settlement that unless the cat did jump very soon, several of those who persisted in stroking its back would go to the wall.

Cool by his actions had weaned the good opinion of some of his best friends. His persistent efforts to overthrow law and order and the consequent injury to his character as a good member of society affected his business, until the bad effects were seen in his loss of credit and standing as a merchant. All this worked against him at home, while abroad he was looked upon as an enterprising man, as well as a victim of tyranny on the part of the Hudson Bay Company. "Dot" having published a long letter showing how Cool and his friends were kept down and abused by the Hudson Bay Company.

Sharp, ever since the night on which he had escaped from jail, began to lose the friendship or good esteem of his neighbours, and he too suffered considerably on account of his evil ways.

It would have required a big jump on the part of these men to bring them in safety out of the mire into which they had fallen. It was therefore good news for both Cool and Sharp when they heard of the Cartier-McDougall mission to England; and mark the first steps taken by those worthies on the receipt of the intelligence.

A meeting consisting of Cool, "Dot" and Sharp, was held in the house of the first named gentleman.

" Ha ! ha ! ha !" exclaimed Cool rubbing his hands, " I knew it would come to this."

" Hi ! hi! hi !" chimed in "Dot," "see what the efforts of a proper man as correspondent can do."

" Ho! ho! ho !" added Sharp, " mark what jail-breaking and defying the laws have done for this country."

" And now," said Cool, "of course one should always look

out for the main chance ; that is what I invariably do on all occasions."

"Of course," remarked "Dot."

"Certainly" said Sharp, "but how is it to be done."

"Listen" replied Cool, "for I see plainly that nothing could be done without me in this matter.   Sharp as you are, Sharp, I'll wager you have no idea what I am going to propose,"

"I'll give it up," replied Sharp.

"Hold," cried "Dot ;" "let me see, Haw! I see—yes! go on Cool I've some idea of what it is."

"Has it never occurred to your wise heads then that there are hundreds of acres of land in this fine country going to waste; and are you not aware that as soon as the country is handed over to Canada, these hundreds of acres will be in great demand by persons wishing to come and settle here."

"Exactly" interrupted "Dot," "Haw! a light beams upon me."

"What the deuce has that to do with us ?" asked Sharp.

"What is to prevent our securing a large quantity of land beforehand, if we lay claim and stake it off into lots.   Will not the Canadian Government be bound to respect our right to them ? Certainly they will.   My idea, therefore, is for us to form a clique, (Twaddle might be allowed into it), and pick out such choice spots as we think will be most saleable.   The more we claim the more we'll get; so don't let us be in any way fastidious about claiming too much."

"Capital," said "Dot ;" "when will we commence?"

"As soon as possible," replied Cool.

"I'm in for it," said Sharp, "for to tell you the truth, it is about the only thing I have to look forward to.   My business has gone to the dogs ever since I got out of jail; but what about Whirl—won't he be one of us ?"

"I'm not very well satisfied with him of late. He is not as he used to be, and evidently wishes to desert us altogether. I say, therefore, let him go, we can get on without him ; and perhaps he'll yet be sorry for leaving us in the lurch."

" Haw! keep the fellow out of course," said "Dot ;" "he mixes to much with those d——d Americans to please me."

"All right then," said Sharp, "only Whirl has been always a friend to me."

Cool now proposed to his two companions that they should go to a certain part of the settlement on the morrow, where he said several choice lots could be procured by a very simple process.

"And what may that be ?" asked Sharp.

"Haw ! Yes tell us," said " Dot."

" Why by a little rum and a few pounds 'of pork and flour."

"How so ?" interrupted Sharp.

"We'll extinguish the Indian title ; in other words, we'll buy the land from the redskins."

" Lord man," said Sharp, "the redskins have no right to that part of the settlement, at least any of the Indians around here now."

" Oh ! that is nothing," replied Cool ; " we'll make them out to have a right, and that will be sufficient. We'll get them to sign a paper giving over to us their right to the lands, and that will prove our ownership."

"But what is to become of the people living there already ? have they not a better right than we can ever show ?"

" Pshaw ! the Canadian Government will listen to our claims before those of the half-breeds, depend upon it."

" Perhaps so, but I'm afraid its slippery ground to tread on. We'd be far better to take claims where it won't interfere with anybody else."

" Interfere, be hanged ; do you suppose the half-breeds will be consulted ?   Don't you believe it ! they'll have to knuckle down, or else leave, you'll see."

" Certainly," said " Dot," " that is so."

The next day the three worthies drove to the place Cool had in view, and by a bottle or two of rum and some pork and flour, they succeeded in getting one or two miserable Indians to sign a paper giving over a right which did not belong to them.

Cool, " Dot," Sharp and Co., thought that they had achieved a wonderful success, but their exultation was of short duration.   The authorities happening to hear of the transaction, took the matter up, and poor Sharp again found himself in the clutches of the law, he being the unfortunate one of the three who was informed upon as having sold liquor to the Indians.   Sharp was fined ten pounds sterling, and being without funds at the same time, he applied to Cool to aid him in his distress.   Cool, however, did not care about paying out such a large sum of money, even for a friend. and, therefore, excused himself.   Sharp, indeed, would have been obliged to go to prison had not some unknown person kindly furnished the means to set him at liberty.   This little occurrence did not stop the land speculation however.   Choice lots were here and there marked out and claimed.   This was done by running a plough round the piece of land, and the name of the person thus claiming it being marked upon a stake driven into the ground.   Other parties seeing Cool, " Dot," Sharp and Co., at work, now commenced staking off land, until at last the settlers finding out what was going on, interfered, and a great deal of ill-feeling was caused amongst the people on the subject.   Indeed, this promiscuous claiming of land on the part of strangers, did more to engender a feeling of discontent towards

Canadian annexation than anything else. The idea became quite prevalent that the rights of settlers to their lands would not be respected, but that every Tom, Dick or Harry might come in and claim land wherever they found it. This selfish and unprincipled behaviour on the part of such men as Cool and his friends did a great deal of harm, and sowed the seeds of future trouble in the settlement. In fact, it became generally believed amongst a large number of the settlers that they were to be ignored, and that strangers were to be allowed to come into the country and do as they pleased ; and that Canada's whole aim in endeavoring to obtain possession of the country was to find a place of refuge for its surplus population, and that the interest of the Red River people were to suffer thereby. All this ignorance of the real intentions of the Canadian government was caused by the actions of a few men like Cool and his party.

"Dot's" correspondence to Canada during his short stay in Red River assisted very materially in augmenting the feeling of uneasiness in the settlement, for it savored so much of arrogance that it seemed like a forerunner of what people might expect under the Canadian rule.

"Dot" and Cool held many consultations together, and during these interesting meetings, the general plan seemed to be to drive the natives of the country back, as they would uncivilized Indians ; but they forgot two very important points, which were, first, whether Canada meant to drive the settlers back in this way ; and, secondly, whether, if so, the Red River people would allow themselves to be so treated.

But, for the time being, both Canada and Red River were forgotten in the absorbing interest of Cool and Company.

One day, as "Dot" sat in Cool's private room, a tall, thin, and rather ragged looking individual opened the door. This

V

person we know as Flyaway, but " Dot " did not know him by this name, he therefore rose and demanded his business.

" Is Cool in ?" was the reply.

" Haw ! Mr. Cool you mean, I suppose ?"

" I've always heard of him as Cool," said Flyaway ; " but I suppose he's risen in life since I saw him last. Where is he now ?"

" Not knowing, can't tell, haw !" answered " Dot."

" You're a queer little fellow," remarked Flyaway. " Where did you drop from ? I suppose Cool is quietly skinning you, like he did me, eh ? What's your name ?"

" You're a lunatic, I should say," exclaimed " Dot," " and you imagine Mr. Cool to be an eel-monger. Haw ! very good."

" You'll find out whether he doesn't skin you before he's done with you ; that is if you're worth skinning, which I doubt."

" Haw ! my dear man, if your business is with Mr. Cool, you had better call again. I am writing, don't you observe ?"

" No, you are talking, and if you don't write better than you talk, you're not good for much. Adieu, my friend, fare-well," and Flyaway turned on his heel to leave, but as he did so he encountered Cool.

" Hilloh !" exclaimed the latter, " where the d——l did you come from at this time of the year ?"

" From the plains, of course," replied Flyaway, " where else could I come from ?"

" Well, how has trade been ?" asked Cool.

" Trade be d——d. I haven't done a thing. I'm dead broke ; and have come to you for help."

"The deuce you have," said Cool. " I thought you had made up your mind to have no further transactions with me."

" Well, the fact is, I am a ruined man, and I want to leave this country, never to return. You, Cool, have made a good deal of money out of me at one time or another, and surely you won't refuse to advance me enough money to get me out of Red River."

" My dear Flyaway, you could not have come to me at a worse time. I am just about broke myself; things have not gone well with me of late."

" A very convenient story," said Flyaway : " but you had just better fork over, else I'll let a cat out of the bag that you won't like."

" Let it out, my dear fellow. I am not particular ; but if you'll take my advice, you'll leave me alone. You are no match for me."

Flyaway threatened, then entreated, but all to no purpose. Cool would not listen to his demand, so the poor Doctor, half enraged and half in despair, left the house.

" I hope I'll live to see the day when you'll be in want," he muttered, as he strode away.

Flyaway left the settlement a few days afterwards, having scraped together a small sum of money sufficient to take him out of the country. He had spent his all on the plains, as Whirl had predicted, in drink, and he left Red River an utterly ruined man. We will not again meet him, so we may mention that he died, a couple of years afterwards, in a low saloon in Chicago, his end being a terrible one, brought on by a continued fit of drunkenness.

" Dot," after his departure, remarked to Cool : "Haw! who the deuce is that queer looking individual ?"

" An old friend of mine," said Cool ; " he used to be a good sort of fellow, but latterly he has gone altogether to the dogs ; but never mind him. I've got some news for you, and I think

I see a chance for making a hit.   The Governor is starting for England in a day or two."

"Haw ! indeed, well ?"

"Suppose you write to Canada that he is going away to escape from the outraged feelings of the people here ; in fact, because he felt the country getting too warm for him."

"The devil !" exclaimed "Dot."   "What if he should come back again ? how then ?"

"Oh ! it will be all forgotten by that time ; it will serve the purpose of creating an impression that he is unpopular here, and let that idea get abroad, it will have its effect."

"Good ! it will be done ; but I must not write to my paper.   Let me see, Haw ! yes, I know ; I'll send the letter to a friend of mine to publish.   That will do ; let us write it now."

The two thereupon sat down and concocted a vile slander on a worthy man.   They made it appear as if the departure of the Governor was a source of joy to the settlers generally; that the wish of the greater portion of them was that he never would return to the country, and so forth.

Now, the fact of the matter was that there was no man in Red River more respected than the Governor ; and when he left the settlement at the time we have reference to, it was the earnest wish of all good men that he should speedily return.

CHAPTER XXVI.

E left George Wade on a bed of sickness, in a strange house. There we still find him still suffering from the accident he had met with, and likely to remain an invalid for some time. The family into whose house he had been carried, were very much respected in the settlement, and George Wade was fortunate to find shelter under their roof during his illness, for they were most kind and considerate in their attentions towards him.

The name of this family was Stone, and like the Merediths, there was an only daughter, a beautiful girl, who proved a gentle and attentive nurse to George. The fracture to Wade's leg, proved a very troublesome affair to him, and one that required the utmost care to prevent his being a cripple for the rest of his life. No means were spared by the Stones to have their guest treated with the consideration they would have shown to a son or a brother ; and George soon found himself very much at home with them. Nina Stone was what is called a half-breed girl ; and, contrary to what " Dot" in his letters to Canada tried to show regarding her country-women, she was a perfect lady in every respect. She never had the opportunity of seeing much of what is called society, still she possessed that innate sense of what is maidenly and proper in one of her sex, that one could not help admiring and even loving her for her gentleness and goodness. In her attendance upon George Wade, she showed such a degree of reserve, without the affected shyness so often adopted by young ladies, that it tended to impress the wounded man with a feeling of respect for his fair nurse.

The residence of the Stones was finely situated on the bank of the Red River, and a great deal of taste had been shown by the family in the arrangement of the grounds around the house. It was a quiet sort of taste, however, having more of a tendency towards comfort than mere show, and this is a characteristic feature to be found around most of the dwellings of the principal settlers in Red River. The Stones were farmers, and ranked amongst the first in the settlement. They were what would be called wealthy in Canada, and had made the principal part of their money in the North-West.

We may mention here a fact which is worthy of notice, namely, that although much has been said against the Hudson Bay Company as a monopoly, exercising tyranical power, yet it is an indisputable fact, that without the existence of that monopoly, as it has been called, the Red River farmers would not be to-day in the position they are.

How few amongst the farmers in Canada, are to be found who have funds invested in bank stock outside of their regular means; yet let one start from Fort Garry and go down the banks of the Red River, or up the Assiniboine, and he will find that most of the settlers in those localities have money invested either in Canada or England. Had the Hudson Bay Company, however, not proved a large consumer of their products, they never could have found a market sufficiently great to allow of their raising or selling the crop necessary to build up their circumstances to the state we have already described.

It is folly, then, to speak of the Hudson Bay Company as having been a drag upon the country ; for in fact that wealthy and powerful corporation protected and kept the settlement in existence up to the present day. The worst that can be said is, that during the early days of the Company, their officers and servants tried in every way to stop free trading in furs, and sometimes the means used for that purpose were not the fairest on record.

Their government was a weak and unsatisfactory one, it is true ; and may have tended to prevent emigration to the country ; but that there was any intentional obstacle placed in the way of strangers coming to Red River, is utterly untrue. Indeed, as has been shown in the case of the Merediths, there are far more instances of facilities having been offered to people to settle in the country, than of any attempt at prevention on the part of the Hudson Bay Company. Then again, leaving its fur trade and governmental qualities out of the question, had it not been for the Hudson Bay Company, the settlers of Red River, instead of being as they are to-day in comfortable circumstancees, would be not much better than frontier squatters, with little else to the good, besides a few acres of land under cultivation, and a log cabin as a house.

The Stone family was a fair specimen of the better class of settlers in Red River at the time of our story. They were what are called half breeds ; their forefathers having intermarried with Indians. They had grown with the country, and when we meet them they possessed money invested abroad, and had a large and well cultivated farm in the settlement, which yielded them a handsome yearly competence.

The Merediths were regular visitors at the Stones during George Wade's illness, and Mrs. Meredith was continually bringing something to comfort her sick son, as she called him.

Jack and Tom whenever they could get away from their work around the farm house were sure to be found at the bedside of George.   The latter, therefore, felt no want of attention on the part of his friends.   There was a blank, however, in the heart of poor George which could never be filled up, and many a silent tear did he shed over the loss of the one so dear to his memory.

Poor Mrs. Meredith began to show signs of her great suffering.   Her grey hair became more silvery in its appearance ; her figure stooped more ; and her sharp features grew more softened in their character.   Her health seemed to be breaking up, and her ways were more childish since the death of Grace.

The two boys were more subdued in their manner ; and often while speaking to George, the tears would trickle down their cheeks when by chance they would refer to their dead sister.

But the one who felt the loss of Grace most keenly was poor Mr. Meredith.   One day, as the old gentleman sat beside George, he sadly remarked " my dear boy,—on the day when our Grace was taken from us, you were about revealing the circumstances of that unfortunate mystery which hung over you so long and unhappily, are you strong enough to speak about it now ?"

"Yes" replied George, " I have wished for some time to open the subject to you, but dreaded to refer to it lest it might bring to mind the harrowing circumstances of that miserable day."

" Well ! well ! my boy, we will have to be resigned, and try to look upon the past with some composure," said Mr. Meredith.

" Had I the silver casket here," continued George, " I would read to you the contents of that paper which we discovered in the second secret drawer."

" Then, my boy, I have brought it with me, thinking that you might wish to look at the paper again, and perhaps free my mind of the load I have carried so long, and which has wrought

so much misery for us all ;—but before you read one word of it,
I wish you to feel that I have not now the slightest feeling of
doubt remaining in my mind regarding you, nor do I blame
you for anything that has happened. I am the only one to
blame, for I ought to have accepted your word, and not have
listened to others on the spbject. You were right, while I was
wrong; but oh! pity me, George. I am indeed a heart broken
man," and Mr. Meredith sobbed like a child.

George was very much affected, yet he tried to soothe the
poor old man. "Give me the casket and I will read you the
whole truth about this affair."

Mr. Meredith then produced the little box from his pocket,
and handed it to Wade ;—and the latter opening it, took out
the paper and spreading it before him read as follows :—

" Believing myself to be upon my death bed, yet, having the
hope that I may not die at this time, I have written this confession, and now place it in the secret drawer of this silver
casket. I have been a coward all my past life-time, and I will
remain one until the moment of my death. I am acting the
part of a coward by not openly making this confession, instead
of hiding it in a secret drawer, where I know that it is apt never
to be discovered. While there is life there is hope, and it
is because I may live through my present sickness, that I take
the course I am now doing. Should this confession be brought
to light before I die, it would bring me to the miserable end I
have dreaded so long. But I trust that this paper will yet be produced, through Divine agency, to free an innocent man from a
foul stain resting upon his fair name. This is my confession :—

"George Wade was my shipmate on board the ship *Nero*, in the
East India Company's Service. He and I became bosom companions, and to the last he remained my firm friend. Our berths
were close to each other. We were in the same watch, and it

often happened that we would walk the deck arm in arm in
conversation, until it was time to turn in.   There came to be no
secrets between us,—until one day when we were lying in the
Port of——————we became acquainted with a young lady
named Edith Rossamer.   Unfortunately for our future peace
and happiness, we both fell in love with this fascinating girl,
and from that moment a coldness arose between us.   George
Wade about this time had a fearful quarrel with a man named
Long, who was a messmate of ours on the same ship.   Fierce
words were interchanged between the two in the presence of
several of our crew.   Now it happened that I discovered Long
to be a favorite with Edith Rossamer, and a deep feeling of
hatred for the man arose in my breast.   I brooded over my
hate, and the more I thought about it the greater became my
enmity towards him.   George Wade, soon forgot his quarrel
with Long, but my memory only assisted in making my hatred
more intense.   As is very often the case, when Long found out
my dislike for him, he returned the feeling with interest, and
although outwardly we were polite to each other, in our hearts
we were sworn enemies.   One night Long and I happened to
be standing beside the taffrail, when we got into an altercation,
one word brought on another, until we became so excited that
we were on the point of coming to blows.   About this time
Long was standing with his back towards and quite near the
taffrail—The ship was then going about twelve knots an hour ;
the night was pitch dark ; and a pretty heavy sea on.   Like a
flash it crossed my mind.   The devil must have whispered into
my ear.   What a splendid chance to finish Long.   At that
moment the unfortunate man used a most insulting word towards me,—The next I planted my fist with such force upon
his breast, that he staggered back, and before he could recover
himself he was overboard.   My God, it is dreadful to recall the

agony of that moment ! I cowered beside the taffrail as I heard the last shriek of the drowning man, and then I peered about in the darkness to see if any living soul was near that could have seen the deed—I knew that the wheelsman was not in a position to have witnessed it. He, however, heard the shriek and sung out,—'Mr. Loving, did you hear a cry astern ;—somebody must be overboard.' 'I did not hear it,' I replied, going up to him, and as I spoke I trembled, but, I continued :—'I'll go and see if anybody is missing.' 'Will I keep on my course, Sir ?' the man asked. 'You can't do anything else in this sea.' I replied. 'All right sir.'

"As I turned from the taffrail I suddenly encountered George Wade, but I did not know him in the darkness until he spoke.

" 'What has happened ?' he huskily demanded of me.

" 'I am going to see,' was my reply, as I endeavoured to push past him.

" 'Stop,' he said, sternly, 'Ralph ! I was only a few feet apart from you and Long. I heard you having words with each other. Now tell me what has happened. Where is Long ? somebody struck a blow. Who was it?'

" 'My God, Wade,' I replied, now completely terror-stricken. 'I never intended to knock him overboard. I struck him because he called me a liar ; and he was nearer the taffrail than I thought. What will I do ? Surely you will not betray me. No one saw it done, and I am sure the man at the wheel could not tell what was going on. Oh ! Wade, think of our friendship; think of my father and poor mother ; think of the disgrace to them; and think of the miserable end it will bring me to. I never intended to commit murder. I only struck a blow in anger and did not look at the consequences. Spare me, Wade ; oh ! promise me that you will.' I knew Wade to be a conscientious fellow, and one who never broke his word.

There must have been a terrible struggle in my messmate's mind, for he walked to and fro some time before he gave me his promise. 'Loving,' he said, 'you have this night committed a fearful act. You say you did not intend to kill the man. I am bound as your friend to believe you; but if you have deceived me, you have but added to the fearful crime of murder—that of perjury—for your word to me at this moment I consider as sacred as an oath. I will never reveal without your consent what I heard this night between you and Long.' I was safe. I kissed Wade's hand; I blessed him, and almost grovelled at his feet. Wade, however, seemed to shrink from me, although he had professed to believe me. The mark of Cain must have been upon my brow. On search being made for the missing man, Long was found to be absent, and an investigation took place the next day. The wheelsman was first interrogated, and he stated that he heard angry voices not far from him shortly before he heard the shriek astern of the ship, but he could not swear whose they were. He thought one sounded like Long's voice; he could not distinguish the other. I breathed more freely after the testimony of the wheelsman had been given. It having occurred in our watch, both Wade and I were examined. I was questioned first, and swore that I never heard any noise on the quarter deck, and had not seen Long during the greater portion of the watch. I fairly trembled when it came to Wade's turn. What will he say, I thought, for he will never tell a lie as I have done. On being asked what he knew about the affair, Wade answered ' I refuse to answer any question that may be put to me on the subject.' He was warned about the consequences that would follow, if he did not speak, but he would not answer one word. I once more breathed more freely, but my guilty heart sank within me when I saw them put the irons on George Wade, and walk him off to close confinement ; but coward that I was, I dared not free him from his position."

"The quarrel between Long and Wade was now discussed to the disadvantage of the latter. When we reached the port of ————, Wade was placed on trial ; but as there was no evidence to convict him, he was set at liberty. Still the brand of murder rested upon him in the opinion of his messmates, and on this account he had to leave the service. Wade never asked me to free him from his promise, and I, coward that I was, allowed him to suffer. I now confess that it was I and not George Wade struck Long the blow which hurled him over the side of the ship. The devil tempted me, and I listened to him, and now the crime of murder is on my soul. I fear to die, and I fear to confess while there is a chance for me to live. George Wade has gone to America I am told. I have never seen him since he left the *Nero*, but I trust that some day this confession will be found, and that it will blot out the unjust stain upon his name. Whoever discovers this secret drawer, let him or her in mercy send this paper to Alexander Wade, Esq., Essexshire, England, and God will reward him. I am a miserable man, and have no hope for the future ; for this reason I cling to life, for after death I am lost forever. I pray the forgiveness of George Wade, should this ever be seen by him.

" Ralph Loving."

" My poor boy, how you have suffered," said Mr. Meredith, when George had finished reading the paper.

" Yes, Mr. Meredith, I have suffered," replied George ; " but that would have been as nothing, had it not been the death of my poor Grace. I could overlook Ralph Loving's falsity to me; but oh ! it is hard to forgive him when I think of our great loss." The tears started to the eyes of the sick man, and his voice trembled as he continued. "It was a fearful struggle for me to refuse you an explanation at St. Boniface of what had been told you. I never broke a promise, and that one was a dreadful one to break, for it seemed as if the life of a human being hung upon my lips being sealed; but Ralph Loving, poor miserable man that he was, has a dreadful account to render at the judgment day."

"Have you any idea how the affair became to be spoken about in the settlement?"

"I have not," replied George; "that has always been a mystery to me."

"Cool told me," said Mr. Meredith, "and he afterwards informed me that Flyaway overheard you speaking to Barron about it."

"Ah! I remember," said George; "I did mention one night to Barron, while he was on a visit to our camp, behind the town, that I had got myself into serious trouble before I came to Red River. I mentioned that I had unfortunately got mixed up in an affair on board ship, for which I had to stand my trial; but anything further I did not say, except that I was innocent of the crime I was tried for, that was all."

"Then," said Mr. Meredith, "that villain Cool has made a handle of what was told him by that miserable creature Flyaway, to try and ruin you; but it is all over now, and what I have heard to-day only shows me how hasty and wrong I was in condemning you so quickly."

"Do not speak of it now, Mr. Meredith; we must try to forget it. I will send this confession to my father, in England, for although he never doubted my innocence of the crime imputed to me, yet the fact of my being unable to clear myself has been a source of great trouble to him."

Mr. Meredith soon after left for home, as Nina Stone entered the room to attend to her patient.

CHAPTER XXVII.

E will now pass over a period of some months be_
fore we again revisit our friends. During that
time winter had passed away, and the beautiful
spring had given place to the warm yet pleasant
summer. That scourge, the grasshoppers, so peculiarly destructive in the North-West, had vis-
ited the settlement and laid waste almost every green field. It
was a trying time for the farmers, for there were very few
amongst them who received any return whatsoever from the
seed sown in the spring. It is a noticeable fact that when the
grasshoppers appear in the fall of the year they do not destroy
the crops to the same extent as they do the following summer.
The eggs are deposited in the ground just before the cold
weather sets in, and remain there all winter. When spring
time comes the young insects, about the size of a common house
fly, may be seen in myriads hopping here and there, feeding on
any green leaf they happen to light upon. The grasshoppers
are always most destructive just before the time they take
flight, and it was so in the case we are describing. Those pests
of Red River were so numerous on the occasion we have reference to, that in some places, especially alongside the houses and
fences, they accumulated in one living mass to the depth of over
a foot ; and around the walls of Fort Garry they were so thick

that men had to be employed with wheelbarrows to cart them away, as the stench which arose from them soon proved unbearable.   It is seldom, however, that they prove so utterly destructive as they did at the time we are writing about.   It was a most disheartening sight, when driving through the settlement during that summer, to see field after field perfectly bare ; —not a green thing in the shape of herbage to be seen anywhere.   It is the general opinion, that as the country settles up, the grasshoppers will disappear in proportion ; and it is to be hoped they will, for at present they are a very serious detriment to the settlements.

Mr. Meredith suffered equally with his neighbours, and it was a great drawback to his farming operations, as he lost his first crop in Red River.   It seemed to the poor old gentleman that his sojourn in the North-West was bound to be unfortunate, and he at last began to regret ever having left Canada. Mrs. Meredith had taken a great deal of pains, assisted by the two boys, in planting a fine lot of vegetables around the house. For some time the grasshoppers appeared to have skipped over her favorite patch, but at last they came, and the old lady in despair hit upon a plan by which she hoped to preserve her cabbages.   Taking the blankets, quilts, sheets and even her petticoats from the house, she carefully spread them over the plants. " There !" she exclaimed, " the pesky things surely will not get through that."

But alas ! for human expectations, the next morning Tom burst into her bedroom, as she was in the act of dressing, and cried out,

" Mother ! Mother ! come out and see your cabbages."

" Sakes alive !" replied the good woman, " how you frightened me Tom—what is the matter with you ?"

" Oh ! come and see."

Mrs. Meredith, throwing a shawl over head, hurried after her son, and as soon as she arrived in the garden, she threw up her hands in amazement, and something akin to horror.

"Gracious! goodness!" she exclaimed "this beats everything I ever heard about. The pesky things will run off with the house next."

And what was the matter? Why the grasshoppers had eaten large holes through her blankets, her sheets, and her petticoats, and had stripped her vegetables as well. Tom roared with laughter, which obtained for him a sound slap on his ear from the indignant old lady.

"There you good for nothing, take that for your pains. What do you see to laugh at I'd like to know?" "Ugh!" she suddenly exclaimed, as she clapped her hands upon her dress and rushed into the house. A grasshopper had got up her clothes.

Many of the better class of farmers in the settlement had laid by for a rainy day, and therefore were not altogether made destitute of grain by this unfortunate year; but others, not so provident, had either sold or used their previous crops, and were consequently placed in a very trying position for the approaching winter. Numbers of the settlers not having sufficient in their barns to feed their families till the spring.

Mr. Meredith now found the benefit of his stock farm, for, unlike many of his neighbours, he had a supply of cattle to fall back upon. He could always sell his beef, and thereby raise sufficient money to purchase grain, both for food as well as seed for the spring.

The stock farm was progressing very well under Jack's careful management. A large quantity of hay had been cut and stacked away; new barns and stables had been built, and a large quantity of stone hauled from the quarry, in case other buildings should be required.

W

Mr. Meredith became so disgusted by the loss of his crop, that he determined upon giving the most of his attention to stock-raising for the future; and few in the settlement had a better opportunity to succeed in that line than he had.

We will now turn our attention to an old friend of ours, whom we have overlooked (but not forgotten) for some time. we mean Mr. Bon. During the month of May, the plain-hunters and traders arrive in the settlement with their robes and furs.

Outside the town of Winnipeg, every spring, the lodges of the plain-hunters cover the prairie in large camps, and the town itself is a scene of bustle and activity. Mr. Bon's store was crowded from morning till night with people, most of whom were his own traders and their friends, settling up the year's business. In the fur trade, although you credit a man for sometimes over two years, yet when he comes in, he will expect the highest market price for his furs, and will not have the slightest idea about paying interest for the use of the money.

Mr. Bon, as we have already mentioned, was a man very much respected amongst the half-breeds, and usually his word was taken in cases were other men would have had some difficulty in making themselves believed. This assisted him very much in his dealings, especially with the plain-hunters. It was a general custom with the latter, when they were indebted to Mr. Bon, to go to him and tell him how many robes they had. If he agreed to buy them, they would at once go and bring in their carts from the camps, and deliver the bales of furs into his store, trusting to his giving them a proper value for them.

The robes are pressed into bales containing ten each, and are brought into the settlement in this manner. It is, therefore, a very risky matter to buy without unpacking, as you may afterwards find out that out of the ten you may not have over four really good ones. Mr. Bon, at the time we are writing about, received in, a very good collection of almost all sorts of furs caught in the North-West, amongst which were Buffalo robes, Black Bear, Grizzly Bear, Cinnamon or Brown Bear, Wolves, Wolverine, Mink, Marten, Red Fox, Kitt Fox, Cross Fox, Silver Fox, Otter, Beaver, Muskrat, Fisher, Badger, Skunk, Lynx, Ermine and Ground Hogs.

The plain-hunters generally remain in the settlement until sometime in July, when they start out once more on what is called the summer hunt, and they do not return until October. Generally, however, when the hunters leave the settlement in July, they do not come back until May in the following year.

It was amusing to observe some of the scenes in and about the town of Winnipeg, during the time that the hunters were in. Their stay in the settlement, as soon as they had completed their business, was turned into a sort of holiday time, and, we are sorry to say, that drinking formed one of their chief amusements. It was no unfrequent thing to see five or six fights occurring in a day ; but fists were the most deadly weapons used on those occasions.

And now we will turn our attention to another and more settled pursuit than that of fur hunting. We have reference to haymaking. It is customary in Red River to set a day aside on which to commence cutting the prairie grass. No one, by the laws of the settlement, is allowed to begin before that time ; and this is done to prevent the choice spots being taken up by a few persons. The 21st of July is the day usually set apart, and it is no unusual thing to see the settlers starting out on the 20th, so as to be on the ground by day-break of the 21st.

The plan adopted by those in quest of hay is, when they choose a place where the grass seems suitable,—to cut a circle with their mowing machine, and inside this none of their neighbours have a right to intrude. It is sometimes laughable to observe the hay-makers in their endeavours to get ahead of each other. It is customary for a farmer, when he goes out to mow, to take with him provisions for several days, as well as a tent and cooking utensils. He then remains out on the prairie until he cuts sufficient hay for his wants during the winter. We have known settlers to remain awake all night, so as to be at work first in the morning, and thus be enabled to make the largest circle. Whenever this is accomplished, the hay-maker can take his time, as no one will think of cutting inside his line or mark. Some farmers make as many as four and five hundred loads of hay each season ; and Mr. Meredith at the time we are writing about, cut over six hundred, as his stock farm required a very large quantity.

There is no scarcity of hay around the settlement at present, but as people from abroad flock in and take up the prairie land, it will become a more difficult matter to secure feed for the cattle than it is now. The plan which will have to be adopted then, will be to keep so many fields for pasture and grass growing. There will be no more marking out of circles—no more cutting hay wherever one can find it. What is open prairie now will then be turned into fields with fences round them to preserve them for their owners, and each man will grow grass for haying purposes, instead of as they do now, cut wherever it suits best.

And now one word about the difference between farming in Red River and in Canada. In the latter it is the work of a life time to obtain a cleared farm, unless by purchase ;—in the former all one has to do is to take a heavy breaking plough with what is called a colter or revolving knife, to cut the sod, and turn up the land on the prairie which you propose to cultivate. A little harrowing is then necessary, after which you put in your first crop. So rich is the land that you do not require to use manure at all, and the second year your farm is in as good order as you ever will get it. This is different from having to fell immense trees and wait for years to have the roots rot in the earth.

We say, therefore, to the farmers of Canada, come here, where you may enjoy all the benefits of prairie farming, without the necessity for changing your allegiance, as you might have to do were you to emigrate to the Western States—and when you come to Red River, if you find the land taken up along the river banks, go back on the prairie, there you can dig a well almost anywhere and find water ; and you can always find wood enough for your household purposes within a reasonable distance from your farm. If fencing is difficult to obtain, adopt the plan already described in this book, and which is extensively used throughout several of the Western States.

For building purposes we recommend brick. The clay in Red River is peculiarly adapted for the making of bricks, and we prophecy that ere long the houses in the settlement will be principally built of that material.

We have almost forgotten Mr. Bon, however, and must now pay him another short visit. As we have said, it was a busy time with him when the plain hunters came in. There were the furs to receive and repack for shipment abroad.

Some descriptions found their way to England, others to the United States, and a few to Canada. Buffalo robes and mink are seldom shipped out of America. As soon as the bales are prepared, they are marked and sent off in carts to St. Paul for reshipment from that point to wherever they are consigned. Besides this, Mr. Bon, about the time his traders arrived, was preparing to send off his brigade of carts to St. Cloud for his goods. Each freighter in Red River always requires a certain amount of advance before he starts on his trip, either for the use of his family during his absence, or for his own while on his journey. The clerks in Mr. Bon's store, therefore, had enough to attend to in supplying the goods required, both by traders as well as by freighters ; and it was not very long before the shelves presented a very bare appearance ; indeed, it is generally the case that the stores in the settlement are completely cleared out of goods long before the new supplies arrive.

Mr. Bon had never lost his friendship for the Merediths, and neither had they ceased to respect him for his goodness and honorable disposition. Indeed, Mr. Meredith learned to consult him on all matters of importance, and he never had reason to regret having done so. During the trouble between George Wade and the old gentleman, Mr. Bon had done his utmost to repair the breach between the two, and he warned Mr. Meredith not to place too implicit confidence in Cool's statements. Mr. Bon, during George Wade's illness, often visited him, and he soon discovered that Nina Stone was in a fair way of falling in love with her interesting patient. He, therefore, thought it right to mention the matter to Mr. Meredith.

"Poor fellow," said the old gentleman, " he seems to have the power of causing everybody to love him. I am not at all surprised at what you tell me."

"I think, however," said Mr. Bon, " that it would be as well to remove him to your house as soon as possible,"

" Well, perhaps it would be the wisest course to pursue," said Mr. Meredith.

Accordingly, he made the proposition to George the very next time he visited him. George Wade, although he could never forget his first love, still began to admire the unselfish noble girl who had nursed him through his illness ; but he little knew how deeply he was loved by her.

Nina Stone was a fair specimen of a Red River lady ; kind-hearted, gentle, and retiring, she won your good opinion at first sight. She had learned to love George Wade soon after he became an inmate of her father's house ; but she never revealed the state of her feelings even to her mother. Mr. Bon, however, who was very quick in judging character, discovered her secret, and he feared lest it might be the cause of heart burnings to the girl, for Nina Stone was a great favorite with him. Mrs. Meredith also became very fond of Nina, and invited her often to spend the day with her. " It reminded her," she said, " of the time when her Gracie was alive, to have Miss Stone near her."

This in itself served to counteract what Mr. Bon had advised for the best, as Nina and George met very often in the Merediths' house ; and it soon began to be evident that unless George Wade returned the attachment of the loving girl, that she would follow in the footsteps of Grace Meredith.

CHAPTER XXVIII.

E will now skip over the summer and autumn months, and pass on into the winter, the most distressing perhaps ever felt in Red River. The grasshoppers, as we have already stated, destroyed all the crops in the settlement, and in consequence of this there was every reason to expect a large amount of destitution amongst the settlers.

News, regarding this state of affairs, went abroad, and many kind friends stepped forward in Canada, Britain and the United States, to help the settlers. Subscription lists were opened in those countries, and money flowed in fast for the relief of Red River.

About this time, Cool and his party, ably assisted by Twaddle and "Dot," thought it was a splendid chance for them to make a big strike, and, in fact, they required something to improve their sinking fortunes. Cool, "Dot" and Twaddle held a private meeting, at which they decided that if they could get the control of the relief supplies expected, they might make a good thing out of it. For this purpose, therefore, it was proposed to form a general committee from amongst the settlers, of which the aspiring and conspiring trio were to be the ruling members. But, alas! for human expectations; while the general committee was being formed, word arrived from Canada and St. Paul, that it was the desire of those donating the relief supplies, that the bishops and clergy, in conjunction with the Governor, should form the committee in Red River for the purpose of distributing the relief amongst the settlers. This was a death blow to Cool, "Dot" and Co., but still they did not despair. The *Buster*, which had made a great ado about the general committee, now professed to recognize it as the only responsible authority on the relief question in the settlement. But as the most of the members of the general committee did not care about acting contrary to the wishes of those who sent the supplies, Cool, "Dot" and Co. began to feel that they had not made such a good thing out of the affair.

They now tried to push themselves into the committee of bishops and clergy, but all to no purpose; they therefore had had to "back down," as it is called, altogether. The *Buster* now began to cry down the relief arrangements, but finding that a useless job, it finally did not refer at all to them.

Cool felt very much chagrined at this most decided defeat, and did all in his power to retard the efforts of the committee. The fact was, he and "Dot" had tried to make it appear in the settlement, that it was through their influence that the relief was sent at all. It was, therefore, a bitter mortification to them when they found themselves entirely unrecognized in the affair, by the people of Canada.

Sharp had sunk so low by this time, that he was forced to close up his store, and leave the settlement for St. Paul, where he remained for a few years, until at last he was reduced to keeping a third rate boarding house near the levee. We will leave him in that *elevating* occupation, hoping that he made it pay better than he did scheming and law-breaking in Red River.

Whirl, as we stated in a previous chapter, began to see the

errors of his ways, for the simple reason that his keen foresight taught him that it wouldn't pay to fight against law and order, and, also, that it was time enough to cry out for Canada or the United states, when either of them possessed some right to the country. Whirl, therefore, settled down to business, and became noted for sharp, and sometimes not over honest dealing; still he throve, and would, no doubt, have been a rich man, but, unfortunately for him, he took to drinking, and one morning he was found dead by the river side, having, it is supposed, tumbled out of a boat, while endeavouring to cross over to St. Boniface, in a state of intoxication, during a dark, stormy night.

Twaddle stuck to the *Buster* until it "busted" him, then he took to growing cabbages and other vegetables for a livelihood, and he was often heard to remark that kitchen gardening was far preferable to trying to "bust" the Hudson Bay Company. One paid; the other did not. Twaddle, just before retiring from the *Buster*, encountered an enraged Canadian, who pitched into the unfortunate editor, for having written such trash about the country, the result of which was a black eye for Twaddle. And there we will leave him alone with his cabbages. Ah! Canada, how your champions suffered for your sake. Ah! Canada, how you have also suffered by their deeds.

Cool and "Dot" were now left alone in their glory. The former was down as far as he could go in the estimation of the people. In fact he entertained serious thoughts of leaving the settlement altogether; and the general wish amongst his neighbours seemed to be in favour of his departure never to return again. Had Cool shown any honesty in his political ideas in favor of a change of government, or had he pursued a proper course in endeavouring to further them, it is quite probable that he would have now many friends both for himself

and the cause he was espousing.   But it was quite apparent
that his only object in preaching Annexation to Canada and
destruction to the Hudson Bay Company, was to promote his
own selfish ends.   He even went so far as to promise certain
parties his influence in obtaining for them *fat* offices under the
proposed change of rulers, thus endeavouring to show that he
was an authorized agent of the Canadian Government and
therefore a representative man.   This of itself did Canada's
cause a great deal of injury in the settlement, for people could
not but condemn a government who would employ a man or
men to undermine the only constituted authority in the country,
instead of openly entering into proper negotiations for a transfer
of power.   Of course many people saw through Cool's preten-
sions, but there were others who believed him to be a Canadian
agent, and therefore condemned Canada for the unlawful deeds
committed by the Cool party in the settlement.   It is no wonder,
therefore, that the settlers dreaded the future to a certain
extent; and although there were persons like the Merediths
who counteracted the evil influence of the Cool party, and to a
great degree removed the erroneous impression left on the
minds of the people regarding Canada, still a great deal of harm
was done.   It is satisfactory to know, however, that Cool and
his friends suffered the most by their operations—and totally
lost the respect of their neighbours.

As we have already mentioned, Cool's business dwindled
down to nothing;—his credit abroad as well as at home became
worthless, and at the time we bid him adieu, he was on the eve
of his departure from the scenes of his many unenviable
exploits.   We pity the community whom Cool favored with his
presence after he left Red River, for assuredly there was
trouble in store for them from the moment they took that arch-
conspirator amongst them.

As soon as "Dot" found that his friend Cool intended deserting the cause, he began to think it high time also to leave. The unfortunate correspondent found to his cost that he had got into bad company, and felt that he was consequently a loser by the connection. His land speculations were frustrated by the action of the settlers in the matter. His expenses while in Red River had been enormous, through his extravagance, and he found that he possessed few friends on account of his untruthful letters to Canada. He, therefore, decided to follow in the footsteps of Cool ; and it is to be hoped when he reached Canada he tried to make some reparation for the evil he did while in Red River. But we fear his malady, so far as speaking slightingly of the North-West people, was beyond redemption. Some unknown wag presented "Dot," on the day of his departure from the settlement, with a leather medal, on which were inscribed the words—

"For Services in the North-West,

"Haw !

"Dot that down."

We may mention here that Cool had unsuccessfully endeavoured to obtain a loan of money on several occasions from Mr. Meredith. Mr. Bon and George Wade having been the means of preventing the old gentleman from being swindled.

And now, that we have politely shown the unruly characters of our story out at the back door, we will return and pay a short visit to those for whom we have a more friendly feeling. But, before doing so, we will relate to our readers some of the dreadful sufferings endured by the settlers of Red River during the winter following the desolating visit of the grass-hoppers. In many cases whole families were forced to subsist on two and a half pounds of flour per week for each person. Horse flesh in some instances was eaten, and we remember hearing of one family collecting old fish-heads from around the door of their house and boiling them up for soup. The rabbits, usually so numerous around the settlement, entirely disappeared ;—the fisheries were a failure ;—in fact provisions of all kinds were scarce during that miserable winter. We know of cases where the freighters who went to bring in the supplies had to subsist, while on their way to Abercrombie, on the bark of the trees. No one can tell how much suffering existed amongst the settlers, and yet there was not a single case of robbery nor pillage by the half breeds during that miserable time. No, although many of them were often on the eve of starvation, they never committed one act of theft from each other to satisfy their desperate hunger—will public opinion now sanction the lies which have been told about the natives of the North-West? Will they not rather be lauded as a good and honest people ? We think so.

As an example of Mr. Bon's goodness, we may here state that one day he killed an ox and instructed his servant man to prepare a large boiler of soup from it each day as long as the meat lasted. To this repast over forty little children used to come and partake of it.

But we will leave this sorrowful picture, and turn our attention to others more agreeable.

George Wade after his recovery from the unfortunate accident that befell him, became a frequent visitor at the Stones', and ere long he became deeply interested in Nina. Her gentleness of disposition and true nobleness of character won his regard, and at last he felt unhappy when away from her presence. It must not be thought, however, that he had forgotten Grace Meredith. Ah ! no, the memory of her sweet face was ever present with him. It was the great resemblance of character between Nina and his lost love, that first drew him towards the kind-hearted girl. At last George found out that he was beloved by the fair nurse who had watched over him so tenderly; and when he made the discovery, he felt very much troubled about it. He knew that his first love would ever remain with him, and therefore he could but offer Nina a share of his heart. He consequently felt uncertain how to act. He did not wish to pain the young girl's feelings, and yet he felt afraid that he had unwittingly won her love, and that it would be cruel to cast it from him. At the same time he did not feel sure how far the memory of his lost Grace would interfere with Nina's happiness, should he make her his wife.

While in this uncertainty of mind, George Wade had recourse to his two friends, Mr. Bon and Mr. Meredith. Both advised him to weigh the matter well, before taking a step that might afterwards cause him as well as the young girl a great deal of misery.

Said Mr. Bon—"I would, if I were you, George, go direct to Nina Stone, and tell her the true state of your feelings; if she will accept you as her husband on your terms, then, my dear fellow, I should say marry her at once."

George followed Mr. Bon's advice, and it is needless to say that he and Nina were shortly afterwards betrothed.

About this time, Wade left the Hudson Bay Company's service, having received letters from England, asking him to return, as his father was failing in health. He, therefore, re-solved upon leaving Red River early in the spring. A day or two before his departure for England, a few friends gathered together to witness his marriage with Nina Stone. The Meredﬁths were there, and although they tried to look cheerful, still the memory of the former marriage hung like a cloud over them. Poor Mrs. Meredith cried like a child. George Wade

was very much affected also, and kissed the old lady affectionately.

" Cheer up, my dear mother," he said, " I will soon be back
to Red River, perhaps never to leave it again ; and then I will
try to be a good and faithful son to you ; and I am sure Nina
will be like a daughter to you."

" Oh ! yes, George," said Mrs. Meredith, " I love you both
well, but my poor lost treasure, I could not help thinking about
her."

Mr. Meredith now came up, and finding his wife in tears,
he quietly led her from the room, and drove her home. The
marriage, from the sad memories attached to it on the part of
the Merediths and George, was, although not an unhappy one,
still by no means cheerful. Nina, who was a sensible girl, understood the feelings of her husband and the Merediths, and
did not therefore expect a merry wedding.

George arranged to leave by the first trip of the steamer
International, and, therefore, on the day appointed for her departure, he took passage with his bride en route for England.

A number of friends accompanied them as far as Fort Garry
to see them off ; and as the steamer slowly moved away, hand-
kerchiefs were waved and good wishes loudly expressed for the
safe return of the young couple.

" You're sure to come back to us," said Tom.

" God permitting, as sure as that the sun will rise to-morrow," was the reply of George.

CHAPTER XXIX.

HE scene is now changed from Red River to England, and there we will ask our readers to accompany us for a short time.

The windows of an old-fashioned country residence, in Essexshire, were lit up, and the sound of merry voices within proclaimed that something unusual was going on. Every now and again a carriage would drive up the avenue and stop before the principal entrance; fairy forms could then be seen alighting and skipping up the stone steps. The large hall door would open, a flood of light would suddenly be thrown upon the trees in the park, and then when the gay guests had entered amidst hearty welcomings, the heavy door would be swung back with a bang.

A ball was evidently being given in this old-fashioned residence, and although uninvited ourselves, we will take the liberty of asking our readers to accompany us within. All except two persons are strangers to us in these large and sumptuously furnished rooms; and who are they? may be asked. We will answer in our own way. The residence in question belonged to Alexander Wade, Esq., the father of George, and the ball we have observed as going on, is given in honor of the arrival of the young bride and bridegroom from America.

The arrival of George and his young wife was the subject of

much speculation amongst the neighbouring gentry ; the rumor of his having married a half-breed lady had preceded him, and a great deal of curiosity was felt amongst the friends of the family regarding the appearance of the expected Mrs. Wade.

The idea entertained about a half-breed was a very vague one amongst the people of that country place, and in fact it was altogether a matter of uncertainty to many whether a young lady, just from the wilds of America, knew how to behave herself at all.

On the arrival, therefore, of George and Nina, in Essexshire, most of the neighbors came to visit and welcome them home ; and old Mr. Wade, although feeble in health, resolved upon giving a large ball in honor of his son's return.

"You are like the prodigal," said Mr. Wade, to George, "and I the indulgent father. I will, therefore, welcome you home with a prodigality worthy of the occasion, and we will spare no pains to make it pleasant."

Invitations were therefore issued, and the ball passed off to the satisfaction of every one, and old Mr. Wade in particular. Our readers will now see that George and Nina were the only two present with whom we are at all acquainted. Nina at first felt rather shy at having to appear before so many strangers, but George reassured her by telling her that she would find the people in England as jolly as those she had been accustomed to in Red River, and that their manners were also very similar. On the night of the ball, Nina entered the drawing-room hanging on the arm of George, and her natural grace and winning manner at once made her a favorite with all present. Her dress was simple and tasteful, and altogether there was not a more ladylike person in the room.

George had good cause to feel proud of his wife, and when he remembered "Dot" and his letters regarding the Red River

X

people, and the ladies of that country in particular, he could have pulled the little conceited correspondent by the nose, had he been near him.

Old Mr. Wade became very fond of Nina, and she in turn showed him all the attention due by a daughter to a parent. George and his father had many conversations regarding the former's previous life ; the unhappy affair which caused him to leave the East India Company's Service ; the sojourn in Red River, and melancholy end of Grace Meredith. The old gentleman sympathized deeply with his son.

" Well, my dear boy, all is well that ends well. I am sure you have reason to be thankful and proud for having gained the love and affection of such a sweet girl as Nina."

Many invitations flowed in on the young pair, and wherever they went, the "stranger wife," as Nina was called, made a host of friends among the kind hearted Essex people.

But gaiety soon gave place to sorrow, for good old Mr. Wade fell suddenly ill one day, and it became the opinion of doctors that he would never rise from his bed again. Nina was unremitting in her attentions on the sick man ; indeed, so much so, that George at last became alarmed for her sake. She looked so pale, and seemed so worn out with the fatigue ; still she could not be persuaded to leave the sick-chamber.

Mr. Wade at last grew so childish in his attachment towards his son's wife, that he never seemed to rest easy when she was away from his bedside. Death finally came and carried off the weary soul to a home of rest ; and Nina, who had at last begun to sink under her continued confinement was saved from perhaps a dangerous illness.

George felt the death of his father very deeply, and as soon as the funeral was over, he hastened away with his wife from the scene of so much sorrow where shortly before there had been so much happiness. He felt that his wife required a change of air to preserve her health. He therefore arranged his business, so that he could leave the property in charge of a competent agent, and started for Scotland with Nina soon afterwards.

The property which Mr. Barron had willed to Grace was a valuable one, and George therefore determined to look after it to preserve it, if possible, for the Meredith family. It was his own proposition to do this, as Mr. Meredith had no desire to possess the property or to claim it from Mr. Barron's relatives. George perhaps had the best right to it, but he had sufficient for his own and Nina's wants, and he did not consider that he could fairly lay claim to what was never intended for him, although there is no doubt but that Barron wished him to become equally benefited with Grace by the bequest.

When George visited the property, he made known his errand to the person in charge of it, and from him he learned that there were several of Barron's relatives in poor circumstances who would be glad to obtain assistance from the rents coming in from the estate. George instructed the agent to do nothing until he sent him word, as Mr. Barron's will was in America, and could be easily proved.

As soon as he returned to Essex, he wrote on the subject to Mr. Meredith, and received an answer, saying that Barron's will had been destroyed, and that, therefore, his relatives were to be allowed to have the property as if no will had ever been made against them.

" This is just like the honourable old man," George exclaimed, when he read the letter, and accordingly he wrote the agent of the Barron property, enclosing a copy of Mr. Meredith's letter. George found that the trip to Scotland had done his wife a great deal of good, but at the same time he discovered

that her heart yearned for Red River; and she often expressed
a wish to return and see her relations and friends once more.
On this account he resolved upon leaving England, and again
visiting the North-West, and accordingly he left Essexshire in
the fall on his return to America.

During the absence of George in England, great changes had
taken place in Red River.   Mrs. Meredith pined sadly after the
departure of Nina and her husband ; it seemed as if the
memory of · Grace saddened her moments so much, that her
health suffered considerably in consequence.   At last she was
confined to her bed, and in a short time she too was laid in her
grave by the side of her loved daughter Grace.

Mr. Meredith began to fail fast, and the loss of his partner
in life caused a deep-rooted melancholy to hover over him.
Jack and Tom did their utmost to cheer up their poor old father,
but it was evident to everyone that he would not live long.

The stock farm had succeeded beyond expectation, and both
the boys now owned and worked separate farms, besides looking
after their father's property.

Mr. Bon had increased his business, and was every day adding largely to his already considerable fortune.

Our old acquaintance, Cool, having left the settlement, his
party had dwindled down to almost nothing, and peace and
quietness reigned in the land.

About this time the transfer of the North-West was spoken
about as likely to take place on the 1st of December, and a good
deal of controversy was going on amongst the settlers regarding
it.   The terms on which it was proposed to hand over the
country were not received favorably by the Red River people,
and murmurings were heard everywhere in opposition to them.

George, however, knew nothing about all this, until he reached Pembina, on his way to the settlement.   There he met an old

friend, Mr. Shorthorn, who described to him the state of feeling in the settlement.   Mr. Shorthorn appeared to take much more interest in the matter than there seemed any necessity for, he being an American citizen.   George was not altogether astonished at what he heard, for he had every reason to fear that Canada had lost instead of gained friends in Red River, through the ill-doings of those who professed to be her champions.

When he and Nina reached within nine miles of Fort Garry, they were stopped by a number of armed men (half-breeds) who had raised a fence, or as they called it a barrier, across the road.   As soon however as George was recognized by several men in the crowd, he was allowed to pass.

" What are you doing ?" he asked of one of the half-breeds.

" We are going to keep Monsieur McDougall out."

" Why ?" asked George.

" Because," said the man—" he and the people who used to break our laws are trying to turn us out of the country.   They want to treat us like dogs and Indians."

" Perhaps Mr. McDougall has no intention of the kind." George said.

" Oh ! we don't know Monsieur McDougall himself ;—he may be a very fine man, but he's not keeping good company."

" Oh !" George said—" There you may have been misinformed.   Perhaps if you see and talk to Mr. McDougall, you will find that he will do what is right for you.   I've always heard of him as a very clever man ;—and depend upon it he knows enough not to cut his own throat, by doing as you think he will.

" Well ! Well !" replied the man.   " I don't know, but they say he has a lot of friends here whom he is going to put over us ; we won't stand that."

"Don't you believe it;—but *bon jour!* Take care what you are doing; you're on dangerous ground." So saying, George whipped up his horse and proceeded on his way.

"Ah!" he said, turning to Nina, "that is the work of designing men. In the first place, the actions of the so called Canadian party have served to misinform the authorities in Canada as to the real state of the people in Red River. It is evident they do not understand them when they think of taking the Government of the country on the plan proposed by the McDougall party. Then it is equally evident that the lawless doings of a few men have impressed the half-breeds with an erroneous idea of the Canadian people. There is a great misunderstanding in all this, and it is a pity that it should be so. I wonder where it will end?"

George and Nina now drove on to the Stone's, and were welcomed heartily by the family. Jack and Tom Meredith, as soon as they heard of Wade's arrival, rushed up to see him; and then George returned with them to see old Mr. Meredith.

The meeting was an affecting one, on account of sad memories. Nina, the next day, went to see Mr. Meredith, and then she and George drove to the churchyard to visit the graves of Grace and her mother. The recollections were sorrowful ones, as they sat for some time thinking over the past. At last George drew his wife to his bosom, and whispered, "The living and the dead will never be rivals." When they returned home they found Mr. and Mrs. Bon, waiting to see them, and the next evening a large party, consisting of the Stones, Merediths, Bons, and several other friends assembled together to welcome the young couple back to Red River.

George soon after this bought a fine farm, and settled down, having given up the idea of living in England, as Nina preferred remaining amongst the friends of her youth. There we will leave them for the present, at the same time we hope that our readers have not been wearied with our story of

"LIFE IN THE NORTH-WEST."

THE END.

EMIGRANT'S GUIDE TO MANITOBA.

S it is more than probable that a large number of persons will take advantage of the opening of the great North-West, and will proceed there during the ensuing spring and summer, it has been deemed advisable to throw together, briefly and clearly, such practical information to emigrants as is attainable.

FERTILITY AND CHARACTER OF COUNTRY.

As to this we need say little. The land is very fertile, and gives back a large, and what would seem to some of our Canadian farmers, an enormous yield of the crops the country is capable of producing. Canadian farmers, who have taken up land in Manitoba, confirm the reports brought them in times past by the Government explorers and the Hudson Bay factors of the splendid crops of wheat, barley, oats, buckwheat, potatoes, and beets. Turnips and carrots are not generally raised.

And while the yield far exceeds in quantity per acre that of the older portions of British North America, the quality is said not to be inferior.

These crops, be it remembered, have been raised year after year from the same land, farmed in what in Ontario would be called a slovenly manner, and without that attention to manuring which good husbandry demands. We may add that almost all correspondents unite in saying that 30 to 35 bushels of wheat per acre is considered a small crop, 40 to 50 being the average.

The land will, in fact, grow in abundance and to perfection any spring crops that can be grown in Ontario. The cultivation is very easily accomplished, compared with that on timbered lands.

The greater part of the country is prairie. The sides of the rivers and lakes are bordered with timber, which, however, is not of so good a quality nor so large as that further south. The prairie extends to almost an indefinite distance north and west of Fort Garry. The land in the neighbourhood of Lake Manitoba is represented as better wooded and eminently fitted for dairy farming. As to the nature of the soil, that on the banks of the Red River, and, with some exceptions, on the Assiniboine, is a heavy clay. In other parts it is a black vegetable mould mixed with sand. A white clay underlies it at a depth of from 6 to 24 inches.

We subjoin statements received from various sources of large crops :—

WHEAT.—1. From 1½ bushels of seed—54 bushels, or at the rate of 70 bushels per acre.

2. From 34 bushels of seed—711 bushels.

3. From 12 " " · 298 bushels.

4. From 12 " " 242 bushels.

5. Average of land on the Assiniboine, west of Poplar Point, last year :—From 1 bushel of seed—17, or 34 bushels per acre.

6. From 30 bushels of seed—684 bushels.

BARLEY.—1. Average 60 to 70 bushels per acre.

2. From 55 lbs. of seed—31 bushels.

This person gives the average of barley thus:—From 1 bushel of seed—15 bushels.

OATS.—Average : from 1 bushel—15 to 20 bushels.

BUCKWHEAT.—From 2 quarts—7 bushels.

POTATOES.—1. From 1 lb., early rose—172 lbs.
2. Average : from 1 bushel of seed—35 bushels.
3. From 5 bushels (besides feeding the family)—250 bushels.

The size of the potatoes is equally remarkable. Thus by different correspondents we have 2 lb., 2 lb. 1 oz., $2\frac{1}{2}$lbs, 2 lbs. 13 oz., as the weight of single potatoes, and it is further averred that no sign of decay has been seen there.

Cabbages are spoken of as weighing 15 or 16 lbs. each ; turnips (Swedes), 15 to 19 lbs. ; beets, 17 lbs. ; and cauliflowers, parsnips, onions, etc., equally splendid.

CLIMATE.

The summer of the neighborhood of Fort Garry is fully as warm as that of Ontario, and the winter is colder. The thermometer goes down to 40° and 41° below zero, though that is unusual. This, to the greater part of the inhabitants of Ontario, would seem perfectly unbearable, as indeed would the milder days of 35°, 30°, and 20°; but we are assured that the very bracing air of that healthy country, renders the cold quite endurable. One correspondent writes that he has driven, without discomfort, across the prairie all day while the mercury stood at from 30° to 40° below zero.

There are seldom any very strong winds, and when there are, they do not last long. This calmness of the atmosphere, and the dryness and absence of change, will explain how the intense cold is borne with so little discomfort. Any one who has lived in Eastern Canada, and afterwards spent a winter in

Toronto, or west of it, can readily assent to the probable truth of what the correspondents write.

One writer says :—" Everything here goes to extremes ; the summer is hotter, the winter colder, the sun brighter, the lightning and the Aurora Borealis more vivid, the thunder more terrific, the vegetation more rapid, the sky clearer, and the birds sing sweeter."

That the weather is not so universally cold during the winter, and that the cold does not set in so early as perhaps is imagined,—to show this, we may add that on the 1st of December, 1870, ladies attended a prairie reunion without extra clothing, the gentlemen present dispensing with overcoats.

HOW TO GET THERE.

There are three routes for Canadians :—1st., from Collingwood by steamer to Dawson Road, near Fort William, thence by land and water communication. 2nd., via Detroit, St. Paul's, Benson, and Pembina. 3rd., via Collingwood, Duluth, St. Paul, etc. The second of these routes only will be available to Canadians during the winter at present. The others, it is hoped, will both be available shortly after the opening of navigation.

To speak first of the route first mentioned, we may say that tickets can be provided in Toronto through to Prince Arthur's Landing, which is the beginning of the Dawson route. Until steamers are placed upon the long stretches of lake and river, 311 miles in all, which intervene between the Lake Superior waggon road and that at the Fort Garry end, it will be necessary for immigrants to provide their own canoes and guides· This will limit the class of travellers by this route for the present to the more hardy. The expedition, however, last year included a lady among its members, and her narrative does not show that hardships were suffered which a moderately robust woman might not endure without liability to injury. Even if the steamers and stages are not immediately placed upon this route, it yet offers many advantages for the class of travellers we have indicated. One gentleman, who has gone to Fort Garry by Dawson's route, says that a party of young men could accomplish the journey at a cost of $20 each. Persons travelling this way are also more independent and able to suit themselves as to the baggage they may take with them.

Whether the Government will have steamers and stages ready in time to be of much service next year is doubtful, but they have given contracts out for the steamboats to Messrs. Dick, who are doing their best at the late hour the contract has been awarded them. There is not the slightest doubt that when this route is thoroughly equipped, it will be by far the best route for summer travel.

The route from Prince Arthur's landing is, for 47 miles, over a road represented as fairly travelled. Lake Shebandowan is then reached, and the water communication, interrupted only by 12 portages (in length 12 miles), is continuous to the north-west angle of the Lake of the Woods, or 311 miles. The lakes and rivers passed through are : Shebandowan Lake, Kashewaboiwe, Summit Pond, Lac de Mille Lacs, Barrel Lake, Windegoostegoon Lake, Kasgasikon Lake, Sturgeon Lake, Lake la Croix, Rainy Lake and River, and the Lake of the Woods. From the north-west angle of the latter lake to Fort Garry is over a very good road for about 90 miles.

It is said that the journey can be easily made by this route in 17 to 20 days from Toronto. Cattle, heavy machinery, or furniture cannot, of course, be taken by this route as yet. Emigrants should go up in parties of eight to ten, and should carry bacon, biscuits, rice, flour, groceries, etc., etc.

The portages are represented as not being nearly so difficult as at first supposed, and it is to be hoped that the Government will have roads, if not tramways, at once constructed.

In leaving this part of our subject, we suggest to enterprising people the desirability of establishing a hotel or hotels on the line of road between Lake Shebandowan and Prince Arthur's Landing. There are several localities where very good land for farming exists on the line of road, and some of these localities are already taken up.

The second, the only winter route, is by way of the Great Western Railway to Detroit, and thence to St. Paul's, Pembina, and Fort Garry.

The third route is by the Northern Railway from Toronto to Collingwood, thence to Duluth by steamer, thence by rail to St. Paul's. It will be seen, therefore, that the two latter routes converge, and were it not that the Duluth route is not open in winter, one would be as available as the other. The Duluth will be probably the cheaper in summer, as it affords more water travel. The ticket by this route to St. Paul's will be about $25. From St. Paul's in summer, whichever route is taken to get there, the next point to be gained will be Fort Abercrombie, on the Red River. This is the most difficult portion, as the journey is performed by stage. Some of the Canadian companies are making arrangements to perfect the connection at this part of the journey ; if they can do so, it is probable that the whole journey to Fort Garry will be performed at a cost of $50, or $75 per passenger, including a moderate supply of baggage. Until some plan is perfected and announced at this point, it would be wrong to offer an opinion of the cost of the journey, as $50 and $60 have been demanded for this portion of the road alone. Once at Fort Abercrombie, a steamer will convey the passengers to Fort Garry. The following minute description of this route was given for the purpose of enabling a lady to go to Fort Garry to meet her husband, and has been pronounced to be correct in all particulars :— The route to St. Cloud is by rail ; thence to Fort Abercrombie, 180 miles by stage, which is fairly comfortable. The first night is spent at Sauk Centre, where is a rather decent hotel. The second night is spent at Pomme de Terre station, where the accommodation is middling. The next night Fort Abercombie is reached. Here the most comfortable place is said to be the establishment of James Nolan, express agent. His wife is a Canadian, and well disposed to Canadian emigrants. It is found necessary to procure a conveyance at this point, Nolan will make himself useful if written to in advance. After this point there seems to be some doubt about the stage, but it runs, at all events, to Pembina. From Abercrombie the next point to be reached by the land route is Georgetown, 52 miles across the prairie, and unless the stage runs, the worst portion of the way. There is, however, a night station at the 25 mile point, at the Jesuit mission. At Abercrombie or Georgetown it will be best to wait for the steamer a day or two in summer, which goes direct to Fort Garry, or if it is not raining, the stage may be on the route to Pembina, when a private conveyance must be taken—55 miles to Fort Garry ; the resting places are not very good, but are half-breed huts. Only 50lbs. of baggage, per person, is allowed by the stage on this route, and the best way to send extra baggage is said to be through Hill, Griggs & Co., forwarders, St. Paul.

We subjoin a table of distances for winter travel, compiled by Dr. Schultz :—

Miles.

Pembina to 12 Mile Point..... ....11¾

12 Mile Point to Grand Point...................17¾

Grand Point to Little Salt...................... 7⅛

Little Salt River to Big Salt Crossing.........10¼

Big Salt Crossing to Riviere Marais Camp... 4

Riviere Marais to Small Lake................... 8¼

Small Lake to Turtle River 3¾

Turtle River to English Centre 10¾

English Centre to Elm Centre.................. 7¾

Elm Centre to Point............................. 2¾

Point to Running Creek.......................... 3¾

Running Creek to Young Bull Creek......... 5¼

Young Bull Creek to 1st Point.................10

1st Point to Goose River Landing.............. 7½

Goose River Landing to Camp Lake........... 7¾

Camp Lake to Elm River....................... 5¾

Elm River to Georgetown......................12¾
―――――
167

For the benfit of those travelling by winter or early in spring
we may add that on the road from Benson to Alexandria, 47
miles, and from Alexandria to Georgetown, about 130 miles,
there are plenty of comfortable houses to stop at for those who
prefer them to camping out; and from Georgetown to Pembina
houses may be met with at the following places :—At Goose
River, 28 miles, the mail shanty; at Grand Forks, 32 miles,
there are five or six houses; at the point between the two
Salts, 37 miles, there is a Norwegian's shanty; and at Two
Rivers (commonly called Twelve Mile Point), 30 miles, there is
a wood-cutter's house a little off the road; Pembina is 12 miles
north; a further drive of 28 miles will bring them to Scratch-

ing River, the beginning of Red River Settlement proper ; and from that place to Fort Garry, 39 miles, the road is thickly settled.

In fact there seems to be no difficulty to a person driving 30 miles a day in finding a resting place by night.

WHAT TO TAKE.

This will depend on the route taken, and the manner in which the journey is conducted. It is safe to say that everything that will pack up in small compass is desirable. Tools, &c., are high priced, and difficult to get in Manitoba. It is hardly safe to advise a settler to carry a stove, and yet a 10 inch "Commonwealth" stove, in Winnipeg, has been sold for $110.

MERCHANTS

will have the opportunity of making heavy profits with quick returns, literally. Even the influx already poured in has, if we may believe the accounts sent, exhausted the stock, and we refrain from pointing out any particular class of goods to be sent in, because all are needed, and a taste for the most expensive must be to some extent cultivated.

LABOUR AND CHANCES OF EMPLOYMENT.

There is in fact an opening for every class of tradesmen, and a few of the following would speedly find employment :—Blacksmiths, carpenters, painters, bricklayers, plasterers, shoemakers, tailors, cabinet-makers, carriage-makers, tinsmiths, farmers, practical engineers, (that is, men who understand the manufacturing of the steam engine) millers, masons and brickmakers. At present there is no cabinet factory in the country, neither is there a foundry, only one tannery, no brick manufactories, no

Y

woollen mills, no flax mills, no soap factories, no potteries, and no oatmeal mill. The country can give employment to about four watchmakers, two bookstores, one bookbinder, one farrier, six veterinary surgeons, a few land surveyors, conveyancers, teachers of music, bakers, confectioners, milliners and dress-makers.

Good wages are paid carpenters, framers, plasterers, say $2 to $2 50 per day; and board is not more than $4 50 per week. The manufacture of household furniture will, it seems to me, from the difficulty of carriage, prove very lucrative. Useful labourers have obtained as much as a dollar a day and board, or a dollar and a half and board themselves. Of course in such a new country a great many business chances in the shape of manufactories are open, and we learn that breweries, grist mills, and saw mills are in course of erection.

One writer sums up the present wants of the country in this respect as follows :—

"There is a capital opening for two woollen mills, there being none at all at present. The country is a magnificent country for sheep pasturage ; sheep farms I have no doubt would pay well. Our country is also well calculated for flax culture ; two flax mills, after the introduction of the cultivation of flax, would doubtless pay well. Portage la Prairie is much in need of a steam grist mill. There are also good openings for one or two soap factories, two or three tanneries, one or two potteries, two or three brick manufactories, two or three foundries, five or six waggon and carriage factories, three or four cabinet factories, and one oatmeal mill."

Of course farmers will have excellent opportunities in the new colony. It is suggested that any persons intending to settle in Manitoba should come without their families if possible, and make things as comfortable as possible before bringing them up.

TAKING UP LAND.

On this point the Dominion Government have not acted with such prompitude as to enable us to speak with absolute certainty. It may be said, however, that any one taking up unoccupied or unclaimed land will be entitled to a pre-emption right. The land is subject to allotments for the Hudson Bay Company, and to those already settled in Manitoba, and to extinguish the Indian titles. The Government will do a great service and avoid much difficulty in having these different land claims marked distinctly. As to the manner in which the land has been hitherto settled, one correspondent writes :—

" The lots in the older settlements vary in width from one chain to three, four, five and six, as the owner had sons ; for, instead of allowing his sons to go and take land in some place else, he would split up his already narrow farm, until, I am told for a fact, there are people living on one chain of land. The fact of the matter is just this, there was so much land they cared nothing for it. It was of no value, for while they had to pay from 5s to 7s 6d per acre for it from the Company, they could not sell it for anything more than the value of their improvements, if for that.

" In the newer settled places the tables are entirely turned, for instead of three to six chains doing them, they must have from ten to twenty chains, and some of them claim five or six miles in length, and some of our Canadians have run furrows around thousands of acres."

We should advise settlers, if possible, to take up their claims in the neighbourhood of the lakes or rivers, as by this means they have greater facilities in getting their wood, which only grows in such vicinities. The shores of Lake Manitoba are spoken of as wonderfully adapted for dairy farming, as one correspondent says :—

"The lake is situated about sixty miles to the north-west of Winnipeg, and the country between is wooded prairie. At the present time the settlement at the lake consists of a small Hudson Bay post, and the dwellings of about a dozen families of half-breeds, but there are circumstances which combine to attract settlers to this point, and the lake is destined to be, I think, the centre of a thriving district. It is a splendid country for stock raising, and already the inhabitants of other parts of the settlement commence to take up claims along the shore for the purpose of stock-farming."

LIVING AND PRICES.

As yet, as may be gathered from what has gone before, certain articles fetch very high prices. Lumber, for instance, brings from $60 to $70 per 1,000 feet, and not very good at that. The saw mills, which are projected, will speedily reduce this. It is said that McArthur & Martin are about building one on Lake Winnipeg, and Lynch Brothers another on Lake Manitoba.

The prices of growing crops are less than in Ontario by one-half and farmers must take that into consideration when looking at the prices subjoined. Wheat is worth $2 25 ; Barley $1 30 per bushel ; Beef, per 100, $10 ; Pork, per 100, $17 ; Butter, packed, 38c. per lb., Poultry, cheese, eggs, and vegetables of every kind, find ready sale at equally remunerative prices. Potatoes average 50c a bushel all the year round.

Cattle are worth about the same price as in Ontario, an ox being worth £15 to £16. Horses are smaller, but about the same price.

The buildings are made of logs laid in mortar, of boards, and of brick. The latter kind will no doubt be more numerous hereafter as there is, we are informed, only one brick-maker in the colony.

HUNTER, ROSE & Co.'s

PUBLICATIONS.

MAN AND WIFE: A NOVEL. By Wilkie Collins. Crown 8vo., 574 pp. Oxford style, $1 ; paper cover, 75c.

KING ARTHUR: A POEM. By Edward Bulwer, Lord Lytton, Revised Edition (in the press). Crown 8vo., 460 pp. Cloth illuminated, gilt edges, $1.75 ; cloth embossed, $1.50.

LIFE OF THE DUKE OF KENT, embracing his Correspondence with the DeSalaberry Family. By Dr. Anderson, Quebec. Demy 8vo. Cloth, $1.

"DOT IT DOWN;" A STORY OF LIFE IN THE NORTH-WEST. By Alexander Begg, Winnipeg. Crown 8vo., 380 pp. Cloth embossed, $1.50.

In the Press.

A HISTORY OF THE RED RIVER TROUBLES. By Alexander Begg. Crown 8vo.

Hunter, Rose & Co.,

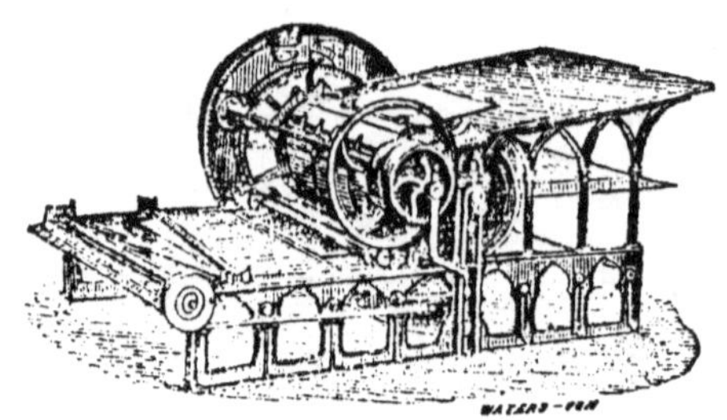

PRINTERS,

Electrotypers, Stereotypers,

AND

BOOKBINDERS,

TORONTO AND OTTAWA.

———————◆———————

ESTIMATES, with sample pages, supplied for Composing, Electrotyping, Stereotyping, Printing and Binding Books, of General Literature, Legal Works, Magazines, Pamphlets Catalogues, Music, &c.